IRRESISTIBLE TROUBLE

COPPER VALLEY FIREBALLS #4

PIPPA GRANT

Editing by Jessica Snyder
Cover Design by Lori Jackson Designs
Cover Image copyright © Wander Aguiar

AUTHOR'S NOTE

Dear Reader,

This book is my love letter to everyone who has been with me in Copper Valley from the beginning. Our beloved hero, Cooper Rock, who has been giving me fits for not only refusing to tell me his story for well over three years, but also for having a first name that's visually confusing with the city of Copper Valley, has shown up in at least seven other Pippaverse books. I'm honored and delighted to finally be able to torture him—ah, I mean, bring you his love story. I hope you adore Waverly every bit as much as I do, and I hope you think Cooper deserves her by the end.

I'm including a list of characters, their books, and how they relate to Cooper here in case you need a refresher, or in case this is your first introduction to the Pippaverse at large.

Happy Reading!
Pippa

Note: Cooper first appeared in **Flirting with the Frenemy**, *Bro Code series #1. The hero and heroine of that book were not given a cameo here, so you have one less couple to keep straight. But if you want to go back and get all of the Cooper Rock easter egg goodness, start with this book.*

Beck Ryder and Sarah Dempsey (aka Serendipity Astrid Darling), from *America's Geekheart*, Bro Code #2. Beck (formerly of the boy band Bro Code, formed by five guys who grew up together in Copper Valley), like all former Bro Code members, is a huge Fireballs fan. He and Cooper are friends both in the city and in Shipwreck, Cooper's hometown an hour away in the mountains, where they have weekend houses next door to each other.

Grady Rock and Annika Williams-Rock, from *Master Baker*, a Bro Code series spin-off book. Grady is Cooper's older brother. Annika was Grady's best friend in high school and has therefore known Cooper a long time.

Tripp Wilson and Lila Valentine, from *Liar, Liar, Hearts on Fire*, Bro Code #3, current owners of the Copper Valley Fireballs baseball team. *Liar, Liar, Hearts on Fire* tells the story of how they came to own the team.

Levi Wilson and Ingrid Scott, from *The Hot Mess and the Heartthrob*, Bro Code #4. Levi is Tripp's brother and the former member of Bro Code who went on to have solo success in the music industry. He's a big fan of the Fireballs, friend of Cooper's and also a close friend of Waverly's in the music business.

Brooks Elliott and Mackenzie Montana-Elliott, from *Jock Blocked*, Copper Valley Fireballs #1 and spin-off from *Liar, Liar, Hearts on Fire*. Brooks is Cooper's teammate. Mackenzie is the Fireballs' biggest fan.

Luca Rossi and Henri Bacon, from *Real Fake Love* , Copper Valley Fireballs #2. Luca is Cooper's teammate. Henri, whose day job is writing romance novels under the pen name Nora Dawn, joined the Lady Fireballs after moving to Copper Valley and falling in love with Luca.

Max Cole and Tillie Jean Rock, from *The Grumpy Player Next Door*, Copper Valley Fireballs #3. Max is Cooper's teammate. Tillie Jean, aka TJ, is Cooper's little sister. Their book involves an epic glitter bomb.

Cooper's other teammates include Francisco "Frankie" Lopez, Robinson "Robby" Simmons, Darren Greene, Trevor Stafford, Emilio Torres, and Deigo Estevez.

Waverly Sweet, aka a top pop queen who still can't hold her nerves, especially when old flames are involved

THERE ARE butterflies in my stomach.

You'd think after this many years in the biz, nerves would be one of those things I'd have mastered, but there they are, whispering some of my unshakeable, ever-present fears.

What if you fall off the stage?

It's been six months since you had anything close to a wardrobe malfunction—maybe tonight will be the night!

This would be a great show to forget the words to "Home Run" again like you did when you spotted you-know-who at the American Music Awards, wouldn't it?

The *Waverly Sweet: Honey and Sass* tour, my eighth full tour, sixth as a headliner, started about a month ago. We've been on this tour long enough to fall into routines.

I shouldn't be getting nervous.

Especially right now. I'm a pro. I've got this.

Right?

Thirty seconds ago, I was fine. But then, thirty seconds ago, I was posing for pictures with members of my Waverly's Braverlies Fan Club at my normal backstage pre-show meet-and-greet. There's nothing like meeting people who are more nervous than you are to make you put your own stress on the backburner while you assure them that yes, you're a normal person like them, and yes, you honestly are thrilled to see them.

One-on-one?

I genuinely am. I love my fans. I wouldn't be here without them.

But when you put thirty or forty thousand of them together in an arena? Or even more in a stadium?

Crowds are a totally different beast.

It's easier to apologize to a group of five people in a private setting for accidentally stepping on some toes while you get in position for a picture than it is to appease them if you get obviously out of rhythm with the backup dancers or forget the words to their favorite songs.

If I could *only* do meet-and-greets and skip the show portion, I would. In a heartbeat. But that's not how this business works.

"Have a great time at the show," I call to Sabrina and her parents as they exit the room.

Sabrina squeals and waves one last time as my security team subtly shuffles her out and closes the exit door.

And then chaos explodes all over the room.

It's organized, streamlined chaos, but it's still chaos, and I recognize *this* chaos.

It's *we're late* chaos.

I glance at the clock.

2

Dammit.

Under an hour until I'm on. Should I change my wardrobe? Wait.

Did we take "Gone Yesterday" out of the setlist for tonight?

I shoot a look at Hiramys, my lead assistant, who's more harried than usual. She's roughly fifteen years older than I am, with olive skin, dark curly hair that's perpetually tied back in a bun, and a pantsuit wardrobe that never stops.

But despite tonight's amazing pantsuit, I can tell something's amiss.

"Trouble in the arena?" I ask Scott Two, a beefy, balding white guy in his late forties who is—you guessed it—the second guy named Scott on my security team.

He hands me my glittery pink water bottle as he points me toward the door behind the tour screen that we use for photos.

"No."

"No loose monkeys?" *There you go, Waverly. Be ridiculous.* It helps the butterflies.

"No."

"Secret nooky happening in a closet?"

"No."

"A diamond heist happening under our noses because no one told me I was the distraction?"

"No."

"You're not even going to ask why I'd think there would be diamonds hidden in Mink Arena?"

"No."

Scott Two has four divorces under his belt, three daughters in my general age range, one grandson, and a secret addiction to eating Junior Mints while playing Mario Kart. He's been with me for a few years, and everything I know about him, I've found out through gossip from other people on my team.

Sometimes I wonder if this is what having a father would've been like. Lots of scowling, lots of *no*, very little opening up to offer personal details, and never enough answers to my questions. And for the record, I only wonder because the people in my life who knew my mom tell me that Scott Two would've totally been her type.

Clearly, she knew what she was doing when she went the sperm bank route.

Far better to not have a father than to have a disappointing one, even if it sometimes makes me wonder where I came from.

"What's up, Hiramys?" I ask while we wait for the next security team to give us the all-clear for my exit to the green room. "I asked The Steel Trap here, but he's not giving me anything."

She clips her pen onto her clipboard, puts a finger to her earpiece, and says, "Yes, tell Zinnia everything's under control."

I wince.

My Aunt Zinnia has been my career manager from day one. Usually she's here with us at every stop of the tour, but she had to dash back to LA for a face-to-face meeting with the brass at my record label.

She can be a lot, so it's nice on occasion when she's not here.

Tonight, though, I'm too stressed that I'm late for my voice warm-ups, meditation, habitual three Haribo gummy bears, snuggles with Hashtag, my cat, and the normal dash to the bathroom right before my cue that it's stage time.

"What about the last group?" Gus, the cameraperson, says to Hiramys.

She shakes her head. "No-shows."

4

He nods and lifts his camera tripod, shutting the legs and tucking it under his arm in less time than it's taking Kiva, my security lead, to work with arena security to clear my exit out of the room. The team printing pictures at the small table near the exit door close their laptop lids and unplug the printers.

And that's when I hear it.

"Wait! Wait! We're here!"

My team doesn't tolerate *late*, which has always created a mixed bag of emotions for me. Much as I need my time to settle my nerves with my pre-show rituals, fans pay a lot of money to come to a concert and meet me. I know how I felt the day I met Shania Twain, and no matter how big of a goober I personally think I am, I logically comprehend that I am to them what Shania was to me.

And I know how disappointed I would've been if Shania hadn't waited those two extra minutes when traffic slowed us down that first time I had a chance to meet her, after my mom was gone and before I launched my own musical career, and when she had no idea that Evelyn Sweet's daughter was the kid who was running late.

Aunt Zinnia always says the good of the many outweighs the good of the few, and it's more important for me to be on time to the stage than it is for me to make sure one last person isn't disappointed when they can't get here on time.

But Aunt Zinnia isn't here, is she?

"Wait," I say.

"Waverly—" Hiramys starts as Scott Two grunts.

I recognize that grunt.

It means Kiva's cleared me for the dash to the green room and I need to move now.

"It's five more minutes," I say.

"Aiden's dad couldn't find parking," someone wails. "Construction! Detours! Giant turtles eating the street signs and causing potholes!"

"C'mon, Hiramys," I whisper with a smile at the creativity involved in the panicked voice. "We're already late. What's five more minutes?"

She gives my stomach a pointed look.

On cue, it gurgles a noise that real butterflies would probably never make.

Scott Two clears his throat and gestures pointedly at my escape route.

I shake my hair back—not easy with this much hairspray in it—narrow my eyes—which makes it almost impossible to see since I'm wearing six layers of fake lashes—and plant a fist on my hip. My fist slips, though, because I'm wearing the glitter dress that's slicker than olive oil on a polished porcelain floor.

But I stand my ground.

Let's be real.

I wouldn't do this if Aunt Zinnia were standing over me, but she's not here. "Five. More. Minutes."

Everyone in the room freezes.

Except my stomach, which is like, *Oh, Waverly, you are going to regret this when we don't have time for our last emergency dash to a toilet before you go on...*

I growl softly back at it. *Fuck you, stomach.*

It cackles in utter glee at my momentary bravado.

"But Percy's mom will never let him out to go to another concert again. This is his only chance," a different panicked, cracking voice says on the other side of the entry door.

The first week of this tour, four kids from my fan group got lost in the tunnels of the arena before the show and missed their meet-and-greet window by three minutes.

Last week, I didn't realize I'd run long during the meet-and-greet, and a half-dozen small groups were turned away.

I'm not supposed to know, but Hiramys let it slip, and I've been wallowing in guilt ever since.

"Let them in." I gesture for Gus to set his camera back up. "One more." Then I point to the team at the printer table. "*One more*."

"Zinnia—" Hiramys starts.

"Is not the boss," I finish.

My Aunt Zinnia is absolutely the boss. She's been making the hard calls on my behalf for almost a decade. I rarely argue. Why would I? She made me and she's certainly never steered me wrong when it comes to career decisions, as my bank account and the *Billboard* charts can attest.

But I can't go on stage tonight aware that I've already disappointed my fans.

I hand Scott Two my water bottle as Kiva pops her head in the door. She has red hair and bright green eyes and went into security after being fired from her preschool job for being too much like a drill sergeant.

I personally adore her.

"What's the hold up?" she asks.

"Me," I reply.

She shares a look with Scott Two, then they both sigh. Kiva nods to Hiramys, who also sighs and opens the door.

A moment later, a dozen or so boys tumble into the room. Some short, some tall, of all skin tones, all wearing matching T-shirts featuring a cartoon lion leaning on a baseball bat and lifting a glove. Most of them I peg as somewhere between nine and twelve.

A tall Black man enters the room behind them. "Thank you," he says quietly to Hiramys. "This was a last-minute opportunity for us, and it's a thrill for all of them, no matter what's about to come out of their mouths."

That's all I hear before my full attention is taken by the boys. I turn on my Current Queen of Pop superstar smile and squat a little to be more on the level of the kids hovering in the small space between the door and the picture screen plastered with my tour logo.

"Oh my gosh, hi! Did you bring your whole team?" I ask.

"She knows we're a team," one of the kids whispers.

"Duh, Aiden, we're *in uniform*," another kid whispers back.

"You're baseball players?" I prompt.

All dozen of them explode in answers at once as they swarm closer, smelling like pre-teen boys always do and making me smile at their excitement.

This is the oldest the boys usually get in the meet-and-greets. Once they hit full-on puberty, the teen years and high school, they're too cool to admit that they like my music. So I make sure to smile at each of them individually, especially the bigger kid who's hovering at the back of the group, staring at me with wide, unblinking eyes.

You never know anyone's full story, and you can't learn it in five minutes at a meet-and-greet.

I'm incredibly fortunate to be here, doing what I do.

It's not only about the music either. My job is to bring a little bit of happiness and inspiration into my fans' lives. I use my music and my platform to sneak into their subconscious while they're still young and help them believe anything's possible, that someone has their back, and that we can all be stronger and better and happier when we're together.

Okay, yes, and that love's hard, but also dreamy.

Which might be a lie.

Feels like a lie to me most days.

"We're the worst team in the Little Sluggers League," the kid I've identified as Aiden finally says over everyone else.

"We lost *every game* last year," the one that I think is Percy confirms.

"A ball hit me in the face one game." Another boy points to his cheek.

"You leaned into the pitch, Harry," someone points out.

"Wow, that was really brave of you," I say. "Did you learn a lot last season?"

"No," Percy says.

Their coach makes a strangled noise.

I smile at him too.

"Can I tell you a secret?" I say.

Twelve heads bob up and down.

"I knew a baseball player one time who told me that the only way you ever truly lose is by giving up, and that you *have* to lose big to fully appreciate it when you finally win big." My stomach rumbles into full-on *we are not happy* mode. Probably because I mentioned *a baseball player*. I ignore it—or try to. He's not here, that was a long time ago, and he can't hurt me anymore. "Are you giving up?"

"No way," Percy says. "We have *potential*. We're even getting a real baseball player as an honorary coach to help us out. But so far, he's mostly fed us pizza, told us we're awesome, and then left."

"Like my dad," one of the shorter kids volunteers.

I hold out a fist and ignore the growing nerves threatening my stomach again. *Simmer down*, I tell it. *You're safe here.* I always schedule Copper Valley on my tour while spring training's going on. There's no way the *real baseball player* I knew will be here tonight, despite being *from* here.

"Hang in there, friend," I tell the little boy. "I grew up without a dad too."

"You did?"

I nod. "And you know what? There are lots of people who love you and who'll be there for you even if you don't have a traditional dad."

He beams at me.

And I hope I'm not wrong.

"My dad says our pretend coach is a hack," Percy announces. "What's a hack? Waverly, are you a hack?"

I love kids this age.

No filters.

They're fabulous.

"Some people think so, and that's okay. I don't believe it though." I turn my focus on one of the quieter boys in the back. "How long have you all played together?"

"One season," he whispers.

"We lost a lot," the kid next to him says.

"She knows. We already told her."

"How can you be the real Waverly when the real Waverly is doing a concert at Mink Arena tonight?" a shorter boy with dark hair asks.

"We're at Mink Arena, Derek," Aiden says. "But for real, do we get to stay to hear you sing?"

"Absolutely, you do."

Two of the kids groan.

And I feel a real smile blooming. Their honesty is refreshing. "But only if you want to. Do you like The Cherry Tomatoes? They're playing right now, and I think they're still on for another forty minutes or so."

Bingo. Both of the groaners light up. "Right now? *Right now?*" one asks.

"Right now." I lower my voice. "I can get you secret tickets to stand next to the stage."

And now *all* the boys are staring at me like I'm a goddess.

Hiramys doesn't blink. I don't do this every show, but I do it often enough that they plan for me to toss curve balls their way.

As the boys' cheers die down, I smile at all of them. "You want pictures before you go? Can I sign anything for you?"

"Do we have to go?" Aiden asks.

"Unfortunately, I have to get ready for the show. But you can stick around and watch my set from our secret seats next to the stage too if you want."

Hiramys gives me a thumbs-up. The coach's face twists in a silent *oh my god, are you serious?* question, and I smile at him again.

I gesture for the program that Derek's holding while Gus moves to start positioning the boys. "Did you want an autograph?"

He nods.

"Do we all get a copy of the picture?" Percy asks.

"Of course. If you want it."

Aiden pumps a fist, and they crowd closer, making Scott Two move in as well as I sign hats, shirts, and pictures.

Then Percy looks at Hiramys and the older man. "Coach! Coach, you have to get in too."

"And Coach Cooper!" Derek says.

I drop my Sharpie, which Scott Two grabs and hands back to me while I tell myself to get a grip.

Coach Cooper is a different Cooper.

He has to be.

Because the Cooper that I pretend I don't know is in sunny Florida for spring training right now, and *not* here in the cold, wet, last-of-winter Virginia foothills, waiting to see a Waverly Sweet concert with a bunch of pre-teen boys.

Percy twists and peers at the door. "Where's Coach Cooper? Sorry, Waverly. He got us in, but I guess he's not a fan. Hack."

"Coach Cooper!" Aiden yells. Derek echoes it.

Hiramys gives me the *do you need a rescue? Is your stomach okay?* look, but before I can unfreeze everything about me, a dark-haired, blue-green-eyed, dimpled, Florida-tanned pirate of a man steps into the room.

My entire body ignites in goosebumps. My pulse rockets into fight-or-flight mode and decides we're picking *freeze*.

"Coach Cooper!" Derek crows. "We thought you left!"

It's been *eight years*.

Why is my body being a dumbass about this?

Get a grip, Waverly. You're a fucking rock star.

Nope.

That doesn't work.

Why doesn't that work?

"Come get in the picture," Aiden says.

"Or maybe after we take one without you, so my dad doesn't see me with a hack," Percy pipes up.

And Cooper Rock, star hometown player for the Copper Valley Fireballs, apparent adopted coach of the worst Little Sluggers team in this city, and the first man to have the distinct honor of breaking my heart, smiles like having a ten-year-old kid call him a hack is the funniest part of his day.

He's a bad bad bad bad bad bad bo-oy! Use him for a toy toy toy toy toy toy to-oy!

My eyelid twitches.

This is *not* the time for song inspiration.

"Don't call Coach Cooper a *hack*, Percy," Aiden hisses.

"But my dad says he is," Percy hisses back.

"Hey, what's the first rule of being the Mountain Lions?" Cooper and his stupid handsome face and stupid adorable dimples and stupid dream-haunting voice says.

"We're a team!" a bunch of the kids crow together.

"Exactly. And we cheer for each other even when we're all being hacks, right?"

"He's such a good guy," the real coach says to me while the kids trip over themselves to assure Cooper that yes, they cheer for each other. "I've been doing this a long time. Nobody ever cares about paying attention to the losing teams in the Little Sluggers, but Cooper—man, he steps up. He's been involved in the league since before Aiden's older brother played, always showing up for the kids who struggle the most, totally flying under the radar because no one pays attention to the losers, especially in the off-season. Don't know if you know or not, but the Fireballs themselves sucked so bad for so long that even the people who knew who he was didn't care. Thought he'd be too busy with the Fireballs having so much pressure this year, but he reached out a couple weeks ago. When he told me he had a hook-up for tickets tonight, I thought he was kidding. But look at us. This is making so many of these kids' dreams come true."

And this is exactly my problem with Cooper Rock.

The man who gave me the best three days of my life eight years ago, ghosted me after promising he'd call, and then made every last gossip page on the planet when he was caught making out with an A-list actress two days later, is the same man who'd adopt the worst team in the Little Sluggers and make their dreams come true.

Also, Levi Wilson is on my *I shouldn't put you on my shit list for this but I'm going to anyway* list. It's not a far leap to guess that my fellow pop star, native of Copper Valley, brother of the Fireballs' new co-owner and known friend of Cooper, was the hook-up that made this meet-and-greet moment happen.

I shoot Hiramys the *no no no no no* look.

But she doesn't see me.

Of course she doesn't.

Not when Cooper Freaking Rock is showing off those sparkling blue-green eyes and that lady-killer smile and those dimples and that swagger that somehow manages to say *I'm just a regular guy who's also a god on a baseball diamond and a heartbreaker off the field.*

Hiramys extends a hand to Cooper. "Oh my god, I *love* you in those Pirate's Booty commercials. You and your grandfather are *adorable.*"

Cooper grins the same *aw, shucks* grin that he wore for his adoring crowd the one time I spotted him at a party a few years back, when I didn't realize at first that it was him having that tumble-off pool-side with Simone Biles, which is one more reason to love-hate Cooper Rock.

The man can do *anything.*

And he knows it, but that humble-not-humble *aw, shucks* grin always feels genuine. "Pop's the real star in those commercials," he says to Hiramys as I sign the last few autographs for the kids who won't stand still for our picture. "Did his own wardrobe and makeup, and every last bit of the script was improvised. I was merely along for the ride."

"You are so sweet. Look at you, passing off all the credit and adopting some kids who could use exactly this kind of baseball role model."

She takes a big breath, and oh, no.

Oh, no no no. *Don't do it, Hiramys. Don't—*

"Waverly and I watch the Fireballs *all the time*, and you are —*shew*." She fans herself.

The boys have stopped to listen, and they all stare at her like she's crazy.

The room is shrinking.

And that's before Cooper's gaze shifts past Hiramys to me, where I'm standing in front of my normal photographer, gaping at him.

Our eyes connect, and an electric current zaps through the air, first making my heart cramp, and then my vagina, who quickly gets over the cramp and starts in with an unwelcome throb.

It's been eight years, I silently remind her. *You don't get to pretend you remember, and also, we're on stage in forty-five minutes since this is running long, so simmer down.*

She also doesn't get a say, because *Cooper Rock.*

Backstabbing heartbreaker who, by all accounts, is master of the one-night stand and yet *still* comes off smelling like freaking roses in the press anytime his name happens to hit the media.

And he's standing there with that smoldery grin, posture screaming, *This is but one more normal part of my day*. He breaks eye contact with me to turn the grin back on Hiramys.

"Eh. I'm just a guy who can catch a ball. Sometimes hit it too. Let's get these pictures and get out of your hair. Really nice of you to let us in even though we were late. I know you didn't have to."

And this is why it's impossible to hate him, no matter how much I want to.

I believe the line.

I freaking believe it.

My gut twists.

It's been eight years—let it go, I tell myself.

He's the gold standard you've held every man to since, my heart replies.

Fuck my heart.

I have a job to do.

Even if it's right.

"Here we go, gentlemen," I say. "Gus, line us up, please."

"With Coach Cooper too!" Derek repeats.

Cool as a cucumber, Cooper makes eye contact for a split second before aiming his self-deprecating grin at Aiden. "You want the picture ruined?"

A chorus of *yes*es go up amongst the boys.

He meets my gaze again, and there it is.

That *zap* of history and curiosity and unwelcome attraction.

It passes as I turn my attention to Gus, who's running the camera and has final instructions for all of us.

Unfortunately, those instructions include me being sandwiched between the two grown men with the team.

Cooper has his hands tucked into the pockets of his jeans. The denim hugs his long legs, and his black Mountain Lions T-shirt is the right amount of tight enough to emphasize his lean torso. A tattoo peeks out from beneath the sleeve wrapped around his right bicep. And I'm trying—failing—to not notice any part of him.

When Gus tells him to scoot closer to me, he's still standing far enough away that we're not touching but close enough that I can smell butterscotch and mountain pine while the hairs on my arms reach for him and fall short.

"Some of them pretend they're not fans, but that's because they haven't had a good enough influence to own it yet," he murmurs to me while Gus patiently rearranges the kids for the third time. They all clearly don't know their own height, which

16

isn't unusual. We see it every day. "You should've seen the room when I told them I got tickets. They *all* love you."

"I've had worse critics."

He looks at me and for just a moment all of his cocky *I'm a baseball god* swagger disappears from his lean face. "Yeah, me too. But I wanted you to know."

My stomach dips.

Cooper Rock thinks about me.

I'm Waverly Fucking Sweet. I sell out arenas and stadiums all over the world. My last record went platinum in a week, and my lead single was certified diamond not long ago. I have a skincare line, a clothing line, a home goods line, and I recently signed a contract to be the new face of a luxury car brand in Europe. The Waverly Sweet Foundation donates over a hundred million dollars to charities around the world every year. I've hosted *Saturday Night Live*, testified before Congress, am probably going to be named a UN Ambassador soon, and I'm about to launch a weekly web series talking with female leaders in all kinds of industries.

On paper, I'm a freaking *badass*. I could date anyone I want —and I have.

And here I am, getting a case of teenage nerves because a baseball player that I fell head-over-heels in love with for three whole days nearly a decade ago still thinks about me.

I jerk my attention back to the kids, who are *still* refusing to take Gus's orders. "They know what they want, Gus," I say. "Think we should snap the picture?"

"I think they'd win more games if they listened to the grown-ups in charge," he mutters while the team's main coach sighs in agreement.

Cooper claps a large hand on top of Aiden's head and gently tilts it. "The man's not wrong, slugger. Two steps to

17

your left. Let Sam in. There you go. Eye on the ball. Or the cameraman. Yeah?"

"I don't want to stand by Bobby," Aiden says. "He smells like Cheetos, and I puked those up last week."

"Bob, my man, can you hold your breath while you smile for three seconds?" Cooper asks.

"I can hold it for seven seconds, Coach Cooper!" Bobby replies.

"Good job. Do that."

We get the picture taken, and as soon as Gus gives us the thumbs-up, the kids turn and fire questions at me again.

But my team herds them toward the exit as soon as the photos are printed. I keep answering their questions the whole time, nodding and smiling and giving their main coach the *you're very welcome, it was my pleasure* nod as he thanks me once more.

Were it not for the Cooper factor, this would be my favorite group of the night.

And speaking of the Cooper factor—while the last of the boys is being herded toward the exit, he hovers beside me.

When I glance up at him—and even in heels, I have to look up—he has the same sheepish grin that he wore the first time I met him.

My stomach tumbles over itself.

This is gonna be a thirty-minutes-in-the-bathroom-with-nerves kind of night, which means it's a very bad night for me to be running late out of my meet-and-greet.

Why isn't he in Florida?

"Could you do a huge favor for a guy who's legit your biggest fan?" he says.

Oh, god.

He loves my music.

He loves my music.

I cannot handle this right now. "S-sure," I stutter.

He pulls a baseball out of—actually, where *did* that come from? "My buddy Diego is *obsessed* with you. He's a rookie on our team this year. Really talented. Going places. He'd basically die of joy if you signed a baseball to him, and if you knew how joyful Diego was on a normal day, you'd know that's huge."

I blink once.

Then twice.

His buddy Diego.

Not him.

Of *course* Cooper Rock isn't my biggest fan.

And he doesn't think about me.

I'm just impossible to miss.

He probably doesn't even remember that we spent three days together in Los Angeles back when he was finishing his own rookie year in Colorado and I was in the baby stages of launching my career.

I snap my spine straight, tell every last one of my hormones *and* my stomach to get a hold of themselves and *get over the freaking past*, and I smile brightly. "Of course! I love making my fans happy."

Our fingers brush when I take the ball, and more sparks shimmy across my wrist and up to my elbow.

Cooper clears his throat and drops his hand quickly, like I'm repulsive.

"Is there anything else I should know about Diego?" I ask.

I know who Diego is. New catcher for the Copper Valley Fireballs. Happiest guy on the face of the planet. He was born with resting delighted face, and he's fun to watch on the

19

promotional clips the Fireballs have put out of him all through spring training.

And for the record, I only watch the Fireballs because Levi Wilson is such a fan, and Levi's the brother I've never had. You do things like that for family.

"Not yet." Cooper grins again. My vagina sobs at the knowledge that this handsome face isn't worth our time, and my heart flips my vagina the finger for daring to acknowledge that he's still panty-meltingly handsome. "Gotta give him a little at a time so he still has something to play for. But can I leave you his phone number so that you can congratulate him when we win the World Series this year?"

"I'll take it," Hiramys says. "I'll also hold it in safe keeping in case Waverly's tempted to call him and ask him out before the season's over. He's cute. A little young, but for that face? And that smile? The Fireballs are winning the hottest team award no matter what happens this season."

I sign the ball to Diego, making sure to put on extra hearts and a personal message that I'll be cheering for him this year and can't wait to watch him hit his first regular season home run, and then I hand it back to Cooper, somehow avoiding physical contact again this time.

He glances at his team, who are all getting passes to go watch the rest of tonight's performances by the stage, and then back at me once more.

Go away, I want to yell.

I have thirty thousand fans to get ready for and a highly embarrassing ritual I don't want to discuss but need to get to work on very soon here.

But Cooper doesn't leave.

I look up into those blue-green eyes, open my mouth to

thank him politely for coming and tell him that I hope he enjoys the show, but instead, he opens his mouth faster.

"Those kids love you," he says quietly, "and they have no idea who your mom was. You're impressive as fuck, Waverly. You did it. Good job."

He claps me on the shoulder, ducks his head, and then steps around me like he didn't drop the bomb of all bombs and leave a permanent warm imprint of his hand on my skin.

They have no idea who your mom was.

Until thirty seconds ago, I assumed there was exactly one person in my life who would understand how much that sentence meant to me.

Turns out, there are two.

Cooper Rock remembers.

And not only the naked stuff.

But the important stuff.

I have no idea what my face is doing while I stare at his retreating backside, but I know I need a bathroom.

Stat.

Hiramys grips my elbow. "What was that?" she whispers.

"A ghost," I whisper back.

A very sexy, very unavailable, very master-of-one-night-stands, very no-longer-my-type ghost.

Whom I will probably not be able to shake for *weeks* now.

Cooper Rock, aka a baseball god who always knows exactly what he's lost

THERE ARE three important things you need to know about me before I tell you my biggest secret.

One, baseball is my life. Specifically, Fireballs baseball. I was four years old the first time I vividly remember seeing the Fireballs on TV and five when Pop, my grandpa, told me that if he hadn't married Nana, he would've pursued his own baseball career with our favorite team. I was seventeen when I was drafted into the Minors, twenty-one when I hit the big leagues in Colorado, and twenty-two when I was traded to the Fireballs in the off-season and demanded a ten-year contract.

And in case you weren't already aware—the Fireballs have historically been the absolute worst team in baseball. If it wasn't for the new ownership coming in at the start of last season, the baseball commissioner would've moved us to

Vegas and renamed us the Craps, which would've been a few steps up from how bad our record was.

Taking the Fireballs from lovable losers to champions has been my entire life's mission, and now that the team has solid leadership, we're going places. This year, we're not settling for getting kicked out of the play-offs one game away from the World Series like we did last year. This year, we're going all the fucking way.

Second important thing—my family is the only thing I love more than baseball. I wouldn't be where I am if it weren't for them. My parents and brother still live back in Shipwreck, Virginia, a little town founded a couple hundred years ago by Thorny Rock, our pirate ancestor who left the sea in favor of the Blue Ridge Mountains when he retired and needed a place to hide the supposed riches we've never found. Shipwreck's about an hour from Copper Valley, the big city home of the Fireballs.

When my teammate and the Fireballs' star pitcher, Max Cole, retires from baseball, he and my sister, Tillie Jean—they started dating in the off-season and are perfect for each other—will settle there permanently, right around the corner from my brother, Grady and his wife, and right around the other corner from our parents. Family and Shipwreck made me who I am today, and yeah, I totally still claim my pirate blood at every convenient opportunity.

And the final detail you need to know about me is that I love women.

Throughout my career, it's been pretty damn convenient that I love women, considering scoring off the field helps me play better on the field. Every baseball player has a superstition.

Score to score is mine, and it *works*.

I don't talk about it a lot—one of my teammates had the exact opposite superstition and was the oldest virgin in baseball until he broke his own curse last season—but it's the truth.

I play better when I get laid. Always have. I tell people my lucky socks are why I always make the All-Star game despite playing for the Fireballs, but it's really sex.

So when I tell you it's been a few weeks since I hooked up with a woman, and that my game is slipping *already*, when the season has barely started, and that for the first time in years, I don't want to go hook up with a woman—a random woman, I mean, like I usually do—and not even for the sake of playing a better game tomorrow, hopefully you understand how serious this is.

From the minute I paused in the doorway last month, sneaking peeks of Waverly Sweet making my adopted Little Sluggers team feel like the center of the universe at that meet-and-greet, and then her dropping that little *a baseball player I used to know* comment with my losing mantra following it, it's been like something critical and essential suddenly appeared, hovering out of reach.

And that moment when her bright, sunny but shocked gaze landed on mine for the first time in years?

Time stood still while my entire world lit up with firecrackers that I haven't felt since the *first* time I laid eyes on her.

It's been a lot of years. I've done a lot of things. Been a lot of places. Slept with a lot of women.

But one word kept whispering through my brain.

Home.

And since that moment exactly three weeks, two days, and four hours ago, I haven't wanted to do anything with any other woman.

At all.

It's like other women don't even exist.

Waverly's in my every waking thought.

She's in my dreams.

She's who I picture impressing when I step up to bat. She's who I hope is watching the highlights reels on the sports channel when I make a diving grab to rob the other team of a double or when I catch a beauty of a throw from Diego to tag a would-be base-stealer out at second. She's who I'm talking to when I'm tapped for pre- or post-game interviews.

And she's the one woman on this earth who is so far out of my league that it's a miracle I survived being in the same room with her again.

The torture that was watching her entire concert from the private wings off the stage was like reliving those three glorious, amazing days together early in both of our careers before her aunt informed me in no uncertain terms that Waverly Sweet was too good for loser baseball players.

There are people in my life who'd probably say I became such a great baseball player to spite Zinnia Sweet.

Or possibly that I became master of the one-night stand—to the benefit of my career—to spite them both. What started as a way to drown the pain—yeah, yeah, lame, I know—turned into a hardcore superstition that might not have existed otherwise.

Not like Waverly tried to get in touch after Zinnia chased me away, and she definitely had my phone number.

I've always wondered if Zinnia was doing the dirty work Waverly asked her to do.

But she's not who I'm supposed to be thinking about tonight.

Tonight, I'm supposed to be focusing on doing what I do best.

Scoring *off* the field.

Bonus if it gets a certain pop star out of my head.

But the mechanical bull in this bar isn't doing it for me.

Neither is any of the rest of the bar scene. Nor was the club scene. Private party scene. Or even the locker room scene.

"Dibs on blue dress," Francisco Lopez says reverently beside me. Frankie's our shortstop, about my height, with brown skin, brown eyes, and more superstitions than the rest of the infield put together.

I'm out with a handful of single teammates, most of them at least five years younger than I am, and we're on the prowl, looking for some post-game fun. We've swept our home opener series in Copper Valley despite my rocky performance, and it's time for me to get fully back in the groove.

This is prime *Cooper Rock gets a girl, celebrates, and satisfies his superstitions before we head off on a road trip* time.

Usually, Blue Dress would be exactly my type. She's laughing—always a plus. She's with a group of friends, which means there are ladies for my teammates to flirt with too. Her vibe says *I'm up for a good time but I don't want your number and I won't be there when you wake up in the morning.* That is a must for the women I have flings with during the season.

And in the off-season too, if I'm being honest here.

But tonight, even watching her tame that mechanical bull like she has the thighs of Xena, Warrior Princess, isn't doing it for me.

Because she's not a curvy, white, sometimes-brunette and sometimes-blonde with pink sparkle eyeshadow, the voice of an angel, the patience of a saint, and the touch of a nymph.

"Check out her friend in the black top," Robinson Simmons says. Robby's in his second season with the Fireballs as our utility man. He's Black, with short hair, a brand new tattoo with his niece's name on his bicep, and he scored three runs for us tonight. "Just...wow."

I'd like to, but I'm now distracted by the television in the corner of the room, where the curvy pop star of my dreams is all dolled up in a sequin dress, pink lipstick, and fancy up-do, smiling and chatting with a reporter from one of those entertainment shows.

I don't know how it's possible for her to get prettier every damn day, but she does.

And she has for the past seven or eight years.

The other thing she keeps getting?

Nicer.

Fucking *nicer*.

Don't need the sound on the TV to guess what she's saying right now as she pulls a second glittery young white woman to her side.

Do you know Aspen? She's taking the music world by storm. I listen to her album on repeat as often as I can. I'm so mad that we haven't had a chance to do a collaboration yet. Next album, right, Aspen?

"Earth to Cooper," Lopez says directly in my ear. "Dude, you're not gonna get laid tonight if you don't get in the game."

I jerk back, recover, and force a cocky grin at my teammate. He caught me mooning over Waverly Sweet like I'm our rookie catcher instead of the veteran on the team who knows how to handle himself in every situation on and off the field.

"I'm practicing letting the universe send me what it knows I deserve."

Normally, saying something like that wouldn't make me want to throw up in my mouth, but tonight, it does.

I don't want a one-night stand with a random bar chick right now.

But what I *do* want, I can't have.

She and her manager made that crystal clear a long time ago, so I moved on, and I made something of myself too.

Dammit.

I look around the bar once again.

Xena the Warrior Princess in the blue dress has finally been thrown off the mechanical bull and is high-fiving her friends. Definitely a bachelorette party. The lady in black that Robby was drooling over is donning a veil, and I take the opportunity to punch him lightly in the arm.

"Don't go for brides, dude. It does *not* end well."

"Shiiiiiiit," he breathes. "My mom would kill me."

"Not saying you couldn't be her getaway car if she decides not to go through with it, but do not, under any circumstance, pick up an engaged or married woman, *ever*."

Diego plops down on the bench across from me, all smiles. He was born in the Dominican Republic, grew up mostly in Oklahoma, and couldn't be happier if he tried. I cut a glance at the television, and yep. Waverly's gone, and some actor is in the hot seat for an interview now.

Diego was probably in the bathroom streaming the interview on his phone.

Which is basically exactly where I considered going too.

Watching her with my adopted Little Sluggers baseball team—*Jesus*.

She stayed the same. All these years, she's stayed who she is.

Or who I always hoped she was.

Smiling. Waiting for a group of kids who were late, even when she had other stuff her staff clearly needed to get her to. And she made a point of talking individually to *all* of them and making sure no one left without getting something signed.

Even the shyer kids who were hiding in back got her individual attention.

And then offering them tickets that I'm well aware are usually reserved for the specialest of the special guests.

Treating them like they were the only kids in the entire damn arena.

And *not* because she knew I was there.

That much was obvious.

"Did you know Waverly Sweet's friend Aspen has a pet guinea pig?" Diego says.

Francisco groans.

Robinson gives the rookie a dead-ass *we don't go to bars to talk about pop stars more popular with teenage girls than with professional baseball players* look.

"Coop. Talk to this boy."

Diego looks at me like he's a puppy and I'm holding out a ball.

"You want to date Waverly?" I ask him.

His face dances with a kind of panic that would be amusing if we were talking about anyone else. It's the first time I've seen a not-smile on him, and it's like I've bulldozed everything he knew about how the world works.

"I can't date a *goddess*, Mr. Cooper."

Mr. Cooper. That will never not make me feel old. "One, she's a regular person, just like you. But where you're a baseball god, she's a singing goddess, so I get the confusion. Point is, under the makeup and dresses, you're the same. You want to ask her out, you can do it. No rules against it. But two, if you're intimidated and think she's above you, then you're right. Don't ask her out. Power dynamics shouldn't be uneven in a relationship. So. What about her friend?"

Now all three of my teammates are giving me the *did he take a ball to the head and we all missed it?* look.

I cock a brow. "Gentlemen, we are worthy, and anyone who thinks we aren't doesn't deserve our time. Life lesson. Get it tattooed on your dick to remind yourselves multiple times a day."

Frankie makes a noise, but I ignore him. "You think you've got it all figured out because you have the arrogance of youth, more money than god, a division championship under your belt, and some of you are getting paid to do commercials for jock itch spray and running shoes. But there are women out there who are still gonna act like they're better than you, like you're some kid who's never gonna grow up because your day job is in sports, like you're too much trouble because we're on the road all the time and they think that'll hold them back from doing what they want to do."

"Some of them are better than us, Coop," Robby says.

I snort. "Fuck that. We're goddamn heroes. We deserve women who fucking *adore* us and are willing to be with us despite how hard it is to love a guy who's on the road half the year. Got it?"

Diego slides a wide-eyed *what the fuck?* look at Robby, who pulls a long, slack-jawed face and shrugs back.

A fry falls out of Frankie's mouth.

And then all three of them crack up together.

"Haha, Mr. Cooper," Diego cackles.

"Bruh. You had us going for a minute there," Robinson adds on a chortle.

Francisco's laughing too hard to even breathe.

Shit.

Shit.

I don't want to get laid tonight.

I don't want to be out with my friends.

I don't want to swagger around here being fabulous, getting hit on, lining up options for the next time we're back home too.

I want—

I want something that I let go a long time ago.

Something I had to let go for my own sense of self-worth.

And I don't want to want that, and I don't understand why five minutes in a damn meet-and-greet room is turning my world upside down during a season when I have much, *much* bigger things to worry about than the pop star I walked away from eight damn years ago.

Yeah, but you haven't talked to her since then, an obnoxious voice that sounds like my grandfather's parrot says in my ear. *You talk to her, you fall for her. Rawk!*

I shove up out of the booth. "Got beaned in batting practice," I mutter. "I should go home. Don't let D get arrested. Or hook up with a bride or that redhead in the corner who's been eyeing all of us. Not a good fit. Trust me."

"You need me to drive you home, Mr. Cooper?" Diego asks. He grins. Of course he does. "I'm designated sober driver. I got you, boo."

I need to get my head back on straight.

Waverly Sweet was a blip in my past. She's not part of my present or my future, no matter how much I can't stop thinking about the way she stared at me when I walked into that room, and the way she stared at me when my mouth didn't get the memo to shut the fuck up and instead started rambling about her mom.

So I'm gonna go home, wallow in my feelings until they pass, and then I'm gonna get back to being Cooper Rock, baseball god, hometown hero, and sexy beast with the ladies.

Have to.

Because if I don't, I'm gonna be worthless for my team this season. And *this* season, of all of them, is the one that matters most. This is the season that will change all our lives even more than last season did.

Which means that I need to get Waverly Sweet and all those old memories out of my head in order to be the player that the team needs me to be.

"Yeah," I tell Diego. "I'd love a ride. Thanks, man."

I don't need a ride.

But D needs to feel needed and like he's an important part of the team both on and off the field.

Also, he's gonna talk about Waverly the entire time.

Can't get over her if I don't face her.

So here we go.

3

Waverly

OF ALL THE parties that I had to bring Aspen to, this is by far the worst option.

It's great for her.

Super for her.

It still feels weird for me to say I found an indie artist and decided to put my star power behind making her into the next big thing, but that's exactly what happened with Aspen. I was on my tour bus one night last summer, licking my wounds after seeing one more report about my ex-fiancé and the diamond he bought for the woman he'd been cheating on me with the last few months of our relationship, and I started randomly perusing iTunes to distract myself before I spiraled into the pit of self-doubt and loneliness that's been my constant companion since Geofferson—yes, Geofferson with a *G-e-o*—left me for a Cirque du Soleil dancer.

Yes, she's prettier than me.

And more flexible.

And I don't want to talk about it anymore, other than to say that that night is when I stumbled across Aspen's self-produced first album and fell head over heels in love with her voice and her style and basically everything about her.

So here we are, at Cash Rivers's annual spring bash, because the networking opportunities for her will be incredible tonight. I'll get to introduce Aspen to some of my favorite Hollywood stars and producers, which could put her on the path to writing music for high-profile projects. Getting pictures of her rubbing elbows with execs from various music labels should help her negotiate better terms for her first studio album when it's clear that she's in demand, or at least get buzz going if she decides to stay indie.

And I have indigestion.

I've done this dance before, throwing my weight behind someone to help their career take off.

This is different, I remind myself.

First, it's intentional instead of accidental. Next, I had my team run a background check to make sure she's the real deal. When they were satisfied, I friended her under a fake profile on TikTok and gushed about her to test out her reactions to a random nobody loving her music, and I found her to be lovely and charming and humble. I arranged a *completely by chance* meeting where I confirmed she's the same in person as she seemed online.

And the final factor in my decision to take her under my wing, teach her everything I know, and help her launch her career into the stratosphere?

There's no chance that I'll fall in love with her.

But unfortunately, everyone's focus is less on the fact that

I've brought Aspen with me, and more on the fact that Geofferson is also here with his fiancée.

It's been almost a year since we split up. Almost a year since we've been seen in the same place.

Almost a year since I was labeled the ice queen, blamed in the tabloids for our breakup, and completely lost my interest in men in general.

You could say dating lost its appeal.

And now here we are, with the whispers swirling all around me and that self-doubt and embarrassment and shame that I didn't see what was right in front of my eyes the whole time welling up all over again and threatening to make my sensitive stomach cause a major scene.

"Ignore him," Aspen whispers beside me.

"That's a lot easier to do when everyone else is ignoring the elephant in the room," I murmur, trying desperately to evade all the curious glances and the way my stomach is gurgling like it needs a bathroom more than it needs to be at this party. "Also, I'm about to change my mind. I can't make you famous if you're going to have to deal with all of this crap too."

"I have an amazing therapist and an unhealthy amount of *I don't give a shit what unimportant people think of me* in my personality. It comes with the kind of rejection I've had all of my life, but that you didn't have until Geofferson. Who didn't deserve you, by the way."

I catch sight of Geofferson's blond head across the wide-open living room in this Malibu mansion, hear his obnoxious fake laugh that he only does when he's working on impressing someone more important than he is, and I flinch.

He shouldn't be here.

You're so high-maintenance, Waverly. You're so picky about what you eat, you spend more time on your wardrobe every day than most people spend in an entire week, you never have time for me, and now that my career is taking off, there's not time for us to have an actual relationship.

I was *high maintenance* because I have stomach issues, the world expects eight costume changes at every concert, and my career is as demanding as it is rewarding.

Meanwhile, his career was taking off after I introduced him to all the right people in all the right places to set everything in motion to *make* his career take off.

Is he that great of an actor?

He's decent, but he'll never win any awards.

And his band on the side?

See again, decent, but it'll never win any awards.

Not that he's not good, or that he doesn't have fans that connect with his style and his kind of talent. But the number of people who've quietly told me he never would've gone anywhere, and definitely not with the speed that everything exploded for him without my endorsement, makes me feel totally used.

I have no idea if any of them are being honest, or if they're telling me what they think I want to hear.

Either way, what I did for Geofferson is giving me not only indigestion, but also the threat of an incredibly embarrassing situation if that gurgling in my stomach moves to my intestines.

And here I am, doing the exact same thing for Aspen tonight.

I tell my digestive system to simmer down and nudge Aspen toward the pool deck outside. Air sounds heavenly.

"Have you met Cash yet?" I ask.

She slides one last look in Geofferson's direction as we cross the threshold to where the real party is happening. "No, but it can wait. I'll give you ten bucks to go back in there, walk right up to the douche and pretend like you're happy to see him, then mutter to someone after you stroll away that you pity the way his career is about to tank without your support."

"I'd do it, but I couldn't handle the press coverage when he gets lucky and I end up wrong. And also, it might make me puke to be that confrontational."

She wrinkles her nose. "We seriously need to get you in touch with my therapist."

"We probably do."

"Fine. What you need is a revenge boyfriend. Someone even *better* than Geofferson."

Cooper Rock's smiling face flashes through my mind, and I instantly squash the vision.

Or try to.

It's been five weeks since he crashed my meet-and-greet in Copper Valley, and I'm hyper aware that the Fireballs have an away series here in Los Angeles this week—they beat my home team about an hour ago—and that he's friends with Cash Rivers, the Bro Code member from Copper Valley, Virginia, who went on to become a movie star after the boy band broke up.

Yep.

Cash is a Fireballs fan too.

So Cooper could be here tonight.

Which would be awful.

I don't want to see Cooper Rock. I don't want to think about Cooper Rock. I don't want to even know that Cooper Rock exists. The man has a way of getting under my skin, and *no*.

Cooper didn't use me the way Geofferson did, but he left abruptly, and I'd never—*ever*—fallen so hard for anyone the way I fell for him in those three days we were together. Not before and definitely not since. When he told me he had to get back to baseball, but that he'd call, and then he didn't...and didn't...and didn't...and then went out and was photographed kissing someone else the same way he'd been kissing me...

It was my first real taste of heartbreak, and it changed me. The whole thing feels like a lifetime ago and yesterday all at once.

Especially being here and having to face Geofferson again.

I shake my head at Aspen. "No. I don't want a revenge boyfriend. I'm working on me first and relationships only when I'm ready and he's right and not a douche." Hence my reputation as an ice queen.

God forbid a woman politely decline a few dates because she needs to put herself first to heal after the trauma of realizing that the man she thought she was going to marry was only using her to kickstart his own success. It doesn't matter how politely you say no. It's still *no*, and I'm apparently not supposed to use that word.

"You should date Davis Remington."

I choke on a laugh, the whole idea startling me enough that my stomach quits gurgling for a moment. "Yes, because dating a reclusive former boy band guy who has nothing to do with the industry anymore and never wants to be seen in public is *revenge*. That'll make so many ripples with the pictures of us that don't exist."

"It would." She grins. "The mystery factor, Waverly. Think of the mystery factor. You probably don't even have to date him. You can just spread the *rumor* that you know where he is and you're dating him."

"I could find out where he is in like five seconds—hello,

we're at his former bandmate's house, and I *have* seen him *in person* in the past two years—and no."

"Can I pretend date him?"

"Not until *after* we've established that *you* can be a star without having to date your way to the top."

Her laugh lights up the entire pool deck, and at least a dozen people turn to stare at us.

And I mean A-listers and Grammy winners and basically half the movers-and-shakers in the film and music industries.

Aspen blinks as her gaze sweeps around at the sudden attention, and she drops her voice, which takes on a slight waver. "I solemnly promise to make you proud."

Which, thankfully, seems to be the only thing that Liv Daniels overhears as she turns from chatting with Dax Gallagher, lead singer of Half-Cocked Heroes, and his long-time girlfriend to study both of us. The dark-haired, slender, white actress has recently been making headlines for declining prominent roles when her male co-stars were banking oodles more money than she was offered on the same projects, and now she's starting her own production company with the backing of some even higher-profile women in the biz.

"I don't think you'll have to try very hard," she says to Aspen. "You're a natural. Liv Daniels. And you're *Aspen*. I'm glad you're here. I've been wanting to chat."

Aspen gapes at her.

"She's happy to meet you too," I tell Liv, "but you'll need to give her a minute."

Liv's eyes twinkle. "Can do. How are you doing, Waverly? I saw the douche showed up. Who invited him?"

"Do we care?"

"We do if we want to avoid working with anyone who'd voluntarily associate with him."

"Oh my god, I love your petty," Aspen gasps.

Liv winks at her. "Thank you. I've worked hard to develop it and use it over the years."

"Okay, I love all of you."

"We should do drinks. When are you free?"

Aspen blinks. And then she flies into motion as only Aspen can, which is one of the things I've quickly come to love about her. "Have your people call my people."

She shoots a look at me, and I see the silent snicker of glee that she got to use that line.

Liv misses it as she pulls out her phone.

Texting her people, I assume.

She pockets it, and the three of us chat for a while, Aspen getting more comfortable with each passing minute until we're surrounded by several actors and musicians who are hanging on her every word.

"So I had a choice," she's saying. "It was either call animal control or chase that armadillo out of my house myself. And then find a new place to live. Not that there weren't already clues with the leaky roof and the landlord being all *don't take that tone with me over text if you don't want to live with buckets in the kitchen for the next six months since I'm not contractually obligated to fix the roof,* but the armadillo sealed the deal."

"Did you get the armadillo out?" Liv asks.

"Hell, no. I blocked him in the kitchen, told my landlord that I left his check on the counter next to the fridge, grabbed the essentials only, and left."

"Where did you go?" Cash Rivers asks her.

"Waverly's house. This was like two months ago. Also, I heard a rumor that my former landlord got arrested for tax evasion. You people do *not* mess around when you want revenge, do you?"

"I had nothing to do with that," I say.

Did my team?

Possibly.

I have no idea. They don't tell me things I don't need to know.

I'm smiling, but it freezes on my face when a familiar voice speaks up behind me. "Sure, you didn't."

Geofferson. Freaking *Geofferson*.

Aspen's mouth contorts. Liv's eyes narrow. Dax Gallagher's girlfriend, Willow, pulls a face that I'm pretty sure she learned from her Viking stepbrothers, and I legit think she might be winding up to punch him on my behalf.

I'm suddenly not annoyed that Geofferson wants to make a scene.

Not on my behalf.

I'm annoyed on Aspen's behalf. Tonight's about *her*. And the only thing anyone will be talking about tomorrow is the fact that Geofferson and I had our first public run-in since our breakup.

I turn slowly.

He's smirking. "Waverly. You look...well."

His fiancée pops her gum and leans into him like she's physically incapable of standing up on her own. "Waverly! We didn't know you'd be here."

I force a smile. "Geofferson. You look exactly the same." I sweep a glance around the party. "Is your new side piece here too?"

Everyone on the pool deck sucks in a breath.

Oh my god.

I said that. Out loud.

"Snap," Aspen whispers.

I have no idea what anyone else is thinking, because the

only thought in my head right now is that loud roar of *and this is why they'll repeat tomorrow that you're a grudge-holding ice queen*.

"Turns out I don't need a side piece when I'm with the right woman." Geofferson isn't smiling when he says it though.

Oh. Em. To the gee.

He *is* cheating again.

That *fucker*.

There are two kinds of people in my world. The kind that lose their way more and more with every dollar that goes into their bank accounts, and the kind that find a way to balance the fame and scrutiny and money with staying true to who they are.

I grew up in this world. I've had my slips. Since Geofferson, I've been trying to find who I really am, but I still feel like an invader in my own skin more days than not.

And I know I'm not the only one.

So maybe there are three kinds of people in my world, and I fit into the lost group.

Which is exactly where Geofferson's fiancée will be in a few months.

If I were the bigger person, I'd warn her.

But *she knew* we were engaged when she started dating him. The entire world knew, and if she was dumb enough to start dating a guy who claimed to be a movie star without googling him—which would've brought me up right at the top of her search results—then that's on her too.

Geofferson jerks his head at Aspen. "This your new little project to find yourself?"

I hate that when I look at him, I still remember the good times.

I hate that when I look at him, part of me still wants him back.

Fuck that part. Fuck all of those parts. I toss my hair back, lift my chest, and look him dead in the eye. "Go find your own spotlight, Geofferson. I'm done letting you use mine."

Two bodies leap between us. I don't know who they are. I can't see straight at the moment.

Conflict?

I *hate* it.

I've let Aunt Zinnia fight my battles for me for years in order to focus on what I do best, which is write and sing songs, connect with my fans, and smile for cameras.

My stomach gurgles again. Someone here will report this whole encounter to the tabloids and they'll twist it to make me look like a spiteful bitch instead of a woman trying to stand up for herself against someone who wanted to ruin her night so he could feel like a man.

Aspen grips my hand. "I am extremely glad you're not with that douche anymore," she whispers.

She's right.

I need to date again.

I need to make new memories with someone who'll make me happy, not someone who will haunt me for the rest of my life. I shift, turning away from Dax and Cash, who're not-so-subtly pushing Geofferson off the porch while flagging security.

Good riddance.

And that's when I see him.

Cooper Rock.

Cooper Rock is here.

Of course he is. No surprise. I *knew* this could happen.

But the irritating part?

My heart jolts and yells *that one. Date that one.*

He's seven million times more handsome than Geofferson. Funnier. Or was, when I thought my soul *recognized* him. And he talked about his family almost non-stop, whereas Geofferson constantly complained that his parents loved his sister more because she was always at their house helping them do things that you do for the people you love when they need help.

Cooper's gaze sweeps past me as if he hasn't noticed me at all. He freezes for a split second while I stare, even though I'm positive he doesn't realize I'm here gawking at him. Then he turns to a pretty brunette standing next to him, whispers something, and the next thing I know, he's dipping her back in a kiss that belongs on a movie screen.

My stomach gurgles the way it does to warn me that if I don't get to a bathroom *stat*, there'll be a lot more being reported to the tabloids than that I ice-queened out my ex-fiancé.

My temper flares.

Heat stings my eyes.

I have everything. Money. Fame. Fortune. Good friends. My aunt watching out for my career. Medication to solve my stomach issues most of the time.

But I don't have taste in men.

And I don't think I ever will.

4

One Month Later

Cooper

I'M IN A SLUMP.

I'm in a fucking *slump*.

Me.

Cooper Rock. The heart and soul of the Fireballs from their losing years. The guy who lets rookies give him sober rides home when he doesn't need them so that they feel like they're an important part of the team. The guy who pranks his teammate and future brother-in-law to make the dude smile, since he's the opposite of Diego and needs to smile more. The guy who spends extra time in the batting cage even though he butts heads with the batting coach because deep down, he knows she's right and he could be a legend bound for the baseball hall of fame instead of a mere god in one small part of the country, and who doesn't want that?

Clearly, me.

If I wanted to be a legend, I wouldn't let something as dumb as not being interested in getting laid this season stop me from playing good baseball.

But it's my thing.

I get laid, I play good ball.

This year?

I'm not doing either.

I'm muttering *stupid stupid stupid* to myself as I slouch through the secret hallways beneath the bleachers at Duggan Field on a rare off day, hoping to catch the Fireballs' resident superstition expert hanging around the stadium without looking like I'm hoping to catch her. I slip out the door next to the players' clubhouse, turn the corner to open the door into our private lounge, and run headfirst into a dream.

"*Ack!*" the blonde-haired, heavenly-scented, glittery eye-shadowed, curvy pop star squeaks as her open glitter tumbler tips and spills liquid all down her jersey.

I stop.

And I gape.

Start to reach out to touch her hair at the same time I try to pinch myself. This is a dream.

This has to be a dream.

Actually, have I had this dream?

I have definitely had this dream.

No matter what color her hair is dyed, I've had this dream.

"Here, sweetie, I've got it." The dark-haired woman that I recognize from the meet-and-greet, the one with round rosy cheeks and the energy of a chipmunk, bustles between us, shoving napkins across Waverly's chest and using her hip to bump me out of the way. "Are you burned? Cyrus! More tea!

Elodie! Wardrobe change! Oh, Waverly, don't you worry. I'll get this cleaned up for you in no time."

"Thank you, Hiramys. I'm okay."

Hiramys eyeballs me, and recognition sets in immediately. "Cooper! Cooper Rock! Aren't you a sight for sore eyes? Mercy. Hello. How did you get past all of the security? Didn't you see the signs? The ballpark is closed."

"Only to some people," Waverly murmurs.

Her voice is cool, but it's not snooty, *I am above you, peon* pop star cool. Or even *you seriously crossed the line with that comment about my mother* cool. It's more *I'm dripping in hot tea and wouldn't be if you were watching where you were going* cool.

At least, that's what my brain says.

Right along with *you are such a dumbass every time you see this woman.*

It's not wrong, which is the only explanation for what comes flying out of my mouth next. "That was my sister. That I was kissing. At Cash's party last month."

Yeah.

That's what I just said.

And it's what I did when the team was in LA and I got invited to a party thrown by a movie star who grew up here in Copper Valley and who's been a personal friend since I made my debut with the Fireballs eight years ago.

I was minding my own business, hanging out with Max and Tillie Jean and a few other friends when I saw Waverly and her entourage and freaked.

Nothing says *big bad baseball player* like freaking out when you see a woman you have a stupid crush on.

Yeah.

I'm *that* kind of mature.

Her aunt was right all those years ago, and that hasn't

changed. *Waverly's going places, and she doesn't need a man who'll never grow up holding her back.*

Hiramys and Waverly share a look that's clearly more conversation than a simple glance. Hiramys clears her throat. "This isn't personal—I adore you on the field, Cooper, and that was so sweet that you've adopted the worst team in Little League to build them up and make their dreams come true the last time we were here in town—but I'm going to have security escort you out. Protocol. You haven't had a background check. Honestly, I don't know how you slipped through. There are signs and security *everywhere*."

Jesus. Hello, bad. Meet worse.

I aim my most harmless grin at her because I need to not leave here.

I need to ask Waverly out.

Mind made up. Right here, right now.

This is the *only* way I'm getting her out of my system. I have to ask her out, and she has to go ice princess and show her true colors, then I can realize that the Waverly I'm crushing on is all a façade who has her aunt do her dirty work for her, and I'll finally be able to get back to doing what I do best: scoring.

Everywhere.

"The signs never apply to me," I tell Hiramys. Like hell I'm admitting to knowing the undisclosed passages under the field and that I didn't see a single damn sign on my entire way into the stadium. That's my little secret. "I live here. Duggan Field is home for a Fireballs baseball god like me."

"You were kissing your sister," Waverly says.

Fuck. I would've preferred she paid attention to the whole *I'm a god* part.

Maybe.

Did that sound conceited?

Shit."It's something we do," I tell her. "*Wait.* No. That sounded wrong. It's not something we do. I mean we fake it when one of us needs to avoid someone. We started it back when I was in high school and playing travel ball and we'd go to these games a few hours from home where guys would hit on her, so I'd kiss her—*pretend* to kiss her—because they didn't know I was her brother and not her boyfriend, and then they'd leave her alone."

My brain says *shut up.* My mouth says *we haven't dug this hole deep enough.* "No one crosses Cooper Rock. Not even back then. I don't like my sister. I mean, I do. She's awesome. Great person. But I don't like her like that. I wasn't even kissing her. I was kissing my hand over her mouth. There was no lip contact. At all. And she paid me back by—actually, that one's embarrassing. Never mind."

Waverly lifts her tumbler and takes a sip of whatever's left in it, bright hazel eyes watching me. "And who were you hiding from?"

Jesus, Mary, and Babe Ruth. I would've rather told the embarrassing revenge story. "Levi Wilson." *Fuck.* First name that slipped into my head, and it's the wrong one. She loves Levi. It's mutual. They're like me and Tillie Jean. Brother and sister. Tight. But not involved. They're not actual blood relations, but they act like, it, and *ew.*

Plus, Levi's madly in love with a local bookstore owner here in Copper Valley and is about to become stepdad to her three kids. They're adorable in that adorable way people in love get adorable.

Jesus.

My brain is short-circuiting.

"You and Levi are having issues?" Waverly asks, clearly not

buying it.

Or possibly hoping it's true, since he was my connection to getting my Little Sluggers team into her meet-and-greet back in March and I'm definitely not welcome back for another of those.

"It was a surprise that I was there at the party," I improvise. "He wasn't supposed to see me yet."

"Doesn't he know your sister too?"

"It was dark. Ish."

"It really wasn't."

A burly security dude with an earpiece and a chest the size of our travel bus approaches.

This.

This right here is why I will be alone once I've retired from baseball. My parents set the gold standard for being in love with your partner. My brother's following in their footsteps. Now that Max has pulled his head out of his ass and quit telling everyone who'll listen the lie that he's not good enough for Tillie Jean, she's following in their footsteps. And I'm great at everything else, but when it comes to talking to women that I'm obsessed with—or rather, the *only* woman I get obsessed with anytime I see her—I turn into a blubbering, incoherent, rambling mess.

"Didn't expect to see you here," I mutter. I glance at the security guy again. "Really sorry about the tea. Didn't mean to make you spill it. I'll go."

"Who were you hiding from?" Waverly repeats.

I meet her eyes again, and angels burst into song in my head simply from making eye contact with her.

She's a goddess.

And not like I'm a god. She's an actual goddess. Not faking it.

And those angels in my head sound a lot like her.

Jesus. I have *got* to get over this woman. And I thought I had. I really thought I had.

Until I saw her being her awesome, amazing self with a bunch of kids who are usually reminded by everyone around them how hard they suck at baseball and too many other things in life.

"Can't remember," I lie.

Her eyes go flat. "So you saw someone else you slept with before and didn't want it to get awkward."

My reputation precedes me. "No. It was—"

You're obsessed, dude. You're so obsessed you hear it as two separate words. Ob. Sessed. Shoot your shot, bro. Shoot. Your. Shot. Then move on.

I glance around the room. Where Waverly goes, her aunt Zinnia is sure to follow, and honestly?

That's who I didn't want to see me.

She was approaching Waverly's group when I realized they were both there, and I needed to not be spotted for my own sake.

I almost have more history with Zinnia than I do with Waverly. She was the messenger when Waverly dumped me. When I ended up at a party in Vegas a year later that Waverly was also unexpectedly attending, Zinnia was the one who appeared out of nowhere basically the minute I spotted Waverly and showed me out. My agent let it slip that I'd lost out on an endorsement deal that my buddy Luca Rossi ultimately got because Zinnia Sweet stepped in and informed the parent company that Waverly wouldn't be following through with her line of skin care products for them if I became the face of their shampoo line.

But I don't see Zinnia in the Fireballs' clubhouse now.

Only the rest of Waverly's entourage, who are all listening in.

I have no idea what she's doing here at my baseball park, but she's *here*.

Fuck it.

I'm done ignoring the signs.

I'm done hiding and I'm done letting Zinnia Sweet in my head. "I didn't want your aunt to see me and make a scene."

Waverly's brows knit together. "Why would—oh my god."

"Yeah. I—"

"Oh my god." The second *oh my god* comes out as a shriek. She shoves the tumbler at her assistant, then lifts a hand that clearly tells the security guard to back off, which he does.

And then she's grabbing me by my shirt and shoving me out into the hallway and slamming the door behind us, demonstrating that she no longer needs her guard because she intends to tear my limbs off all by herself, which, yeah, is also hot.

"You slept with her, didn't you?" she hisses.

"What?"

"You slept with my aunt! Oh my god. *Years*, Cooper. For *years*, I've thought you decided to ghost me because I was an annoying little brat who got too attached because you were good in bed, even though I *totally* restrained myself from texting you every single minute of those days right after since Aunt Zinnia kept telling me no one wants a desperate woman, but that's not it at all. *You couldn't keep it in your pants and you slept with my aunt and neither one of you would tell me."*

"Ew," I gasp. I might gag a little. Okay, I definitely gag a little. "No—*ew*."

Waverly plants a hand on her hip and glares at me. "What, now she's *too old*?"

"No, she—" I blow out a slow breath aimed at the ceiling. "I don't sleep with women who tell me I'm not good enough, and I don't sleep with women who give off the needy vibe, and I don't sleep with women when they're related to the woman I'd really like to date."

She blinks, clearly surprised and unable to hide it, and I realize her lashes are plastered thick enough to be seen four states over, and her eyeshadow glitter is rainbow glitter, and that's not my obsession talking.

She's actually wearing rainbow glitter eyeshadow and eyelash extensions, and I'm so fucking drunk on being near her that it took me this long to notice.

Those gorgeous eyes waver over her smooth, round cheeks, questions and doubts written all over her expressive face. "Aunt Zinnia told you you're not good enough?"

Fuck.

Zinnia wasn't Waverly's messenger. She was running interference all on her own.

And I get it.

I've been *that guy* telling dudes they're not good enough for my sister for years, and I almost fucked up the best thing that ever happened to TJ because I was reinforcing some self-doubt that Max already had when I went after him in the off-season. I don't get to judge someone else for doing it to me.

Especially when she was right.

I swallow hard and look at the wall behind Waverly's head, featuring a photo of me diving for a line drive between first and second base. Making me out to look like a hero when really, I'm as much a fuck-up at heart as anyone else.

"It was a long time ago," I mutter to Waverly.

"How long?"

"A long—it doesn't matter."

"What did she say to you?"

"It doesn't—"

"Let me decide if it matters."

I finally grow a pair and look her straight in the eye, because that's what you do when you're not afraid of everything that's currently terrifying me. "She wasn't wrong. That's what matters. I *wasn't* good for you. You were going places, and you had—*have* a reputation that shouldn't be tarnished by a guy like me."

I need to shut up. I need to shut up, but also, I need to get it all out. "I wouldn't have cheated on you, but I would've been gone every year from February to October, you would've been on tour all the time, we never would've had time for each other, we both would've been explaining that all those pictures in the tabloids weren't what they looked like every time we found five minutes to talk, and the most important part—the thing she knew and I knew and that I always assumed you knew too—was that I would've held you back."

She makes a *you're being ridiculous* noise, but I press on.

If I'm spilling my guts, I'm spilling all of them. "You didn't —don't—you're basically the best thing to ever happen to music and you're an awesome role model to more people than you probably even realize, and I'm—look, the point is, I didn't sleep with her. I wouldn't sleep with her."

Her eyes are as round as I've ever seen them.

But I'm in it. I'm in it, and I'm not bailing now. "I like you. I'm not that stupid, secretly insecure kid who'll let someone's opinion stop me from going after what I want anymore, but I am the dumbass who's finally realizing I never had the balls or the courtesy to go ask *you* if you wanted to break up with me or not instead of leaping to the same conclusion as the other people in your life who care about you. I didn't have the guts to tell you to your face that I had to leave so you could shine. I owed you that. And I'm sorry I didn't do it."

She finds her voice, and it's soft and condemning. "You left because Aunt Zinnia told you that you weren't good enough for me."

I rub the back of my neck. "I was young and dumb and out of my league, and I'm sorry. I'm still bad for your reputation, but fuck it. I'd like to take you out. Or in. In works. I can cook. I'm fucking awesome in the kitchen. Here. My number. Call me if you're interested. And I'm sorry about the tea. And kissing my sister. Which wasn't a real kiss. I swear. That was— never mind. I'd offer to buy you a new outfit, but clearly, you don't need me to—here."

I pull a Sharpie out of my back pocket, steal one of the napkins still stuck to her jersey—*Braverlies*, it says. She's wearing a jersey for Waverly's Braverlies, her fan club.

That's fucking adorable and awesome and I want one.

"Aunt Zinnia broke us up," she repeats, again, like it's never occurred to her that anyone in her inner circle would've protected her from guys like me.

"Long time ago," I mutter again. "It's in the past."

She blinks at me, and I want to wrap her in my arms, kiss her senseless, and drown in every bit of her in a way I've *never* wanted to drown in *any* woman.

What the *fuck* is wrong with me?

Concentrate, dummy.

Right.

I'm scribbling my digits while she stares at me, suddenly feeling like I'm still that stupid, immature kid who didn't understand the world he was living in. I'm a small-town family guy at heart. Always have been, always will be. And Waverly was my first brush with celebrity.

She was starting her career then. A few wins under her belt, but overall, a relative unknown. I knew it wouldn't stay that way long. Anyone could look at her and see not just star power, but staying power.

She had her singer-actress mother's genes, but she also had this magical mix of girl-next-door vibe and sheer determination to prove she was worthy on her own without the lingering influence of her mom's name in the industry.

The entire world recognized that she was the whole package the minute they finally looked at her. She has this way of *being* that's impossible to miss.

And the thing that makes Waverly most awesome?

She's *still* the girl next door. You see it in every interview she does, every video she puts out, and you hear it in every song she writes.

"Always good to see you, Waverly. I thought all my heroes were baseball players, but that was before I met you."

I tuck the napkin into her jersey, resist the urge to pin her to the wall and kiss her until she can't breathe and desperately needs to climb me and tear my clothes off in the nearest closet, and instead put my hands into the pockets of my sweatpants and head back down the hallway like I was never here.

I don't know why she's here.

I don't know if any of that actually happened.

But there's a pretty good chance this is the last time I'll ever see her.

I have blown my last shot.

And I'll be spending the rest of my day off getting drunk, and then getting her out of my head.

At least, that's my plan until I turn the next corner.

And then—well, then, I don't know if things get better or worse.

5

Waverly

"OH MY GOSH, your barrette is the cutest! Do you love mermaids?" I smile at the wide-eyed little girl whose *Waverly's Bravelies* poster I'm signing at the edge of the baseball diamond at Duggan Field while the crew behind me regroups and repositions the lighting for the final sequence of the video we're shooting here today.

Aunt Zinnia keeps circling past and making noises like I need to be involved in creative decisions about the shoot, but I'd rather talk to my fans.

Also, the last time I tried to help directorially, the video ended up as my most-commented-on YouTube video ever. And the comments are not glowing reviews.

People say much more when they don't like something, and they did *not* like that video.

"Your earrings are pretty," the girl whispers.

"Tell you a secret?" I whisper back.

She nods.

"They're *heavy* and make my ears hurt sometimes. And I don't think they go with my jersey at all, but smarter people than me said I should wear them, so I am."

Her nose wrinkles. "Mommy says fashion isn't worth it if it hurts."

"Listen to your mommy. *Always*. She's a very smart lady."

"We're ready for you, Waverly," Hiramys says, suddenly at my side.

I smile one last time at the little girl, who's probably eight or nine. "Stay true to yourself, okay, Olivia? Don't let people make you wear heavy earrings unless you love them so much you can't help yourself."

"Thank you," her mom says as I straighten.

"Thank you for coming." I wouldn't be here without my fans, and it's the one thing I try to never, ever forget.

"We wouldn't have missed it for the world. I *loved* your mom's music, and now Olivia loves yours, and—I'm sorry. I'm rambling. You need to—"

She cuts herself off as Hiramys slips her arm through mine.

I smile and wave at Olivia, remind myself that I really have made my own career despite getting a leg up in the start because of who my mom was, and then it's back to work.

Video shoot days are always long but totally worth it when we can pack the stands with members of my fan club. Today should be bonus fun—Levi Wilson and I teamed up for a duet on a song called "Always Play My Maybe," and when he suggested we shoot the video at his favorite ballpark, I said yes before thinking it all the way through.

Today, I'm very much wishing I'd thought it all the way through.

Duggan Field is available that day does not mean *the players will be away*, as I assumed it did.

Or, at least, that the *private event, stay out* signs all over everywhere would mean the players wouldn't be wandering through. Or that they, too, had been *told* by management to stay away.

As if that would've worked.

Nothing stops Cooper Rock.

You'd think I would've learned that by now.

I want to take you out. I cook. I wasn't good for you then.

"Ballpark sucks that bad, huh?" Levi says as I join him at home plate.

I realize I'm scowling and quickly take my face back to neutral. "You try wearing bowling balls in your ears."

"I think he did that fifteen years ago," Ingrid, his girlfriend-slash-love-of-his-life, replies with a smile. I adore Ingrid. She's a total hot mess in all the best ways. Like right now, her dark hair is falling out on one side of her ponytail, undoubtedly the work of her son, the youngest of her crew, but she's patting it like she knows and doesn't care. "I saw pictures."

"Levi wore *earrings*?" Zoe, his eldest stepdaughter-to-be, gasps.

"Anyone can wear earrings, but I don't know why they'd want to," his middle future stepkid, Piper, replies. She's obsessed with hockey and is extremely disappointed in all of us because we didn't bring in any of the Copper Valley Thrusters hockey players for cameos in the video.

Stu, our video director, approaches. "How about some payoff for a long day?"

"Define payoff," Levi replies.

Stu grins at him. "Take the pitcher's mound. You want the

kids in the shots? Time for fun. Waverly, you know how to hold a bat?"

"Sure." I take the wooden baseball bat from him and grip it the same way I've seen—ah, *people* do.

Yeah.

The way I've seen other *people* hold bats.

Not any particular people. Whose games I've watched too many of over the years, because I'm a sap who still wishes people well even when they hurt me, and who has a massive sucker streak for lovable losers, especially when my best friends cheer for those loveable losers.

See also: part of me was happy to hear that Geofferson, who got most of our friends in our split, got a role in the next Marvel movie.

Okay, fine. Full disclosure here. I was happy that he's a supporting henchman, and not a primary henchman. It's like I get to revel in seeing him show his true colors on-screen, and not even being the primary henchman is like the biggest insult to what Geofferson wants to do. Secondary henchmen are throwaway roles. Primary henchmen go on to star in slasher films.

Also?

There's something about holding this baseball bat that makes me feel powerful. Maybe I need to release one or two more of those breakup songs I wrote last year and pull a Carrie Underwood in my next video.

"Beast mode," Levi says as I test the weight of the bat. "Try not to take my head off when I pitch it to you, okay?"

I laugh. "I am *not* going to take your head off."

"Right. You're standing there like you're going to the World Series, and you're not going to take my head off."

"I can *hold* a bat. I can't *swing* it."

He takes a baseball and a glove from the production assistant, then waves the glove at me. "C'mon, killer. Let's see it."

Levi Wilson is the big brother I didn't know I needed when I got into the music business. My mom was huge before cancer took her from us when I was in third grade, and Aunt Zinnia had been critical to managing her career and talked to me about it all the time, so I thought I knew all the important parts already.

I did not.

Some things never change in this business, but other things change rapidly. Opening for Levi on my first tour was one of the best things that could've happened to me. He's one of the good guys in the industry, and he taught me a lot.

And while I have a lot of great friends back home in LA, Levi is the closest thing to a *normal* friend that I have.

He grew up here in Copper Valley as the younger of two sons of a single mom in a middle-class neighborhood, got famous by accident, and never really let it go to his head. Definitely falls into that *stays grounded* category of people in my circles.

His fiancée is a single mom of three who runs an independent bookstore and still gawks anytime Levi brings her to a big Hollywood event.

I often tell him he's half the reason I relate to my fans. He taught me how to maintain a sense of *normal*, which turned out to be easier than I was afraid it would. He says that means I'm actually normal myself, and also a natural people person.

I'm apparently afraid of a lot of things.

Maybe too many things.

Maybe if I wasn't afraid all the time, I wouldn't carry anxiety in my stomach and I'd take a chance and date again.

He arches a brow at me while I wiggle the bat the way I've seen *batters* do it on TV.

And then I swing.

His face contorts while Piper cracks up. She's pretty funny herself, but not right now.

She's really bad, she signs to Levi.

Zoe shoves her. "Knock it off, Piper. Waverly knows sign and can understand you."

"Piper. First base," Levi says. "Ingrid, wanna try third?"

Ingrid laughs. "Absolutely not."

"What if we get you some help?" Stu nods to the dugout. "You promise not to hurt them, and they promise to not be assholes about signing NDAs and having cameos?"

What seems to be the entire Fireballs baseball team is waiting in the dugout. Half of them are wearing pink Waverly's Braverlies jerseys. The other half are in black jerseys that match Levi's, with TEAM WILSON printed across the front.

"No way," Levi says. "Tripp'll kill me."

Tripp. His brother, who's in his second season as co-owner of the Fireballs, and yes, I know *entirely* too much about the team.

I blame Levi even when I shouldn't. But he isn't aware of my history with Cooper, and I intend to keep it that way.

"I'll only kill you if you injure one of them," Tripp himself says through a bullhorn from somewhere in the outfield. "Also, we get to use footage for promotional purposes once the video's live."

"Why's he hiding back there to talk to you?" I ask Levi.

"Either his wife doesn't know he approved this, or one of his kids is using the bathroom in the bullpen."

"Absolutely not." Aunt Zinnia charges out from the opposite dugout. "We are *not* giving free publicity to this baseball team."

I glance at the dugout again.

Diego Estevez is there. The rookie catcher that Cooper asked me to sign a baseball for.

Luca Rossi. I know him from his shampoo commercials. My skincare line is produced by the same parent company. I've known who he is for years but didn't realize he played baseball until he got traded to the Fireballs last year.

"Who's the best hitter on the team?" I ask Levi.

"Toss-up," he replies, which isn't what I expected him to say. Everyone knows Brooks Elliott has the best batting average and the most runs batted in. "Stats say Brooks Elliott, but Cooper Rock led the team for *years*. Still smacks the shit out of the ball even if he's playing second fiddle to the newer guy."

"You are *not* batting with professional baseball players," Aunt Zinnia tells me.

I can count on one hand the number of times I've stared my aunt down in the years since she re-introduced me to the president of my mom's record label when I was in high school. But I'm in a mood.

She wasn't wrong. I was bad for you.

Aunt Zinnia chased Cooper away and then manipulated me into not messaging him until she could manipulate me into deleting his number from my phone when we saw the pictures of him with the actress I refuse to name.

Do NOT give that man any more fodder for the press, she'd said. *God only knows what he'd tell the tabloids if you message him now.*

What would've happened if she hadn't interfered?

Did she interfere more?

Did she *set up* his meeting with that actress?

"What's the harm in getting some fun shots for the video?" I ask her. "My fans *love* it when they see me being real. Is there anything more real than making a fool of myself with professional sportsers?"

"You could get hurt."

"We could've all tripped anytime today," Levi says. He's never been overly warm with Aunt Zinnia, but he's never been rude either. I assumed his focus was more on his music than on the whole teams of everyone around him, but now I'm wondering if he has opinions and won't air them because she's my only remaining family. "Nobody's throwing the ball hard at Waverly. She might chip a nail though."

I fake a massive eye roll that I don't really feel but am compelled to do anyway, lest anyone catch on to the emotional turmoil setting me off again. "Oh, the horrors."

"Cooper!" Ingrid calls.

I flinch.

Aunt Zinnia lets out a low growl.

Levi shoots us both a look, but Ingrid continues, distracting all of us. "Bring a helmet for Waverly!"

"You want a clean one or a lucky one?" Cooper calls back like he wasn't under the stands telling me he liked me a few hours ago.

Aunt Zinnia turns and stares at him, and her face goes the kind of annoyed that I only see when she's dealing with incompetent staff or her own ex-boyfriends.

Decision made.

"Lucky," I call for myself. "I always want lucky."

Cooper's gaze locks with mine, and my breasts aren't the only part of me tingling.

And that's a problem.

He's not wrong about my reputation. Or his.

And while I'm trying to help launch Aspen's career and get over the ice queen thing, my media coverage needs to stay squeaky clean.

My reality is a sucky reality.

"Have you met any of the players before?" Ingrid asks me.

"A few," I reply coyly.

Aunt Zinnia whips her gaze to mine again.

She's formidable when she wants to be.

Unfortunately for her, I learned from the best.

"Here, Miss Waverly, it's brand-new, but it's still lucky, because we—I can't talk about it." Diego rushes to home plate holding a massive helmet with a face guard. "Usually you wear it to catch, but you should wear it to bat. Protect as much of you as we can. I love you. You're my favorite. I listen to all of your songs. All the time. I love you. Max! Happy Max! Come pitch gently!"

"What am I, chopped liver?" Levi asks Diego.

"You're too pretty. You probably can't throw." Diego flashes a dimple and sparkling dark brown eyes at my friend, and I want to pinch his cheeks.

He's even more adorable in person than he is on television.

If he were in the music biz, I'd adopt him as my little brother and show him the ropes. But not for a few years. He's too precious to ruin him yet.

"How old are you?" I ask him.

His cheeks flush a deeper brown. "Nineteen."

"And you're already in the Majors? That's amazing. Good for you, Diego. *You* stay safe too, understand? The Fireballs are gonna need you for a *lot* of years." I take the helmet from him.

He takes a giant step back. "Thank you, Miss Waverly."

"Did you get that ball I signed for you?"

He bites his lip and looks down. "Yeah. That was—wow. I have to go. I can't stand in your glow. I'll go blind."

"I'm a regular girl under all this makeup. Promise. Next time we're both in the same city, I'm finding you and taking you to a party myself so you can see what a dork I am."

He makes a noise and darts back to the dugout, heading straight for Cooper, who grins at him and rubs the young man's dark hair, same as I've seen him do to many of his teammates over the years that I've watched the Fireballs play in the name of supporting the team my friend loves.

And then all of the guys I've watched play ball on television file out of the dugout and onto the field.

Am I squealing to myself?

Yes, I do believe I am.

They're *real*.

I get it. I'm a pop star. I grew up in Los Angeles. I get a front-row seat at the Grammys and even won an Oscar for a movie score once. People think *I'm* not real, or that I should be taller, or that I wear glitter eyeshadow and eyelash extensions even when I'm sleeping.

I should not be dazzled by a team of baseball players.

Obviously they're real people.

But this particular team has done something amazing since opening day last year, and I'd be lying if I said I wasn't enthralled with their skill and dedication.

"You any good?" Brooks Elliott asks Piper.

She flexes a tiny arm. "Don't mistake smallness for weakness."

"Never," he replies. "I have a terrifying sister-in-law not much bigger than you. Learned my lesson already, I promise."

"Cameras rolling!" Stu calls. "Act natural. Have fun. Levi, take the mound. You. Lopez. Go play second. Cole, on deck. Rossi, you're on mascot management. Simmons, first base coach. We're gonna get Waverly on base. Rock. Go show her how to hit a ball."

"Nuh-uh." Levi waves Cooper off. "You don't touch my little sister."

"Are we seriously doing this?" I ask.

Cooper spreads his arms. He's sporting the black TEAM LEVI jersey. "Dude, I have a sister. I know how to behave around women."

"I've seen what you do with your sister," I tell him.

"What do you—" Diego cuts himself off as his eyes go wide and he looks at Cooper. "Happy Max will *kill* you."

Cooper claps him on the shoulder. "Never quit calling him Happy Max. He loves that. You playing pitcher? Show Levi how it's done?"

Diego grins. "I don't pitch."

I smile at him. "That's okay. I don't bat."

His face erupts with a smile so big that it's impossible not to smile back. "Waverly's taking me *to a party*," he says out of the corner of his mouth to Cooper.

"Lucky duck," Cooper replies as he moves to squat behind home plate, giving Levi some kind of signal that's probably *I'm not touching her*.

Dammit.

All this opportunity, and he won't take it.

I've spent the past month dropping hints to anyone who'll listen that I'm open to dating again, but I haven't found anyone who's caught my eye.

Not the way my past has.

"Is Diego always that cheerful?" I ask Cooper.

"Always," he confirms. "Best thing to ever happen to the

Fireballs. He really is. You're gonna wanna choke up on the bat."

I blink at him. "Choke up?"

"See how your left hand is right at the bottom end of the bat?"

I look at the bat. "Yes."

"Slide both of your hands up about four inches."

I slide a look at him.

He's straight-faced, like he's not telling me how to hold a bat, which I'm gripping about the same way I gripped *his* bat a few times many years ago.

I creep my fists slowly up the bat, stretching and flexing my fingers and basically molesting the barrel of the bat. "Like this?"

His Adam's apple bobs. "Yes—no. Stop there. Back down about two inches."

"You messing with her swing, Rock?" Levi calls.

"Hush. I'm sabotaging the enemy," Cooper calls back. "Team Levi here, remember?"

"How do I line up to the plate?" I ask. "Like this, right?"

I tilt my upper half over the plate, bending my knees and sticking my butt out.

Levi swipes his forearm over his mouth, his eyes dancing like he's trying not to laugh. "Knees apart, Waverly," he calls.

"Maybe I hit really well like this," I yell back.

"Cooper, *help her*," Zoe wails.

I'm openly flirting with danger. I *want* Cooper to step behind me, line his chest up to my back, wrap his arms around mine, and show me how to hold and swing a baseball bat.

I don't want to marry the man, but I have an itch and I want to scratch it.

"This is about fun, not scoring," I tell Zoe as I adjust my stance again.

Ingrid's next to her, and her eyes tell me she doesn't believe me.

And she shouldn't.

"Are you going to pitch that ball or what?" I call to Levi.

"I'm suddenly worried you're not the one in danger," he replies with a grin.

He's not wrong to worry.

Not wrong at all.

"C'mon. Pitch it," I taunt.

"Cameras are rolling," Stu reminds us.

Levi squeezes his eyes shut, mutters something to himself that's most likely *I'm going to regret this*, and then he lobs a soft pitch my way.

I swing the bat and almost smack Cooper in the head with it.

"Ball one!" Diego yells.

"*She swung*," Levi says.

"You've clearly never played off-hours Fireballs baseball," a blonde in the dugout responds.

Cooper waves at her while he retrieves the ball from its spot against the wall. "Mac! Get out here and play umpire."

"No way. My dads will *kill* me if they see me in this video and realize I didn't invite them too."

"C'mon, babe," Brooks Elliott calls. "I'll protect you, and we need someone who knows the off-hours rules behind home plate."

Three other women in the dugout shove Mac, and she finally trots out to cheers from the entire team and Levi and his family too.

I smile at her. "You're very popular."

"Biggest Fireballs fan *ever*." She pumps a fist to her chest. "They have to love me or I'll hex them. Cooper, if you don't show Waverly how to swing a bat, I'll have to have Brooks do it, and that could end poorly for my marriage, and you don't want that, do you?"

"You know I'd fix it all for you," Cooper replies.

"Yeah, I've seen how you *help*. C'mon. Show Waverly how to swing the bat."

He meets my eyes again, and could the man for one minute *not* be this damn handsome?

"I have to help you now." He shrugs. "Sorry. Can't be helped. Everyone thinks Tripp and Lila and the coaches run the Fireballs, but it's really Mackenzie."

"Oh!" I drop my bat and spin to face her. "You're the one who led the protests over Fiery being retired and the new mascot options all being terrible."

Her baby blues blink twice and then go wide. "Oh my god, you know who I am?"

"I was *riveted*. And also, that meatball mascot contender?"

"I stole it," she whispers.

"You are my *hero*. I would've given up the Fireballs forever if it'd won."

"Oh my god, you love the Fireballs?"

Dammit. My face gets hot, but I quickly hook a thumb toward the pitcher's mound. "When your adopted brother is a fan…"

Total lie.

Total and complete lie.

I have never once in my life told Levi that I'm a Fireballs fan, even when we were on his tour bus and he was watching games, because I didn't want him to find out that I was once hung up on Cooper Rock for six months after he broke my heart.

They're friends, and I'm well aware that Cooper does a lot of good around here.

A *lot* of good.

Often with Levi at his side. I'm not messing that up.

"Okay, Waverly, first, we're fixing your stance." Cooper squats at my feet, taps my back foot, and helps me move it about six inches.

And suddenly all I can think about is that his head is right next to my crotch.

"Other foot," he says. "And now bend your knees. Good. Like that."

He leaps back to his own feet, but instead of telling me to take a test swing, he does exactly what I want him to do and exactly what he most definitely should not do, and he lines himself up against my back, gripping my hips to indicate I should lean over the plate while pushing my butt back into his crotch.

That's a cup. That's a cup. That's a cup.

He *has* to be wearing a cup.

Has to be.

"Squat a little lower." His breath tickles my ear. He pulls his hands off my hips, and then does the absolute worst thing he could possibly do.

As if what he's done already isn't bad enough.

But when he closes his large hands over mine around the baseball bat, a full-body shiver that I can't even pretend to hide races from my fingers up my shoulders and down to my breasts and lower.

My neck has goosebumps. My scalp has goosebumps. My pussy has goosebumps.

"Bring it back like this," he says, pulling the bat back over my right shoulder and nudging my elbow higher at the same time, "and then when you swing, you step forward with this foot—good—and let it all flow however it feels most natural."

He walks me through a swing that I don't remember because his breath is tickling the side of my neck and my butt is nestled in his crotch and his hands—*god*, his hands.

His hands are warm and strong, and his arms are solid, and I want to lick every inch of them up to that tattoo that I know he has under his sleeve, and I very much should've found a fling a month ago when Aspen told me I needed to get back on the dating train.

Aunt Zinnia is glaring daggers.

Levi clears his throat. "You about done, Rock?"

"Pitch it," Cooper calls back.

"We might be having words later."

"Baseball first. You know I can't stand seeing people play poorly when I can help."

"I believe him, Levi," Mac calls. "He knows we'd all kill him on Diego's behalf if he makes D's favorite musician look bad. Also, did you hear? Management says they've sold more of Diego's jerseys than Cooper's this season?"

Cooper jerks behind me. "The fuck they have."

"Everybody already has yours," Levi says with a laugh. "And you're getting oooooold."

"So old," Piper agrees.

"Pitch the ball or we're replacing you," Mac orders. "And quit with the potty mouth, Cooper."

Levi mutters something.

Cooper mutters something.

Then there's a ball flying my way, and a solid baseball player who smells like butterscotch and sunshine on the beach guiding my hands and arms to swing the bat, until—

Crack!

"I hit the ball," I gasp.

"You hit the ball!" Mackenzie crows. "Run, Waverly! Run!"

Cooper's body drops away from mine. "Run," he echoes, giving my shoulders a gentle push, and I realize I'm standing here like a doofus who knows nothing about baseball despite the number of games I've watched.

I have to *run*.

And so I do.

I run like someone's chasing me, which is basically how I feel almost all the time.

Someone wants something from me. Someone wants to hurt me. Someone wants to take my success from me.

But right now, I'm running so that Levi's stepdaughter doesn't throw me out at first base.

I never played baseball. Or soccer. Or did swim team.

And as I dash down the first base line, laughing with the joy that came from the feel of that ball smacking the bat, I decide to ignore the disappointment at not having Cooper cradling my body, and instead, embrace the excitement of trying something new.

Something new.

That's what I need in my life.

Something new.

Robinson Simmons catches the ball at first base and hands it to Piper while Ash, the Fireballs' new baby dragon mascot, makes the *keep running, go to second base* motion. I shriek and swerve away from Piper and Robinson, missing first base completely, which I'm well aware is against the rules.

"Run, Waverly!" someone yells in the crowd.

More people join the chant, so I turn and keep running, all

the way to second base, where Glow the Firefly, another of last year's mascot contenders who hasn't found a new home yet, is chasing away anyone who might try to catch the ball and tag me out.

"Safe!" Mac yells from behind home plate three feet before I step onto the base.

"What?" Levi yells back.

"She is totally out!" Piper shrieks.

"I demand a video review!" Francisco shouts.

And while they're arguing, and at the urging of the mascots, I take off running for third base.

Lying to myself the whole way that I don't also want to see if I could get to third base with Cooper Rock.

6

From Cooper Rock's text messages...

SOME RANDOM NUMBER: I can't stop thinking about this, despite trying very hard for literal weeks, so I'm going to come right out and say it. We should talk. I feel like I missed some very important information a long time ago, and it's keeping me up at night, and I'd like to move on. So I'd like to chat. In person, if possible. But no one can see us together for obvious reasons, if you've seen the gossip pages today. I don't want drama, and I don't want this to be a THING. I just want to talk.

Cooper: Hello, you have reached 1-800-Talk-To-A-God. For Zeus, press 1. For Mars, press 2. For Ra, press 3. For Brahman, press 4. For Cupid, press 69.

Random number: Okay. Noted. Never mind. Bad idea.

Cooper: Undo. UNDO. Control-Z. UNDO.

Cooper: That was for my sister.

Cooper: In-law. My sister-in-law. I'm not always a weirdo with my sister.

Cooper: Waverly?

Cooper: For the record, you're the only person I ever embarrass myself in front of. I had dinner with an actual king of an actual country right before the season started and I spilled mead all over myself and called him Mour Yajesty and accidentally hit on his wife and I wasn't as embarrassed as I am right now. And it really was an accident. I was complimenting her necklace. Not her breasts. I didn't know there was a word in their country where jewels meant the same thing as breasts. I was framed. Set up. Made the pawn for everyone's entertainment. And I know better now. Except when I talk to you, apparently.

Cooper: *gif of himself stealing second base and landing face-first in the other team's second baseman's crotch*

Cooper: ^^ Not as embarrassing.

Cooper: *gif of himself doing the funky chicken in the dugout at Duggan Field*

Cooper: ^^ Also not as embarrassing. Or embarrassing at all, actually. I own that one.

Cooper: *gif of himself with his pants falling down on the ballfield*

Cooper: ^^ That one was almost embarrassing, but only because I was wearing a belt from a clothing line my agent was trying to get me an endorsement deal for and it looks bad when you have a belt fail for a company you're hoping to endorse, and also, I have cake. I HAVE CAKE. The cake should've kept the pants up. Total cake fail. Usually I'd get myself de-pantsed on the field on purpose and it would be way harder than that.

Random number: Cat got stuck in the cat door. I had to rescue him. Also, HOLY MOLY, how do you not sprain your thumbs typing that much in thirty seconds? Don't you need your hands to play baseball? Does your management know what you do with your fingers and your electronics when you're unsupervised?

Cooper: Practice. I'm a finely-honed texting machine.

Cooper: But that doesn't mean I'm annoying. I know when to quit.

Random number: *doubtful emoji*

Cooper: Correction: I do my best to know when to quit. It's sometimes hard due to being cursed with such a big personality.

Random number: I honestly thought I'd have to ask for proof that this is you and not some spoof number you gave me just for kicks, and yet here we are.

Cooper: *selfie of himself wearing a 1980's headband in front of a fountain*

Random number: I'm trying so hard to not be amused by this entire conversation.

Cooper: Resistance is futile. And way less fun.

Random number: Where are you? And what are you wearing?

Cooper: It's Richard Simmons Day in the clubhouse. I'm jogging in Reynolds Park and wearing tiny shorts for my warm-up before the pre-game warm-up. Wanna see?

Random Number: I feel like there's no correct answer to that question.

Cooper: Good point. I'll save them for dinner so you can see them in person. Pictures don't do them justice.

Cooper: And by THEM, I mean the whole ensemble. Shorts. Wristbands. High socks. How I look in the shorts.

Cooper: But I promise to change the shirt. I'll wear your face instead of mine.

Random Number: I didn't say dinner. I said TALK. But

weirdly more important right now - YOU'RE WEARING A SHIRT WITH YOUR FACE ON IT?

Cooper: *selfie showing his shirt, which does, indeed, have his face on it*

Cooper: You don't wear shirts with your face on them?

Random Number: No.

Cooper: I'm gonna need a selfie to confirm I'm talking to who I think I'm talking to before I send you any more photos that might end up on a gossip website.

Random Number: Do you know what those gossip websites would say about me if I wore a shirt with my own face on it?

Cooper: Yeah, unfortunately. Sorry about the attacks on your jewelry, by the way. That's dumb.

Random Number: *picture of a wrist with a kitty cat charm bracelet and a hand petting a black-and-white cat's head*

Random Number: Eh. I like the jewelry, so I don't much care. And it's free publicity.

Cooper: It's still dumb. Bet you a home-cooked Cooper Rock Dessert of Fabulousness that if I launched a line of charm bracelets, people would think it was the coolest thing ever, and that's not because I overflow with awesome. Double standards make me want to give someone a wedgie.

Random Number: And how many wedgies do you give out in a year?

Cooper: Sorry. That's super secret. Classified. NDA-level stuff. All I can say is, Beck Ryder asked my opinion about a new line of shorts for his fashion empire, and I know he'll be calling any minute now to ask me to be the official spokesperson of his wedgie-proof underwear. I haven't been able to give ANYONE a wedgie with those things. They're a modern miracle.

Random Number: Beck's wife is one of my favorite people on the entire planet.

Cooper: Whoa. You know Sarah?

Random Number: We grew up next door to each other. She used to help babysit me when my nanny was having a rough day.

Cooper: No. Fucking. Way.

Cooper: Wait. Am I allowed to say fuck around you? Is that against the WSCOE?

Random Number: Yes she did, yes you can, and what is the WSCOE?

Cooper: The You Code of Ethics.

Random Number: *selfie of Waverly making a *what the fuck are you talking about?* face*

Cooper: Oh, hey! Those are your real eyelashes! Do the other ones make it hard to keep your eyes open? Sometimes I see you on TV and I'm like, "Is she squinting, or did someone go overboard with the fake lashes?" But when I ask my lash-extension-wearing friends and relatives, they tell me it's a secret.

Waverly, henceforth known as Baseball Cheater in Cooper's phone: It is definitely a secret.

Cooper: I like your real eyelashes.

Baseball Cheater: You can't even see my real eyelashes.

Cooper: That's why I like them. They're real.

Baseball Cheater: I...don't know what to say to that.

Cooper: It's a good thing.

Baseball Cheater: Very few people compliment my real eyelashes.

Cooper: You're hanging out with the wrong people. Want me to tell you that your knuckles are adorable too?

Baseball Cheater: Sadly, you wouldn't be the first.

Cooper: WHAT? Whoever it was doesn't think they're as adorable as I do.

Baseball Cheater: Stalker.

Cooper: I am many things, Lady Baseball Cheater, but I am not a stalker. Unless we're talking about those secret mascot costumes that management thinks I don't know about that were delivered to Duggan Field under the cover of night three weeks ago that might or might not be related to that awesome Fiery the Dragon fanfic that's going viral right now. Then I'm a stalker.

Baseball Cheater: No, I meant it was a stalker who liked my knuckles.

Cooper: *jaw dropped emoji*

Baseball Cheater: It's fine. I mean, it's not, but that's what my security team is for. It's fine.

Cooper: That is NOT fine.

Baseball Cheater: I know, but it's normal.

Cooper: ALSO NOT FINE.

Baseball Cheater: And I repeat: that's what security is for.

Cooper: The fact that I'm jazzercising in the middle of the park dressed like Richard Simmons and don't need security while you do because you have cool knuckles is messed up.

Baseball Cheater: Go back to the part about the new mascot costumes and the fanfic. What fanfic and what new mascots? I thought that was over.

Cooper: Seriously? You haven't heard about the Fiery the Dragon fanfic? It's the biggest thing to hit the internet since that video that took Bro Code viral back in the day. Hold on. You need a sample.

Baseball Cheater: The MASCOTS, Cooper. The MASCOTS.

Cooper: Management will kill me, and they LOVE me, so you know it's serious if they'd kill me if I tell. But you can trust them. They won't be pulling another poo ball or obscenely-genitaliaed mascot out of their pockets.

Baseball Cheater: You really don't have any self-esteem issues, do you?

Cooper: Look, this is my favorite bit from the Fiery fanfic: "Fiery the Dragon, the once-powerful, unstoppable mascot force behind the Fireballs' heart, was suddenly conflicted. For the first time in his life, he'd seen something he could see himself loving more than baseball. Her name was Brimstone, and she hated him." Isn't that awesome?

Baseball Cheater: My English tutor's eyeballs would've twitched at the repetition of see/seen in that sentence.

Cooper: Yeah, but for fanfic, it's good, right?

Baseball Cheater: I've read better fanfic. Is the whole thing like that?

Cooper: The whole thing is AWESOME, even though it's not done yet. I can't wait for the next episode. Fireballs fans are the best. And yes, we'd have to throw down and wrestle in a vat of Fireball red Jell-O if you try to say your Braverlies are the best.

Baseball Cheater: You still have the Jell-O fantasies, I see.

Cooper: What can I say? Once a Jell-O wrestling addict, always a Jell-O wrestling addict. I'm not that different these days. Just have a little more pressure to win. That's it.

Baseball Cheater: Okay. You've convinced me. We can talk in person.

Cooper: Well, yeah. That's a given. I'm bringing dessert. And dinner. And wine. Do you drink wine when no one's looking, or do people still think you're nineteen and perfect and would never do something as normal as drink a little alcohol?

Waverly: TALKING. Just talking. I looked at your schedule, and we have an overlap in Denver on Thursday night. Can you meet me after your game?

Cooper: When you say "TALKING"...?

Baseball Cheater: *link to a gossip website with a picture of Cooper and Waverly standing over home plate at Duggan Field with the caption THE DOWNFALL OF A POP STAR?*

Cooper: Wow. You really sold your love of baseball. That reporter should know baseball might break your heart, but it'll also put it back together.

Baseball Cheater: They're talking about your reputation. And the sad truth is, if we get caught talking, and then you go off and hang out with other women, I'll get painted as a high-maintenance man-killer despite your reputation for a short attention span when it comes to women, and the tabloids will go mad again. So. Talking. TALKING. In secret. I'll let you know what to do when it's time.

Cooper: *wincing emoji* You don't mince the truth. Mad respect.

Baseball Cheater: If it was only me I was worried about, I'd say who cares and do whatever I want. I could literally go buy a private tropical island tomorrow and live there singing songs to myself and my cat for the rest of my life. Except for the part where I'd get lonely. I don't like being lonely. And I think my gifts are meant to be shared, not hidden. And I don't think I'd really belong there. Not that I have any clue where I do belong. Also, I'm twenty-seven freaking years old. Anyone who still expects me to be a saint all hours of the day is ridiculous. I get to live my life too. But half of my schedule right now is supporting a young musician that I believe in with every bit of my being while she launches her own career, and being seen with someone labeled as "the wrong person" after the disaster that was my break-up with Geofferson is a bigger story that would overshadow Aspen's career launch. I won't do that to her, and honestly, I don't want to live through all of the WAVERLY IS SUCH A BITCH coverage again either. It's not you. It's the world I live in. I couldn't talk to half the single, eligible, age-appropriate royalty in the world in public either, if it helps.

Cooper: People have no appreciation for dating dudes who like sheep anymore.

Baseball Cheater: What?

Cooper: Oh. Never mind. Thought we knew the same royalty.

Baseball Cheater: You'll have to introduce me sometime. I'm curious now.

Cooper: You and your private island and cats, him with his hatred of people and love of sheep? No way. You'd cancel with me for this week and go fly to see him instead.

Baseball Cheater: *laughing emoji*

Cooper: So. Denver. Thursday. You. Me. The cover of darkness. And the best date you've ever been on.

Baseball Cheater: TALKING. You're doing this to annoy me, aren't you?

Cooper: I can talk your ass off. But in case you forgot, you're talking to Cooper Rock. Yeah, there's some annoying here, but there's also FUN. This talking? It's gonna be the best talking of your life.

7

Cooper

I'VE HAD two days to contemplate this, and I don't have a fucking clue where I'm taking Waverly for our *talk*.

For the record, I'm keeping my hands to myself, and I will only do talking. And listening. Only the listening part even, if that's what she wants.

But also for the record, I can be one charming bastard when I want to be, and if my *talking* happens to inspire her to want to do anything else, I'm game.

Make no mistake.

She says *talk*.

I say *holy shit, I've been attacked by the bee swarm of love, and for the first time in my life, I want to be a one-woman man, and that woman is her, and I will not waste this second chance to prove it to her*.

I can dream up the world's best pranks in the blink of an eye. I can be standing in my house up on Thorny Rock mountain back in Shipwreck and sense that one of my family members needs a helping hand with one of their businesses downtown. I can be in a bar and sort through which women would be clingy and which women would be up for a night of fun and which women need a guy to slide in next to them and play the jealous boyfriend for a hot second to get a douche who can't take the hint off their back. I've had rooftop dates and ballpark hookups and rendezvous in zoos and quickies in parking garages.

And I have no idea where I can take Waverly to impress her.

"Is the air thin up here?" I ask Luca Rossi in the locker room before the first of our four-game series in Denver. He's a tall white dude with the best hair in baseball. Or that's what his shampoo sponsor—which should've been mine—would like you to believe. "It's thin up here, right? My brain feels like a balloon. Like an awesome balloon filled with confetti and rainbows, but still like a balloon."

Darren Greene snorts on my other side. He's a bulky Black dude who's been with the team second longest after me, and I think he's having the same *what the hell do I do with my life if we pull off the win of the century?* nerves that I'm currently claiming whenever anyone asks why my game's off this season.

It's not a lie.

But it's far from the whole truth

"Air's not thin," Darren says. "You're getting old."

I gasp.

Diego gasps.

The rest of the guys crack up.

"Holy shit." My words are barely audible, even to me, as the truth finally penetrates my skull. "I'm getting old."

That has to be it.

I can't figure out where to take a woman who I have the biggest crush on of all the crushes I've had in my entire life.

I have a massive crush on a woman.

A single woman.

A woman who broke my heart once a long time ago, but let's face it. I was young and naïve and not nearly as confident in myself back then. That doesn't count. Not when I had a lot of growing up to do still.

And I've fastidiously made it my mission to never grow up, which is why this concept is even more shocking.

This crush could only be happening if I'm getting old.

I pull out my waistband and look down at my junk.

Is it—is it hanging lower? Is gravity pulling my balls down? Are my—*are my swimmers getting slow?*

Is this crush on Waverly about some primitive part of me telling me we're running out of time?

"If you want to consult a real oracle, you're not gonna find it in your pants," Emilio Torres calls.

"It's Cooper. His balls *are* his oracles," Max replies.

"Are they malfunctioning?" Diego angles closer, but not close enough to intrude on me-and-my-balls time. "Mr. Cooper, do you need help with your oracles? This is serious. Your game doesn't have game. Are your oracles broken?"

Luca looks at me closer while I let my shorts snap back to my waist. "Hey, you missed that throw from D yesterday," he says.

"And you struck out every time." Darren's looking at me closer now too.

"What're you doing differently?" Brooks Elliott asks.

As if I'd tell him.

He's a stocky white guy, and he's who I was talking about

when I mentioned the player who came to the team a virgin at the beginning of last season.

Superstition.

Didn't think he could hit the ball if he scored with a woman.

Married to Mackenzie, the Fireballs' most superstitious fan now, and together, they've broken his curse.

Still, *my game sucks because I haven't gotten laid since spring training* isn't something I'll be sharing with him.

Or anyone. Including—or maybe especially—his wife. I thought I could talk to her about it before I ran into Waverly filming her video at Duggan Field, but now—no way.

"Maybe someone washed my lucky socks," I say.

The locker room at large gasps.

Fuck.

Now one of the equipment managers is gonna get in trouble. "By accident," I add.

"We're doing a de-cursing," Darren says. "Tonight. After the game."

Shit. "I have plans."

"Cancel them."

He stares at me.

I stare right back. "I'm Cooper Fucking Rock. I can play a good game without lucky socks."

The entire locker room gasps again.

Except Darren.

Pretty sure he knows my issue isn't my lucky socks. "Prove it."

The oracles in my pants are definitely sweating now. "I will."

"Will you?"

"*I will.*"

He smirks.

If anyone on this team knows what *really* helps my game, it'll be Darren. I knew him before he met Tanesha. Watched him fall in love, fight it, give in, and now they have the cutest toddler on the entire damn planet.

I can say that because my brother's baby is new enough that he still looks like a creepy alien. And not only in pictures. In person too.

Which I did *not* say to his wife when I saw them in the hospital last week, for the record.

Point is, loyalty's gonna be a lot harder when both Darren's kid and my nephew are in preschool. Preschool is when they get seriously cute.

"Who is she?" Darren asks quietly.

I snort.

He smirks harder.

A few of the other guys lean in.

"Holy shit, did Cooper fall for someone?" one of them whispers.

"Management's aging up Baby Ash," I announce.

Tattling about what's going on with the Fireballs' new mascot gets them. We are *all* suckers for the baby dragon who took over for Fiery, the grizzled old veteran mascot, after the team's new owners tortured the fans with horrible alternative mascot choices all season last year.

And the entire locker room is obsessed with the fan fiction about Fiery's love story.

Which is excellent. I love team spirit.

"What?"

"*No!*"

"She's perfect as she is!"

"Are they gonna change *Go, Ash, Go* too? I'm not forking

over another fifteen bucks for a new card game to—fuck. *Dammit.* Of course I am, and they know it."

"I sent the baby plushies to all my nieces and nephews! They can't change her! Not yet!"

"Saw the costume myself," I tell them. "She has pigtails, and she's a full foot taller."

"We're stealing it," Brooks announces.

"*You're* not stealing it," Francisco retorts. "You and Mackenzie would do some freaky sex thing with it."

"*We would not.*"

With everyone giving Brooks the dubious eyeball, pressure's off me.

Except I still don't know where I'm taking Waverly. Or what we're doing.

Besides talking.

We can talk and also have a lot of fun. And definitely good food.

Shit again.

She's eaten stuff all over the world.

Good stuff.

How do you impress a woman who can literally have anything flown in from anywhere at the drop of a hat?

I hear my grandfather's parrot tell me I'm screwed while my mom's voice echoes in my head too. *Be your charming self, sweetheart. If she's worth it, that's all she needs. And that's all she's even asked for.*

She wouldn't say that if she knew I was talking about bringing Waverly Sweet home.

She'd tell me I was out of my league and I definitely need something better than a lobster dinner. She can get herself a lobster dinner.

What the hell can I get her that she can't get herself?

Fun.

I can get her fun.

Can't buy fun.

Not the Cooper Rock way.

That's what she dug about me eight years ago. Let's see if she'll still dig it now.

8

Waverly

How is it that my aunt can be halfway across the country, working hard on projects that are good for the Waverly Sweet brand, making me feel happy because she's my family and I love her, and still drive me up a flipping wall?

"No," I say for the fourteenth time. At least. "I am *not* going on a date with *any* of the Mercy Brothers, I don't care which one is *cutest*."

"If you're going to throw your own career away to help other young musicians—"

"I'm not *throwing my career away*. And I'm *only* invested in helping Aspen. Aspen, who's an amazing musician who simply needs a little boost, and then she'll take over the rest of the world all on her own. She's not a boy band who are already hitting the top of the charts because *they're cute*. She's the real deal."

"Waverly, your video with Levi is dropping in a week, and we need—"

"*Stop.*" I pace my hotel suite and stifle an irritated growl while Hashtag, my black-and-white tuxedo cat, tries to trip me. It's ten forty-three. The Fireballs game ended exactly nineteen minutes ago. Cooper will be here imminently if he's any good at following directions, and I'm way more eager to see him than I should be. Some parts of me more than others.

Even though I was very firm with him that we need to *talk*.

"We need to put the focus on *you* for a while," Aunt Zinnia says, gentler now, her words laced with innocence, which I used to believe but lately am starting to question.

Is she playing me?

Has she been manipulating my entire life and I never noticed?

"I don't *need* this much focus on me. The song is good. The video is amazing. My fan base combined with Levi's is massive beyond belief, and this is exactly the type of art my Braverlies want from me. Why don't we let it do whatever it's going to do *without* baiting the tabloids and gossips too? Let the music speak for itself?"

There's a rare moment of silence on the other end of the phone that makes the hairs on my arm stand up.

"We can't let them say that you're involved with some second-rate, playboy baseball player."

Now the hairs on the back of my neck are standing up too. My stomach rumbles. "Why not?"

"You're Waverly Sweet. In the world of celebrities, you're on top of the mountain, and—"

"And the *second*-best member of a boy band is worthy of me?"

"Do you know how much press coverage you'd get for

Aspen for her being in the picture if you and Xyler Mercy became Britney and Justin two-point-oh? How long has that been? The world will eat this up."

I'm not a suspicious person.

I'm really not.

But ever since the moment that Cooper Rock dropped that little bomb that Aunt Zinnia was the reason he disappeared, things have been shifting into focus in my brain, and I don't like the picture I'm getting.

And that's why I want to talk to Cooper.

No, that's why I *need* to talk to Cooper. Alone. Without witnesses. While he's bound by the NDA that my security team is making him sign before he gets here, and when I can look him straight in the eye and decide if he's trying to cash in on my fame for some reason of his own—he's turning thirty this summer and can't play baseball forever—or if he wants to add my more-famous-now name as another notch on his bedpost, or if he's telling the full truth when he says that Aunt Zinnia told him to go away.

I launched my career on my mother's name and with my aunt's management acumen behind me. Both of them were in the music industry long before I was born, and I wish every day that Mom were here and that we could do this together.

But lately, there are things I'm starting to question that I've never wondered about before.

And this is *not* a good combination with my already over-sensitive stomach, which seems to be getting worse by the day.

Freaking stress.

"I don't want to fake-date a boy bander," I say firmly.

"You haven't dated anyone at all since that awful *Geofferson with a G-E-O*. I'm worried about you."

I must be in a mood, because my first thought is that she

hadn't said a word about it until she overheard Aspen saying the same thing at the studio last week.

And the other thoughts that have been swirling are that throughout my entire career, every single big event has been surrounded by massive tabloid coverage—*something* being said about me in the media anytime I launched a single, an album, a video, or was in consideration for an award.

I used to worry that I only broke into music because my mom was Evelyn Sweet and no one wanted to tell her daughter no. Mom would've been a legend if cancer hadn't taken her too young, sitting among the greats like Madonna and Mariah Carey and Annie Lenox, with a healthy acting career on the side to boot.

Now I'm starting to worry that after my mom's name got me in, it's only gossip and not my talent that's kept me here.

"You're not playing games with the press to get my fan base riled up and talking about me so that the single will launch higher in the charts, are you?" I ask Aunt Zinnia.

Her exasperated sigh echoes around the room.

Hashtag glares at the phone and yowls.

"Waverly, *everyone does this*."

It's a punch to the gut, and my gut *cannot* tolerate punching right now.

The right answer? *Waverly, you can't hit higher than number one, and that's what you've built. You've built an empire that will take you to number one every time.*

The truth?

My entire musical career is a fraud.

"I am not *everyone*," I say quietly.

"No. You're Waverly Fucking Sweet. The fact that the press takes the bait when it's you and not when it's the Mercy

Brothers proves we're justified. They know who's big. They know who matters. They know—"

"Oh my *god*, Aunt Zinnia. What happens when you leak a story to the wrong person and *we become* the story for manipulating the press to make me who I am today?" I rise, start to pace, feel that warning in my gut, and head for my medicine bag instead. "What will *that* do to my career? To *your* career? When they find out you've been playing them?"

"You're twenty-seven. How many female artists stay relevant much past thirty? You're wasting the last few years you have in this industry helping other people, who *also* won't last, instead of yourself."

I miss the rest of whatever she says next because my phone lights up with a message from Cooper.

On my way to submit to my fate. See you in five.

I glare at the phone.

Not because I'm mad at Cooper. Any other minute the past two months, I'd probably smile.

But right now, I'm mad.

He gets to be a goofball, send ridiculously funny messages that won't be construed wrong because he's *Cooper Rock* and everyone knows that's how he is, then dash off into the night and hang out with whoever he wants with no judgment, no worries about anything other than possibly local gossip. The worst he gets is the occasional mention on the news if he happens to hook up with someone like me, and in those cases, he comes off looking like a stud.

Whereas I'm stuck in a hotel room waiting for my security lead to sneak him in here and then sneak him back out without anyone seeing to avoid my reputation being *tarnished* by proximity to a *player* and to keep the tabloids from going crazy trying to make me feel bad for looking like a woman who wants to have a fling with a guy who could be a lot of fun.

"I'm done talking about this tonight," I tell Aunt Zinnia. I *want* to ask her what she told Cooper, but I don't want her to know I'm thinking about him. I don't want her to know I'm talking to him. I don't want her to know that I remember he exists. Not tonight.

Tonight, I'm too angry with her and too overwhelmed at finding out she's been using underhanded methods to make me famous. "I'm going to bed."

"That's a good idea," she says. "You haven't gotten enough sleep lately, and Hiramys tells me you're going through Pepto like it's candy."

I shouldn't be irritated that she knows my stomach's been acting up, but I am. "Night," I say shortly.

"Love you," she replies.

I hang up, feeling like a complete disaster. When's the last time I took a vacation in a small country where I'm not recognized? Or even spent two days by myself somewhere?

Is that why I'm irritated with my aunt? Because I need a break?

Or did she really cross a line?

She's probably right. Everyone uses the paparazzi for publicity. It's annoying, but it can be mutually beneficial.

Until it gets out of hand.

"Let it go," I mutter while I shake one hand out. With the other, I text Cooper back.

See you soon.

He texts back a gif of himself in his baseball uniform, flashing a grin and a thumbs-up.

"Why does he have to be so freaking handsome?" I grumble to Hashtag.

My cat yowls his response. I make a face and head across the room to the champagne and shrimp I had sent up from room service.

Not to impress Cooper while we talk, but because it sounded good an hour ago. Now, I'm shoving the half-eaten tray out the door so that I don't have to look at it anymore.

"You want a charcuterie board instead, hon?" Hiramys asks me.

Naturally, my suite doesn't open into a hallway.

It opens into the antechamber of the entire top floor of the hotel where half my security team and my personal assistant are waiting to be at my beck and call.

And when Hiramys says *charcuterie board*, I know she means *a lot of crackers with a little bit of cheese and bananas if you're up for it, and a side of ginger ale since that's your favorite when your stomach acts up.*

"That would be lovely. Thank you."

She rises from behind the small desk where she was madly typing on her laptop and moves to the phone. "You got it, sweetie."

I disappear back into my suite and settle on the couch. Hashtag crawls onto my lap and meows at me.

"I *am* taking it easy," I tell him.

He twitches his tail like it's a lie detector and I'm testing positive for falsehoods.

"And tonight, I'm reconnecting with an old friend," I add.

That's honestly what it feels like, and I latch on to that hope as if it's my life raft.

I don't think about how I need to ask him to tell me exactly what he remembers of Aunt Zinnia calling things off between us back before both of our careers exploded.

Hashtag yawns and settles in my lap, his thick, deep purrs vibrating against my legs and belly.

"He is *too* an old friend," I mutter.

An old friend you want to get naked with, I can practically hear my cat thinking.

Or possibly he's thinking I need a vacation, since there's probably little chance my cat is actually accusing me of wanting to sleep with Cooper, which, let's be honest, is possibly the only thought that could distract me from wallowing in my sudden questions about my aunt's integrity and the validity of my own success.

And there goes my stomach grumbling again.

Hashtag eyeballs it, then me.

"Stop with the judgment," I tell him. "I have one life to live and I'm making the most of every minute."

If you were making the most of every minute, you'd quit pretending you only want to talk to Cooper tonight, my cat replies.

Silently.

With all kinds of imperious know-it-allness in his green eyes.

"Quit putting your horniness on me," I tell him. "I heard you singing your head off for that tiger on TV who couldn't give you the time of day yesterday."

He lays his head over my lap and gives a sigh-purr-*harumph*, like he's done talking about this.

And I look at my sweatpants.

Should I change?

Is this too casual for a talk?

I didn't want to do leggings for fear he'd get the wrong impression if I was wearing tight clothing—plus my stomach's in no mood for tight clothing—but an oversized crop top hoodie and sweatpants might be a little too sloppy.

There's no way I'm doing jeans. I don't have a single pair that has enough give in the waist to accommodate my angry stomach tonight.

"Should I change?" I ask Hashtag.

He blinks one long, slow blink.

Cat experts tell me that's his way of saying he loves me, but I feel more like he's calling me a dumbass.

And Hashtag is right.

I'm *talking* to Cooper. I don't have to get fancy for him. He texted with me while dressed like Richard Simmons and told me he liked my eyelashes.

"He'll be hungry after the game, won't he?" I ask the cat. "I should ask Hiramys to have a hamburger sent up too. Or a quinoa bowl. He eats healthy during baseball season, doesn't he?"

And there goes my stomach again.

Hashtag flips onto his back—yes, still in my lap—and stares at me with one ear stuck under his head and his teeth hanging out weird.

"Okay. *Okay.* I'm overthinking. If he wants food, he can order it himself. Happy now?"

He yawns, then bats at an invisible pixie somewhere above him, roll-jumps to his feet, and takes off like something grabbed his tail.

My phone dings with a text message from Kiva, my favorite person on my security team.

They're here.

The butterflies in my stomach flutter harder, and a very unladylike noise grumbles out of my midsection, this one louder than anything I've dealt with previously today.

Hashtag looks up from attacking a cloth mouse in the doorway to the bedroom.

"Shh," I whisper to my stomach.

It gurgles and twists.

My cat abandons his toy and heads over to me to investigate, hopping onto the couch next to me and sniffing toward my face.

"Who's a good boy?" I scratch his ears, and I'm rewarded with his distinctive purr as he tries to crawl back into my lap again.

My stomach rumbles.

He springs up like he's seen a terrifying cucumber, and once again, dashes away to bounce off the walls, ultimately skidding into the bathroom.

"Hashtag," I say, "don't—"

Thump.

"—run into the wall," I finish.

I rise, the door clicks, and then I feel it.

That's *not* my stomach.

That's my intestines.

And this isn't normal angry belly.

The realization smacks me in the chest and jolts every organ in my body south of my ribs.

This isn't nerves. This isn't sensitive stomach.

This is bad shrimp.

And bad is about to get much, much worse.

9

Cooper

BREATH MINTS? Check.

Deodorant? Check.

Condoms? Check.

No pressure, I'm telling myself as Waverly's red-headed, resting I-take-no-shit face security team lead stares me down on the way up the service elevator at the back of the hotel. *Take it slow. We're here to talk. Let her lead. Don't spook her, but don't be afraid to commit if talking goes well. The condoms are break-in-case-of-the-best-kind-of-emergency only.*

Shit.

Shit.

My balls heard me think *commit*, and now they're shrinking.

C'mon, buddies, I coax. *This isn't the end. This is trying something new.*

Not helping.

Let's be real.

Waverly Sweet isn't interested in sleeping with me.

She probably knows I'm even better in bed today than I was eight years ago, but also, she knows my reputation. And while I'm starting to suspect she's a closet Fireballs fan, that's probably more out of some kind of loyalty to Levi Wilson, or because half the country has been watching our transformation, than it is because she's been curious about my career.

And she will definitely not be interested in climbing the Rock to help me get over a little baseball slump.

But on the infinitesimally slim chance that *talk* is, in fact, code for *I want to ride the Cooper Train*, this needs to be the best trip she's ever had.

I need her to never want to get off.

Wait.

That came out wrong.

I want her to get off. Over and over and over again.

Courtesy of the Cooper Train.

"Shut up," I mutter to myself.

Her bodyguard lifts both pale brows. It's a small lift, like a blink-and-you'll-miss-it lift, but she heard me, and now she thinks I'm the kind of guy who talks to himself.

Rudely.

Good thing she can't hear what's going on in my head.

"You come here often?" I ask her as much to distract myself as because I'm curious about Waverly's schedule.

Her gaze settles into a flat-lined *you wanna rethink that question?*

"Denver, I mean." I gesture around the service elevator, which is slowing, *thank fuck*. "Not service elevators. I meant Denver. Mile-high city. Mountain views. Good art scene. You get to Denver often?"

"Mm."

"I ramble when I'm nervous, and you remind me of Levi Wilson's lead security agent. You know Giselle? She's awesome. And terrifying. She scared the shit out of my brother the first time Levi came to visit me up in Shipwreck. Probably because I told her he had a secret file of photos of Levi on his computer, so she was doing her job. I'm a bad influence. Terrible, really. You heard how my sister and her boyfriend had that little glitter incident before they hooked up, right? Everything my little sister knows about pranks, she learned from me."

Shut. Up.

My mouth doesn't get the message.

Also, now I feel a challenge. It's the *win Waverly's bodyguard over* challenge. "Wait. Duh. Of course you know Giselle. Do you know Rhett Elliott too? He's my teammate's brother. Has his own security firm. Total badass. And his wife—she's scary. You ever meet Eloise, do *not* underestimate her. I made that mistake once, and I had to get a totally new computer with new log-ins for everything. And change my social security number. And my legal name. And don't ask what happened to my cleats. Pro tip: She doesn't like being called short."

"We're here."

"Sweet ride. Nice. Appreciate you driving."

In a dozen years in pro baseball, counting my years in the Minors, I've never had a game that's made me sweat more than this elevator ride has, including last year's play-off games. Never met a woman who's put more nerves in my stomach either.

And I'm not talking about the security lead.

I mean Waverly.

Pretty sure it's not that she's more famous than I am. Richer than I am. In better shape than I am too.

I get paid to stand around for ninety percent of every game, run hard to first once or twice—three times a game if I'm on fire—and chase grounders maybe a dozen times in any given game, and while I work out hard regularly so that I can do all of that, she can get up on a stage and sing *and dance* for two solid hours.

Okay, yeah, maybe all of that is part of why I'm nervous.

But the other part?

You don't get past Waverly Sweet's entourage unless she thinks you're worth it.

For the first time in my life, I *want* to go to the trouble. I want to be worth the trouble.

And for the first time in eight years, I'm wondering if I can measure up.

The bodyguard holds a key card to a door. "If she screams, I won't knock. I'll come in ready to do whatever I need to do."

"Ah—thanks." Mental note: find the balance between my A-game and Waverly screaming loudly enough that her security team decides to investigate.

And there go my balls, retracting the rest of the way back into my body.

Awesome.

Probably a good thing she only wants to *talk*.

Is this fear of rejection?

Is this why I've exclusively stuck to one-night stands with women who give off serious *I do not want a relationship but I do want to have fun* vibes?

Because no other woman will ever measure up to what Waverly was in my memories, or because I'm afraid I can't live up to what the woman I really want to date deserves to have in a long-term partner?

Or both?

The bodyguard pushes the door open and gestures for me to enter.

I slip into the suite and let the door shut behind me, taking quick stock of the textured ivory walls, the massive television, the upscale white sectional centered around it, the Turkish rug under the coffee table, and the gilded mirror over the entryway sideboard.

But what really catches my eye is Waverly's reflection in that mirror—baggy black sweatpants, short pink hoodie, her light brown hair tousled, feet bare—dashing across the room before the bathroom door slams shut.

I blink at the closed white door.

Do I say hi?

Do I follow her?

Do I—*oh*.

Oh, no.

I recognize that noise.

"Oh, god," she whimpers, her voice echoing behind the door.

I angle closer. "Hey, you okay?"

"Go away. Go away, pretend you weren't here, and never, ever, *ever* speak of this to *anyone*."

I won't tell you how she punctuates that statement, because I'm not here, I don't know what's going on, and I'm never ever, *ever* speaking of it.

As directed.

"And don't eat the shrimp." Her voice is shrill, which isn't a sound I've heard from her either.

I glance around, spot her cat batting at what looks like a shrimp tail on the floor, though I don't see any other evidence of a tray, and sprint across the room to shoo him away.

He hisses at me, which is not unlike the way my brother's

pet goat reacted the first time we met, but while I was setting up a surprise that Grady's goat had full reason to react poorly to back then, today, I'm making sure Waverly's cat doesn't get sick.

"Just looking out for you, little buddy," I tell him.

He hisses again.

Fantastic.

I make my date puke and her cat hiss within thirty seconds of walking into her suite.

This is not auspicious.

At another sound from the bathroom, I head back to the door, where I practice active *not listening*. "This is me not being here and not hearing anything while I ask if you want me to go get your security team. Or some water. Or—well, anything."

"This is *not* happening," I hear her say softly.

Dude.

For real.

"Do you really live life on the road if you don't live the consequences of eating some bad shrimp every now and again?" I ask. "There was one time, my second season with the Fireballs, when we ended up staying at a new hotel that was so excited to have us that they laid out a private reception for us, but the meatballs weren't cooked all the way through and the whole team was sick for two days afterward. Weirdly, we lost those games less badly than normal, but I think the home team took pity on us."

"Has anyone ever told you that you talk a lot for a guy?"

"Usually my sis—" *do not say sister, idiot* "—kabob. My sisk-abob. My food. It talks to me."

"You have a very weird relationship with your sister."

It's a good sign that she knew what I was going to say, right? That means she digs me enough to pay attention. Even when she's indisposed. "Only on occasion, and unfortunately, those occasions overlap with me seeing and talking to you more often than statistically probable."

There's another ominous noise from the bathroom that I am definitely not hearing but that makes me wince. "You sure it was the shrimp?"

"Only thing I ate this after—" She cuts herself off, and you don't want to know why.

"Please don't tell anyone," she says when she can talk again.

"I'm getting your security people."

"Cooper—"

"Tell me which one if you have a preference. And it's not because I can't handle you not feeling well, okay? If we were both normal people living next door to each other and I heard you through the apartment wall and I came over to check on you, I could totally handle everything you're dealing with. But we're not normal people. On a scale of my brother's goat to the Queen of England, you're right up there with the queen, which means if you so much as sneeze wrong, I'm obligated to notify the people who can get you to a doctor."

Do I want to be her hero and stay and make her feel better?

Fuck me.

I do.

But she's not a normal woman.

And the sigh on the other side of the bathroom door says she knows it. "Five minutes," she says.

"Waverly—"

"*Five damn minutes*, Cooper. I won't die of dehydration in *five damn minutes*." She pauses again to do what she's doing, and I pause to let her.

Her cat gives me the hairy eyeball of *I'm mentally clawing your fingers off and feeding them to my pet piranhas*.

I don't know if her cat has pet piranhas, but he has this look about him that suggests he'd love them if Waverly would get them for him.

"If you quit making noise, I'm getting your people," I tell Waverly.

Not even kidding. If she needs to go to the hospital and I'm the reason she doesn't get there, I will never forgive myself.

And that'd be true whether she was Waverly Sweet or some random person who started getting sick on the street next to me.

But I can't take her myself because she doesn't want to be seen with me.

For good reason.

"They'll tell," she says.

"They'd tell *the fucking gossips*?"

"*No*. They'd tell Aunt Zinnia. Just—five—"

I curse to myself while she quits talking.

To me, at least.

She's talking plenty to the toilet.

I head toward the door that I'm pretty sure leads to the other part of her suite, where her entourage is most likely hanging out, but before I get three steps, her cat leaps in my way and hisses again.

"You too?" I say to him.

He bares his teeth.

I mutter another word that I learned from my grandpa, then set a timer on my watch.

But I don't give it the full five minutes, and I don't care what she's afraid of or what her cat's opinion of me is.

Not when her voice gets fainter after another thirty seconds.

She needs help.

And I can't be the one to do it.

Fuck.

10

Waverly

COOPER DIDN'T LEAVE.

If I were him, I would've snuck right back out the way I came in if I'd walked into what he walked into, but not Cooper Rock.

When I'm finally done with what the shrimp decided to do to my insides, Hiramys and Kiva hover until they're sure I won't do the same with the Pedialyte they're making me sip.

Yeah.

Pedialyte.

How's that for a badass pop princess?

But finally, I'm showered and wrapped in a fuzzy robe with my teeth brushed and my face bare and my stomach feeling like it completed a marathon, but instead of running it did sit-ups for twenty-six-point-two miles, and Cooper Rock is still here, sitting on the couch after apparently charming my cat, who's splayed across his lap.

"You didn't say you wanted him to go," Kiva says.

Cooper salutes me with a bottle of Gatorade. "I like to be absolutely sure I'm being thrown out. Gotta be way more dramatic to get through this thick skull. You like home renovation shows? This couple found—never mind. Nope. That's not for tonight."

"He is aware of exactly what will happen to him if word of this leaks to the press," Kiva says.

He nods to me and jerks his head toward Kiva. "She's officially scarier than Brooks's sister-in-law."

"High praise," Kiva says dryly. She scans my forehead with a thermometer, nods once, then shoves a fresh bottle of Pedialyte at me. "Drink slowly. Mr. Baseball, time to go home."

"Do you have curfew?" I forgot to ask him that in text.

"Eh. When you're Cooper Rock, it's more of a suggestion than a requirement."

I don't believe him. His eyes are too twinkly and his dimple too dimply.

I try to give him Kiva's badass bodyguard glare, but I don't really have the energy. "I'm not a baseball expert, and don't take this the wrong way, but I'm not sure you're playing well enough this year for that to be true."

He clutches his heart, sinking dramatically deeper into the sectional couch, his grin getting bigger. "*Ouch.* If this singing thing doesn't work out, you could join the team as our pep talk person."

Kiva clears her throat.

Cooper slides a look her way, then looks back at me. "Right. I need to go so you can get to bed."

"Stay."

Kiva gives me the *you have a full calendar tomorrow and you're going to hurt like hell* nostril flare.

111

Cooper's way less subtle.

His brows shoot up to his hairline and his lips part.

"Please," I add.

I wanted to talk to him, and I have no clue when I'll get another opportunity. Plus I don't want to be alone.

Not that I'm ever alone when Hashtag is around and my entourage is just a room or two away, but it's different when there's a person who has no financial interest sticking around to keep me company.

And tonight, I'm feeling decidedly unsure about who likes me and who likes that I make money for them.

Including my one and only blood relative.

"Sure. I can stay." He grins, popping out that dimple that was irresistible trouble eight years ago and might still be. "I love giving management heartburn and then playing so good they let me get away with anything."

"Didn't we just establish that your game—"

"Zip it, baseball cheater. I'm gonna play my ass off tomorrow. Yours too. You watch."

If I were a normal woman with a normal job and a normal life, I would be in mortal danger of falling for Cooper Rock again.

But ego is a dime a dozen in my life, and while his is amusing, it's still ego.

I nod to Kiva. *He's staying.*

She nods back. She also gives Cooper the universal sign for *I have x-ray vision and I will see if you set one errant arm hair out of order, and then I will bust in here and ruin what's left of your career.*

She doesn't mess around with signs.

"One hour, and then neither of you get a choice in the matter," she informs us.

She doesn't leave until I'm sitting on the couch though.

Can't blame her.

My legs aren't as solid as I'd like them to be.

I tuck them under me and glance at Cooper.

"You okay?" he asks. "For real?"

"Definitely been worse." Hashtag makes a fuss of lumbering to his feet and sighing heavily while he moves from Cooper's lap to mine, where he plops down immediately, purring louder than my tour bus engine. I rub his head and let mine drop back against the sofa. "Why did you stay?"

"I don't leave teammates behind."

I blink at him once, and then I crack up, which unfortunately makes my sore belly jiggle in all the wrong ways. "I am *not* your teammate."

"Are we on Team Wooperly or what?"

"Team *what*?"

"I mean, we could be Team Waper, or Waverper, or Cooly, but I think Team Wooperly has a better ring to it."

Hashtag looks at him, makes a weird low growl noise, and starts swishing his tail like he's annoyed.

"We are *not* doing this celebrity name thing. You came here so I could ask you a few little questions. In *secret*."

Gah, that grin. "It's so clandestine—we totally need a code word. Like Team Wooperly. And clearly once we start talking, magic will happen. I'm awesome. You're awesome. Together, we're like, awesome quadruplified."

"*Quadruplified*? That is not a word."

"My sis—"

My brows raise, and his grin goes all kinds of self-deprecating.

"Ah, fuck," he mutters. And then he plows on ahead. "*My sister* got me a word-a-day calendar, and *quadruplified* is too a word. Also, I dare you to put it in a song."

You did this to yourself, Waverly. Also, why is it this easy to smile at him when he's being ridiculous? "You really are always like this, aren't you?"

"Fantabulous? Hells, yeah. We're a lot alike that way. I wake up every day and choose to be the baseball version of a rock star god, you wake up every day and choose to be the pop star version of a rock star god..." He sets aside his Gatorade and rises. "But you can't wake up if you don't go to sleep. C'mon. It's sweet dreams time."

"Is that a code word?"

"Nope." He twitches his fingers at me, offering a hand to help me up. "I won't be able to sleep unless I know you're getting the rest you need, so do me a solid and let me tuck you in. Total complete vulnerable honesty here? If I don't sleep, I'm all talk on having the best game of my life tomorrow."

"Are you being...responsible?"

He winks. "Don't tell anyone. That'd totally blow my reputation."

"Hate to break it to you, but I can't move." I point to Hashtag, who's still twitching his tail like he's debating if he wants to eat Cooper's face. "Cat's on me. It's a rule. I only move when he moves."

"Huh."

"I know. It's a hard life."

He studies me, then my cat, and then he lifts a finger in the air and starts drawing on an invisible chalkboard. "Carry the two," he mutters. "Cross-pollinate with the baby dragon mascot, divide by zero, combine an acid and a base, throw out McElroy at first, and multiply it all by infinity..."

"What are you doing?" And why am I grinning like this?

"Complicated life equations, and the answer is... Yep. I can totally do this. As if there was ever any doubt."

"Do what?"

He squats in front of me, slips one arm under my legs, the other around my ribs, and carefully lifts me.

I squeak.

My stomach questions if any movement is a good idea and decides to let me have this one.

Hashtag meows in protest but doesn't hop off my lap. He stares at Cooper, highly offended that anyone would move his throne.

"Problem solved."

There's no arrogance in his expression. It's pure amusement. I wrap one arm around his neck and the other around Hashtag, barely resisting the urge to run my fingers through Cooper's thick, dark hair. "How do people tolerate you on a daily basis?"

"Your words try to wound, but your smile says you'd love it."

"Such ego."

"Why, thank you. I've worked hard to perfect it."

Despite his grin, I know he's not kidding.

Not totally.

I used to watch the Fireballs lose game after game for dumb, dumb reasons and wonder how the players kept their mental health strong. Especially the players who voluntarily stayed and weren't publicly begging to be traded.

Cooper's ego?

Undoubtedly a coping mechanism.

But if he were all ego and only ego, he wouldn't be carrying me and my cat into the bedroom and setting us gently on the king-size bed. "Are you a bedtime story or a lullaby type person? Either way, you can't go wrong. I can deliver both. At the same time, even. All you have to do is ask."

"I'm a *fall asleep with the TV on* person."

He sighs heavily. "That is *not* the recipe for good sleep."

I gesture for the TV remote.

He hands it to me, then plops onto the bed next to me. "What're we watching?"

"*I'm* watching something I'll enjoy, and *you're* going back to your own hotel after you answer one question for me."

"No can do. Can't sleep unless I know you're sleeping."

"Cooper."

"Baseball cheater."

Hashtag sneezes on him. Swear to god, my cat *aims* his sneeze.

Cooper looks at the cat snot all over his lean, muscular forearm, then back up at me, shrugging. "It's a secret rule of clandestine meetings. When your secret discussionist has had a rough night, you fulfill the duties of the good friend, because you don't do secret late-night discussionism with people you wouldn't be friends with."

"Where are you getting all of these rules? And all of these words?"

"Luca's girlfriend, Henri. She writes romance novels. Ever hear of Nora Dawn? That's her pen name. And she has friends so she makes good recommendations of other romance novels. I've studied them all meticulously to make sure I get it right. I can do fake short relationships, enemies to temporary lovers, friends to temporary lovers, secret flings, and I'd probably even do a marriage of convenience—for like two weeks max—but I draw the line at secret babies and accidental pregnancies. Clearly, I've got sports hero covered, and I could be on a romance novel cover, but I won't do paranormal romances either. Not interested in getting busy with a witch or a vampire or a demon when human women are so fascinating. And actually exist."

Is he for real?

He sounds for real.

Hashtag twitches his tail again. He's still in my lap, but he's shifted to make himself more comfortable, and he's purring extra loudly.

That either means *I'm still worried about you, mama* or it means *I'm plotting someone's death.*

I've had him for four years and I still can't tell.

Cooper's ears go adorably pink, and once again, I want to wrap myself around him and hold on for dear life.

"Was that too much personal information?" he asks. "I'm not embarrassed to read romance novels. I read a lot. Don't tell my sis—my family. They have this perfect image of me as a brainless baseball god. Don't wanna ruin it."

"You're tight with your family."

He grins, and this time, it's not an ego grin. It's a warm, *you brought up my favorite subject* grin. "They're awesome. We're like the eighty-fifth generation of Rocks to rule Shipwreck. Not in the dick way, but like, Shipwreck is awesome, and we want everyone to experience the mountain pirate joy. I ever tell you about my family? My mom runs the local coffee shop. Dad has the most popular restaurant in town. Tillie Jean used to manage it for him, but now she's on this path to one day take over as mayor. Grady makes donuts and muffins that are so good, you see heaven when you eat them, and he and his wife, Annika, have a new baby. Wanna see?"

He's already reaching for his phone, and I'm leaning in to watch him pull up his photos. "This is Miles. He's basically brand-new. Eight pounds, fourteen ounces, twenty-one inches long, and he can cry like a champ. That's Annika—

she's a total rock star. Twenty-three hours of labor. Twenty-three. Jesus. I get whiny when I hit a grounder that goes foul when I'm already halfway to first and I have to go run again."

"I remember that," I murmur.

He pauses in swiping photo after photo of his adorable baby nephew and his happy family. "Wait, what?"

I mentally rewind, and then I feel my own face flush. "Someone said something—"

"You watched me mic-ed up in spring training."

"Only for the whining. You went viral for whining that you were tired after getting halfway to first. The entire *world* saw that."

His grin comes back in double-force.

I fumble for the remote. "You really like your family." I remember that about him. This isn't the first time he's shown me pictures of his siblings and parents, and I remember entirely more about them than I'd admit.

"I won the family lottery."

"Lucky," I say before I can stop myself.

He tilts a look at me, and then sighs, like he's caught on to what I'm talking about. "I didn't mean to cause trouble with you and your aunt."

"I really liked you," I whisper. "A *lot*. And then you were just gone, and I didn't know why, and I thought it was me. I thought I got too clingy, or I was annoying, or—"

"It wasn't you." He's sitting right next to me, but not touching me at all, and I'm not sure if it's because he doesn't want to, or because he thinks I don't want him to.

Honestly?

I don't know what I want, besides *different*.

And I endure a massive wave of shame and guilt for ever

wanting anything different. I have the world. *I have the damn world*. And it's not enough.

What does that say about me?

"All of this?" Cooper waves a hand around the suite. "Who you are now? She knew you had this in you. And it's not about what's in your bank account, Waverly. It's about the difference you make for your fans. The world needs music, and you do it in a way that makes a bunch of kids in really awkward stages in their lives feel seen and appreciated and valued. My Little Sluggers team? They won a game last night, and they dedicated it to you. They said they played *for you*. Those kids winning? That was a fucking miracle."

"They did it for you too."

He shakes his head. "Three of them know who I am. Those aren't baseball nut kids. Those are *we're looking for where we fit and haven't found it yet* kids. *All* of them were playing for you. And they're only twelve kids out of the *millions* whose lives you touch. Zinnia was right. I would've held you back. Don't hold that against her."

"Why are you defending her?"

"She's your family."

I squint at him. "And what are you? Why did you humor me and come here tonight? To do it all over again? To tell me you're not good enough for me and that I deserve better, but in person this time instead of letting the ghosting do the talking for you?"

My stomach turns over.

Hashtag meows and softly butts my belly with his head like he can protect me.

And Cooper doesn't blink. "No," he says softly. "Not gonna lie here. I've never—no, scratch that. For a long time, I haven't been interested in relationships. I had a team to turn around, and I couldn't have done what I needed to do professionally either if I had too many distractions. And I never—I've seen what my parents put into making a good marriage work. I've never had time for that, and I don't want to half-ass the one thing that's supposed to make life worthwhile."

He clears his throat and shifts closer to me. "But we're going all the way this year. The Fireballs are going all the fucking way. And then all my dreams will have come true, the dreams everyone told me were impossible, and as great as that feels, it's fucking terrifying too. I have to find a new mission in life. Can't play ball forever, and even if we—nope, not gonna say that. No matter what happens tomorrow, the day after, whatever, I was already there to help turn the Fireballs around. Winning the World Series? Yeah. That's gonna feel fucking fantastic. But what the hell do you follow that with? What comes next?"

"What do you mean?"

"I mean I've never *not* had a mission, and it's always been to take the Fireballs all the way. The idea that I get to the top and find out it's all downhill from there—it has me feeling like a little bit of a disaster. And I like you. I like you a lot. But I don't want my disaster rubbing all over you."

I drop my head to his shoulder. "We look like we have it all."

"How do you do it? How do you find the next dream after you win seventeen Grammys and go platinum with every album?"

I freeze.

Oh my god.

That's what's wrong.

I'm in autopilot. *Go go go. Do more. Get bigger. Grow. Be unstoppable.*

What if I...stopped?

Am I living my life for me, or is my irritation with my aunt that I've never told her what I actually want, forcing her to bulldoze ahead, trying to find the next thing in my career to make me happy?

Do I have any idea what I need to be happy?

"Sorry," Cooper mumbles. "Talking too much again."

"No, you're really not."

"I am. You need sleep. And look, you have my number. You can call anytime. Or text. I give really good text. Especially when I copy-paste wrong. I sent Diego a GIF of Ares Berger lifting a Zamboni when I meant to send Luca a GIF of me shaking my butt, and poor Diego thought I was telling him that he'd never be as good at baseball as Ares is at hockey, and we almost lost him for a whole game. Never saw him not smile before that."

My eyes get hot.

Cooper has *fun*.

And the day all his dreams come true, he'll get up the next morning, even not knowing what his new dream is, and he'll still have fun.

I don't have fun. I work. I have friends, and when we get together, we compare battle stories of who had the worst write-up on a gossip site and whose label or production company is trying to cut them the rawest deal and which of us had run-ins with stalkers. I have anxiety. I have stomach issues. I have insomnia.

What am I even doing?

"Can we be friends again?" I ask and then realize how lame that sounds.

Hi, I'm an internationally-known pop star on top of the world. Will you play dolls with me at recess?

"We've always been friends."

"*Cooper.*"

"Friends who don't talk and had a really awkward last parting because I was a dumbass chickenshit, but I'm older and wiser and better and cockier now. Now, I'd at least organize a flash mob under your hotel room to tell you that I was leaving because you deserve better friends than me."

He takes the remote from my hand. "But we don't have to worry about that tonight. Tonight, you're going to sleep, and tomorrow, I'll text you weird shit and you'll pretend it's normal, and maybe we'll be in the same city again sometime."

"You'll text me?" I ask.

"Nothing can stop me. Not this time. I solemnly promise with every ounce of pirate blood in my veins that I will text you, tomorrow, without question, no matter what, even if I'm dead."

"You are such a goofball."

He smiles softly and points the remote at the TV.

It blinks on at full volume right in the middle of an episode of *Who's Your Family?*, startling us both so badly that I jump, Cooper yelps in surprise, and Hashtag yowls and launches off my lap.

He hisses when he hits Cooper's lap, miscalculates as he jumps off the bed and lands on a nightstand, where he knocks a lamp off before dashing at a dead run into the sitting room and tearing around, bouncing off the walls and furniture.

I snag the remote to dial the volume down as quickly as I can.

"Sorry," Cooper mutters. "*Jesus.* I am *not* smooth around you. And I was making good progress with your cat too."

"Don't be smooth, please. I've had enough surface-level smoothness for one lifetime."

Hashtag bolts past the open doorway, fur fluffed from his neck to the tip of his tail.

"He'll settle down in a few minutes."

Cooper eyes me, then my cat, then me again like he's still stuck on what I mean by *surface-level smoothness.* "This is normal?"

"He has a big personality."

"That's what my mom says about me too."

I smile and shift on the bed to crawl under the covers. "He'll come back when he decides it's bedtime."

He starts to say something, but this time, I shush him and point to the TV. "This is my favorite part."

On screen, the host is asking a woman if she's ready to meet the family she never knew she had.

"Is this that show about family secrets people find out after taking DNA tests?" Cooper asks.

"*Shh.*"

The woman nods, and the host leads her to a blue door.

"Why isn't she opening it?" Cooper whispers while the woman hovers with her hand above the doorknob.

"Because her whole life is about to change," I whisper back.

He shifts closer to me on the bed, but I don't pay much attention. The poor woman on the television is shaking. "I don't know if I can do it," she tells the host.

"You've come this far, Mary," he replies.

"But do they *want* me?"

"Only way to find out is to open that door."

I hold my breath.

She takes a few audible breaths, wipes her eyes, and then turns the handle and pushes the door open.

Two people are waiting on the other side, a man with white hair and wrinkles and a woman wearing a Christmas sweater and thick glasses. She's younger than the man, but I'm pretty sure her hair's only brown because it's dyed.

All three of them gasp and stare at each other.

The man breaks the silence. "Sandy…she has your eyes."

"My baby girl," the woman whispers, and then the three of them are hugging and laughing and my eyes are hot and Cooper's staring at me.

I try to flop lower in the bed and blink fast to keep him from noticing.

"I like it when they have a happy ending," I whisper.

"They don't always?"

I shake my head.

He doesn't reply, but I can feel him watching me.

Quiet Cooper is odd. He's never quiet. He always has something to say.

Always.

But not right now.

Now, he's watching me like he wants to ask questions, like he knows something's weird, but even though he's here because we're supposed to *talk*, and we sort of agreed to be friends, he doesn't want to push.

Or maybe I'm reading too much into this and he's right, and I should go to sleep.

"I'm a sperm donor baby," I whisper. "Sometimes I wonder…but it's not really safe to go find out, you know?"

He stretches out on the bed next to me, our legs and hips and shoulders touching, mine under the covers, his on top, but still touching.

And he *still* doesn't say anything.

"Swear to god, if you're thinking about sneaking a DNA test on me—"

He rolls to his side and hooks one leg over mine. "Boundaries. Right and wrong. I wouldn't do that."

I believe him.

That's the thing about Cooper.

He sleeps around. He doesn't commit. If we're spotted in public together after the media coverage of him helping me hold a baseball bat for the video that drops next week, *dozens* of women would come out of the woodwork to tell stories about him and their time with him.

Possibly hundreds.

But in my experience, and from what I've heard and seen while watching his career the past several years, he keeps his word, he goes all-in when he cares about something, and his heart's in the right place.

He has an ego, but he's also grounded.

The only time he's ever let me down was the time Aunt Zinnia chased him away.

"You know where you came from," I say quietly.

He settles his arm across my hips, and I can't help wondering if he's intentionally avoiding my belly. Like he knows it's tender.

"I picked my family," he says.

I make a face at him. "You picked your parents and your grandparents and your brother and your sister?"

"Not the first time. Not when I was born. But after I left for the Minors, there was this time when I felt totally disconnected. Like I was becoming someone different and they weren't there all the time, but they were all with each other, and it was like I didn't fit anymore. Not like I used to. So I picked them again. I decided to get to know them again."

"Get to know them again? Like, they changed? Not you changed?"

"They did. We all changed. The people my siblings are as adults, the people my parents are when they don't have to parent me as much. The people my grandparents are when they're not the babysitters who spoil me with candy and pirate swords when my parents drop me off. They're different, you know? And it turns out they're awesome people. Like my baseball family is full of awesome people. And my neighborhood families in Shipwreck and Copper Valley are awesome people. And my Fireballs teammates are awesome people. And my favorite coffee shop family in the city is full of awesome people."

"Aspen's my found family," I whisper. "I've only truly known her for six months, but she feels like my sister more than almost anyone I've ever met. Aunt Zinnia doesn't get it. She thinks I'm lost. That I forgot where I came from and what I owe to my mom's memory and to the world that's given me so much and that I'm going to throw it all away while I try to find where I fit in. But I don't even know where I came from. Not really."

He opens his mouth, but I put my fingers to his lips. "Don't tell me it doesn't matter where I came from when I clearly know where I am and where I can go, and don't tell me I have all the money to find out what I want to know without anyone else realizing it. Okay?"

And there's that Cooper Rock smile again. He takes my hand in his and presses a soft kiss to my fingers. "I was going to say you clearly came from somewhere awesome."

I smile back. "No, you weren't."

"Waverly Sweet, expert in Cooper Rock. Hm. Didn't see that coming. I mean, I should've. I'm a truly remarkable member of the species. Well worth learning and studying, which you've clearly done. But I always thought you outranked me on the awesome scale, and that you knew it."

"Are you calling me full of myself?"

"More like self-aware."

"You would be terrifying if you worked somewhere that let you use all of that brainpower."

He blinks at me like he's honestly startled.

"I don't mean you don't have to be smart to play sports," I add quickly.

"No, I know."

"You always have something to say, and you're quick on your feet, and—"

He moves my fingers, pressing them to my own lips instead. "And you need to go to sleep."

Hashtag hops onto the bed, walks across my body, and wedges his big, furry butt between us.

"You don't have to go," I whisper.

He holds my gaze with those bright blue-green eyes, and I wonder if he's thinking I'm getting too clingy, or if he's thinking he doesn't want to go either.

"Pretty sure I do," he finally says. He kisses my forehead, earning a disgruntled snort from a squished Hashtag. "But not quite yet."

11

Cooper

I'M BEING *that guy* again. The one slipping out of a hotel room at five in the morning after accidentally falling asleep in a woman's bed.

Know how long it's been since I fell asleep in a woman's bed?

Years.

Learned early on not to do that. Falling asleep means you're at their mercy when you wake up. *Want breakfast? Here's my number. Call me next time you're in town. We could hit the shower before you go. You still in town tonight? Want to do it again?*

And *if* you manage to sneak out while they're asleep, you feel like an asshole for sneaking out while they're asleep, knowing they'll wake up wondering if you're there or if they did something wrong or if you're really that kind of asshole.

Even when you're clear—*I'm not looking for a relationship, this is for fun*—and even when you've gotten good at reading women and which ones mean it when they say fun's all they're looking for too, sleeping over adds an extra degree of intimacy that complicates things.

Today, I'm not that kind of asshole—I left a note and followed it with my promised text after making sure Waverly's phone was on silent so it wouldn't wake her if it dinged—but I *feel* like that kind of asshole.

Doesn't help that her cat kept staring at me like I was that kind of asshole.

That cat has *expressions*. And he uses them to his full advantage.

"You talk in your sleep," Kiva says as we ride back down the service elevator.

If it's a subtle *I saw you sleeping and could've done anything to you in your sleep* threat, I don't take the bait. Waverly wanted me there last night. Therefore I stayed.

Instead, I nod to her. "I was considering a career in the CIA, but I flunked out of try-outs for accidentally spilling the beans about the UFOs while I was being monitored in my sleep. Or so I assume. Wicked awesome dream that night about chilling with the aliens. We made soup and they told me the secrets of the universe. Stupid dream brain didn't let me remember them when I woke up though. Makes sense I was talking about them too. Only thing besides underwater basket weaving that I've ever failed at in my life. Did you know you don't have to put on SCUBA gear and find a lake to do underwater basket weaving? Mind. Blown."

She gives me a furry eyeball, which sounds weird but isn't. She has the thickest red eyelashes, and you add in the blood-shot eyes, and they legit look like red furry beasts. "So it's not only in your sleep. You basically never shut up."

"Shh. Don't tell anyone." I grin.

She doesn't.

Waverly would've.

We're talking, Cooper. Just. Talking.

We'll see, Waverly Sweet.

We will see.

Should I have left her to be ill in private? Fuck, no.

Have I been there through food poisoning and too much partying and the random actual stomach bugs for my teammates? Damn right. Of course I can handle it.

Do I feel like a useless slug for going to get Kiva to help?

Yep.

When you're watching the world's biggest pop star get violently ill, yes. Yes, it's necessary to notify her team. And it pisses me off to admit I'll never be enough on my own, even if she's willing to give me another date.

Yes, *date*.

I want to date Waverly Sweet.

I, Cooper Rock, baseball god, favorite son, king of the one-night stand and secret killer latte maker, hereby vow to be the kind of man who deserves Waverly Sweet.

Starting right now, I'm cleaning up my reputation. Not only clean it up, but be squeaky clean. I want to be the kind of guy she can trust. I want to be the kind of guy she can go out with in public. The kind of guy she can date without seeing rumors that I'm dating other people behind her back. The kind of guy she turns to first when she wants to talk, when she needs a shoulder, or when she's ready to unwind and blow off steam.

And for the record—sex isn't the only trick in my bag.

I know *tons* of ways to blow off steam, and I intend to use every last one of them and dream up a few more until that always-wary, always-exhausted look fades from her eyes.

Once Kiva opens the staff elevator on the bottom floor, I sneak out of the hotel unnoticed and walk the three blocks to the hotel where the team's staying. Still have time to get a couple more hours of shut-eye, which I need if I'm gonna pull off the game of my career.

Good luck with that, my junk mutters to me.

Shut up. I'll give you a few yanks in the shower and then we're gonna play the fuck out of this game today, I mutter back.

Silently.

For real.

I can be quiet when I want to be.

And I have plenty of secrets.

Okay, fine. I have like three. And no, I'm not telling you what they are.

Not yet.

I duck into my hotel's back entrance and hit the stairwell, head down, shoulders slouched, and make it all the way to my room without passing another person. Takes me two swipes of my card to get into my room, and the second the door shuts behind me, I'm stripping out of my shirt.

"*Gah*, put it back on!" a voice screeches.

My hands fly to cover my nipples. Not because I'm ashamed of having nipples or because I'm modest. It's more that the screech belongs to Tillie Jean. She's clearly been sleeping on the couch in my suite, and I know math.

Tillie Jean plus sleeping on my couch plus not enough sleep equals a very dangerous Tillie Jean, which puts my nipples at risk of a twister.

Big brother instincts kick in a split second after self-preservation. "Where's Max, and how hard do I have to kick his ass?"

"Ugh, is he naked?" another voice says.

"Mackenzie?"

"Oh, don't even think you're getting off easy, you lazy-ass team saboteur," a third voice says.

One, *saboteur?* It's way too early in the morning for words like that, and I'm the guy with a word-a-day calendar who likes to toss out big words. And two, as I head deeper into my suite, it becomes obvious that there's at least five of my teammates' wives and girlfriends here. Yes, I'm counting my sister more as a teammate's girlfriend than as my sister at the moment.

"Marisol? Tanesha? *Henri?* Jesus. What did Max do that all of you had to come get me?"

"Max isn't the problem," Tillie Jean says. "*You* are."

"Don't act so surprised." Henri pulls a face at me. "Being the least confrontational of all of us doesn't mean I'm not mad at you too. I get mad sometimes, and I'm mad now."

"Missing curfew while your game's in the crapper?" Tanesha snorts. "You have a *lot* of explaining to do."

I retrieve my shirt and pull it back on. Getting caught in any state of undress with five of my teammates' wives and girlfriends is the exact opposite of cleaning up my reputation.

"Can't talk about it."

"Why?" Mac demands, and honestly, right now, I miss the days when she used to go totally mute in my presence.

Okay, I don't. That was awkward for everyone. Tell myself I'm a god in my head to pump myself up? Yes. Get stared at by a totally silent woman decked out head-to-toe in Fireballs gear every time we ended up in the same room after her BFF started dating one of my buddies in the city? Nope.

But right now, I wouldn't mind if she wanted to pretend I didn't exist.

"Don't be rude," Tillie Jean says.

Yeah. She knows what I was thinking.

I pretend I don't know she knows, though. "It's not rude to not talk about the things you can't talk about. I'm aware my game's in the shitter. You think I want to be the guy who tanks our chances after everything it's taken to get here? Fuck, no. I'm working on fixing it, and that's why I'm out past curfew, and that's all I can say without cursing it."

That should take care of Mackenzie. She never met a superstition she didn't believe. Ask me sometime about the lengths she went to back when Brooks joined the team and she found out he was planning to give his own superstition the middle finger since he didn't want to play for the Fireballs.

Before she decided to marry him, I mean.

Things changed then.

But that's the only superstition she's ever given up, and I think she took on fourteen more to replace it.

"Liar," Mackenzie says.

Henri sucks in a breath.

Tanesha and Tillie Jean both snicker. I might've grown up with TJ, but I've known Tanesha longer than any other Fireballs wife, which unfortunately means she's known me that long too. She's my baseball sister.

Marisol crosses her arms and taps her fingers against her bicep. "Give me one good reason we shouldn't tell management you're not getting your sleep while your game's total shit."

"Because then I'd have to have meetings with them instead of going to sleep so I can play like the god that I am today? And my game's not *shit*. It's more...having a little breather."

Whew. Five glares is a lot of glare for this hour of the morning.

"What's your superstition?" Mackenzie asks.

"Lucky socks. They got washed two weeks ago. By accident. Not the equipment manager's fault. Don't blame him. I shouldn't have left them out."

Mackenzie's glare gets glarier. "I already talked to Theo, and he swears up and down no one's touched your lucky socks. Everyone's worried about you, so he's personally checking to make sure they're in your locker or your bag before they start laundry both before and after every game."

Fuck. "Okay, yeah, I washed them myself. My nose can't tolerate what it used to. Getting old sucks."

All five of them suck in a breath.

Yes. I can run with this story. "I'm turning *thirty* soon," I say solemnly. "That's like—"

"If you say *old*, I will remember this and pay you back the minute we walk off the field with the World Series trophy," Tanesha, who has me by two years, says.

"—A milestone that I'm not prepared for." I clear my throat and glance at her. "I'm a spring chicken in normal-person years. But in baseball years, being thirty is like being fifty-eight."

Henri's brow furrows. "Fifty-eight?"

"Don't let his specificity distract you," Tillie Jean says. "I don't fully buy this *old* bullshit. And Mom says you're having bad dreams again."

The *traitor*. "She thinks I'm having bad dreams because I asked for cotton candy during that post-game interview three weeks ago. Remember? She was like, *you only want cotton candy after bad dreams*, but really, this dude behind home plate was eating it *all fucking game*, and it was on my mind. You know how hard it is to watch every single batter, waiting for them to hit a grounder your way, but instead, all you see is a big fluffy ball of pink moving behind him? How can anyone endure that and not want cotton candy? This is my normal mid-season craving for junk food."

"The more he talks, the more he's making up stories," Tillie Jean says to the room at large.

I like my sister.

I like Max.

I wasn't initially in favor of the two of them dating, because Max would be the first person to tell you he was a shit and didn't do relationships, and even though I knew he was wrong, *he* didn't know he was wrong, which basically meant he wasn't wrong.

I didn't want my sister dating someone who needed her to be his self-esteem. That shit has to come from within, because we all have a hard enough time with our own self-worth before taking on the responsibility of someone else's.

Max pulled his head out of his ass and realized he can both struggle sometimes and still be a committed partner. Now as long as I don't find my sister crying in my hotel room over him being a dick—which I haven't—we're cool.

Huh.

I do talk a lot.

And my point was, I don't like my sister being on the road with me when it means she's telling all my secrets and hacks. "Can I please go to bed so I can play like the god I am in a few hours?"

Praise the ghost of Babe Ruth, it works.

"I'm calling Mom," Tillie Jean says as she heads to the door.

"You know believing in yourself is bigger than any super-stition, right, Cooper?" Henri says as she follows.

Mackenzie snorts. "Oh, to be so new to the game that you still believe that... *Call me*, Cooper. I can help. And you know I will. Anytime, day or night." She punches me lightly on the arm. "I'll even quit being pissed that you haven't asked for my help yet."

Tanesha gives me a no-nonsense mom glare, which has gotten mommier since Andre was born last season. "Do. Not. Fuck. Around. You know what happens when you fuck around."

"You find out," I finish.

"You will so find out, and if you find out and make us lose, I will *never* forgive you," Marisol says. She's been with the team about five years now. I mean, Emilio has, but Marisol's been his boo as long as I've known him, and we all went to their wedding in the off-season.

"Nice pep talk," I say as they file out of the room. "I know it'll help."

TJ makes a face at me. *You don't need pep talks, Mr. Ego*, that face says.

For most of my life, I would've agreed with her.

But today?

Today, I think I need a pep talk.

12

Waverly

"ARE YOU SURE YOU'RE OKAY?" Aspen punctuates the question with a cool hand on my forehead and a wrinkled nose. "You still look pale."

We've been all over Denver today, recording interviews for morning shows that will air later this week, making celebrity appearances at museums and zoos, recording sessions for my webcast, and now we're in the green room at a nightclub where Aspen's about to perform three songs off her upcoming album.

I'm not going on with her, but I'm still backstage for moral support. "I'm fine."

She squeezes my hand. "You should go back to the hotel and rest. I've got this, and you've gone above and beyond. You really have."

"Hmm, go back to the hotel all alone and watch TV and take texts from Aunt Zinnia, or watch one of my favorite artists on the entire planet charm a full nightclub of people while I get to listen to her perform?" I squeeze back. "No-brainer. I'm staying. And I'd stay even if I *didn't* have to deal with Aunt Zinnia's texts."

"Why's she in such a mood?"

"Because she's Aunt Zinnia and she has resting cranky mood?" Because someone on my team told her Cooper Rock was in my hotel room last night.

Of all the things I didn't want to deal with today, having her flip out over me being an adult and capable of making decisions about my life and my career for myself is pretty much top of the list.

Aspen squints at me.

"What?" I reach for my compact mirror. "Oh, god, do I have something on my face?"

"Yeah. It's called *a big fat whopper*. I'm still new to using big speakers and I really like those ear thingies that protect my drums. No hearing damage yet. And I love tea. And when you're like *she's in a mood* when I overheard a nameless someone on your team whispering about being pissed that they didn't get an autograph from Cooper Rock when he came to visit you last night before your digestive system turned you into an audition for the next *Exorcist* movie, my overactive imagination gets the better of me."

I jerk my head around to make sure we're still alone, then pull her to the couch and force her to sit before leaning in close to whisper. *"Who?* Who was whispering?" I demand.

"I didn't get a good look."

"Aspen."

"I didn't! It was right before we went live at the zoo and I didn't tell you this before, but I'm terrified of giraffes, so I was faking it the whole time, but like three hours later, I remembered. I googled the guy and *holy hells bells*, Waverly. Sportsers are a dime a dozen for someone like you, but that *smile* and those *eyes*. Either the man doesn't live up to the promise in those dimples, or you have the worst timing in the world for getting sick."

I gape at her. "Focus, Aspen. *Who was talking?*"

"They were in a group, and I don't know all your people yet. But as far as rebound relationships go, this is a good one. I mean, assuming he can do in private what his face promises. And then I googled some more, and he is very popular with the ladies, so I think you've got a really good chance of being satisfied if you go the hot athlete route there. And I don't care that the average athlete isn't as famous as like, Iron Man. Athletes are *ripped*. Ripped beats rich in the game of vengeance boyfriends. And I mean *ripped* in the *has stamina* way. I didn't go googling shirtless pictures or anything. I have boundaries."

This is not the time to glare at her. It's not.

Not if I want more information.

But my face can't help it.

"So is that why Zinnia's in a mood?" Aspen whispers. "Because she hates it when you date people that she thinks are beneath you?"

I have on sixteen layers of fake eyelashes and enough glitter on my lids that I cannot even press my palms into my eyeballs in frustration right now without causing major damage, never mind the fake nails. I have older friends that I could talk to, most of them either stars themselves or kids of stars who get how valuable privacy is.

But I'm freaking tired of the secrets and pretending I'm some kind of perfect superhuman.

And after what Cooper did for me last night, there's no way I'd call him beneath me.

Not even close.

I've been actively avoiding thinking about it all day, but I can't anymore. I don't *want* to not think about it.

My team is paid to hold my hair when I puke. With Aunt Zinnia taking me in after my mom died, and the stomach issues I've had all my life, she's been there for my more awkward moments more times than I can count.

And yes, Cooper handed management of me over to my staff, but he stayed. And he made it super clear that if I wasn't *Waverly Sweet, most important person in the world*—gag me—he would've left them out of it and stayed on his own.

But the biggest thing?

He texted like he said he would.

Ignore me if I said something about Oompa Loompas in the driveway last night. Weird dreams. Totally normal. Thanks for asking to talk. Felt good to hang out with you again.

He added a gif of himself blowing a kiss that the Fireballs used in a promotional video last year.

And I've been pretending I don't want to swoon all day long.

"Cooper and I had this little fling like eight years ago," I whoosh out.

It's the first time I've said it out loud.

Ever.

When you're nineteen and you think you're in love with the first guy to give you an orgasm, and then he disappears with no further contact, you assume you're high maintenance. Not worth it. That he wanted one thing, and then he found it better somewhere else.

And when your aunt basically confirms all your fears out loud and says it'll be better if you forget it ever happened, you feel so much shame and embarrassment that you want to do exactly that.

You don't want people to know your failures.

Not when it's critical that you come off looking perfect.

"Oh my god," Aspen whispers.

"And there's apparently a lot more to the story of why he disappeared than I thought there was, so I asked him to come over last night to talk about it, and then…well, then there was *revenge of the small crustaceans* in my gut, and he didn't bail. He stayed, and we barely got to talk about what I wanted to talk to him about, but he stayed and made sure I was okay and comfortable, and now I'm both super confused and super clear on what I want."

"He ghosted you? *Why?*"

I wave the question away. "Would you give someone a second chance if it turned out that they had a good reason for leaving and you could forgive them for being young and stupid since you were kinda young and stupid too, and you thought they wanted a second chance, which it felt like he did, even if he's known for not *ever* seriously dating anyone and your last serious partner was cheating on you and neither one of you really has time for an actual relationship right now?"

"Why did he ghost you?" she repeats.

"That's not an answer to my question."

"But it's critical information in order for me to answer your question."

"You are such a hard-ass."

"I don't earn friends by dancing around the hard stuff."

This one's tough.

If I tell her, I feel like I'll be on the cusp of betraying the only family I have.

But if I don't talk to someone about this, I'm afraid I'll be betraying myself.

So I find the best compromise I can. "He felt like he'd hold me back if we took things any further, and he thought I could —well, that I could do *this*." I wave my hand around the room, around my outfits and makeup and the crew waiting outside and the entirety of my larger-than-life life.

"He decided all on his own that you were going to be on top of the world and that dating him would hold you back?"

I roll my eyes.

She doesn't blink.

"Fine," I say. "He might've had some help coming to that conclusion. And I might've had some help coming to the conclusion that it was my fault for being *me* when it wasn't. Also, he didn't exactly apologize for it, but he *has* told me that he's older and wiser and won't walk away this time. Not that we've defined what *this time* means, but…"

Aspen bites her lip.

"What?" I ask.

She shakes her head.

"*What?*"

"You remember that day after I finished recording, and you walked in on the studio engineer trash-talking one of my songs, and you told me to fire him?"

"Oh my god, tell me you're not dating him." I cringe, because that's exactly what Aunt Zinnia's been saying to me all day. *Tell me you're not dating Cooper Rock again. You know he's not good enough for you. You know he'll break your heart again. You know you're so high above him, he doesn't even deserve to look at the soles of your feet.* "Never mind. None of my business. I didn't say that. Go where your heart is, do what makes you happy, and I promise to be here for you if he's a dick-turned-knight-turned-dick-again."

She laughs. "No. He's a dick. Through and through. But all of that?" She waves a hand like she's capturing my words back from the air. "All of that *believe in yourself, be happy, I support you*? I just...do you ever...*argh*."

"Do I ever what?"

She shakes her hands out, stands, and paces toward the door in her heels and her sparkly black dress. "We're talking about you. And Cooper. And why he left. And what you're not saying. Waverly, look, I know she's your aunt, and I shouldn't say anything, but all of this extra stuff she lines up for you makes you utterly miserable, and every time you follow your gut, you *nail* it, but you don't follow your gut without second-guessing yourself all the time because—never mind. Never mind."

"No, don't stop." My body is flushing hot and cold and hot again, and it's not from last night's shrimpmageddon. "You think I should fire my aunt."

Her shoulders hitch. "All I'm saying is, if she weren't your aunt, would you still want her to be your manager?"

I swallow hard. "That's a big question."

"Please don't hate me," she whispers. "I—you're doing so much to help my dreams come true, and I don't think I could be your real friend if I didn't tell you that I think you deserve better. It's what you've told me every step of the way, and I know there's still a ton that I don't understand about the business, but you're—you're *at the top*, Waverly. You're *it*."

I grimace.

She grabs my hand and squeezes. "You deserve to be surrounded by people who love you and want what's best for you. And on top of that, you deserve to be free to date the people you want to date, or to *not* date the people you *don't* want to date, and I get the impression that you've never had any of the freedom to do the things that normal people in their teens and twenties should get to do, and I want that for you. I want you to live your life for *you* and make mistakes and learn from them and fall head over heels in love because it's *love*, and not because you both want the same thing or someone put a stamp of approval on your love life."

"You don't think my aunt wants what's best for me?"

"Please tell me to shut up."

Of all my friends, Aspen is the newest and the one that I should be most circumspect with. Her access to my personal life should be limited, and everything she's saying shouldn't resonate this hard.

But maybe that's why I need her.

Maybe she'll tell me things no one else in my circle dares to say. The things that everyone else assumes I won't listen to, either because they've tried or I've given off the wrong vibe in the past or they're so used to Aunt Zinnia still being such a major part of my life that no one questions it.

I shake my head at Aspen. "You shouldn't feel like you need to be anyone other than *you* for you to succeed either. If being you means saying the hard things, then you should say the hard things."

"This is awkward."

"No, it's—okay, yes. It's awkward. But it's also...good? You're a fresh perspective. I don't get those often."

She bites her lip again, then grabs her phone, thumbs over the screen, and lifts it for me to see.

It's a text from Aunt Zinnia. *Tell Waverly you don't approve of this Cooper Rock nonsense. She'll listen to you. God knows why, but she will. You owe her this after everything she's doing for you.*

I flush all over again. "I—"

"You're a grown-ass woman, and if you want to go screw an entire baseball, football, soccer, whatever team, then I'm gonna be right there handing them STD test kits and you industrial-size boxes of condoms."

I make a face.

"She's holding your personal life hostage over your career. I know, I know. She's looking out for you. But…is she? Look at Liv Daniels. She's the *It Girl* in Hollywood, and she has a life. Avery Hart too. Your friend Levi Wilson slowed his schedule way down for love but is still making new music and doing more online events for his fans, and they love him for it. Your career shouldn't be your entire life, and you get to make mistakes, Waverly. You get to *live*."

"And if I make a mistake in public, the gossip pages and the tabloids pick it up, and then all of the positive attention *you* deserve becomes negative attention on me instead, and I love your music, and I want to see you succeed."

"If I'm going to survive this industry, then it won't be about what everyone's saying in the gossip pages. It'll be about me writing and performing the music that people want to hear. Like *your* career is about you writing and performing the music that people want to hear. Not about you doing everything and being everywhere and using up everything you have to give at the expense of your physical, mental, and emotional health."

I flinch.

I still have my doubts about how I got to the top.

But Aspen doesn't stop the way that Hiramys or anyone else on my team would at the sight of me flinching.

Nope.

She keeps giving me what for.

And I hang on to every word.

"There will *always* be someone bigger than me getting more attention and publicity. *Always*. If it's not you, it'll be an actress or a social media influencer or another performer with a different scandal. There will always be roadblocks that have to be overcome, just like you're on top and there are still roadblocks you have to overcome."

"But—"

"Waverly, I love you. I adore you. I don't know why you picked me, or why you still keep picking me, but every day I feel more and more like you're the sister of my heart. And I can't stand watching you put the rest of your life on hold to put me in the spotlight. *You deserve to live*. Not in a bubble, but the life you *want* to live."

"I…do." Even to me, it sounds lame.

Aspen doesn't roll her eyes though. She leans in closer instead, totally ignoring my weak protest. "Date. Travel for *fun*, not because some politician asked you to highlight something or because another actress told you that you have to be an activist too. Watch the movies you keep saying you want to watch and read the books you keep saying you want to read. Go to a freaking baseball game. *Live*."

I gape at her.

Go to a baseball game.

She thrusts her hands into her hair, which is a horrible idea, because it's sprayed within an inch of its life for her performance. "Stop, stop." I reach to help her untangle her fingers.

"Dammit," she mutters. "Now I'm spun up."

"Channel it. You'll do great."

"*Go to a fucking baseball game*, Waverly."

"That thing with Cooper isn't serious. It's not even a thing. It's—"

"Hey, Siri, what is Waverly's most used app on her phone?"

"Voice memos, and you know it."

"*After* voice memos and text messages. What's that, Siri? It's the *baseball* app? Because Waverly *is a secret baseball junkie*? And a *secret Fireballs baseball junkie* at that? Gasp. No. Say it isn't so."

She gives me a one-eyed glare from under thick lash extensions that both make her look incredible and also shouldn't be necessary at all.

We get her fingers untangled, and I sigh. "Why am I doing this to you? Why am I getting you all dolled up to go up on stage and do the one thing that's making me a little crazy right now?"

"Because you say I have talent, and apparently some people with a lot of money and connections and control agree with you, and also, *hello*, this is fun."

Her smile lights up her whole entire face, and I can't argue.

Even on its worst days, this is the best job in the world.

She grips both of my hands. "Make a phone call to whoever on your team will make it happen fastest and go watch a baseball game. *In person*. You'll love it. It's great pre-press for launching your video with Levi, and even Zinnia can't argue."

I make a face.

She makes a face.

And I realize she's right. About everything.

So what am I going to do about it?

13

From the text messages of Cooper Rock and Baseball Cheater

COOPER: I would like to formally submit my resignation from the Ego Hall of Fame. I have been put in my place, with witnesses (aka you), and I can no longer pretend I know how to play baseball.

Baseball Cheater: You were literally robbed by a squirrel. Freak occurrence.

Cooper: And I struck out every at-bat.

Baseball Cheater: The pitcher was on fire. Who gets eighteen strike-outs in a single game?

Cooper: You were clearly his good luck charm.

Baseball Cheater: Are you sulking?

Cooper: *selfie of himself pouting in the Colorado visiting players' lounge* No.

Baseball Cheater: Is that Diego behind you? I was so excited when he hit that home run last night.

Cooper: Our saving grace. He robbed that asshole of a perfect game.

Baseball Cheater: And you got to see Jarvis. Looked like he said something funny to you when you were up to bat that second time.

Cooper: Yeah, he made a joke about how it sucked to get traded away when we were finally winning, but he was taking solace in us getting our asses kicked.

Baseball Cheater: OMG. Please tell me you reminded him that the only reason it was him and not Lopez was because he was worth more and got the Fireballs a better utility man.

Cooper: Wait. WAIT.

Cooper: YOU'RE A FIREBALLS FAN. And not just a fan. YOU FOLLOW US. YOU OBSESS OVER US.

Baseball Cheater: When my team called to ask if there were any private suites available last-minute, Tripp Wilson found out, and he and Lila insisted I sit in their suite. You know owners. They talk a lot about business. They talked all about trades last night.

Cooper: YOU FOLLOW THIRTY-TWO INSTAGRAM ACCOUNTS AND THE FIREBALLS ARE ONE OF THEM.

Baseball Cheater: Is this all-caps texting really necessary?

Cooper: YES.

Cooper: Sorry. No. I yell when I'm excited. Not angry yell. Excited yell. Like, normal voice won't do it when I'm this excited. I have to use excited voice. Shit. I'll probably make some dumb typos now too. Anything I say that's weird, blame autocorrect.

Cooper: How long have you followed the Fireballs?

Baseball Cheater: Tons of celebrities don't control our own Instagram accounts.

Cooper: But you do.

Baseball Cheater: That's a leap.

Cooper: I can do math. As I demonstrated last night.

Baseball Cheater: What you did last night was NOT math.

Cooper: Agree to disagree. Serious question – do you know anyone who specializes in breaking curses?

Baseball Cheater: Serious answer – there's no such thing as a curse. Everyone has an off night. Especially when they don't get enough sleep the night before.

Cooper: Lack of sleep is not the problem.

Baseball Cheater: I'm going to pretend you didn't imply that sitting in a hotel room while a pop star puked her guts out was the problem.

Cooper: I was ABSOLUTELY NOT implying that.

Cooper: I had a nice time last night. You're fun to hang out with.

Cooper: Clearly, I don't mean I enjoyed that you weren't feeling on top of the world. That part sucked. For you. Definitely sucked for you. And I didn't enjoy it, but I like hanging with you no matter what we do. Or don't do.

Cooper: Pretend I deleted and didn't send that last message.

Cooper: Am I typing fast, or are you typing slow? Have I lost you? Did a miracle happen? Did the wifi die here? That would be best. Then I haven't sent any of these messages.

Baseball Cheater: I think we should have a fling. (And yes, it took me that long to work up the courage to type that.)

Cooper: You have my full and undivided attention, and I should definitely not be sitting in a public place right now.

Baseball Cheater: We didn't end our last fling the right way, so I think that, for closure, we should do it again, and then stay friends. I know you don't settle down, and I don't think I'm in a place to settle down either right now. As a friend pointed out, I've kept doing the next big thing for my career for so long that I haven't stopped to think about what I want with my life. I schedule in days off but then spend them writing songs or obsessively reading articles about myself on gossip sites so I can figure out what not to do next time. I need to figure out who I am when I'm not working. So it'll be no big deal when you move on and I move on, because I'm not relationship material right now either, but I never got to say goodbye, and as hard as this is to admit, I think it's made me go for all the wrong guys since the last time I saw you. I didn't want to hurt like that again. And instead, I hurt in entirely different ways.

Baseball Cheater: You've been silent way too long. It took me half an hour to type that out.

Cooper: *selfie in an elevator* Got stuck downstairs. Forty-three seconds, and I'm all yours. Call me maybe?

Baseball Cheater: Can't. I'm on a conference call.

Cooper: With who?

Baseball Cheater: Potential endorsement deal.

Cooper: Isn't that what you have people for?

Baseball Cheater: I like knowing what I'm endorsing.

Cooper: Me too. And my agent knows I'll fire him if he signs me up for something dumb.

Baseball Cheater: This is important.

Cooper: More important than you having the life you literally just said you wanted rather than working all the time like five texts ago?

Baseball Cheater: I'm suddenly regretting opening up to you.

Cooper: No, you're not. You're regretting not telling them you have to go and hanging up and letting your team handle this so that you can go read that awesome Fiery fanfic. There's a new episode up.

Baseball Cheater: No!

Cooper: There is. And it's spectacular.

Baseball Cheater: In the train wreck kind of way? I read a bunch of the episodes after you mentioned them, and they're all train wrecks, but also like the good kind of train wreck. I can't look away. It's like a train wreck of butterflies and cotton candy.

Cooper: LE GASP. Love on Fire is literally the best fanfic in the entire universe.

Baseball Cheater: You have no idea what a relief it is to know that you're secretly in love with a dragon.

Cooper: And Zing! She gets me. Hang up. Call me. I need to hear your voice so I know this isn't one of your well-meaning assistants pranking me.

Baseball Cheater: *clandestine selfie taken from under the table showing three staff members behind her*

Cooper: Say you got an urgent call from a friend going through a rough patch in his relationship with his soulmate, then sneak to the bathroom.

Baseball Cheater: You are a terrible influence.

Cooper: Which is exactly why you're texting with me and not any of your other friends.

Baseball Cheater: You can never meet Aspen.

Cooper: Mental note: Meet Aspen.

Baseball Cheater: GAH. Okay. OKAY.

Cooper: Ah, hell. Tripp's asking if we can talk. And when the owner wants to talk…

Baseball Cheater: Tell him you can't talk. That you have a friend going through a rough patch in his relationship with his soulmate.

Baseball Cheater: You totally didn't tell him, did you?

Baseball Cheater: You really are a terrible influence. I'm sitting in the bathroom after I made that excuse, and now you're not answering me.

Baseball Cheater: Although, I'm all caught up with Love on Fire now, and I also got to stream an episode of Who's Your Family, so this wasn't all bad.

Baseball Cheater: I have to go or I'm going to be late to an appointment to read books to preschoolers. Text me later. And let me know if you're actually in trouble with management. I might know a guy who can help. *winking emoji*

Baseball Cheater: But before I go – on the off-chance all those rumors are true about you hitting a rough patch with your game because you're afraid of success, then I wouldn't be a good friend if I didn't tell you that success is the last thing you should be afraid of. When you hit the top of one mountain, it makes it easier to see the peaks of the mountains you never knew existed before. You know what you want. What you've always wanted. You want to win it all for the team you've loved above all else forever. So do it. Win. Bask in the glory. Enjoy every fucking second. And yes, I said fucking. Worry about what's next when you get to what's next. Trust me, it'll be clearer when you get there. It always is. Don't miss the sign to get off the mountain to travel to the next continent's mountains. I think that's the mistake I made.

Baseball Cheater: And also, thanks for being so cool about the other night. I'll talk to you later. Xoxo

14

Cooper

"You shaved."

Diego's statement startles me, and I almost fall off the bench in the locker room when I open my eyes and find him squatting three inches from my face. I'm meditating with noise-canceling headphones, looking for my focus and trying to tap the warrior inside.

Something's gotta work.

So far, extra workouts aren't doing it.

Fewer workouts aren't doing it.

I've tried both.

Trading nights at the bars with going to bed early so I can make extra trips to pet shelters and children's hospitals and nursing homes and playgrounds and Little Sluggers clinics and camps isn't doing it. And I'm doing all of that without press coverage, for the record.

Self-improvement comes from within, not from external

gossip validation. If they catch me there, so be it. But it's not for the cameras.

Yet none of this is working to pull me out of my slump.

And if this isn't working, I can't talk or work my way out of what my problem is.

Celibacy is *not* good for my game.

Neither is the pressure of being first in our division as we get closer and closer to the All-Star break.

This is when every other team in the league will be after us.

We can't let up. This lead is ours to blow, and if there's one thing the Fireballs are historically exceptionally good at, it's blowing.

It's such a long climb to the top. I don't know what I'll do if we fuck it up. If *I* fuck it up. And I'm still terrified about what's waiting on the other side if we *do* make it all the way, but there's no way in hell I'm letting that stop me from wanting it all.

This is what I've dreamed of my entire life.

I'm not letting up now.

If only I could get my game back.

"Lucky socks are failing me. I'm trying something new," I tell Diego.

He wrinkles his nose. "You still smell like lucky socks."

"You smell like rookie noogies." I reach for him, but he darts away like he doesn't spend hours a day squatting behind the plate. Hope the kid's knees last long and prosper.

The bench shakes beside me as Max sits down. He's digging into a bag of popcorn. "Dick broke?" he asks.

"Didn't look close enough in the shower to see for yourself that I'm better than fine?"

"I don't like to squint in the shower. Also, if that's where you're showing off…"

I reach for the popcorn.

He pulls it away before I can grab any. "This is winner popcorn. I won yesterday. You struck out twice and popped out once."

"I scored."

"Dude, you got walked, and then you got walked in. They gave that to you."

"You were my idol when I was in the Minors." Diego's down the way, sitting in front of his locker, but he's clearly listening in, and he's staring at me the same way he stared at Waverly's photoshoot in *People* last week.

Waverly.

Waverly.

We've been texting every day for over a month now. Sometimes she leaves me a voicemail. Sometimes I leave her a voicemail.

We're both hella busy. It's annoying as fuck, and every day, I'm realizing more and more how right Zinnia was all those years ago.

We would've held each other back.

Or worse, we would've started resenting each other for our schedules, and then what was a three-day thing that we seem to have overcome now would've turned into a lifetime of hating each other.

And I don't like to hate people.

"Sorry you had misdirected hero worship, Diego." Max shakes his head. "Always happens. The rookies worship ol' Coop here, and then they get to know him."

"It's okay, Happy Max. I like knowing my idols have layers."

"Makes us more awesome," I interject.

Diego doesn't agree.

Instead, he makes a deer-in-the-headlights face and turns to grab something out of his locker.

Francisco snorts. "Taken down by the rookie. Nice, D. Nice. But, Coop, seriously—is your dick broken? You haven't been out with us after a game practically the whole season. We're missing our wingman."

"He got old," Luca offers.

"The Rock only gets more fabulous with age," I reply.

"I love The Rock!" Diego looks up from his phone with a massive grin. "*Baywatch* is my favorite movie. He's so good. And he keeps getting better."

I hook a thumb toward my chest. "*This* Rock, Estevez. The *Cooper* Rock."

Brooks throws a stuffed Baby Ash at me. "Don't talk about yourself in third person. It'll make you strike out again."

I catch the stuffy and cuddle it like I was cuddling Miles a couple hours ago. Cutest baby on the face of the planet. Fight me. Miles, I mean. My nephew. My very real, human nephew. Ash is now a close second for cutest baby, and I'm pissed at what management is doing to her at the end of this year.

"Disrespecting the baby dragon mascot will make *you* strike out," I say.

"TJ says your mom says you're having bad dreams," Max pipes up.

"I'm not having bad dreams."

"Being trapped in a bubble with a cat chasing you and trying to pop the bubble while you're floating ten thousand feet in the air doesn't ring a bell?"

"Nope." Jesus. She's ratting me out *again*.

"My abuela interprets dreams," Emilio says. "Want me to ask her what it means?"

"Being trapped in a bubble is a metaphor for feeling

trapped in life," Diego says, peering at his phone. "And being suspended in air without a parachute or wings means you're afraid you're going to fall. Cooper's having performance anxiety because the pressure's getting to him."

"Your phone tell you that?" I deadpan.

"My sister has bad dreams, so I learned how to help her understand them." He smiles, angels invent new melodies on their harps, self-cleaning glitter spontaneously erupts from the sky, and everyone in the locker room smiles too.

Even Max, who had a very rocky start with Diego's optimism this year. "You ever have bad dreams, D?"

"Never. Except I did once dream that Waverly Sweet wrote a song about me and it included the word *mustard* six times. That's as close to bad as it gets."

"What's Waverly up to today?" Emilio asks.

Every molecule in my body tenses, and it takes superhuman effort to not look super interested in the answer. Or into how I missed that Diego is *that* obsessed with the woman I'd like to date if I could find the freaking *time*.

I know what Waverly's up to. She's going on a national morning talk show to hype up Aspen's album and tour, and then she has a charity lunch in New York for a pet foundation, followed by recording another one of her webcast episodes, and then she's doing a photo shoot for the makeup line she's launching next week, followed by a quick dinner with her management team to discuss tour schedules two or three years out, and then she has a writing session with one of her favorite music producers.

I have all of these songs in my head and snippets on my phone and no time to get them out, she told me on text last night. *I don't write well after a full day, but if I don't hook up with Emily tomorrow night, it'll be three more weeks before our paths cross, and that's like a year in songwriting time for me.*

And she's butting heads with her aunt. *It's just this publicity thing* or *We disagree about a song on my next album* or *She didn't like the dress I had made for the Queen Tribute Concert.*

You ask me, her aunt needs to pop an edible and go spend a week at an all-inclusive getting her knots unwound.

"Waverly hosted a puppy prom." Diego flashes his phone out at the clubhouse at large, and we all *aww* over a picture of Waverly lying on the floor with dogs crawling all over her. She's in a princess crown, and the dogs are wearing bowties and tutus.

And now I'm irritated all over again.

She didn't send me pictures of that.

Why didn't she send me pictures?

"Dude, my prom did *not* look like that," Brooks says.

"Wish mine had," Emilio chimes in.

"She got twenty-four dogs adopted yesterday." The pride in Diego's voice makes my shoulders twitch. "She was there with her boyfriend."

"*What?*"

Everyone turns and stares at me.

Boyfriend? Fuck, no. She's *mine*. "Twenty-four dogs is *huge*," I improvise.

Max stares at me a beat too long while Diego takes the bait and rattles on about how Waverly's *boyfriend* adopted the dog that was missing one ear.

She doesn't have a boyfriend.

She doesn't. It's a publicity stunt. Has to be.

She would've told me if she was dating someone.

Wouldn't she?

Yes. Yes, she would've. She's starting to step out of her

comfort zones in public, but dating one guy and coming to my house to do what she's calling *finishing our fling* isn't her style.

Also, that *finishing our fling* thing?

No way.

No fucking way.

This is only the start. Come November, I'll have a few months off.

If she can wait four more months for me, I can date her pants off.

Figuratively.

And literally. That's part of dating. But figuratively first.

Assuming I can figure out a way to impress the fuck out of her during our supposed fling-finishing.

She can buy herself the whole entire world, and here I'm hoping my personality alone will win her over.

Don't say it. It's bad enough I'm thinking it. I don't need you to say it too.

Maybe the problem with your game is that you've finally realized you're not all that.

Dammit.

I told you not to say it.

The problem with my game is that I play better when I'm getting laid, and I'm not getting laid because I found someone I'm so obsessed with that I don't even notice when other women are in the room anymore, and because I've always been *me*, she doesn't think I'm worth her time for anything more than getting *closure*.

Max pokes me. "Dude. It's *puppy prom*. Who scowls at that?"

"I'm gonna hit a fucking grand slam today," pops out before I can think. This is what I do.

I talk big.

I deliver big.

Usually.

And historically, I talk big, deliver big, and the game lets us down, because we're the Fireballs. But this year, I talk big, I deliver small, and the team comes through anyway.

The whole clubhouse goes silent.

"I'm gonna hit a fucking grand slam," I repeat.

My teammates all exchange glances.

Diego's even dropped his phone like puppy prom and Waverly no longer matter.

That's kinda huge.

Luca clears his throat. "Maybe you wanna start with a single?"

Darren grabs him around the neck and gives him a noogie. "If Cooper says he's hitting a grand slam, we're fucking setting him up to hit a grand slam."

Luca's flailing. "I'm just saying, maybe we start with baby steps."

"What if you get on base, and I hit a grand slam?" Brooks says.

Fucker's usually behind me in the batting order.

He's right.

That's more likely.

I surge to my feet. "I'm going to talk to Coach Addie."

And now the entire clubhouse is sucking in a collective breath.

I flip them all off and head out of the clubhouse toward the coaches' offices.

Coach Addie and I butted heads again last week when she caught me replacing the bats in the batting cages with bats painted like Thrusty, the Copper Valley Thrusters hockey team's rocket-powered bratwurst mascot. *Can't improve your swing with that paint job,* she said.

And she was unfortunately right.

Santiago, our head coach, gave me a long side-eye a few hours after the Lady Fireballs ambushed me in my hotel room when I missed curfew a couple weeks before that, and he benched me two games later after a piss-poor performance.

But the team won.

Without me.

Tripp Wilson keeps stopping by to check on me. We were friends before he and his wife became co-owners of the team, so while there are lines in our relationship that weren't there two years ago, I still consider him to be my friend first.

Not really fond of the hints he's started dropping. *Only two years left on your contract. Do we need to talk about what's coming next? You'll always have a spot in the organization of course. Name where you want to be.*

Translation: Dear Cooper, your best days are behind you. Wanna join the coaching staff so your old ass doesn't drag the team down after we've worked this hard to build it up?

My agent will have some things to say about that, and I'll let him, but since we're not even close to negotiation time, I'm taking this as Tripp being my friend first and the Fireballs' owner second.

I stop at the assistant coaches' door and knock. It's open, and all four of them inside look up at me.

Pretty sure Coach Dusty's eyeball twitched, and not because I've apparently interrupted a round of *Go, Ash, Go,* the card game that management commissioned to celebrate our new mascot last fall.

Coach Dusty's our fielding coach. I'm giving him heartburn this year too. Still snagging the hard balls to catch, but I've let too many easy grounders go past me.

I lock eyes with Coach Addie. "I'm gonna hit a grand slam today."

All four of them share glances.

Coach Dusty coughs.

"Big Ben's pitching for Atlanta," Coach Addie says.

Shit. Big Ben's a legend. I've never hit a home run off him. *Ever.* He's struck me out more than any other pitcher in baseball, matter of fact.

"Can't wait to see the look on his face when I knock it all the way out of the park."

The four coaches share a look again, then Coach Addie throws down a card. "Kid fan. I'm protected. House rule—if I get back and only one of you is left, I win by default." She rises to her feet while the other three groan, and she nods to me. "Your call, slugger. Let's see how you're swinging today to make sure you've got it in you."

"I've got it in me."

But do you? the doubt whispers.

I punch that fucker in the face and put it in timeout.

I'm a fucking professional baseball player.

I'm doing this.

And then, tomorrow night, I'm giving Waverly the fucking date of her life.

15

Waverly

THE WINDING ROAD up to Cooper's home in the Blue Ridge Mountains an hour outside of Copper Valley is quiet and dark. I spend most of the ride texting with Aspen about how her show went last night and with my producer about something that isn't sitting right on a track I recorded last week, but between texts, I can't stop looking behind us.

It's not worry about the tabloids or gossips or Aunt Zinnia.

It's more that I'm too excited about tonight, and I don't want anything to ruin it. And no, I don't want to talk about what being *too excited* might mean for the state of my brain and my heart when I thank Cooper for a nice time and leave tomorrow with a handshake.

"Are you sure—"

"No one followed us," Kiva says from beside me in the back of my SUV while Scott One guides the vehicle around a corner. Scott Two's in the passenger seat.

"And Cooper's house—"

"Is secure," she confirms. She makes a noise that I've learned over the years means she's vexed. "It's nearly as secure as your houses."

"That bothers you?"

"He's sports-famous, and I realize this house is mostly empty during the baseball season, but he's on a secluded mountainside outside a small town with a low crime rate, yet he has a security system to rival yours."

"That makes sense to me, given some of the pranks he's pulled. Remember the headlines about Max Cole showing up to spring training with glitter in his hair? And how he's still glittering now? Once you launch the glitter bombs, you have to step up your security game if you want to avoid retaliation."

Kiva gives me another look.

"He won't prank me," I assure her.

Her look gets *lookier*.

I ignore it. "No one's leaked this to Aunt Zinnia?" That's the only thing threatening to upend my stomach tonight.

"I plugged the hole."

"Thank you."

I don't ask who the hole was. My team feels like family, so I don't want to know.

There were three departures from my staff in the past week, but I tell myself it was only one of them, and there's no way for me to identify which one if I don't ask.

My SUV turns onto a tree-lined driveway and follows it up a hill and around a bend to where Cooper himself is hanging out on the porch of a large, two-story mountain manor, sitting on the steps between stone pillars, hands dangling between his knees.

He shaved. His hair looks freshly trimmed. He's wearing a button-down with the sleeves rolled up his tatted forearms, and every erogenous zone in my body jolts to immediate attention. I can't tell if he's in dark jeans or a pair of slacks, but those are definitely wingtips on his feet.

He dressed up for me.

At his own house.

My heart lodges in my throat, and my veins suddenly feel like they're full of Dr Pepper. Chills race down my arms, and my clit tingles.

We're doing this.

We're getting naked together and working off all our history in order to be friends again.

That's not how this goes, my brain whispers.

I tell it to shush and trust me, even though I don't actually trust myself.

I do trust that there'll be some stress relief involved in naked time with Cooper though, and the pop gods know I could use some of that.

"We'll be circling outside," Kiva says as Scott One opens my door for me.

"Thank you."

"I put extra condoms in your purse."

"You have always been my favorite. Don't tell Hiramys."

Kiva doesn't respond.

Cooper rises, descends the stairs, and greets me with a kiss on the cheek that sends a thrill over my skin. "Hey."

Hey. It's the simplest greeting ever, but it makes the butterflies in my stomach take flight, and I'm suddenly nervous all over again.

Not *I'm going to embarrass myself* nervous though.

Excited nervous.

"Oh my gosh, how's your butt?"

I cringe before the last syllable is out of my mouth.

Not how I meant to start the evening. I can hold my poise through the most awkward live television interviews, but I can't greet a guy I'd like to shag tonight without asking about his ass.

He takes it in stride, though, flashing a Cooper grin. "You mean how's the ball?"

"You took a ninety-six-mile-an-hour fastball to the ass at home plate. And then you limped to the dugout after you finished circling the bases when Brooks followed you with his grand slam, and you didn't go back in the game after that."

There's a dip in his grin, but it comes back as quickly as it wobbled. "Dramatics for the fans. I'm fine." He slips an arm around my waist and steers me up the steps. The subtle scent of his cologne or aftershave or whatever it is wraps around me like a hug.

It reminds me of warm towels on a sandy beach, and it makes me feel *home*.

No, Waverly. Not home. This is temporary, for fun and closure, with a guy who's perfect for temporary because he's not the settling down type.

See also: He's been the talk of social media for the past twenty-four hours after taking that aforementioned fastball to the ass while he was up to bat. Someone zoomed the video in all the way so that his ass and the ball that hit it were the only things in the camera view, and that firm muscle flexing to send the ball flying in another direction without a hint of butt wobble has been watched millions of times on each of the social media platforms.

Not that I looked at them all. That'd be preposterous.

Aspen checked out the one or two that I hadn't and filled me in too.

But the bigger point here—there are *way* too many women weighing in and wishing his ass well, and I'm nearly certain a reasonable percentage of them have had up-close-and-personal experience with Cooper's ass.

At least, that's what the comments indicate.

"Is it bruised?" I ask.

"Eh. Had worse. The bigger question is, how much have you been thinking about my ass?"

Totally caught. "It's hard to miss."

"Awesome always is."

"I meant the video coverage is hard to miss."

"Excuse me, but you're missing the most important element of this story. Bases were loaded when I took that hit. My butt got an RBI last night. How many other players do you know who can say that?"

There's a catch in his voice that tells me he's not as happy about his butt getting credit for a run batted in as he's pretending to be.

But I've slipped on stage enough times—hello, forgot the lyrics to *my debut single that I sing at every concert* one night about a year ago—to not ask about it.

Also, not gonna lie.

I was glued to the television when I finally got to watch the recorded game last night, and when he stepped up to bat with the bases loaded, all I could think was *hit a grand slam, Cooper. Hit a grand slam.*

It had to be going through his mind too.

I look up at him and smile. "Do you have any idea how many women have dueted and stitched your TikTok video about it? Like, half the female population of the world. And a solid portion of the male population too."

"And you know because you can't get enough of my ass in baseball pants, hm? Told you I have cake." He wiggles his brow as he pulls the door open, but it's hard to miss the strain in his expression.

Even in the dim light up here.

My butterflies turn to full-on panic birds. "Cooper, don't lie. Did you get hurt worse than you're letting on?" I've seen games where players have been pulled for getting hit in the helmet, but I've seen way more guys shake it off.

It even looked like Cooper was shaking it off during the game. At least, until he hit the dugout after Brooks's homerun cleared the bases.

"Hit pretty close to my hip bone, and then the muscle froze up, so they pulled me for X-rays. All fine now. Cross my heart. Hope you're hungry. I made crackers and dried fruits and a chocolate platter."

I squint at him. "Is that magic ass bruise-curing food?"

He laughs at that, and I silently high-five myself.

Cooper being a big mischievous dork and causing trouble? That's a given. Cooper laughing? I'm not sure that I've heard his laugh nearly as much as I've seen the smile. "Yep. And bonus, they all rarely cause food poisoning and still taste good. Mostly. Are crackers ever delicious on their own, or are they just handy edible spoons for more delicious stuff? Officially regretting the crackers. Who needs crackers when you have chocolate?"

"I like Saltines."

"Seriously?"

"They remind me of my mom. I don't know why. But I think of her every time I eat them. And I can pack them away."

Crackers.

I'm here to jump his bones on the one night that I was able to squeeze in a side trip near Copper Valley while he's here on a day off between two home series, and we're talking about bruises on his ass and *crackers*.

He gestures me to go ahead of him through the door he's still holding open, but when I peer inside, I don't see anything. "Why is your house dark?" I whisper, halfway surprised that my security team isn't running in to check things out.

"Superstition," he whispers back.

"Are you afraid tonight won't go well if we turn the lights on? I can handle seeing your booboo. I might even kiss it if you ask nicely."

"I might let you." He pulls the door shut behind us and grabs my hand.

Tingles race up my arm when our palms connect. His fingers are long, wrapping all the way around the top of my hand, and his skin is warm, and I'm already struggling to catch my breath.

Don't do it, I remind myself. *Don't think of this as anything more than a one-night thing.*

"Diego went nuts before the game yesterday over the pictures of you at puppy prom."

I cringe in the dark. No one told me that Phillip Nash would show up, and now everyone thinks I'm dating the rock star, which Cooper undoubtedly saw if he saw the stories about puppy prom. "Puppies never take bad pictures."

"Was that your first prom?"

My brain screeches to a halt at the hint lingering in his voice.

No.

No.

I swallow hard. "I guess, kind of."

"Kind of?"

"When you have your first meeting with record execs at thirteen, traditional high school kinda goes out the window. I never had an actual prom, and that's okay. I had something else." We're still in the entryway to his house in the Blue Ridge Mountains not far outside of the city, just standing here, holding hands in the dark and talking about puppies and prom and high school while I squash the panic attack that's suddenly building at the suspicion of what might be waiting for me in the dark.

He didn't.

Tell me he didn't do what I'm afraid he did after he brought up puppy prom with that subtle suggestion in his voice, when Cooper is *known* for things.

I should kiss him. Right here in the dark. And then I don't have to find out.

But what if I leap on him and accidentally hurt his ass?

It has to be bruised. It *has* to be.

He's quiet again, and that's unsettling. Cooper's never quiet.

I squeeze his hand. "Let's go upstairs."

"Waverly, I—"

He cuts himself off like he's nervous.

Maybe he hurt his butt and he can't operate his equipment right now. He's injured and needs to heal. Thrusting won't work, and if I remember anything from eight years ago, it's that he gives very good thrust.

"I think I fucked up again," he says, his words rushed and so unexpected that they barely register. He shifts, something clicks, and then fairy lights glow to life all around us.

They're woven in the banister on the stairs in front of us.

Draped across the walls in the living room off to our left, around the fireplace, over the front of a table overflowing with plates of crackers and dried fruits and bowls of chocolates, and into the open kitchen at the back of the massive room. Balloon bunches are tied up and hovering in clumps around the room, and streamers in pink and ivory are draped from the corners, twisting up to a twirling disco ball in the center of the room.

There's a massive bowl of punch on the island in his kitchen, right between a small tower of champagne glasses and an ice sculpture of two swans whose necks make the shape of a heart.

Soft music flows out of built-in speakers.

Ed Sheeran. He's playing Ed Sheeran's "Perfect."

My stomach turns. My heart thuds to the floor.

He did.

He absolutely *did* do the last thing I expected him to do.

And I do what I've been trained to do, and I turn a brilliant smile on him. "Oh my gosh. You did all this for me?"

He's watching me like he knows I'm faking it, and his ears are going pink. "My mom says I have too much energy and too many ideas. Sometimes, I try to use my powers for good."

"Instead of on glitter bombs?"

He doesn't take that bait either. "You don't like it."

"I do!"

"Waverly."

"You nailed what would've been my high school colors."

He crosses his arms and glares at me, which is also an unusual Cooper expression. "I don't care if you don't like it, but I do care if you lie about it."

"Geofferson recreated prom for me the night he proposed," I whisper before I can stop myself.

His eyes go wide. "Oh, fuck."

"And yesterday was the most awkward promo stunt of my life." The floodgates have opened. "Aunt Zinnia arranged it all. Puppy prom was her idea. Phillip Nash was her idea. I didn't know he was coming. We are *not* dating. His publicist called in a favor because he wants to expand into acting and needed a higher profile event to prove he can pull it off. He's a complete ass in private, and if anyone on my team *ever* suggests I work with him again, they're fired. My cheeks still hurt from faking the smiles and I haven't felt that used since Geofferson dumped me for a gymnastic dancer the minute the ink was dry on his first major movie role."

Cooper rubs his slack jaw. His gaze darts around his living room, our prom dance floor, panic flashing across his features. "More energy than sense, and you have prom trauma. I can fix this. Two minutes. Go hide in the bathroom."

"Cooper—"

"Second door on your left. Down the hall."

"*Cooper.* You don't have to fix anything. This was super sweet. It's a replacement for every other bad prom."

"It's overkill. I should've just pulled out the pizza and left the massage chairs in here so we could watch TV until we decided to make out. I'm kinda addicted to *Who's Your Family* now. It wouldn't be a hardship."

"This is completely you." I smile—this one way less forced —and squeeze his hand again. "Let's dance."

His face does as many acrobatics as he usually does on the baseball field when he's diving for line drives that should be impossible to catch. "We can have a pool party. Dumb to have a pool when I'm not here in summer and probably never will be, so we should use it. That's hella practical. I'll go naked too since you didn't bring a swimsuit."

Kiss him, dummy.

Poor guy's flustered.

And honestly? The more flustered he gets, the more I want to kiss him. And touch him. And dive into his pool naked with him.

I push up onto my tiptoes to do exactly that when Ed Sheeran is abruptly cut off and suddenly we're being blasted with—is that polka music?

Cooper jerks his head to the control panel on the wall, then clears his throat. "Ah, bug in the system," he says over the music. He vaults to the panel, fiddles with the screen, and a moment later, the polka is gone and we have Adele at a much lower volume.

"C'mon." He tugs on my arm. "You hungry? Name your favorite food. Betcha I have it in the fridge. We can eat out on the deck."

I gesture to the streamers and signs and the punch and the disco ball. "How long did this take you?"

His gaze connects with mine, and there's something unusually serious lurking in his eyes. "Not long. Just struck me that it might be fun. Already had most of it here in storage because…well, because I'm me."

"There's an ice sculpture."

"I know a guy." He flashes that grin that makes my panties try to melt themselves off.

I shake a finger at him. "No, you don't. You don't get to use the dimples against me. Put them away."

"Can't. I made a deal with the devil to get them, and now I have to use them or I'll lose them. Painful process, dimple extraction. You don't want to know." He shudders, but he's still grinning as he pulls me to the food table. "Here. Try the Ritz. It's no Saltine, but it's pretty good. And you still haven't told me your favorite food. I could google it, but I need confirmation it's your *real* favorite, and not what you think someone wants to hear."

"I'm not sure I know my real favorite food."

"How can you not know your favorite food?"

My face flushes hot. "I have this theory that when you can have whatever you want anytime you want it, nothing's as special as it could be if it was an honest-to-god treat. Not to be all *I can afford anything*, but—"

A breathy moan cuts me off.

A breathy, female moan, followed by a deep, "*Fuck, yes, give me that hot, wet pussy all over my big, hard, massive dick.*"

Cooper's eyes go wide.

Mine too.

He dives for the corner again.

"*Oh, god, plumber-man, you have the biggest cock I've ever seen.*"

"*My name is Stanley. Say it. Say my name.*"

"*Stanley. Oh, god, STANLEY. Stick it in me, pipe boy. Let me ride your—*"

There's a soft *pop*, and then silence. The disco ball's still turning.

"What—" I start, but I stop when I realize Cooper's entire face has gone pink.

"I probably shouldn't have planted that speaker that made farm animal noises under my brother's bed when I was home last month."

At least, I'm pretty sure that's what he said.

He's mumbling. And yanking more cords out of outlets. And moving to tap on the control screen near the front door.

The sound system starts again, and that has to be someone faking an orgasm.

It has to be.

I've never screamed like that during sex in my entire life. I've never *wanted* or *needed* to scream like that during sex in my entire life.

There's a banging like a headboard hitting a wall.

More banging like the neighbors are disturbed on the soundtrack.

More banging like he's totally railing her.

She goes soprano.

I try to stifle a giggle. Doesn't work, so I head for the food tray.

Do not choke on a cracker, Waverly. Do. Not. Choke. On. A. Cracker.

The sound abruptly shuts off again, and I'm still trying so hard to not laugh that I inadvertently snort spit out of my nose.

"Sorry," Cooper mutters. "I know you hate pranks."

It's true.

I do.

I toured once with an artist I won't name who went as overboard as I hear Cooper likes to, and I've had a strict *no pranks* policy on my tours ever since I got big enough to make the rules.

But watching Cooper squirm as he gets some of his own medicine?

Can't deny this is amusing.

And let's be real.

I'm still totally stripping for him and riding *his* pipe tonight.

"Would that have happened at your high school prom?" I ask him.

He studies my face as I lean against the food table, grinning at him, and he slowly starts to smile back. "Yeah, there was this kid in my class who would've instigated something like that."

"Did his name rhyme with Pooper Mock?"

He blinks once, and then he busts up. He starts to speak, but he has a case of the man-giggles, and it's clearly causing him issues.

I lick my finger, touch it to my own ass, and make a sizzling noise. "Nailed it. This girl is on *fire*."

He's still laughing as he stalks across his living room. "Let's take this party outside. I have this life goal of talking a sexy woman into skinny dipping with me in my own pool."

A full-body shiver of anticipation slinks across my skin and every part of me silently choruses *yes, please*.

And suddenly The Chipmunks are screaming Christmas songs all around us.

I jump, hit my hip on the table, and send a plate of crackers sliding against the plastic table runner.

Cooper's face twists, and then I hear it.

Knocking.

"Hide," he hisses in my ear.

"That's not—"

"*Hide*," he reiterates before I can finish asking why I need to hide from my security team.

The front door swings open, and I leap into action, diving for the nearest hiding spot I can find, which is, unfortunately, under the food table.

It's what I've got. The hall's too far away.

But as I fling myself against the wall, hidden by the table-cloth, I hear something that tells me he was correct.

That's not my staff leading the way inside.

That's a bleating farm animal.

16

Cooper

THERE'S a time for a man to atone for his sins, and while I'm happy to pay up, I'm gonna give my brother hell for deciding that now is my time.

I catch Sue, Grady's pet goat, in the middle of my living room, grab it by its one horn, and drag it out the door. On the porch, I come face-to-face with my grandfather, who's decked out like a grim reaper pirate.

All in black, with an eye patch, a black pirate hat, and his parrot sitting on his shoulder wearing a black cape too. Everything's dark beyond my lone porch light, the weather sticky and warm, and none of this is good.

Especially the part where he's *not* my brother, which means Grady's around here somewhere else, tying up Waverly's security.

"Hey, Pop. Good to see you. Where's Grady?"

Pop's eyes twinkle, but it's not nearly as endearing as

Waverly's eyes twinkling, which they haven't been doing nearly enough tonight because I'm a massive fuck-up.

Probably could've googled *Waverly Sweet Prom* and found out that's how her ex-douche proposed.

Jesus.

Could I have picked anything more likely to spark bad memories?

Pop scratches his pirate hat. "Grady? Probably home sleeping. Or watching that cute little baby so Annika can sleep."

The freaking Chipmunks are still singing that Christmas song inside the house.

It's *the first of July*.

I grin back at my grandfather like my balls aren't sweating at the wrong turns my date with Waverly has taken, which is fully and completely my fault, because I'm me and I got a big idea I had to run with before stopping to ask if it was a good idea or a bad idea or an *already done* idea.

"You know how to shut off the music, Pop? It's scaring the real chipmunks."

One of Waverly's security team comes running. "Mr. Rock—"

"He's harmless," I say at the same time Pop turns and says, "That's Mr. Pirate Rock to you, sonny."

The man looks between us.

"He's my grandfather," I add.

"Who're you?" Pop asks.

"*Rawk! Who the fuck are you?*" his parrot, Long Beak Silver, echoes.

Yeah.

Pop takes the pirate ancestor thing seriously. I normally do too, but not when I have a pop star and her bodyguards around.

Huh. Should've set up a private pirate party. Bet she's never had one of those before.

Or maybe she has.

Google it first this time, nincompoop.

"He's a friend, Pop. Nana know you're up on the mountain this hour of the night?"

"Shoot, she's with me. We know how you get when your game's in the crapper, and we wanted to surprise you."

I'm not a guy prone to having his eyelid twitch. I'm the guy who's usually making other people's eyelids twitch.

Guess my medicine time came due. "Grady *and* Nana are with you?"

He grins bigger. "What? Grady's not with me."

I hook a thumb back toward my house and the awful music. "C'mon, Pop. You're good, but the last time you tried to work my sound system, you gave yourself a bruise on your finger from hitting the control panel too hard." I wink at him. "Who's making the Chipmunks sing? Promise I won't tell you told me."

He chortles, gets ahold of himself, starts to chortle again, and then finally succeeds in straight-facing me. "Whoever stuck their hand up the chipmunks' butts, I suppose. Chipmunks are puppets, aren't they? Oh, hey, did I tell you that Neveah's back in town? Bet she could help you with your game."

He winks right back and adds a nudge to my arm.

And I realize Waverly's all alone inside, Pop could've brought a dozen of my relatives, and I'm enough of a fun guy —I refuse to call myself a *problem*—that there's a high likelihood they're approaching on more fronts than Waverly's people would've expected.

A Rock family intrusion wasn't on my radar for tonight.

Shit.

I fling open the door and head back inside, rip the damn sound system controller off the wall, which finally stops the music, and catch my sister about to lean down and look under the refreshments table, where I can also see Waverly's heel-clad feet huddling as far back as they'll go behind the tablecloth.

"Tillie Jean, you are so *busted*. Nice try, sis. That really worth leaving Max alone for?"

She jumps back up straight, wipes the guilty look off her face fast enough that it's *almost* like it was never there, then gestures around the room. "What are you *doing*?"

"First rule of superstitions."

"What's the first rule of superstitions?"

"Can't talk about it or it won't work." I jerk my head toward the door. "If you want the Fireballs to win tomorrow..."

"Dude, you have an *ice sculpture*. Where'd you even get that? Did you drive an ice sculpture all the way in from the city? And you need pink balloons and streamers for your superstition? *Why?*"

"To make you ask why when you crashed my private party for one."

The disco lights hit a speck of glitter in one of her eyebrows while she peers at me. "You're stressed."

"You're here. Of course I'm stressed."

She grins.

I grab her by the arm, realize Grady's goat is loose in my house again, that Waverly's hiding beneath the table with all the food on it that Sue will undoubtedly want to eat, and I have lost all control.

A walkie-talkie buzzes to life on Waverly's dude. "Cloud Six, we've apprehended an elderly woman on the west—"

"Who're you calling elderly, you poophead?" Nana's voice interjects on the walkie-talkie.

"Oh my god," Tillie Jean whispers. She wrenches free of my grip and dances across the bare living room floor. "Pop, Cooper's got a celebrity up here. Does Beck know?" She lifts her own walkie-talkie. "Grady. Go see Beck and Sarah. They might have the—*hey*."

Waverly's guy has her walkie-talkie now. And the goat. "Leave," he says.

"Don't talk to my girlfriend like that," Max growls from my stairway. "Who the fuck do you think you are?"

My stairway. How did he get in here? Did he climb the fucking wall? How long has he been in here?

"Teammate rules," I say. "The big guy belongs. Can't talk about it. Need you to leave. Take TJ and Grady and the goat and whoever else is up here before you ruin the rest of the season for me."

He frowns at me and folds his arms over his chest.

Can't blame him.

I'm rarely this straightforward. I always have an excuse for everything and never let my weaknesses show.

It's a curse and a gift.

"You know all these people?" Waverly's security guy asks. Pretty sure he's the second in command, but I don't know his name. And while the rest of my family looks goofy with the disco ball lights flashing over their faces, he looks downright scary being irregularly lit by a rotating mirror ball.

Good quality in a pop star's bodyguard.

He'd probably be terrifying in a glitter accident too.

"Family," I say. "If you catch a middle-aged couple—"

"Got a middle-aged couple making out on the north border," his walkie-talkie announces. That sounds like Kiva. "What the fuck's going on?"

"Nosy family, according to Rock," the guy next to me answers her.

He's angling to the table too, like he knows where Waverly's hiding and he'll protect her privacy at all costs.

I'm not enough.

Shit.

I will *never* be enough for Waverly all on my own.

She needs *more* merely because she's Waverly.

"Why do you have an ice sculpture?" Max asks.

"Dude." I make the *don't fuck with my superstitions* face.

He gives me back a *this isn't your superstition and I know it* face. "This guy's an ice sculptor and he's holding you hostage?"

"Oh my god, Cooper, why didn't you say so!" Tillie Jean throws herself at me. "We have to get you out of here. They have sharp instruments and they'll start with your pinkies!"

"Would you please go away?" I mutter to her. "I have *a thing*, okay? I'll tell you later."

Much later.

Much, much later.

She snorts. "In three years? Nope. Not leaving. Your game's shit, you're refusing to go out to bars after the games with the younger guys like you used to, you're disappearing every morning when you used to sleep in, going god knows where and doing god knows what, and we're here to help. So let us help. What do you need?"

"Privacy."

"Cooper—"

"I need fucking *privacy*, okay?"

I don't snarl. I don't get cranky.

Not my style.

But I'm snapping at my sister and scowling at my team-mate and silently wishing scurvy on my grandfather and watching my brother pop his head in the door with a look that says he knows something's wrong, I'm being a shit, and if I want donuts for breakfast from his bakery in the morning, I'm gonna have to spill my guts.

"Let him go, TJ," Grady says.

"How many more of them are there?" Waverly's guy asks me.

I lift a brow at Grady.

He's the oldest of the three of us, and the one who'll have the biggest heart attack if anyone's arrested.

Or disappears.

"Aunt Glory and Aunt Bea and Ray and Jacob and Georgia," Grady reports.

"Fuck," I grumble.

Grady grins.

And it's not a simple grin.

This is a classic Rock grin, full of *I'll call them off, but you will PAY for this favor.*

He lifts his walkie-talkie. "Code shit, team. I repeat, code shit."

"What?" Annika's voice echoes through the room, coming from at least three walkie-talkies. "I've had enough shit for one night. You know how hard it is to change a diaper in the dark?"

"Probably harder than pulling a controller off the wall," Grady replies with a side glance at where my built-in speaker controller is hanging by a wire.

I flip him off.

He and Max both smirk.

Fuckers. They were both in on it.

"Have we met?" Max asks the security agent. "You look familiar."

Shit.

Shit.

He would've been with Waverly the day she and Levi shot that video at the ballpark. Max *has* seen him before.

"He's been traveling with me as my personal guard since that incident in Atlanta," I say. "He's so good, you don't even notice him on the plane most of the time."

"*Rawk!* Don't lie to your elders, shithead. *Rawk!*" Pop's parrot interjects.

"Pop, the language on that bird," Tillie Jean says.

Pop straightens. "What? He's smart. He says what he's thinking."

I fake a yawn. "Welp, time for me to get to bed. Need my batter sleep. Get the fuck out."

Max looks at my feet.

Grady looks at my feet.

Tillie Jean starts to bend to look under the table again.

I reach for her, but the security guy is faster.

"Oh, come on," she says to him as she tries to tug her arm out of his grip. "It's not like he has some secret princess in here."

"Don't tell anyone," I stage whisper, which is basically the only thing I *can* say to throw them off the scent.

They never believe anything I tell them, and much as I love my family, I like it that way sometimes. Like now.

The hairs on the back of my neck stand up, and I realize Max is staring at me.

And that's not any stare.

That's a *holy fuck, I know who you're hiding* stare.

My body flushes hot, then cold, and hot again in the span of two seconds.

I spent the better part of the off-season reinforcing Max's idea that he wasn't good enough for Tillie Jean.

Dude got glitter-bombed twice, caught in the cross fire of my prank war tradition with my sister.

I flipped the fuck out on him when I found out they'd been sleeping together behind my back.

He owes me.

He owes me so much shit.

And he knows who I'm hiding.

I'm dead.

I'm a fucking dead man, and my chances with Waverly are over.

Don't do it to her, I silently telegraph to him. *She's innocent. Torture me, but she's fucking innocent.*

His lips curve up, and that is not a pretty smile.

It's not comforting. It's not reassuring.

It says I will never, ever, ever have a good night's rest again.

"TJ," he says to my sister, "I ever tell you about the time Cooper ordered an ice sculpture and jacked off all over it in his hotel room to try to break a curse?"

Fuck. Me.

I did *not* do that, but any denial will be met with embellishments and lies.

Why?

Because I fucking deserve it.

Grady's eyes flare wide, but then he looks at my feet again, and he starts grinning too. "You didn't tell me. But I remember a time in high school when he got caught whacking off to some documentary on roller skating."

"They can leave now," I tell Waverly's guy.

He smirks at me and makes the *go on* gesture at my family.

"There was that time he was on the float with me for the Pirate Festival parade back when he was three, and he was sitting on the back of it playing with his willy for all of Black-beard Avenue to see," Pop offers.

That one's unfortunately true.

My mother was horrified.

"Can we stop talking about Cooper's penis?" Tillie Jean pulls a face. "I'd rather talk about the time he got caught flirting with his student teacher in English class to try to get all the answers to the test."

"Which English class?" Grady asks.

"The one where every test was an essay."

Also unfortunately true. Turns out there's no answer key to essay tests. Dammit. "I took a ball to the head in a game the night before that happened." I gesture around the room. "Anyone else?"

Sue the goat bleats.

"Good one, Sue," Grady says. "What he did to your brother was *totally* unacceptable." He lifts his walkie-talkie. "I repeat, code shit. We'll rendezvous at the rendezvous point."

"Is that Grady's bakery?" Nana asks over a walkie-talkie. "I can ninja a bodyguard, but I can't remember shit these days."

"She didn't ninja me," Kiva's voice says over the security guy's walkie-talkie. "But she did tell me a fascinating story about Cooper and a donut that I can't decide if I want to repeat or remove from my brain permanently."

"Rendezvous without us," my dad says, his voice echoing

over the multiple walkie-talkies used by my family in my house now. "Libby and I suddenly have other plans."

"Aww, I hope we're as frisky when we hit our fifties as they are," Tillie Jean says to Max.

"Annika and I will be," Grady says. "But you know, if two of us are, that's gonna leave no frisky for Cooper. It's like a rule. One of the siblings has to have a sexual dysfunction. Sorry, Coop. Probably a good thing you're getting in all those memories now."

"I got a secret for you," Pop whispers. "Your grandma thinks it's a little blue pill, but it's actually a regular ritual of select movies and magazines with an herbal mixture that's a classified pirate recipe passed down from Thorny Rock himself."

I scrub a hand over my face.

Max is snickering.

TJ's headed to the door, making noises like she's trying very hard not to laugh to the point of snorting.

Grady's flat-out chortling. "C'mon, Pop. Let's let him do whatever it is he thinks he needs to do to fix his game. Not sure why it involves a thousand crackers, but—"

"Mother*fucker*," I yelp.

"*Rawk!* Polly wanna cracker! *Rawk!*"

Long Beak Silver takes flight in my living room, soaring over my head to land on the food trays. He pecks at the entire spread while I try to shoo him away without shaking the table too much, finally deciding on a fancy cracker with lots of seeds, and then he lifts off again.

Right over my head.

And yes, the damn parrot leaves me a present in my hair.

"Oh, shit," Tillie Jean whispers while I stand totally still, cringing, afraid to move for fear it'll slide.

Parrot shit is gross.

"Told you he went nuts when you say the C-word," Pop says to Grady, who's laughing so hard he can't breathe.

"Out you go." Max hustles them both toward the door and grabs Sue by the horn to hustle *him* out the door too. He's grinning bigger than anyone on the team would ever give him credit for, and if this wasn't the absolute worst thing my family could've done right now, I'd snap a picture of Max's smile to send to Diego to have framed in the clubhouse. "Tillie Jean. Our work here is done."

Waverly's security guy looks at me, and I see exactly what he's thinking too.

Their work is *definitely* done.

I'm screwed.

And not in the way I'd like to be.

17

Waverly

THE SILENCE IS DEAFENING.

It's not total silence, but it *feels* like total silence.

Like that moment when you're standing in the middle of the stage in an open-air arena with forty thousand people in the crowd and your sound system is blasting out loud enough to be heard by all of the people in all of the apartments a full half mile away, and you just accidentally sang *trop that fuck* instead of *stop that truck* and you know they noticed and it'll be viral in the next four seconds, and *I'm high on cough syrup* won't make it any better and you're sure you're still singing because you're a damn professional and it's what you do, except you can't hear a thing over the horror.

It's that kind of silence.

Cooper's family has departed, goat included.

Scott One is still standing in front of the table where I'm hiding, legs spread. Scott Two checked in on comms a moment ago—he was tied up with Cooper's aunts and cousins, who have now been escorted to their car.

Kiva's arrived. I can hear her talking about ignoring making the rounds and staying put on the doors to the house instead.

I'm stuck with this feeling of utter mortification, unsure if it's on my behalf or Cooper's.

His family is hilarious, and he's undoubtedly earned everything they're dishing him.

And instead of owning what I'm doing and popping out to say hi and enjoy everything myself, I stayed hidden.

Like a total chicken.

Afraid that one of Cooper's relatives would view this as a moment to grab their five minutes of fame-by-proxy.

Afraid of what Aunt Zinnia would say.

Afraid of what the tabloids would say.

Afraid that I'm falling for this man who went out of his way to make a special night for me, with no idea how much baggage I carry around the idea of prom, and then trying to shift on the spot to fix it as much as he could.

When he doesn't settle down.

And I have no idea what he *wants* from me.

He does a ton of good for the Fireballs, and then he has the *man*-factor working for him, so while everyone knows he's king of the one-night stand, and that he indulges in them all the freaking time more or less without judgment, he's treating me like I'm the very best thing to ever happen to him.

Because I'm famous?

Because he likes me?

Or because he would do this for anyone? And does, in fact, do it for many women over the course of any given regular season?

He said himself that he has too much energy and too many ideas. He *would* do this for anyone. Wouldn't he?

The tablecloth hiding me from view lifts, and I wince and grab my knees tighter.

Cooper's eyes sweep over me, wary and full of regrets, which looks totally *wrong* on him. "You okay?" he asks.

"This is exactly where I probably would've been anyway if this were my real prom." I force a smile that I almost feel.

He winces, then points to his head. "Parrot left me a little present in my hair. I'm gonna go take care of that, and then I'll be right back. There's rum by the punch if you want to spike it. And I won't blame you if you quietly bail while I'm gone."

He's not hitting his normal carefree goofball attitude, and seeing him struggle makes me ache. "Cooper."

He ducks back down. "Yeah?"

"I know they were making up all of those stories about you. Except the ice sculpture one. I believe that one."

His eyes flare wide for half a second, and then he cracks up. "Yeah. Yeah, that one's plausible. Make yourself at home. I mean, even more at home than hiding under tables. I have massage chairs behind the curtains along that wall, and I'll drop the banner covering the TV if you want to chill. Back in five. I gotta fix my hair. I'd help you out, but my hands are, erm, contaminated with pirate bird...stuff."

I scoot out from under the table easily myself. "It's okay. I'm pretty flexible."

"Yeah. Thanks. Back in a minute. And if you decide to bolt —I get it. No harm, no foul. I mean it."

He heads for the stairs without wincing even a little at the fact that there's been a fowl foul in his hair. That could've been a really great joke, and Cooper rarely misses the opportunity to make one.

I glance at Scott One and Kiva, who are standing on opposite sides of the room, one ready to head to the front door, the other ready to take the back.

Scott One doesn't crack a smile, but Kiva's lips wobble.

It takes a lot to make her break.

"Didn't see a thing," she says. "In this room, that is."

Scott One grunts. It's the same as *neither did I*. He's more or less the same as Scott Two, but with a different number of ex-wives and no grandkids quite yet because he's seven years younger.

Kiva glances up the stairs, where Cooper's disappeared. "If you intend to spend any more time here, we'll need to have a long conversation with Mr. Rock about the number of people who are able to disarm all the parts of his fancy security system."

I don't know if that means *my demand for working security systems has been tested past my tolerance for things being other people's problems*, or if it means *I approve of you spending more time with Cooper Rock*.

"Have you met any of Cooper's family previously?" she asks.

I shake my head. "Not unless I met them without knowing who they were. I met Max Cole the day we shot my video at Duggan Field. If Cooper's sister was with them, I wasn't introduced to her then."

"The aunts worry me."

A normal puff of dread threatens to gurgle in my belly. "This isn't Cooper's first brush with fame. Either he'll deal with them, or we'll deal with him."

Kiva lifts a brow. It's a very clear question.

How do you know?

"Can you please send Hiramys a message and ask her to block all gossip sites from my phone?" I ask.

The second brow joins the first.

It's like she's pointing out that self-improvement isn't something you expect to happen when hanging out with Cooper Rock.

"Of course," she says.

"Thank you." I nod to her, then to Scott One as well. "If you'll both excuse me, I'm going to check on someone who's not having a very good evening."

Kiva hasn't commented on the décor.

Neither has Scott One, but then, he wouldn't.

Scott Two would, but only because he used to work for Geofferson and participated in executing the proposal.

Grateful as I am that I got Scott Two in the split, I'm more grateful that he's still outside.

"Stay away from windows," Kiva tells me before she ducks out the back door.

Scott One grunts again and takes the front door.

And I head for the stairs.

One night. I'm telling myself I get *one night* with Cooper, no rules, just a chance to work him out of my system while enjoying the thrill that is all of Cooper's energy focused on making sure everyone around him has a fabulous time, and the minutes are slipping by.

But when I get to the top of the steps and finally locate his bedroom after guessing wrong the first two times, I realize he's not alone.

There's *still* someone else in the house, and he's talking to them in his bathroom.

What?

"You're gonna have to get on board, big guy," he's saying.

"Yeah, you're right. We had a deal. But the thing is, every-thing's changed. I'm freaking the fuck out. Everything I thought I wanted—it's all changed. But we can't keep doing this. You can't hold me hostage. We have to find a different solution to getting what we need, okay?"

Oh.

My.

God.

What the hell is going on?

I wait for the *big guy* to answer, but all I hear is silence and the quiet hum of betrayal building inside of me.

Who *else* is here if he's throwing a prom for me?

And why is Cooper talking to him like they're in a rela-tionship?

Oh my god.

Am I about to walk into some kind of poly situation?

"I'm not saying we'll never have fun again," Cooper says. "But I am saying you need to step out of my game, and we need to cool it for a while longer. Okay, yes, maybe a *long* while."

Is he on the phone?

Why the *hell* is he calling someone in the middle of our date?

Holy shit.

Is Cooper in gambling trouble?

Am I a pawn?

Or is he seeing someone he can't claim in public?

A… *Big. Guy.*

Oh my god.

"C'mon, big guy. Don't look at me like that. I have *never* neglected you. This is a little something you can do for me, okay?"

Fuck this.

Fuck *all* of this.

I march into the bathroom, ready to tell him *exactly* what I think of being lied to, but the moment I realize who—or *what*—he's talking to, a startled shriek flies out of my lips.

He leaps off the closed toilet seat and to his feet, jerking an ivory towel around his bare hips and hiding his *companion* from view while his face goes the color of lava. His dark hair is wet and tousled, his chest and arms still damp from what had to be the world's fastest shower. I get my first full glance at the tattoo that's perpetually teasing me on his bicep—*oh*, it's Fiery the Dragon, done in black ink—along with a pirate flag tattoo on his left pec and script that I can't read scrolled down the side of his ribs.

"Did you—" he starts.

I'm momentarily speechless as I start to put together the *actual* pieces of what's going on here, and I don't mean how fast he cleaned the bird excrement from his hair, and how often that must happen for him to have gotten it all done this efficiently.

I stare at his face.

Then at his towel, which is only hiding so much of what his *companion* is up to.

And I do mean *up*.

"I wasn't—" He drops the hand not gripping his towel closed. "Okay, I was, but it's not what it sounded—okay, yeah, it's exactly what it sounded like, but I'm not a perv. Wait. I am a perv. But I'm also a good guy."

"You were talking to your penis."

"I'm on a sex hiatus."

I gape and fumble for words.

Apparently tonight isn't what I thought it was. "Hey, so sorry. I didn't realize—"

"I don't—I mean—I'm not—*fuck*. Having sex is my baseball superstition. I have to—you know—to play good."

"*Oh my god.*"

"But I like you. A lot. And I—"

"Your message says, *having sex is my baseball superstition*. Ready to send?" Cooper's phone asks from the sink.

"No!" he shrieks.

"All right, message sent."

He mutters more *fucks* than you probably hear in the entirety of the Fireballs' locker room after a brutal loss, lunges for his phone, showing off yet another tattoo—oh my god, he has Baby Ash on his shoulder blade—slips, and hasn't quite regained his balance—which he does with all the speed and grace you'd expect of a professional athlete, for the record—before the dinging starts.

One ding.

Two.

Three more right on top of each other.

"Shit fuck shit fuck shit fuck *stop*," he orders his phone.

It dings three more times and crows once, then lets out a loud *Arrrrggggh, Matey!*

I clap a hand to my mouth.

Do I want to laugh?

Yes.

Do I want to cry?

Also yes.

"Shut. The fuck. *Off.*" He finally mashes his phone right to make the noise stop, cuts a glance at me in the mirror, and then drops his face, eyes squeezed close. "I haven't hooked up with

197

anyone since I saw you again right before the season. I don't *want* to hook up anymore. And now I can't hit regularly, I'm missing the easy plays and sometimes the hard plays, and management's starting to ask what my plans are after my contract is up and hinting at *coaching* if my game doesn't get better."

His body shudders, which he doesn't seem to notice. But of course he's shuddering.

Baseball is Cooper's entire life. It was when I knew him eight years ago, and it's been apparent in every interview I've seen with him, in every endorsement deal he's had, and you can *see* it in every game he plays.

"Facing the prospect of being done as a player shouldn't be a big deal," he mutters. "I said the same thing—*you should coach*—to my buddy Trevor last year, but this is different, and it's not a *but I'm me* thing. He's a pitcher. Pitchers don't last as long. I'm supposed to have more good years."

I don't say anything. I don't know what to say.

Athletes have superstitions. I watch enough baseball that I hear all about them. Publicly, everyone talks about Cooper's lucky socks.

I never considered that was a euphemism for a sock hanging on his hotel door.

He shakes his head, then lifts it and looks me straight in the eye. "I don't want to use you. You wanna go, I get it. Rather watch TV and have a night off here in a comfy chair, I'm game. I *like* you. Yes, I want to bang you until you can't walk, and no, I don't want *just one night*, and yeah, I'd really like to find my game again. I *need* to find my game again. But tonight I'd rather just…be with you. And that's scary as fuck, because I haven't wanted to simply *be* with someone, hang out, be friends, talk, put all the naked stuff second, since…well, since the last time I was with you."

My heart melts.

I know I should guard it better. I know I'm probably signing up to get hurt all over again.

But *I missed him*.

I missed the man I thought he was—the man I thought he could be, the man I'd convinced myself he never was—when we spent our short time together all those years ago.

And here he is. Again.

The same but better.

He'll hurt me again. There's no question. Both of our schedules are crazy. He lives for baseball, and I live for my fans.

But I can't walk away from what might happen if he *doesn't* hurt me.

So instead, I walk straight into what I want.

18

Cooper

IF TONIGHT HAD A BATTING AVERAGE, I'd be in the negative. And negative batting averages are a mathematical impossibility.

Throw a prom for a woman whose ex-fiancé proposed with a fake prom? Check.

Get invaded by a nosy family who still owes me more revenge pranks? Check.

Bird shit in the hair? Check.

The woman of my dreams—when I didn't even know I *had* a woman of my dreams six months ago—catching me talking to my dick? Check.

Group texting my family my biggest secret? Check, check, check.

So why is Waverly walking straight toward me and untying my towel and letting it drop between us?

And going up on her tiptoes?

And brushing her lips against—*holy fuck me with a baseball bat*.

Her lips.

God.

Her lips.

They're plump and soft and warm and perfect, teasing mine while her fingers thread through my wet hair and she pulls me tighter.

I don't deserve this.

I don't deserve her.

But I wrap my arms around her, lifting her, my cock getting harder and heavier as she hooks her legs around my hips and kisses me deeper.

"Why?" I groan out against her mouth despite the loud voice in my head ordering me to shut up and not ask questions.

"You're so damn irresistible," she replies between kisses while her hands explore my skin.

I'm a fucking disaster. But if that's what she likes, I'll be a damn disaster every day of the week.

I turn, take two steps to carry her to bed, and slip on a wet spot on the tile floor.

Waverly shrieks. Our teeth mash together, and suddenly, she's gripping my whole body with her whole body like I'm a tree she's climbing to get away from danger, even though this tree is in danger of toppling itself.

"*Fuck*," I say.

She buries her head in the crook of my neck and giggles.

Giggles.

God, she smells good. And her giggle—she should release an album of just that giggle. To me. Personally. No one else.

I find my footing and head for my bedroom again, but almost drop her a second time when she nips at my neck.

"Five more steps, cheater," I manage to force out.

My dick is aching like it hasn't ached in centuries.

I'm getting lightheaded.

And she's squeezing my hips even tighter with her thighs, which is making both my dick and my head do more of what they're doing.

Are my eyes crossed?

I'm not even inside her yet, and my eyes are crossed.

"Maybe I should be carrying you," she says, and *fuuuuuck*.

Why does that make me even goddamn harder?

"You could, couldn't you?"

"I might be short-ish, but I'm very strong."

"You're fucking perfect."

She presses a kiss to my neck as I cross into my bedroom, one hand gliding down to trace the skull and crossbones on my chest, and I swear on sweet baby Louisville Slugger, I'm gonna blow right here. I clench my jaw, take a deep breath, and almost get myself under control.

"Why did the baseball player cross the road?" I blurt.

Waverly shifts in my arms, her legs tightening around my bare hips, and she giggles again. "I don't know. Why?"

"To get to the baseball park."

There's a beat of silence as I get two steps closer to the bed, and then she bursts out laughing.

Crisis *not* averted.

"What—*oh*." She wiggles her hips.

I make a very unsexy and very unhuman noise.

"Cooper Rock, am I driving you wild?" she whispers.

"Yes."

"I haven't even taken my clothes off yet."

"I know."

"I really wanted to ask Max for his autograph earlier. He's my favorite Fireball."

"*What?*"

She rocks her hips again.

My eyes cross and my balls tighten.

"Hm," Waverly purrs. "Nope. That didn't work. How about this? I think about Panther when I masturbate."

My brain takes a second to catch on. "The aging rock star?"

"Yep."

"Fuck. That *does* work."

She laughs again. "It really does, doesn't it? He's not my type. And he's old. Well. Guess you have your work cut out for you to turn both of us back on again."

I climb onto my bed with her still clinging to me. "Tell me more about you masturbating."

Her cheeks flush pink. "I was joking."

"You never pleasure yourself?"

She squirms as she lets herself relax back onto the bed, her legs still around my hips. "I've been…uninterested."

I didn't know she could have any more of my attention, but here we are. "Uninterested?"

"I had a bad breakup and I've been really busy and I'm not sleeping well, and—"

I rotate my hips to rub my hard-on against her pelvis—and yeah, I know *exactly* what I'm hitting under that dress—and her eyes cross and drift closed.

"More, please," she whispers.

"Why aren't you sleeping?" I murmur against her neck while I continue the slow torment over her black dress.

"Too much thinking."

"About what?"

"Everything."

Fuck.

I sometimes lose sleep thinking about the team, but that's small potatoes compared to the empire Waverly's running.

I brush a kiss to her jaw. "This is a no-thinking zone. Feeling only."

"But—oh, no, don't stop."

"No-thinking zone," I repeat, hovering above her while she tries to tilt her hips back up to cradle my cock.

She pouts. "Fine. No thinking."

"Very good."

"Bossy."

I grin as I go back to teasing her neck with my lips. "I take orders too."

"Strip me naked and make me feel good."

"Metaphorically or literally?"

"*Cooper.*"

God, her skin tastes amazing. It's like she's made of cotton candy and steak, which are basically my two favorite things in the world, put together in a way that works because she's Waverly and everything works on her.

"I'm a full-service friend," I tell her delicious skin. "Whatever you want. And you're going to have to be very specific."

I rub my cock between her thighs again.

"Unzip my dress." Her order is breathy, her eyes drifting shut once more while her hands explore my neck and shoulders and chest.

"With my hands? My mind? My teeth?"

Her soft laugh fills my bedroom. "Yes."

"High standards."

"Yes."

I like that about her. *You want me, you earn me.* Self-worth is fucking sexy.

I find the zipper behind her silky dress and take my time shifting her beneath me, rolling her over onto her belly while I run my hands over the exposed skin on her neck and shoulders. Goosebumps pebble under my touch and she gasps softly.

"Touch me more," she pants.

I test the zipper on her dress while pressing kisses to the sharp angles of her shoulder blade. "Where?"

"Everywhere."

I tug her zipper down slowly, following it with my mouth and tongue while she gasps and writhes beneath me.

She's either acting, or she loves being touched *this* much.

Make no mistake—I have the ego to believe this is all my talent. But not when it comes to Waverly.

Her zipper goes all the way down to the top of her curvy ass, and I finish my exploration of her back with my lips pressed to the top of her beautiful globes.

"*God*, Cooper," she gasps as she thrusts her ass up into my face.

"Yes?" I murmur against her flesh.

"*More.*"

"More what?"

"More everything."

"Everything?" I slide my hand over her back, tracing the hollow of her backbone. I can't help myself. I have to touch her. "You want to eat a sandwich and watch TV too? While doing yoga?"

"*Cooper.*"

My name comes out of her lips with a breathy laugh, and I

smile as I nip at the top of her ass. "More specific, please, Waverly."

"I want you to do—what you do—with a woman."

"That always depends on what she wants. So you have to tell me what you want." I squeeze her cheek and drift my hand lower over the back of her thigh.

"*That,*" she says faintly.

More goosebumps.

Can't fake those.

But I'm suddenly having performance anxiety.

Can she fake them?

Goosebumps don't mean I can actually give her an orgasm.

Didn't she just say that she hasn't been interested in sex? In like a *year*?

What if I'm not enough? What if I can't make her come?

Shit shit shit.

Get out of your head, Rock.

My fingers drift to the back of her knee, and she yelps and jumps. "Tickle!"

"Sorry!"

Shit. Fuck.

She drops her head into my pillow, her body shaking, and then I hear it.

She's laughing. "Oh my god, I can't even be properly seduced."

At least, I'm pretty sure that's what she says.

It's a little muffled.

"Do you *want* to be seduced?" I ask.

"*Yes.*" She turns her head and looks at me, those glorious dark eyes still glittering with hunger, her lips parted. "I don't...let go...well. I get all up in my head, and..."

I scoot back up the bed to line myself up with her. "What turns you on?"

Her cheeks go a lovely pink. "Like, specifically?"

"Boobs turn me on," I tell her. "A lovely set of breasts, begging to be squeezed with lickable nipples... Yeah. That does it."

Thank fuck, that *is* doing it. My hard-on is re-rising to the occasion.

"So does that smile." I brush my thumb over her lips as they tip up.

"I like kissing," she whispers.

"What kind of kissing?"

"All the kinds of kissing."

"Like this?" I tease her lips with mine, barely making contact.

She hums softly. "Yes."

"How about this?" I suck her lower lip into my mouth.

She moans and grips the back of my neck, holding me there and taking charge until her tongue is dancing with mine and I'm once again on the verge of losing control of my dick.

I am no longer seducing this woman.

Instead, she's seducing me, and I'm like a clumsy teenager who can't tug her spaghetti straps off her shoulders despite how loose her shimmery black dress is.

And I haven't even seen her bare breasts yet.

Fuck, I want to see them. I want to taste them. But mostly, I want to not blow my load before she comes all over my cock.

"I like that," she gasps as she pulls out of the kiss, lifts herself onto her knees, and tosses her dress over her head.

Oh.

My.

Holy.

Sweet.

Baseball.

Diamonds.

She's braless, and those beautiful mounds are tight and perky over her ribs, her dark rose nipples tight and pointed straight at me, and it's pure instinct to pull her across my lap, sit up, and suck one of those buds into my mouth.

"*Oh my god*," she gasps.

My cock surges.

I picture myself missing an easy line drive, and he shrinks.

But only a little.

Still in the danger zone here.

"God, Cooper, *yes*," she breathes, her hips bucking against me as I worship her gorgeous breasts. "I... missed...this."

She's still wearing panties.

I have to rectify this.

Get a condom.

Go slow next time.

"What else turns you on?" I ask between kisses to her sternum as I change to her other breast.

She wraps both arms around my head and tilts hers into my hair. "*You.*"

Never has a single word been both all the best music in the world yet said with all the wrong timing.

I'm not sure my cock can take much more of this.

If I'm gonna have any chance at all of convincing her that one night won't be enough for either of us, I have to give her the night of her life and make her want more.

Fuck, I like this woman.

Can I go down on her and give her the orgasm of her life?

Probably.

I give good fingers too, and if she wants to break out some toys, I'm cool with that.

But any asshole with an internet connection can YouTube how to lick a clit to make a woman come all over your face.

I want to be buried up to my balls inside her when she comes.

I want her to know that my dick is the dick of all dicks, and that she'll never have dick like mine ever again.

I want to be the only dick she ever wants for the rest of her life.

And yeah, that's scary as fuck, but it's also turning me on like I've never been turned on before.

Waverly Sweet has bewitched me, and I'm here for it.

She shudders in my arms as I suck her nipple into my mouth. As she grinds against my cock, unintelligible sounds come from the back of her throat.

I rake my fingers down her back to grip her ass and hold her tighter against me.

I can do this.

I can blow my load and still get it up again.

Swear to fuck, I will if I have to.

"*Cooper,*" she pants.

That's my cue.

I slip my hands under her panties, and in one smooth motion, I have her completely naked, on her back on my bed, while I snag the condom from under my pillow and roll it on.

Her eyes widen slightly, but I capture her lips before she can say what she's clearly thinking.

You're good at that.

You've obviously had a lot of practice.

None of the rest of it matters. I don't want to think about *practice.*

I only want to think about Waverly.

Here.

Right now.

In my bed.

Kissing me back, wrapping her legs around my hips and pulling me into her slick, bare pussy.

She shivers. Goosebumps race across her skin.

I shiver. Goosebumps race across *my* skin.

Being wrapped up in Waverly feels like being home.

"*This*," she says, tilting her hips and taking me deeper. "This turns me on."

Our gazes lock.

I want to look away. I don't know if she can see how desperately I want to hold onto this moment for eternity, and I don't want to know if this one moment is honestly all she wants from me.

I don't want to know if she's giving me a pity fuck so that I can play ball good tomorrow.

I don't want to know if she's giving me the revenge fuck of a lifetime and will ghost me tomorrow.

I do want to be here. With her. In this one, perfect, holding-nothing-back moment.

"You turn me on." Jesus. My voice is raw. I can't hide anything from her.

She flexes her hips, our rhythm coming naturally as I slide out of her and thrust back inside, one of her eyelids closing and the other eye crossing when I find that magic spot deep inside her.

"You are so good at this," she murmurs.

Wow, you've had a lot of practice, Coop. Appreciate it.

I mentally swat the voice away, but it won't completely disappear.

"I like you for more than baseball," I gasp as I drive inside her again.

She tightens her pussy around me. "You—so—*more*."

I can't.

Jesus.

I can't give her much more. Not when she's hot and tight, squeezing my cock harder and tilting her hips just right with every thrust, her eyes going darker and glassy with need, those plump lips parted as she pants my name.

She grips my hair and pulls my face to hers, her tongue finding mine while I slam into her again, and then she moans in my mouth, and that's it.

I'm done.

I can't hold back any longer, and I come so hard my eyes cross behind my lids, a frustrated groan emanating from the back of my throat as I feel her tighten impossibly harder around me, and then she's wrenching out of the kiss, her neck arching, head thrown back, legs holding me tight while her sexy pussy squeezes and squeezes and squeezes my oversensitive, exploding cock.

"Oh, god, yes yes yes *yes yes* YES," she moans, eyes pinched, breath coming fast and short while relief floods me.

We did it.

We made her come.

And next time, I'm eating every sweet inch of that pussy, and then I'm licking her head to toe, and I'll order whatever damn dildos and vibrators she likes so I can play with her body for days on end when my own body can't take any more.

Which is pretty likely when we both have to scrape a few hours together anytime we want to see each other.

"*Fuuuuck*," I breathe out as my cock finally slumps over and plays dead inside her.

Her whole body sags too, except for those gorgeous breasts rising and falling rapidly under my chest. "Oh my god," she whispers.

"Fuck," I mumble again.

"Forgot—how good—oh my god."

I wrap my arms around her again, shifting to not totally squish her when the last of my strength leaves me and I collapse on top of her. "Goddess," I say. "Fucking goddess."

And that's the last thing I remember before I do the last thing I've ever done in this situation, and that's fall instantly, unquestionably, completely and wholly fast asleep.

19

Waverly

ONE UNEXPECTED SIDE effect of sex with Cooper that I had *completely* forgotten about?

The man makes me hear music.

Maybe I should try masturbating and see if it has the same effect. I truly *have* been uninterested since Geofferson, even in giving myself an orgasm or two.

I think he broke me more than I thought. Or else my life did.

"Or maybe you should make room in your schedule for more booty calls with this guy," Aspen says in my ear.

She called me after I texted to ask how her show went tonight, and I now have seven paper towels with half-scribbled lyrics all around me, the complete run-down on Aspen's first show interruption thanks to her first mega-fan trying to climb onto the stage in the middle of her set, and my own complete summary of my date with Cooper.

"Pretty sure I still have a month open sometime late next year," I tell her as I scribble out a note on one paper towel and grab another off the roll. I'm hearing a melody, but it's way more crisp and upbeat than my usual love ballads, and I don't know if this calls for a ballad or a straight-up party tune.

"*Waverly.*"

"Do you know most of my friends in the industry are all like ten to fifteen years older than me? All except you. You're the only one who isn't totally jaded on love or in a committed relationship."

"Which is why you should listen to me when I tell you to clear your schedule, take the man to a private island, and spend two weeks exploring all the things he can do to your naked body."

I glance around Cooper's kitchen.

It basically takes up half a wall of his open concept living space, with an island the size of Australia adding more workspace. At least, when there's not a melting ice sculpture on it.

I couldn't find paper when I slipped out of bed after I was sure he was completely and totally dead to the world, but I didn't look closely at the paper towel holder either.

Not until now.

"Aspen," I whisper.

"What?" she whispers back.

"All of his kitchen thingies are Fireballs-themed."

"*Kitchen thingies?*"

"Like the paper towel holder. The top knob is the baby dragon. And he has a crock on his counter that has all of last year's mascot options on it. Oh my gosh. I wonder if he has custom Fireballs plates." I hop up and start digging, and I squeal when I'm rewarded with exactly what I was looking for. "Oh my god. *He does*. His plates have Fiery the Dragon on them. Hold on. I have to look at all of them. After all of this Fiery fan fiction, I need to know if he has Brimstone on these too."

"Those are a recent addition," the man himself says behind me.

I squeak and drop the plate, which clatters to the granite countertop but doesn't shatter.

"Did you get caught?" Aspen whispers.

"Yes," I whisper back.

"I'm out. Go jump him again. You haven't sounded this relaxed or excited about anything in the entire time I've known you."

She hangs up.

I look over my shoulder, and there's Cooper, hovering behind me without touching me. He's in nothing but low-slung boxer briefs, bedhead, tattoos, and a five o'clock shadow, and no small part of me wants to climb that body and kiss him senseless.

He doesn't have to do a damn thing beyond stand there, and he turns me on.

I am in deep trouble.

He rubs his neck self-consciously. "I thought you left."

"Oh. No. No, I just—I had to write something down. You were sleeping soundly, and I didn't want to wake you." But I couldn't lie next to him without wanting to rub my hands all over him either, so I put my energy to good use rather than disturbing his sleep.

"I don't usually crash like that."

"You worked hard and you need to be in tip-top shape for your game later today."

He grins, but it's not full-strength. Whether that's because he has something on his mind, or because it's three in the morning, or because I was *supposed* to take some hint and leave but didn't, I don't know.

But I want to.

I want to know if tonight changed anything for him.

I feel like it changed everything for me.

"You like my kitchen?" he asks.

"It's so Firebally."

His grin gets bigger. A little more Cooper-ish. "Mac—Mackenzie, Brooks's wife—she's the world's biggest Fireballs fan. You met her when she umpired for your video. And since I've been...not my usual awesome self this year...she decided I needed a home makeover. But I draw the line at putting the Baby Ash toilet paper in my bathrooms. For the record."

"I thought you were just being nice when you gave her the world's biggest Fireballs fan title that day we shot our video. I mean, I knew about the mascot thing last year, but really, I would've thought half of Copper Valley would've turned out to do the same."

He shakes his head. "I'm an amateur compared to Mackenzie. You should see her car."

He's still not coming closer, and there's a wariness in his eyes that pokes at one of the softer parts of my already too-soft heart.

Is he giving me space because I told him this was a one-time thing?

Does he want space because *he* wanted this to be a one-time thing?

Is this about his superstition, and he's afraid he's still broken?

Was this *all* about his superstition and I was the idiot who thought it might be about more?

Was I too needy and too wishy-washy and a disappointment in bed?

Oh, god.

Am I bad in bed?

"Did I do something wrong?" I blurt.

"What?" His brows shoot up to his hairline. "You—no. *No.* You're like—you're perfect. I just—I didn't know—*Jesus.* Do you know I don't stutter in front of anyone but you? It's like you make my brain short-circuit because you're so fucking amazing and I feel like a gnat next to you. Like a giant, dorky, athletic, fabulous, top-of-the-gnat-chain gnat, but still a gnat."

I don't need a mirror to know my hair is doing some crazy-pants stuff right now. I haven't washed my makeup off, and it's undoubtedly smeared with a lot of it left behind in his sheets. And I'm wearing an old Fireballs jersey that I found in his closet, along with a pair of his boxers that I dug out of his dresser that are too tight on my hips, because my hips are definitely a size bigger than Cooper's.

Even with his six-two stature and that lovely ass.

"If either of us is a gnat right now—"

He makes a noise accompanied by a red-hot glare. "If you call yourself a gnat, I'm calling your aunt myself to tell her how much she fucked up by not telling you how amazing you are."

I blink.

"And I don't mean your paycheck or your fan base, Waverly. I mean *you*. You and your big heart and your belief in people and your loyalty and fearlessness. *You.*"

"You wouldn't really call her, would you?"

"Say you're not a gnat."

I cross my arms.

His gaze dips to my chest, then to my bare legs. His

Adam's apple bobs, and he lifts his gaze to mine again. "Say it."

His voice is husky, and I feel it in the pull between my legs.

"I will when you do too," I reply.

"You first."

"Together."

He plops a fist down on his open palm. "Rock-paper-scissors. Whoever loses has to say it first."

My lips twitch. "Are you going to best-three-out-of-five me when I beat you the first two games?"

"No."

"Liar."

He taps his fist on his palm.

I let a full smile slip out as I do the same.

"Rock-paper-scissors," he chants, and then we both throw down.

He plays rock.

Predictable. I'm glad I went with paper.

"Best four out of seven," he announces.

"*Cooper.*"

"I like you and I want to do this again."

My heart soars at the same time my brain whispers *you know better. Don't do it*. I lick my lips and study his intensely serious blue-green gaze. "Play rock-paper-scissors?"

"*No*. See you. Talk to you. Sleep with you. Laugh with you. Try to impress you and utterly fail and then try again. Catch you writing songs in the middle of the night and sit with you until you're done and then toss you over my shoulder and carry you to bed and eat your pussy and bang you in the shower and then sing you to sleep."

Yes, please, my vagina agrees.

"You're busy. I'm busy. But I want more time with you whenever I can get it. However I can get it. *I like you.*"

This. This Cooper.

This is the man I fell hard for eight years ago. The one who'll put his heart on his sleeve and say what he wants.

Until he disappears.

Nothing's changed.

Both your lives are too hectic for this.

He just wants your pussy for his game.

"One day at a time, Waverly." His eyes bore into mine, and there's a thread of pain in his voice, like he knows what I'm afraid of and he feels it too. "Can we take this one day at a time and see where we go? No press. No publicity. No pressure. Just—I like you."

I like you.

It's such a simple sentiment, but I can't remember the last time I heard those words when someone was talking about *me*.

Not the made-up superstar Waverly.

The sometimes disastrous, not-quite-sure-where-she-came-from, cat-loving, reality-TV-watching Waverly who just wants to believe she's loved for everything she is underneath the glitz and glamour.

And he's said it several times tonight when I haven't said it back once. "I like you too," I whisper.

His shoulders sag, and then I'm being strangled in the best kind of hug.

It's a full-body, wrapped-up, Cooper-scented hug that makes me feel safe in ways I haven't felt since my mom was alive. It's the *I've got you* hug and the *you're special* hug and the *I'm memorizing how this feels so when we're apart, I can close my eyes and come back here and feel you despite the distance* hug.

And I hope I'm giving half as good of a hug back as he's giving to me.

"One day at a time," he repeats quietly.

I squeeze harder.

"Can I carry you upstairs and eat your pussy now?" he adds.

Only Cooper.

"Yes," I manage through a very aroused laugh.

He shifts, and then I'm being tossed over his shoulder as he heads for the stairs.

And for the record—if I thought Cooper hugs were good, they're nothing compared to Cooper's talents with his tongue.

20

From the text messages of the Rock Family

COOPER: Having sex is my baseball superstition.

Mom: Oh, honey, you know you don't need your penis to play baseball. This is all in your head.

Pop: Got an old pirate cure for that.

Tillie Jean: EW. God. Why would you—wait. WAIT. OH MY GOD. You're serious. You haven't been out with the guys in months, and your game is getting a little saggy, and I thought it was because you're getting old, but wait again. Do you need some medical intervention?

Max: I hate that I believe this.

Dad: Don't listen to them, son. Any of them. Including your penis if it's telling you that you can't play without it. You don't need superstitions. You're Cooper Fucking Rock.

Tillie Jean: 1. Dad, please don't stroke his ego. 2. I AM SO ANGRY RIGHT NOW BECAUSE NOW I'M THINKING

ABOUT OTHER PLACES THAT NEED TO BE STROKED IF THIS IS TRUE AND GRRRRROOOOOOOOSSSSSSS.

Grady: It's only true if you believe him. I don't.

Annika: But if he's not going out with the guys and his game's shit...

Mom: Annika! That's not how we build him up. I thought we got over this town rivalry thing and you support him now.

Grady: Do NOT come after my wife on that one, Mom. Cooper's game IS shit. And Annika's spending every minute of her waking hours feeding and burping and changing YOUR grandson. Back. Off.

Dad: Don't take it personally, Annika. Libby worries about her kids, and Cooper's had it rough for a few years. Not that you haven't. I know you've had it rough too. But Cooper's... ah. You know what? I'm not gonna finish that. Love you, Annika. You're the daughter I never had.

Tillie Jean: OH MY GOD.

Dad: The OTHER daughter I never had, next to the daughter I DO have, who's amazing.

Mom: How about we talk about Cooper's sex life some more?

Grady: No.

Tillie Jean: No.

Annika: No.

Max: Where IS Cooper? He's gone silent.

Pop: Hopefully he's getting some.

Grady: Can I leave this conversation too?

Annika: I have to go feed Miles. And I'd rather watch a reality TV show about wannabe porn stars than talk about Cooper's sex life. So maybe everyone who wants to continue this conversation can start a new group text without me?

Grady: It's my turn. It's my turn to feed Miles. You go to bed, honey. I've got the baby. And not this group text message, which I'm deleting RIGHT NOW.

Tillie Jean: Do NOT include me in the new family chat, please.

Pop: Family has to support family in its time of need.

Max: And to think, I used to wonder what I was missing with not having a normal family.

Tillie Jean: This isn't the normal part of our family. This is... crisis mode. Also, who was that hiding under the table? I feel like I recognized the bouncers, but I can't place them.

Grady: Cooper hired them so we'd think it was someone important.

Pop: I think he finally found his pirate princess.

Max: I'm leaving this conversation now as well.

Mom: Max, don't go. You know who he was hiding, don't you?

Dad: Grady told me you were having lots of silent communication with Cooper there at the end like he and I used to have before he left Shipwreck to go have a life of his own on the road and get closer to you than he is to me. *sad puppy emoji*

Pop: Miss those days when he was around all the time. So does Long Beak Silver. Instead, he's family with the Fireballs now. *sad parrot emoji*

Tillie Jean: Stop, all of you. Cooper texts as much as he talks. It's like he never left, and you all know it. Quit playing games with Max to get him to talk.

Grady: Do we really want to know who Cooper's trying to score with? Honestly, I sleep better at night when I don't have that information.

Pop: I need to know if she's worthy of the Rock family name.

Dad: *laughing emoji*

Mom: Pop, I hate to break it to you, but I don't think *wedding bell emoji* is in the future for Cooper. Not until he's done playing baseball, anyway. At least. I sometimes suspect his house is a front, and he really lives at Duggan Field. And I'm not sure I'd be okay with seeing him settle down with someone who's willing to live under the bleachers at a baseball park with him forever.

Annika: Wow. I never knew you all trash-talked Cooper. I thought it was a myth.

Pop: My grandson wouldn't get an ice sculpture brought up to his house for just anybody.

Tillie Jean: Pop, Cooper would get HIMSELF an ice sculpture if it made him happy.

Dad: But it was two swans. It wasn't anything Fireballs-themed. Pop might be right. Cooper might have an honest-to-god crush on the woman he was hiding.

Max: Fuck.

Grady: I'm throwing up a little in my mouth as I type this, but if she's willing to, ah, score with him regularly, and that's really what his game needs...

Annika: Ew.

Tillie Jean: *barfing emoji*

Mom: I want all of my children to have healthy sex lives, but I also don't need to know specifics. For the record.

Dad: What if Cooper's curse is the anti-Brooks Elliott curse, and if he settles down with one woman, his career is over?

Max: All right. Enough. Cooper's still gonna get all of these first thing in the morning unless one of us is brave enough to go break into his house, steal his phone, and spare him this entire conversation, which I'm not volunteering for because I don't want to know what else he's doing up there. But my point is - I personally like to WIN. And the team needs him. So you can all take this SOMEWHERE ELSE that I don't have to see and Cooper doesn't have to see, or you can risk taking on those bodyguards again. Me? I'm going to sleep. I'm pitching in two days, and I plan on fucking winning.

Tillie Jean: It's so hot when you get bossy on behalf of the Fireballs.

Grady: Cooper, if you get this, and I'm wincing as I type it... Call me if you need anything. ANYTHING. Even if it's gross.

Annika: I love you, Cooper, but please don't call me. Or Grady, no matter what he offers. Miles and I both need him to keep us sane. Call Max. He's got your back. The rest of us are sending you baseball thoughts and positive superstitions. Go kick ass, because that's what you do, you egotistical motherfucker.

Tillie Jean: Aww, Annika, you only call Cooper a motherfucker when you're really tired. Go get some sleep. Max and I are going radio silent on this chat now. Mom, Dad, Pop—you should do your WE SUPPORT COOPER ritual and get off text too. Night, everyone.

Dad: I just got a tingle of excitement. We haven't done this since his third year with the Fireballs.

Pop: I'm in. Let me get the parrot dressed.

Mom: *facepalm emoji* Suppose we should've thought of that all on our own. Love you, Cooper. Do what you need to do, and play good tomorrow! We've got your back, even if your penis doesn't.

21

Cooper

I FEEL THE SWAGGER.

I *am* the swagger.

The Rock Machine is back.

I stroll into the Fireballs' Clubhouse under the Duggan Field stands feeling like I'm riding a golden unicorn through streets lined with diamonds and rainbows and baseball fans.

There's no Waverly coming unexpectedly out of the Clubhouse, but I get to see her again over the All-Star break in another week or so.

Consolation prize for not making it into the All-Star game myself for the first time in six years—yeah, that hurts.

A lot.

I'm not ready for my baseball career to be over. I love baseball. I always make the All-Star game, and as much as I'm excited about my plans with Waverly, I'm seriously bummed to not be considered among the best this year.

But Diego's super popular with the fans and is going his rookie year, which is crazy awesome. Brooks's bat always gets him in, and Darren's having his moment in the sun, so those three are headed to the festivities on behalf of the Fireballs this year.

Plus, there's this asshole playing for Seattle this year who's out-acrobatting me at second base who got more votes than I did.

Fucker.

He didn't get a kiss goodbye from Waverly this morning though.

That kiss.

It was like she wouldn't be able to breathe without me, and she's already texted a picture of her snuggling her cat as proof that I still have competition for her affection.

Heh.

As if I won't find a way to win the cat over to my side regularly so she has to compete for both of our affections instead. And as if she won't love every minute of it.

Her laughter is the soundtrack in the back of my brain. The scent of the caramel latte I made for her to go with donuts this morning is still lingering in my nose. And the little bit of glitter at Max's hairline that catches in the light when I make my way into the lounge reminds me of the way Waverly glitters and shines from the inside out.

I have it bad.

I have it so bad.

And for right now, I'm way okay with that.

"Dude." Emilio stops stuffing his magic fruit into the blender behind the swanky new bar that management installed for us over the winter break and gives me a once-over.

"You okay, Coop?" Francisco asks.

"You look...weird," Robinson adds.

"Did you see a ghost?" Baby Ash, our team's new mascot this season, asks from the beat-up old couch that we refused to let management get rid of when they redid the clubhouse.

Sounds like Brooks is inside the costume.

And I'm not gonna judge whatever he needs to do to get his game on. Or whatever he and Mackenzie did if he took that costume home with him last night and is only now returning it.

"Feeling great, gentlemen," I announce to the room.

"Ah, hell, Cooper," Luca chimes in. "Your favorite coffee shop didn't add a little extra something to your cappuccino this morning, did they? Are we gonna have to ask management to put you on the injured list to avoid drug testing?"

Max stares at me without saying a thing out loud but with saying a crapton of other stuff silently.

Yeah, I saw the whole text thread from my family.

I know Max knows who was in my house last night.

He clearly hasn't breathed a word of it either, which I appreciate on Waverly's behalf.

I tip a *thanks for not being a dick* nod at him.

He keeps staring.

"No coffee," I say. Forgot to drink mine. I was enjoying watching Waverly drink hers too much to think about my own.

The whole room gasps.

"I'll go get you one, Coop!" Diego leaps to his feet. Didn't see him there behind the couch. Wonder if he was meditating.

"Thanks, D. No need. I got this."

"You said that last game," Robinson says.

"Lay off, Robby," Ash says. "It's not like he made that pitch go wild and hit him in the ass on purpose."

Darren's watching me as intensely as Max is. "You want to talk about it?"

"I'm good. Thanks, big guy. Got this."

"Fucker," he mutters. "I don't want to know."

"Did you lift your curse?" Diego breathes.

I snag the hat of awesome from the top shelf behind the bar and plop it on my head. And when I say *hat of awesome*, you don't want to know. Unless you were here for the mascot wars, in which case, yeah, it's the pornographic Meaty the Meatball hat.

And then I wink at our rookie catcher. "Guess we're gonna find out today, aren't we? I. Am. On. Top. Of. The. Fucking. World. Who wants to get their asses kicked in *Go, Ash, Go*?"

"It's going to have to wait, Mr. Rock."

All of us turn to look at the social media assistant hovering in the doorway. He's pretty new. Basically his rookie season too. You can see the kid trying hard not to trip over himself when he has to talk to one of us in here, so we're doing our best to be real to help him out.

I tip the full-package hat at him. "Percy! What's up, my man?"

He clears his throat. "We need you for another episode of *Advice with Cooper*."

"Awesome. That's my favorite part of the day."

Several groans go up in the locker room.

But there are a few cheers too.

I grin at Percy. "Lemme go change quick."

How high am I riding today?

So high that I completely miss the signs as I head into the locker room to grab my jersey.

I pop the door on my locker, and a million foam mascots spill out.

And then a ceiling panel opens over me, and a million more foam mascots crash down over my head.

Another ceiling panel opens next to the first, and—you guessed it.

More foam mascots.

Not just any mascot, and not any of the Fireballs mascots either.

"Cooper's standing in a pile of dicks!" Francisco shouts behind me.

I grab one of the squeezy bratwursts—they're four-inch Thrusty stress balls, modeled after the rocket-powered bratwurst mascot for the Copper Valley Thrusters hockey team across town—and throw it at him.

"Nice one, Frankie! Now I know who's at the top of my TBGB list."

"I helped, Cooper," Diego yells. "I want on your TBGB list too!"

"Dude, you already shit glitter just by living," Luca says to the catcher. "Don't ask to go on Cooper's to-be-glitter bombed list."

"But then I'd match Happy Max."

Max's eyelid twitches.

I fling a Thrusty stress ball at Max too. "The team that glitters together are winners together, Happy Max."

"I sincerely wish I had doubts about if you got laid last night," he mutters.

"Maybe I meditated with my ice sculpture and found baseball enlightenment." Shit. Walking through a locker room full of stress balls isn't as easy as walking through an actual ball pit. Is it bad luck to squish your sister team's mascot? Even if it's a stress ball? Well, a stress dick?

Nope, I decide.

Not gonna let *anything* ruin my mood today.

And for the record, it's not about getting laid.

It's about living in the glow that is Waverly's attention. She's a giant sparkly rainbow of happiness who's been having a few clouds dull her shine lately, but she's trusting me to help her find her full megawatt radiance again.

You know that feeling when you touch a light switch in the dead of winter and it shocks you and brings you to life?

That's how I felt the first time I met her. Like, *whoa*. This woman *has* something, and the parts of me that want to be the best me *crave* being near her. And then we spent a few days talking and laughing and banging and laughing and talking and banging, and I would've given up baseball for her.

For a hot minute, I really would've.

She was this Hollywood princess, raised in the shadow of her mom's memory, with more talent in her pinky toenail than I had in my entire baseball god body—yeah, I had ego about my skills on the field even back then—and yet she was *real*. Down to earth. Relatable.

I could see her rocking a concert in front of a hundred thousand people and then going home with me to eat gold nuggets and potato pirate swords in my dad's restaurant while we chatted with all the locals about Shipwreck gossip.

And that's what makes her a star.

She makes everyone she encounters feel like she's their best friend.

Like she can fit fully into their world without even trying.

So maybe this is all a dream and I'll wake up again and realize I'm not more special than anyone else. That I'm merely the guy she's shining on today, and one day, she'll decide I'm not worth the hassle.

Again.

But today?

Today I'm gonna live the fuck out of being in this dream.

I do a quick-change into my promo jersey, swim through the stress balls, tell the janitor I'll clean them all up in an hour, and head upstairs to the PR department.

They gather questions from kids looking for advice on everything from how to get out of eating their vegetables to what to do when their siblings annoy them to how to get me to come to their birthday parties, and I answer on camera for broadcast across Duggan Field between innings and on our socials a few weeks later.

It's usually hella fun, and bonus, it earns the Fireballs points with local parents, who may be enticed to bring their whole families out to more games than they normally would, which keeps the stands packed in ways they weren't two years ago.

Especially when I sometimes crash those birthday parties I'm invited to or talk my buddies into crashing when they're requested.

But today, when I step into the suite overlooking the field where we do the filming, everyone does a double-take.

Am I glowing that bright today?

Is it that obvious?

Can they tell I got laid?

Inappropriate, asshole, I remind myself. *Head in the damn game, Rock. Let the vibes flow and ignore the rest of it.*

I lift my brows. "Ah, man, do I have a coffee bean stuck in my teeth again? Hate it when that happens. Hey, Sally. Morning, Keisha. Got good questions for me today? Let's rock these kids' worlds."

The next hour is hilarious. I love these kids' questions.

Cooper, what would you do when your teacher makes you do homework and you don't want to? Cooper, what do you do when your best friend stops talking to you? Cooper, how do I get over my fear of spiders?

Full disclosure—that last question was courtesy of Zeus Berger, the large-and-in-charge former defenseman for the Thrusters.

I don't call the PR and social media team out on using Zeus.

He's basically a big kid himself.

A big kid who now has baby quadruplets at home with his wife, but still a big kid. Also, yeah, Miles is cuter than all of the Berger quadruplets put together.

Don't tell Zeus I said that.

He's one of the few guys who really could crush me if my mouth ran away with me and said *fight me.*

Once I'm released from PR duty, I head back to the locker room, bullshit around with the guys, clean up the stress balls, saving a couple boxes to send to various places around the world where I either owe someone a random foam phallic-shaped mascot as a prank-back or where there are pockets of Thrusters fans who'll flip over them, and yeah, some for Waverly because she'll think it's hilarious that I got attacked by a bunch of four-inch foam dicks, and then it's time for warm-ups.

And then it's time for the game.

And then it's time for my first at-bat.

I'm grinning as I leave the on-deck circle. The crowd starts cheering. The home plate ump gives me a once-over and sighs.

The catcher mutters something that sounds like *oh, shit* and repositions himself.

Trying to fake me out.

Make me think they're throwing me a curve ball.

First rule of baseball: Don't ever swing on the first pitch.

But I know this pitcher.

He knows me.

He thinks he's smarter than I am.

He's probably right.

But the Rock is riding a high today, and I know the moment that ball leaves his hand that he's giving me a pitch he thinks I won't swing at merely because it's the first pitch.

Sucker.

I swing.

My bat connects with a sweet, sweet *crack* that my family can probably hear all the way up in Shipwreck.

And that ball goes sailing into the wind, higher and higher, deeper and deeper, until it bounces off the top of the goddamn scoreboard over center field.

Cooper Rock is fucking *back*.

And Waverly Sweet is the goddess who made it happen.

22

Waverly

THIS HAS BEEN the longest four days of my life.

It's been all back-to-back meetings, photo shoots, promotional appearances, charity appearances, webcast recordings, and harried moments of scribbling lyrics and melodies any chance I can get during the days, plus a travel schedule for said meetings and photo shoots and appearances that have me wondering who on my scheduling team hates me. Which means it's four *whole days* after I leave Cooper's house before I get five minutes to myself to make the phone call I've been wanting to make since the moment I saw him hit his second home run of the night that first game after he tried to salvage prom for me.

And when I finally get him on the phone, he doesn't tell me what I want to hear.

"I'm headed to the bus in ten."

The apology in his voice helps. And it's not like we haven't communicated. We've had an ongoing, drawn-out, hours-between-replies text message conversation going for the past four days too, covering everything from the latest *Love on Fire* fanfic episode to my fingernail malfunction in the middle of an interview.

Usually it's me who can't answer right away, which means I've gotten way more messages than he has.

And those messages?

Sometimes they're normal *hey, thinking about you* messages.

Saw you on the news. Who the fuck calls your outfit ugly while you're reading stories to sick kids in a hospital?

Don't watch Who's Your Family? this week. No, really. Don't do it. Not unless I'm there or Aspen's there or one of us is on the phone. Trust me.

Hey, next time we get together, can you do that little dance that you're doing in this GIF? I keep watching it because it makes me smile.

And sometimes, they're something completely different.

He left me a voice message of himself singing a song he made up about wanting to see pop stars in baseball pants, and I'm still not sure if I was surprised or not to discover that Cooper can carry a tune and has a pretty great voice.

He sent me a photo of a drawing he made of Baby Ash during a Fireballs promotional visit to a local preschool, right next to a drawing one of the kids made that put his drawing to shame.

And then there was the selfie.

Selfies are normal, right?

So why did the one of him sitting by himself at the top of the bleachers, hat backward, sunglasses on, *Shipwreck Pirate Fest* logo on his black T-shirt, with the Blue Ridge Mountains peeking up over his shoulder, and the simple *Wish we were watching a game together here* message he attached to it send a shiver all over the most vulnerable parts of me?

Was he implying one day he'd be retired and I'd take some time off in the summer, where we'd both pretend we were normal people who liked to watch a game together?

And why do I think that I'd walk away from everything if we could do it tomorrow?

We can't, of course, which is probably why I've convinced myself that we would if we could. It's easy to say you'd do things that you obviously can't.

He's still under contract for another two years after this season, and my life is planned out for the next three years as well. Everything I give my fans, he gives to his fans too. And it's well-documented that when he's done playing, he has every intention of continuing to live and breathe Fireballs baseball. As a coach, a scout, an analyst, booth announcer, the weird guy who's always running around the outside of the park with face paint and a megaphone yelling that the crowd isn't loud enough for the team.

Any one of those. He'd do it.

It's as much a part of him as music is in me.

But that's all a worry for another time, because right now, he's on the phone and I'm hearing his voice and even my cat in my lap seems happy about it.

"I think I have twenty before someone realizes I'm not just in the bathroom," I tell him.

"You feeling okay?"

"Yeah. Normal nerves before doing the late-night circuit, but nothing a little Tums can't handle."

"Ever think about skipping it all?"

"Oh my gosh, no. My fans would be super disappointed.

And missing something I've committed to—no. That's a recipe for Tums not being strong enough."

"Yeah, but you get to have a life too."

"Where were you yesterday morning? What's that? Doing a photo shoot for an energy drink endorsement before dashing off to volunteer at a pet shelter and then almost being late for practice? Hi, pot. It's me, kettle."

"That's different. I'm an endless font of energy still in my prime. You're...well, Waverly, I hate to tell you this, but you're a very old twenty-seven. You might as well be *twenty-eight*."

The teasing note in his voice makes it impossible to suppress a smile, even though he's right. Pop stars age faster. I swear we do. "You are such a goof."

"Guilty." He laughs. "And you're not old. You're perfect."

"No, I'm old. I feel about eighty-six today."

"At worst, you look twenty-four."

"At worst, I look like someone who needs to stop with the glitter body suits and booty shorts on stage."

He makes a noise.

"What?" I ask.

"*What* is that you can wear whatever the fuck you want to wear no matter how old you are. My grandmother showed up to the Pirate Festival in Shipwreck a couple weeks back dressed as Catwoman. In leather and everything."

"How does that relate to pirates?"

"Pop's parrot pissed her off, so she decided to go parrot-hunting as Catwoman. At least, I think that's what my sister said. She was laughing so hard, even Max couldn't understand her, and he's supposed to understand everything, including what she's thinking when she doesn't even know she's thinking it. I told him he was getting marked down on his grade for being a good boyfriend for the day, and then—well, then he helped boobytrap my house and crash it while I was in the middle of bombing a date with this woman I keep thinking about."

Hashtag rolls his eyes and lets out a loud, bored yawn.

"Was that your cat?" Cooper asks.

I laugh as I stroke my pet. "He has incredibly high standards and is not yet impressed."

"I have an incredibly big ego and an endless font of motivation to get what I want. Watch out, Hashtag. You're gonna love me as much as everyone else does one of these days soon. And not just here or there. I mean *all the time.*"

If anyone else in my life said that, I'd call them an egotistical ass.

But Cooper's self-deprecating delivery makes me laugh.

Also?

He's earned his ego. How many people work their ass off for the worst team in baseball for *years* without losing both the will to perform and the belief that the impossible could happen?

And then be there when the impossible *does* happen? To be a major part of making the impossible happen?

He can boast as much as he wants.

But the thing I like most about Cooper?

You watch any one of his interviews, and he gives all the credit to other people. *Eh, my glove was in the right place at the right time. It was really the pitcher setting me up and the batter playing right into his hands. That catch in the fourth inning? That was all Diego's throw. Kid never misses. Don't challenge D's arm, you know? My two home runs? Yeah, the wind was with us today, and you know, all of us have those games where we find our stride. Brooks did it yesterday. Frankie last week. Just my turn, I guess.*

He does it with an eye twinkle and a grin that says he loves his job.

Is there anything more irresistible than someone who loves his job? And his family? And his life?

"What would you do if Hashtag never loves you?" I ask him and regret it the minute the words are out of my mouth. *We'll be together forever, Cooper, so how will we deal if my pet still hates you in ten years?*

Like he's not going to play baseball for the next ten years and I'm not going to be booked up for the rest of my life. Like we might actually have time for each other, which we both know we don't.

But he takes it in stride. "Challenge accepted."

God, he's fun. Two words, and they're overflowing with *life*.

Do I live?

Do I?

Or am I wasting it all while trying to find *that thing* that will make me next-level happy when I already have the means to buy myself anything that can be bought?

"How do you do that?" I ask.

"Do what?"

"Be *happy* all the time."

"I'm not happy *all* the time, as I believe you've witnessed."

"But you always come back. *Always.* How do you do that?"

"No idea. I was born like this."

I stroke Hashtag and try to smile, but it doesn't quite come. "I'm serious. Too many people in our positions aren't *happy*. But you..."

"Are you happy?"

"Cooper, I'm on top of the world."

"So that's a *no*."

"You're ignoring my question."

"I grew up with the best parents ever—retrospect speaking, for the record—in a family that was well-respected in our community because we earned it generation after generation. Maybe not that first generation, or even the second. But we earn it now."

"Why not the first or second?"

"I hear Thorny Rock was a real bastard, but he was an actual pirate who had to choose between his love of the sea and living with his treasure in relative anonymity away from the bounty hunters, so that probably went with the territory. Also, if I grew up the kid of a total bastard, I probably would've been a pill. But we've steered the ship back in Shipwreck for a lot of generations now, even if we've never found the legendary pirate gold, and really, community's more important than gold."

I truly do smile now. I'd forgotten the legend of Shipwreck and its pirate founder and his supposed booty that he hid somewhere in the Blue Ridge Mountains after giving up his life on the sea.

Cooper's still going. I like that about him. He's not afraid to talk, and that helps you know where you stand with him. "I learned early on that my parents and grandparents *kept* earning it every day, and then I learned how much they sacrificed to give me what I had, and then I learned what it feels like to *not* get what you want, and how much work it takes to put in the time to make your dreams come true, and how important it is to believe."

Believe.

That's Cooper. He *believes*.

"I might not be living full-time in Shipwreck now," he says, "and I might not ever again, but I always find time to go home. To stay in touch with my roots and the people who've been there for me in the hard times, and to be there for them when they're having hard times. If you've got family and community, what's there to not be happy about?"

"Not knowing where your dreams will take you next?" I say softly.

"Yeah." His voice goes husky. "There's that. But a very wise woman reminded me that's not my hill to climb yet. Maybe in a couple months, but today? Today, I'm happy. Plus, I eat right, exercise, and get enough sleep. Pretty sure the sleep's the key."

Hashtag rolls his cat eyes like he knows Cooper's trying to get out of super deep territory when we only have a few minutes left.

Or maybe he doesn't want to go deep with me.

"So the true key to happiness is sleep, hm?"

"Can't trade the sleep. That'll do you in every time."

"Clearly, you have no trouble with sleeping."

"She swings, and look at that ball go. *Zing!* Home run. She got me. I told you. I don't usually fall asleep *that* fast. Four more nights, and I'll prove it to you."

That makes me happy. My heart does a butt-wiggle dance, and I couldn't stop my smile if I tried. He's flying to LA to hang out at my house while I have a rare three full days of operating out of my hometown that happens to coincide with his time off for the mid-summer All-Star break.

"Speaking of swing and a home run—" I say.

"Waverly Sweet, have you been watching my baseball games?"

"I have a vested interest in making sure you're still performing well."

"*Waverly Sweet, are you betting on baseball?* Insider knowledge. I'm telling the commissioner."

It feels good to laugh again. That's what this is supposed to be. *We'll enjoy this as long as we enjoy it.* "So you're a tattletale?"

"Nah. More, I just want to make sure you know my interest in you doesn't lie in my game. I'm over the superstition. If you want to hang out with our clothes on, I'm gonna keep being the fabulous kick-ass baseball player that I've always been."

"So you're saying you *don't* want to get naked?"

"Ah, shit."

"Hey, you get that I'm teasing, right?"

"Yeah, but now I'm thinking of you naked. And I'll be boarding the bus in five minutes with a hard-on."

I shiver.

I like his hard-on.

"Do you need help taking care of that?" I ask.

"Where are you?"

"New York."

"Can you teleport? I'm in Boston. And is it really worth the effort of teleporting for a three-minute quickie? That's dedication. You must like me a lot."

"Cooper."

"I hear music when you say my name."

I drop my voice and add a seductive lilt, not sure if I sound like a total goofball or a goddess. "What are you wearing?"

"It's gangster suit day for team-building. Mine has Baby Ash printed all over it. I'm the dragon gangster."

I burst out laughing.

"Matching hat. Want a picture?"

"Later," I tell him. "Right now, I want you to unbutton your pants."

"Swear to the baseball gods, if you suddenly appear in this hotel room..."

"Stop talking and take your pants off. I'm trying to talk dirty to you here."

Hashtag yowls in protest, gets something stuck in his throat, and then flies off my lap, which undoubtedly means he's about to hark up a hairball.

Cooper sighs. "Good call. Way less pressure. But there's a baby dragon staring at me from my arm, and now I feel like the bad kind of perv."

"Stop looking at the baby dragon if you want to have phone sex with me." I'm trying to be serious, but it's utterly impossible.

"Okay. Okay. Jacket's off too, but *shit*. I forgot I have Fiery all over the sleeves of my dress shirt. He's angry. I showed his baby girl my hard-on, and now I'm a dead man."

"*Cooper*." I'm cracking up. "They're not real."

"I've never had phone sex and I'm getting very nervous right now."

I choke on my laugh. "Wait. You've never had phone sex?"

"I, ah, have always been more of an in-person for a couple hours kind of guy."

I'm momentarily stunned. He had no problem talking dirty in the bedroom. I never considered phone sex would be different.

"And there goes Mr. Happy," he sighs.

I need to say something, but I'm startled and can't figure out what to say that won't sound completely wrong. *Come back, Mr. Happy* is not the last thing I want to say to him before he has to go.

"I have a code." His words come out rushed, and it's not hard to picture his ears going red at the tips or those fascinating blue-green eyes darting around the room before settling on me to own up to his truth. "*Had* a code. One night only, just for fun and to fuel the superstition. If I got the needy vibes, I bailed before we got to the hotel. If I got the freaky vibes, same thing. Hotels only, even when I was home. No baseball groupies either, because they'd show back up the next time I was in town, and I meant it when I said *one night only*."

"You don't have to explain this to me." Translation: I don't want to know.

"When I talk dirty to you, I want to be able to look you in the eye and feel the way your body's responding, and I want you to be there with me, one hundred percent, not checking your calendar or watching TV or getting your makeup put on while you tell me to jerk myself off."

Well.

My panties are sufficiently soaked now.

"I want to know you're getting off too, and that you're all-in, and my hand is no substitute for you. Not even close. And—"

"*Jesus*, Cooper, put that thing away," a voice barks on the phone. "*God*. My eyes. *My eyes*. You're fifteen minutes late and you're jerking off in front of Baby Ash? What the fuck's wrong with you?"

I jolt to my feet and look at my own hotel door, which is thankfully shut.

Pretty sure that's Luca Rossi.

"I'm not jerking off!" Cooper sputters. "I thought I had a spot on my dick but I can only look at it when I'm hard!"

"*Call the fucking team doctor*. Let's go. And don't you dare have a bad game today. Jesus. I am *never* drawing the short straw again. Darren rigged this. That fucker. I'm telling Henri, and she's gonna make this even worse in a book for you. *Jesus*."

"I don't have a spot on my dick," Cooper whispers. "Text me later. Please. *Please*."

"Tell Luca I said hi," I manage to push out. I'm caught between wanting to laugh and wanting to cry.

But I most definitely want to hop in the shower myself and have some time with a special friend hiding in my suitcase.

Unfortunately, my own hotel room door swings open too.

Aunt Zinnia looks me up and down, and her gaze finally lands on my phone.

Her lip curls.

"Do *not*," I start.

"Ritz-Carlton wants to discuss an endorsement deal. We need you on the phone on the way to the airport."

I sigh inside.

"You've never had an offer this large," she adds.

This is usually a no-brainer. Get endorsement deals, deposit my paycheck into the foundation I run for my favorite charities, expand it, and do more good in the world.

But I'm freaking *tired*.

"You're only young once, Waverly," Aunt Zinnia adds. "This one won't come around again."

I glance at my phone.

I'd rather be talking to Cooper, whether we're laughing or switching to a video call so he knows all of my attention is fully on him.

But that's not an option.

His team owns him until the season's over.

Might as well go do a little more good in the world until I can see him in person next week.

23

Cooper

I PLAY MY ASS OFF, go two-for-four at bat, rob three guys of base hits, and help Diego throw out four would-be base-stealers tonight in Boston, thank fuck, but I'm feeling off as I board the bus back to the hotel after the game.

Coach Addie gives me a side eye as I start to walk past her. "Lucky socks go missing again?"

I drop into the open seat next to her instead of heading to the back of the bus where I usually sit. "What are you talking about? I was on fire."

"Your swing sucked today."

She's not wrong. The only reason I hit the ball was because the pitching sucked worse than my swing, which made it easy to hit.

And I'm finally over getting cranky when I'm told I can improve. You go six or seven seasons playing for coaches who care more about sucking up to shitty management than they do about improving the team, you learn to self-motivate. And when you go those seasons self-motivating and being the best because of it, it's hard to break old habits and trust that the new coaches really do care more about the team than they do about going clubbing later with the owner.

But these coaches care.

And look where we are now.

"Almost missed that throw from Estevez in the fourth too," Coach Dusty says as he takes the seat across the aisle.

For the record, I still maintain that I played my ass off.

Realizing phone sex with Waverly wouldn't satisfy me personally and what that means for how hard I'm falling for her when being with her would basically mean I have to quit baseball was quite the smack upside the head.

And the heart.

So playing as well as I did is something I'll privately commend myself for while still taking the feedback from my coaches. "Hard hotel bed," I say. "Requested a softer one. Should've been switched while we were gone. I'll be better tomorrow."

Neither coach buys it, even though we do, in fact, stay at hotels that'll switch out our mattresses if we go all pampered high-maintenance sportsers on them.

"Someone sick?" Addie asks. She has four older brothers, and I'm convinced Tripp and Lila hired her as much for being able to see through all our bullshit as they did for her baseball skills and knowledge, which are top-notch. I know she wants to manage her own hometown team someday. The Fireballs are a stepping-stone for her.

I consider lying, but I've got enough I'm hiding right now and don't have the brain power to keep it all straight. "Nope."

"Money problems?"

"Nah."

"If you're hiding an injury—"

"Cooper Rock doesn't get injured, Coach. Injured gets Cooper Rocked."

She makes a face like she'd rather be having her eyeballs plucked than listening to my ego talk. "So it's a woman," she says.

That's an understatement. Realizing the Fireballs might be a stepping-stone for me too? That they might be only a phase of my life instead of my entire life?

That's fucking terrifying.

I've never wanted anything else.

Ever.

And I'm not ready to quit. Not by a long shot. But I don't know how to balance having two things in my life that I want to be my entire life.

This time, I do lie. "Nope. Not a woman. Wanna know a secret?" I drop my voice. "It's writer's block."

Dusty coughs. Addie blinks.

And Hugo Sanchez, our conditioning coach, turns around from his seat in front of me to stare. "Writer's block," he repeats.

I grin at all of them. "A guy can't have depth?" I twist in my own seat to holler at the back of the bus. "Darren! Tell these people about my novel."

"It sucks," Darren calls.

Luca leans into the aisle. "Because he hasn't written one."

"Have too," I call back.

Darren winces. "I wish I didn't know that was true."

"Wait. Seriously?" Might be horror on Luca's face. Might be awe. Probably both.

"Some fantasy novel," Max says as he passes my seat on his way to the back of the bus. He cuts me a look.

My nuts shrivel.

He knows about Waverly, and he *definitely* knows I got caught solo in my hotel room with my pants around my ankles before the game, and he owes me.

He owes me so big.

The minute he decides to pay me back for all the shit I gave him in the off-season when he was secretly seeing my sister, and then the glitter bomb incident…

I'm a dead man.

In the best of ways, I mean. I take my medicine when it's dished out. I deserve it.

But I don't know if Max will keep Waverly from the blast impact whenever he finally gives me what's coming.

And I don't know *when* what's coming will finally come.

I think he's enjoying the torment it causes me to constantly be anticipating his revenge. Not getting revenge when I'm braced for revenge might be his revenge.

Fuck.

"No," Luca says. "If Cooper wrote books, he would've told me. He would've told Henri. No one can resist telling Henri everything. Not even *him*." Luca's girlfriend writes romance novels for her day job, but this is only his second year on the team, and I really have had writer's block on my fantasy novel for like three years.

Also?

I don't like not being good at things. And I am really *not* good at writing this novel. Started it because I fell in love with a fantasy cartoon about a pickle while I was killing time on the road a few years ago, got the bug, realized it was harder than I thought it would be, and it's simmered on the back burner since.

Mostly.

I might've dabbled in another project or two over the years after chatting with the Thrusters' goaltender, who's also a Copper Valley local, and who's self-published some stuff, but I refuse to admit to anything.

Luca's giving me the suspicious eyeball that reminds me of his Nonna and her love-curse eyeball. "This is another of Cooper's pranks, right?"

"Tillie Jean's read the first half," Max says. "He calls it *Punkball in Space*. It's about half-human, half-alien baseball players who have to save the universe with the game."

"That's why I can jump so high," I call back down the aisle. "I'm pretending there's no gravity as research."

"Maybe we spend more time pretending you don't have writer's block so you can play baseball," Dusty says.

Brooks Elliott climbs aboard the bus, and the doors shut.

Finally.

We can get back to the hotel, I can take a nap, and then I can wake up around two AM to call Waverly, since that's about the time she'll be heading to bed out on the West Coast, which is where I think she'll be at the end of the day today.

Wait.

Was she filming the late shows in New York or in LA?

Shit.

I can't remember.

Brooks pauses instead of taking a seat, which means the bus isn't moving, and I can't find out yet.

"Everybody has off days, Coach," he says to Dusty. "I'll take Cooper's off days if they mean he gets base hits and doesn't let anything through the infield."

My knee bounces.

Coach Addie looks at it and raises a brow.

I force it to stop.

"Did you prank the wrong person?" she asks me.

"Yes." That's actually true.

I think I pranked myself.

I mean, if falling this hard for a woman who has so little time for me that I'd have to trade in my baseball glove to be with her counts as pranking myself, then yes, I have most definitely pranked myself.

And this bus could run on the power of all the coaches' sighs.

I practically sit on my hands the entire ride back to the hotel. Can't check my phone without risking someone overseeing who's in my text message history. I'm not dumb enough to put Waverly in my phone as *Waverly*, but my new code name for her might be too easy for some of these guys to figure out.

I had to change out *Baseball Cheater* for fear someone would think I was hanging with someone who'd get me into Pete Rose-level trouble, but *Hot Trouble* is basically transparent.

Isn't it?

Or is it?

And am I paranoid about this because I get the feeling Max is plotting something, or am I paranoid because I have no idea how to handle how much I like her?

But finally—*finally*—we reach the hotel. I'm nearly the first off the bus, and I head to the stairs instead of risking getting trapped in the elevator with any of my teammates or any of the women who sometimes hang out in the lobby of our hotels when we're on the road.

Takes me three swipes to get my key card to work on my

room, and when I push in, I have my head down, typing out a message to Waverly, telling her to call me no matter when she's done tonight, and it takes me more time than it should to realize something's off.

Off-off.

"Cooper Rock, you are *such* a dead man," Mackenzie says.

She's standing in the middle of the living area of my suite, flanked on one side by Tanesha and on the other by Marisol, whose nostrils are flaring as she glares at me.

I want to know how people keep getting keys for my hotel rooms, but this isn't the time.

Not when I'm under fire from the three most powerful Lady Fireballs.

I gulp, then force a smile. "Aw, it's my three favorite ladies."

Marisol growls at me. Tanesha's murdering me with her eyes.

"I don't even know where to start with you," Mackenzie says.

"I'm so disgusted right now." Marisol's nostrils flare again. "If you'd ever told me I'd have to walk into Cooper Rock's room and *tell him to have sex for his game*, I would've—you know what? I *do* want to puke right now."

"*And then you damage Waverly Sweet's reputation,*" Tanesha hisses. "I *cannot even* with you."

I freeze.

Hard freeze.

There's no amount of charm buried in my depths that will save me now.

Tanesha throws her hands up. "What the *hell*, Cooper? You're the *one guy* I could always count on for *years* to do what was right for the team, and now we're finding out you're giving your superstitions the middle finger and secretly hanging out with Diego's crush and very *favorite person* in the entire universe, and do you know what he'll do when he sees the news and what they're saying about her because she's associating with *you*? I've wanted to help you *all season*, but I am so *mad* at you right now for all the secrets you're keeping that are hurting everyone around us."

I open my mouth.

Then shut it again.

Tanesha *harumph*s. Marisol lifts her perfectly sculpted brows, silently asking what I have to say for myself.

"What news?" I croak out.

Tanesha shoves her phone at me so I can read the headline.

Waverly Sweet—Role Model Out of Control! From Hollywood Hunk Fiancé to Baseball Bad Boy Fling.

I skim.

It gets worse.

Superstition. Sex. Fallen role model. Beneath her. Mental breakdown.

Mackenzie pokes a finger so hard in my direction that it makes an actual breeze in the hotel room. "We're having a ritual. Tonight. *Now.* And then you're going to apologize to— where are you going?"

I pause with my hand on the doorknob. "I'll take my punishment, Mac. Swear I will. Tanesha, you know I'm good for it. Marisol, you too. But first, I really need to make a phone call."

I dash out of my room and down the hall to bang on Max's door.

He opens with cranky face on full display. "What?"

"I need your room."

"No."

He shuts the door.

And I realize there's something else I need to do.

I dash the other direction down the hall and bang on a different door.

This one opens slowly.

Diego peers out at me with hurt and questions lingering in his brown eyes.

Fuck.

"I'm treating her right." I talk softly. God only knows who's listening, but my teammate, *my friend*, needs to hear this. "I promise you, I'm treating her right. I know you like her. I like her too. I didn't mean for this to happen, and I know it's complicating the hell out of everything, and I know I should've told you, but I need you to know I have no intention of hurting her."

There's no smile.

No *it's okay, Mister Coop.*

Just a wary raised brow.

"You know that feeling when you call the right pitch or you throw out someone trying to steal a base or you hit a home run, and it's like, the world is even more magic for that split second when you're even happier playing ball than you are just to be on the field?"

He nods slowly.

"That's what this is like, except all of those split seconds of magic are lasting for minutes and hours and days. She's incredible. I like her a *lot.*"

"You're Mister Cooper," he says. "You don't have to tell me."

"I do, bud. We're teammates. I know you like her. I *knew* you liked her. And I started dating her anyway. I should've told you. I should've given you that courtesy. I mean it, D.

I'm doing everything a good boyfriend should do. She's special."

He blinks once, and then his smile lights up his face again. "You think we're equals."

"Dude. *Diego*. We're teammates. *We're equals*."

His smile gets bigger. "I'm happy for you, Mister—"

"*Cooper*," I mutter.

"Be good to her, and I'll be happy for you. I like being happy for my friends. I still love her. Too much, like you said at the bar. She's your equal. Not mine."

Jesus. This kid. "We're good?" I ask.

And now his smile is blinding the hallway. "We're good, Coop."

I clap his shoulder as my own door opens and Tanesha peeks out at me. I have *got* to get inside a safe room. "Thanks, man." And then I dash back down the hallway and bang on Max's door again.

He flings it open again and shoves his phone in my face. The screen shows a text message from my sister. Tillie Jean's not on this trip with us because she's filling in for staff on vacation at Dad's restaurant back home.

One day she's gonna run all of Shipwreck.

Right now, she's running my worst nightmares instead. And I once dreamed I was on the all-you-can-eat buffet inside a tree, being eaten alive by a flying giant panda-slash- praying mantis. I have some pretty fucked-up nightmares when I'm stressed.

You were right. It was Waverly Sweet, and that dumbass has been hiding it from us. Also, Pop got totally suckered by a reporter in pirate gear and overshared about Cooper's superstition. Has Diego seen the news? Don't even make that face. I know you secretly like him and you know this is important both personally and professionally.

"*Fuuuuuuuuck,*" I breathe.

I shoot a glance down the hall.

Reporters know where we stay.

This isn't good.

Max grunts out a frustrated sigh, grabs me by the collar with his non-pitching arm, and hauls me into his room. "Why can't you use your room?"

"Lady Fireballs ambushed me and I didn't think they'd leave and I really don't want the press reporting that I host my teammates' wives in my room all the time." Mostly because they'll twist it to make Waverly look worse when *I'm* the damn hornball.

"Do you seriously have to have sex to play good?"

I wince. "Yes."

"How long?"

"Basically my whole career."

"No, dumbass, I mean, how long can you go between games without having sex? Because your game was shit until last week, and if this thing's serious with Waverly, which it has to be since *you don't fucking redecorate your house with ice sculptures and streamers for women ever*, then you're fucked. She's busier than we are, and she won't be—god, I can't believe I'm saying this—regularly available to help you with your—" He cuts himself off by gesturing to my crotch.

This is not getting better. "Can I please make a phone call in private in here?"

"No."

I turn to go. I'll try Luca. Henri's traveling with him, and she's a softie. The fact that she wasn't involved in the ambush gives me hope that she'd take my side.

Unless they're screwing.

He had a good game.

They're probably screwing.

Fuck.

"How serious is this, Cooper?" Max repeats.

The bathroom.

I duck under his arm, slam the door shut, lock it, and then squat on the floor and drop two towels over my head while I'm dialing Waverly's number.

Towels are important.

They muffle the echo.

Not that I've done this before to plan a prank or anything.

I dial her number, and miracle of miracles, she picks up on the first ring. "I didn't leak to the press," I blurt.

"Cooper Rock," a voice that is not Waverly's answers.

This voice makes my nuts retract into my body at a speed and depth that make me believe I might've just gone through puberty in reverse.

I'm a little afraid to hear my own voice, and I wonder if the beard I started growing last week is spontaneously falling out too.

No hair on the floor.

Good sign.

Although, it's a little dark under these towels. I'll have to check again in a few.

"Do we need to repeat this same conversation?" Zinnia Sweet asks.

"Nope."

"Good."

"We're having a different one instead. Waverly's a grown woman, and I'm no longer a kid you can push around."

"Your arrogance won't get you far with me."

"Same."

I hang up.

Arguing with Zinnia Sweet will get me nowhere, and I clearly can't talk to Waverly at the moment.

Doesn't mean I'm done for the night though.

Being the guy who deserves whatever time she'll give me is all that matters.

24

From the text messages of Team Wooperly

WAVERLY: Hey! You around?

Cooper: This is a test of the emergency broadcast system. If you're a pop sensation after a concert, show me your favorite GIF of me. If you're anyone else using her phone, please fuck off and send me the receipt.

Waverly: *selfie, wincing* Aunt Zinnia answered when you called during taping.

Cooper: I'd answer that call from you right now, but someone made a zillion copies of my hotel key and I keep finding my teammates' wives and girlfriends waiting in my own room to give me an earful, so I'm currently hiding in an unnamed teammate's closet and they don't know I'm here and I don't want to make any noise to alert them to that fact.

Waverly: So the entire Fireballs organization has seen the gossip.

Cooper: Yeah. They're pissed at me.

Cooper: And I don't blame them. I'm a bad look for you.

Cooper: For the record, I would've written that article a lot differently. POP STAR TAKES PITY ON BASEBALL PLAYER WHO KNOWS SHE'S TOO GOOD FOR HIM. Today, we discovered that Waverly Sweet is truly the best among us as she demonstrated that she, too, is a normal human being who is sometimes attracted to fun-loving men who wear horrible colors on their baseball jerseys and have demonstrated all season long that they're only good when compared to how badly their team normally plays.

Waverly: Oh, stop. You're worthy. EVERYONE is worthy. I get why people think I'm special, but I'm really not. And you don't like the Fireballs colors? Seriously?

Cooper: You definitely deserve better than some fuckwad insulting your wardrobe while praising my ass. You look a gajillion times better than me any hour of the day.

Waverly: *gif of Cooper laughing with Baby Ash at Duggan Field* You look pretty great here.

Cooper: They caught my good side. On the other side, I looked like a monster. Plus—don't tell anyone, I'll deny it—this new Fireballs orange doesn't do good things for my ass. But baseball gods shouldn't worry about that. And I should worry about you. You okay? You didn't get shit from your aunt over all of this, did you?

Waverly: We had a disagreement over whether this should be used as a promotional opportunity before my makeup line launches in two weeks, or if she should shut up and stay out of my personal life. Also, I have to apologize. I'm almost positive she's the one who leaked everything.

Cooper: My pop—my grandpa—was the one who spilled the beans about my superstition. That's on me. I talked to him and told him not to trust anyone, even people in pirate costumes.

Waverly: Poor guy. Is he okay?

Cooper: Oh, yeah. Hometown hero. Everyone's celebrating him for being the guy who's going up to my house every night to do a pirate ritual to break my superstition curse. Don't ask. Wait. Actually, you should probably know, in case they twist it to make it look like your fault too. He likes to garden in the nude and he swears it evens out the bad energy in the universe. Also, probably don't head out to my house in Shipwreck unannounced. Not that you're not welcome at my houses. The ones I live in, I mean. Not the ones I use as rental property. I never know when they're occupied and that could get awkward. You're welcome anytime in my actual inhabitances though. The one in Shipwreck or the one in Copper Valley. Not that you need them. I know you have a million houses of your own. But if you want mine, feel free. Door code's the same on both of them. Shit. I'm rambling on text. And here I go, sending without deleting, because you already know what you're getting into, so it's not like this'll make me look worse, and if I retype it and send a single sentence instead, you'll know I was rambling anyway for how long it took me to just say YES.

Waverly: *laughing emoji* I honestly appreciate how real you are.

Cooper: And I appreciate that you appreciate it.

Waverly: Oh, god, you're probably getting shit from Fireballs management too, aren't you?

Cooper: Nah. Tripp and I had a talk, and we're good. But if Levi calls you, it would be great if you could tell him you're going through a playboy baseball player phase and you'll be the one stomping my heart into dust. Not that he has any say in what happens to the team, but when your brother owns the baseball team that employs the guy who's not good enough to be dating the pop star they both consider to be their adopted little sister...

Waverly: I think I followed that... Why do I get the feeling you and Tripp are not, in fact, "good"? Do I need to call him after I text Levi and tell him neither of the Wilson brothers are entitled to opinions on who I hang out with in my free time unless they have evidence you're secretly a pop star killer?

Cooper: Nope. I looked Tripp square in the eye, said, "Waverly's a grown-ass woman. You're not trying to run a grown-ass woman's life, are you?" And then his wife cleared her throat, he looked properly chastised, and Lila informed me that if my dick causes her headaches, she's calling my mom. But Lila can't chastise Levi the same way she can chastise Tripp, so it's like, one brother down, one more to go.

Waverly: I can't decide if you're paraphrasing or if that truly happened.

Cooper: It happened. The entire Fireballs organization knows my mom. She's awesome. She also knows how to push my buttons like nobody else, because she's my mom. Also, she says she's going to be very upset if either of us hurt the other, and that you looked beautiful in the picture of us leaving my house.

Waverly: *eye roll emoji* I looked fine. But it was a flattering photo of you. You'll get some great attention out of this.

Cooper: I don't need attention.

Waverly: Maybe this is a good thing. If we're not hiding, you could go with me a few places next week. Like the movie premiere on Thursday night?

Cooper: You'd want me to go?

Waverly: Why not? It would be fun, and I'd honestly get

endless enjoyment out of watching Geofferson's fiancée ogle you. You should wear your Ash suit, and we can take bets on how many tabloids will say you looked fabulous and daring while I was trying too hard to outdo my last red carpet look.

Cooper: You could go in jeans and a tank top and you'd look amazing.

Waverly: So it's a date?

Cooper: Yeah. Let me tell my agent, and it's a date.

Waverly: You have to tell your agent?

Waverly: I mean duh. Of course you should. Your people should always know if you're doing a big public event. They hate being caught off guard.

Waverly: It's not like you're going with me so you can up your visibility and get some better endorsement deals.

Waverly: Ignore me. I'm being ridiculous.

Cooper: Sorry. Made too much noise and Robinson got suspicious. Had to go quiet a minute. My agent got me this sunglass endorsement deal a few months back, and when I told him I was going to LA for the All-Star break, he moved the photo shoot up to the same night. I'll have him move it back again to after the season's over. Not a big deal. Figured I'd be flying solo while you were out doing your things. Happy to be wrong.

Waverly: Oh. Duh. Right. You do this all the time too.

Cooper: Not quite as often as guys on teams that win more regularly than we do, but yeah, I get around a little in the endorsement circuit.

Waverly: Do you like it?

Cooper: Usually. I like that I've basically bought a whole mountain off of my endorsement deals. Feels like I'm following my pirate ancestors' footsteps in letting companies pay me stupid amounts of cash to pose in their shoes or sunglasses or whatever so that I can buy one more bit of land where my great-great-great-to-infinity grandfather supposedly buried his treasure.

Waverly: You… bought a mountain.

Cooper: Ninety percent of Thorny Rock Mountain. Not to brag, but I'm literally king of the Rock. Even if Beck Ryder's house technically sits at a slightly higher elevation than mine does. I'll convince him to sell one day. But now that he and Sarah have the baby, and with it being a better environment for her bees than his penthouse in the city, they're out there more and more. Gonna be an uphill battle to win that house. Literally.

Waverly: What do you do with it?

Cooper: My mountain? I rent out the houses. Mostly vacation rental stuff. Funnel the profits back into running the Pirate Festival and some Little Sluggers leagues in the county. Stuff like that. Don't tell a soul, but I anonymously started sponsoring the Unicorn Festival in Sarcasm a few years ago too. Seriously pissed off all of Shipwreck when Sarcasm announced it, but the two towns picking back up with their feuding means both festivals get higher attendance, and now, with so much of the world going digital and people being able to work from anywhere, population's growing both places too. Not saying I single-handedly reversed a few decades of our towns going into slumps, but I'm not saying I didn't either.

Waverly: *eyeballs bulging emoji*

Cooper: Figure I'll donate the mountain back to the town when I die so they can keep using the profits wisely.

Cooper: And now you know my deepest, darkest secret.

Waverly: That's really sweet. All of it. And way more than the world gives you credit for.

Cooper: Not kidding about that unicorn festival thing. It

needs to stay a total secret. While it would score me points with my sister-in-law, the rest of my family would disown me.

Waverly: Your secret is safe with me.

Cooper: Appreciate it.

Waverly: Oh, other question—anyone you want me to hold backstage passes for on Friday night? Any other Little Sluggers' teams you've adopted that I don't know about? Or maybe you know this secret author of the Fireballs' fanfic and they want a meet-and-greet?

Cooper: Can I get back to you?

Waverly: Always.

Waverly: What would you do if you didn't have your family?

Waverly: Sorry. Left field. Never mind.

Cooper: That's sexy as hell that you use baseball analogies. And I hope I never have to find out.

Waverly: They ground you.

Cooper: Shh. Don't tell them that either. They think I'm an egotistical hornball, and I like it that way. Means they don't expect as much from me.

Waverly: Why don't you let them expect things from you?

Cooper: Better to under-promise and over-deliver than over-promise and under-deliver. And I'm gone so much…

Waverly: You think you'd let them down.

Cooper: I mean… yeah. They're awesome. They do the work to keep the community running. I just drop in now and then and throw cash around. It's not the same.

Waverly: And you're out in the world representing your hometown with everything you do. When you talk about where you're from, it's like you have this bigger purpose beyond baseball that you never let anyone see.

Cooper: They made me. They supported me in following

my dreams. And now—shit. Now, I'm part of a team that's going to do what everyone thought was impossible, and this wouldn't be happening if all of us weren't there fighting for it together. You know how many times my agent tried to get me traded away in the dark years and I wouldn't let him? I know I'm only one guy, but I BELIEVE. I'm a fucking leader on the team. And I wouldn't be that guy if my family hadn't believed in me and taught me how. So the Fireballs being on fire the past two years? That has roots in my family. In my community. Giving back is the least I can do.

Waverly: My aunt made me.

Waverly: It's okay. You don't have to reply to that. I know it's awkward and weird. And since I'm being awkward and weird, I want you to know that how much you love your family is one of the most attractive things about you. To me. And also probably the thing I'm most jealous of. I don't have paternal relatives. Clearly. Sperm bank kid here. Aunt Zinnia never had kids of her own. It's just her and me. And I have friends, but I don't have FAMILY. Not the way you do. Anytime I wonder if my life would've been different if my mom hadn't died, if she'd lived and met a wonderful man who deserved her and if she fell in love and had more kids, if I'd had siblings, if Aunt Zinnia could've lived her life without having eight-year-old me dumped on her, I feel like a spoiled brat, because I have fame and fortune and everything we're supposed to want, and I still just sometimes feel... empty.

Waverly: Right. Shutting up now. It's late. You need your sleep. I need my sleep. Key to happiness, right? If I never know the other half of where I came from, my life won't change a whole lot, and I really am grateful for what I do have. I'm glad you had a good game today. I think I can watch at least half the game tomorrow. Night, Cooper. Thanks for chatting.

Cooper: Money and fame aren't a substitute for love and family, and anyone who'll judge you for wanting both is a dick. Especially when you'd be the first person to give up the fame and money to have family.

p.s. Remind me tomorrow to tell you the sound Robinson makes when he finds someone hiding in his closet. Hope you're sleeping well. *heart emoji*

25

Waverly

THERE COMES a point in every woman's life when she realizes she's tired of waiting for what she wants and needs to go grab all of her desires by the balls and hold on for the ride, and for me, that moment is exactly right now.

"This is a terrible idea," Kiva mutters to me as Scott Two steers my SUV into the parking lot of a local Little Sluggers baseball diamond.

"Only maybe a little." I'm supposed to be downtown in the middle of a meeting about...actually, I forget what.

The point is, I blew it off.

It's an endorsement or product line or costume blah blah blah something, and I have somewhere I'd rather be.

You'd trade the fame and money for love and family.

I stared at that text from Cooper for *hours*, my pulse slowly working its way up into panic zones at the idea of all the people I'd let down if I walked away from my career.

And then my intestines worked themselves into a tizzy over who'd lose their jobs and what people would say about me if I canceled concerts and tore up my recording contracts and walked away from the entire Waverly Sweet empire with all of my side deals and endorsements and offshoot companies and honorary titles and podcasts and movies and appearances and and and and and...

Would I trade in what I've made of my life if I could spend the rest of it living with Hashtag in a little cottage by the sea, playing my guitar or my piano and singing, living and eating and breathing with people I could laugh with and talk to and love, knowing that they loved me not because I was *Waverly Sweet, pop sensation*, but because I was a human being who wanted to be there for my family in all of their big and little moments?

Could a family like that even exist for me? I don't have grandparents. I might have siblings, but they would be half-siblings, with no history between us and the complicating factor of a lifetime of being told I have to be careful who I make friends with because everyone wants something from me, and no one is interested in getting to know *me*.

But that's what I want.

I want a big, massive family that knows *me*, who won't care if I misspeak when I'm telling a joke or if I wear something unflattering.

I want it so bad my heart's in more knots than my stomach is.

Or maybe that's the Cooper effect.

I blew off my meeting this afternoon because Cooper's here. In LA. Spending his first All-Star break afternoon volunteering at a baseball clinic for little kids with some of his buddies from my home team while I'm supposed to be in a meeting.

"Don't look at me like that," I say to Kiva. "If Aunt Zinnia gives you crap—"

Kiva's face basically cuts me off.

If Zinnia gives me crap, she gives me crap, and you'll politely ask her not to do that again, and she'll ignore you.

I believe my aunt wants what's best for me. She *is* my family. My only family.

But I'm realizing we have very different opinions of *what's best for me*, and for the first time in my life, I'm realizing that perhaps I've let someone else make all of my decisions for far too long.

Early in my career, I needed an adviser to help me learn who to trust, what was a good deal, when to sign a contract and when to walk away.

Aunt Zinnia wasn't just my aunt. She was my guide. My mom had pulled her into the industry back when she was a rising star of her own because she, too, wanted the family she could trust around her. By the time it was my turn, Aunt Zinnia knew the players. The game. Who would lie to your face and who would get things done, when to push and when to quietly sit back and wait for the opportune moment to get what you wanted. She knew everything and I knew nothing.

I have more than enough experience to run the Waverly Sweet empire on my own now, but I still let her tell me what to do and when, because why argue or reinvent the wheel when those orders don't conflict with where I think I want to go and what I think I want to do?

But the past few months, especially after talking to Cooper so much about what *he* wants next if all of the only dreams he's ever had come true, I feel different.

What is my goal? Does this project make me excited? Do I want to do this? Where do I want to be in five years? Or even in two? Where does my career end and my life begin?

"You think I shouldn't do this," I say quietly to Kiva.

And by *this*, I don't mean randomly skipping a meeting to show up at a baseball diamond where no one has any idea *Waverly Sweet* is coming and we might accidentally end up getting mobbed and have to make a super fast getaway.

I mean having a wild public fling with Cooper that leads me to making all kinds of choices that reflect poorly on me as a professional musician and businesswoman.

She doesn't break eye contact. "You're the boss, and this is your life."

For once, I'm not sure how to interpret that.

It's your life to fuck up?

Or does she mean *it's your life to live?*

Or maybe both?

I text Aspen as Scott Two drives us through the parking lot toward the section reserved for buses closer to the field. *Am I an idiot to blow off work to hang out with my playboy baseball player quasi-boyfriend while he's teaching little kids how to hold a bat?*

Her reply is instantaneous.

No. You're an idiot to not immediately kidnap him away from there, take him back to your place, strip both of you naked, and enjoy the hell out of playing hooky in a more grown-up way than hanging out with a bunch of kids.

I shiver.

That *does* sound good.

What would happen if I marched onto the diamond, signed a few autographs, then told Cooper to let the rest of the professional ballplayers handle the kids, and dragged him out of there?

You'd disappoint the children, Waverly. You would disappoint the children.

And that's what has me sighing as I climb out of the SUV between Kiva and Scott Two.

You'd get bad press and be labeled a sex-crazed ball of hormones wouldn't bother me, because it's what they say if I even talk to a man *wrong*. I will never escape that kind of judgmental headline, and I should quit worrying over it.

Your aunt would have a coronary. Meh. Whatever.

The kids who came here to see Cooper Rock would be very disappointed.

And that's the one that will get me every time.

He made a promise to be here, and he's one of the highest-profile players in the league, thanks to being the hometown hero who not only stuck with his team because he believed in their bad years, but who's historically been one of the best players in the league to boot.

Even during his off days.

It doesn't matter that we're in LA and not Copper Valley.

There will be kids who are here *because* of him.

There are three diamonds on the field, and we make it to the closest one to the parking lot before I'm spotted, and even then, it's clear that the parents who notice me are questioning if they're seeing what they think they're seeing. Sunglasses, jeans, and a hat over a ponytail really do wonders for anonymity when you're not expected.

No one's pointing their phones in my direction yet.

Most of them are paying attention to the pro ball players and the kids on the field, which is exactly what I want to do as well.

Especially when I realize why I didn't spot Cooper right away.

He's basically hiding, kneeling at home plate, a black baseball hat turned backward covering his dark hair, his face dusted with the start of what promises to be a thick beard in another week or two, in jeans and a *Little Sluggers – Team Sea Cows* t-shirt, helping a little girl in an oversized helmet position her bat.

Unlike when he helped me bat, he's in front of her, tapping her shoes to indicate that she needs to reposition her feet and holding the top of the bat to show her where to hold it.

She's giggling at whatever he's saying, and he's grinning right back at her like his entire life's purpose is being here to help her learn everything he can teach her about baseball.

He goes back on his heels, gestures for her to swing, and when she chops the bat awkwardly, he falls back into the dirt with a dramatic flair. "Holy smokes, Leandra! Look at that swing! The wind off it blew me over! You're gonna take the skin right off that ball!"

She giggles harder.

"Is there anything hotter than a man who's good with kids?" a woman near me murmurs, fanning herself with her left hand.

No ring.

Single mom.

Back off, lady. He's mine.

"I'm reserving judgment until I see if he's full of shit or if he can actually help her hit the ball," the woman next to her mutters.

I almost gasp in outrage, but Kiva pushes me closer to the baseline. "Are you going all the way out there or not?" she murmurs.

We are so going out there, my vagina votes.

Yep. We're going out there, my heart agrees.

But I don't move.

The minute I interrupt everything, these kids lose out on the reason they're here today.

And I'm not here to leap all over him, even if the mere sight of him is making my nipples perk up and my panties damp.

This is his natural habitat. He doesn't know I'm here. He's not pretending to be anything other than who he is, doing what he does, and it's *magic* watching him with the kids.

"Excuse me," a quiet voice says, and I realize it's one of the women who spotted me a few minutes ago.

I put my finger to my lips with a smile.

She smiles back and looks away, out at the field. "My kids and I sing 'Pedal to the Metal' at the top of our lungs every time we drive up the PCH to visit my in-laws," she whispers.

"That's so cool," I murmur back. "It was supposed to be a ballad, but then my producer started playing with that beat while we were writing, and she was so right. It's a total driving song."

"Are you really dating Cooper Rock?"

"That depends on the day and the tabloid reporting the news, doesn't it?" I add a harmless smile, the kind that usually works well to deflect personal questions with people who seem to understand boundaries.

But the lady keeps talking. Quietly. "I grew up in North Carolina. Closer to Copper Valley than Atlanta, so the Fireballs were our team. My family adores him. My sister got to meet him once when she took her kids to hang out in his hometown —you know, the pirate town in the mountains?—and she said he was the nicest guy in person. Everything you expect of him when you see him play baseball. I hope you're dating him. And I hope he's as nice as everyone thinks he is. You deserve someone nice after...you know what? I'm shutting up now. Really nice to meet you. I hope you have fun today."

She drifts away.

Kiva shifts a look my way, and this one is clear as day. *She's not wrong. He's a nice guy, and you deserve it after Geofferson.*

I glance at Cooper again. He's backing up, still talking to Leandra as he signals the pitcher to toss a ball.

And a minute later, when she gets on base, he cheers loudest.

When the little boy after her takes seventeen pitches to even connect with the ball after a ton of coaching on batting position and keeping his eye on the ball, Cooper gives him the biggest *yeah, dude, I knew you could do it! That's the first step!* and a massive fist bump.

When his team moves to the outfield for practice throwing and fielding the ball, he's straight-up enthusiasm, *wow, you almost took my glove off!* and *yeah, I totally miss first base all the time too,* even though he does not, in fact, *ever* mis-throw to first base.

He teaches them the baseball shuffle, which vaguely reminds me of old MC Hammer dances and has both me and the kids giggling nonstop while they all stop ground balls like champs before their time is up.

All of the parents here fanning themselves over Cooper with the baseball players-in-training are right.

There is nothing—*nothing*—sexier than watching a man spend his afternoon donating his time and talents and enthusiasm to build up a group of kids.

When someone comes over the loudspeaker and announces afternoon camp is over, Cooper pulls his kids in for a huddle and starts whispering things none of us on the sidelines can hear.

A minute later, they all stick their hands into the circle, and yell, "Go, Sea Cows, *moo-bubble!*"

Freaking. Adorable.

Cooper straightens, looks straight at me, grins and winks, and that's all the warning I get before one kid yells, "WAVERLY SWEET!" and charges me, leading the pack as the rest of the kids cheer and screech and run faster than *any* of them ran to chase baseballs or to get onto base for the entire past two hours.

"I don't care if he's a nice guy, I hate him right now," is the last thing I hear Kiva say before I'm surrounded by kids.

And their parents.

And the other baseball players and event organizers.

Kiva and Scott Two organize lines and make a buffer around me while I take pictures and sign autographs one at a time and in small family groups, and when it becomes clear news has spread that I'm here and non-baseball people are starting to arrive, they do what they do best and hustle me out of there.

"But—" I fell so quickly into *Waverly Sweet, don't disappoint the fans* mode that I have zero idea where Cooper is, even though I've wanted him next to me this entire time.

And then I spot him.

He's chatting with that mom who talked to me and her kids, and they're very, very close to my SUV.

A snarl wells up in my chest.

Should I have told her he's mine?

Should I have told her to back off?

Should I have been more clear?

Am I overreacting? Is that a wedding ring on her finger?

His gaze slides my way, and the kind smile he's been aiming at the mom and her kids turns into a full-blown, dimpled, I'm-so-glad-to-see-you, lady-killer Cooper Rock special.

It's like he's just stepped onto a stage and had every spotlight in a five-mile radius aimed at him.

He's *glowing*.

Kiva shoves me into the back of my car over my squeak of protest.

Cooper nods to the small family around him, casually strolls away like it's no big deal, and before Scott Two has the engine cranked, my blue-green-eyed heart-stealer is sliding into the back of the SUV beside me.

Kiva's on my right. Cooper's on my left. And I'm in the middle, squished right up against him.

"Hey, do I know you—" he starts, but he doesn't finish.

Mostly because I've thrown my arms around him and smashed my face to his, and now I'm kissing him like I've been living underwater and kissing him is my first full breath in weeks.

He smells like salt and sunshine and he tastes like joy and he feels like the solid wall between me and every worry I've had in the past few weeks. His face is prickly and perfect, setting all the nerves in my lips on fire as his rough beard scratches me while I try to make up for too many weeks of not seeing him in a matter of seconds.

"Cameras." Kiva pulls me off him and folds me over, pushing my face toward my legs.

Cooper slides a hand to my knee and squeezes.

I'm panting for breath and mad that I'm not kissing Cooper and mad that LA traffic is the worst and mad that I have zero privacy. "I thought you didn't see me."

"I knew the minute you climbed out of this car."

"You didn't let on."

"Parents get mad when you pop a boner in front of their kids."

Scott Two sighs. Kiva doesn't respond, but she keeps pressure on my back, making me stay low. And then she insists that I put on my seat belt when it's clear for me to sit back up.

Cooper slings an arm around me, and I lean into him. "Thought you had a meeting," he says.

"Canceled."

He presses his lips to my hair, and I close my eyes and sigh.

Not like Scott Two did.

My sigh is heavy on the relief. "I missed you," I say quietly.

He presses another kiss to my hair. "I'm all yours until break's over."

Days. Mere *days* until his break's over.

That's not nearly enough.

I officially have it bad.

26

Cooper

WAVERLY HAS freckles on her belly.

Not many—just a smattering—but I'm connecting them with my tongue, and let's be honest here.

There's no better way to wake up than a rousing game of connect-the-freckles-on-Waverly's-belly-with-my-tongue. Especially when this rousing wake-up game will be followed by more orgasms posthaste.

Her skin wavers beneath my mouth as she giggles. "That tickles."

"Good or bad?"

"Good, but you're getting close to—*ooooh, yes*."

I smile into her softness as my thumb brushes her clit and her legs part wider. I don't know what time it is. The sun's shining brightly through the gauzy curtains in her second-floor bedroom in the Hollywood house she grew up in. Everything's ivory and gold, with arched windows supported by columns, and if it weren't for the very down-to-earth woman running her fingers through my hair grounding me in this plush, silky-sheeted, massive bed, I'd feel a little out of my league.

I grew up here, she told me when we got here yesterday afternoon. *I don't think I'd pick it if I was house-hunting, but it makes me feel close to my mom whenever I get back to LA, so I keep it. I still sleep in my old bedroom. Wanna see?*

And I'm going to quit thinking about how I'm fingering Waverly in her mom's house in her childhood bedroom and concentrate instead on the fact that I'm with Waverly.

Period.

"This is way better than the All-Star stuff," I tell her belly button.

"You're *my* All-Star."

I slip one finger into the slick heat between her legs, and her breath catches.

Yeah.

Definitely better than all of that All-Star stuff. This is helping my bruised ego over not being there this year.

"I'm—*oh, yes*—canceling every—*god*, Cooper, *how*?"

My lips drift lower, and I shift in her silky sheets to move my whole body down. Her pussy's bare—*freaking costumes and societal expectations*, she said yesterday when I asked—and I'm fascinated. "How what?"

"How—so good—*everything*—but not—so big?"

I choke on an unexpected laugh and lift my head to look at her face. Her neck is arched, head tilted back, hands still gripping my hair. "What?"

"You're not—*big*."

I push up on my elbows to look down at my very happy cock, who is by no means small.

Then back up at her.

She pushes my head back to her lower abdomen, squirming and offering me more of her bare skin and pussy. "I'm not saying it's a bad thing. You *definitely* know how to use everything you've got. And you're not like, less than average or anything. But I remembered you…bigger."

I stare at her.

My dick swells in indignation, but not… massive…indignation.

Fuck.

He's not like, a muscle, is he? Gets weaker and smaller without use?

That's not how it works.

Is it?

Did I break my dick?

Did I neglect it too much? It's not like I don't jerk off. Regularly.

"Oh, god, I just killed the mood, didn't I?" She sighs. "My brain started running again and then I couldn't remember what time my final fitting is for my gown tonight, and I feel like there's something on my calendar I'm forgetting, and I don't want to go to whatever it is, I want to stay here and be naked all day, and now I'm insulting you when I'm trying to say that you leave a big impression by being you and mastering everything great and small, which you're not, and can we pretend it's ten minutes ago and I'm still asleep and you're about to decide you need to be my body's wake-up call?"

"Are you going to call me small again?"

"You're *average*. And I said that's *good*. Do you know how many people with bigger equipment can't use theirs a fraction as well as you use yours?"

I prop my hand on my fist and watch her.

She squeezes her eyes together. "Shit. Please make me quit talking."

"Usually I'm the one overtalking when we're together. This is fun."

"You are *not* having fun right now."

"Okay, yeah, I'm having some pandick attacks right now, but I think they'll pass."

"Panic?"

"No, pandick. My dick is panicking. But you're not kicking me out of bed, and clearly, you know dudes with bigger dicks that you're not calling right now, so…"

She shrieks and rolls, and *fuck*.

I forgot how freakishly strong she is.

But I like it.

And now I'm beneath her, her breasts hovering between us while she straddles me and rubs that bare pussy all over my straining cock. "Cooper Rock, my very favorite thing about you is that you make the most of every talent you have, regardless of whether or not anyone thinks you should be able to do what you do. And *that* is sexy. Are we clear?"

I brush her cheek with my thumb. "I will never get over how gorgeous you are without all of that makeup on."

"That was not an answer."

I tilt my hips, shamelessly enjoying the feel of being between her thighs, a little voice in the back of my head reminding me that I need to grab a condom, but all of my hormones drown that voice out with loud cheers when her eyes cross.

"You like me," I murmur.

"I absolutely—*oh, fuck*—do, and I—*why* do you feel so good?"

I flex my hips and slide my dick in that glorious slickness between her thighs. "Because you like me."

Her lips brush against mine. "I do," she whispers.

"I like when you say *fuck*."

"I would like you to fuck me until I can't see straight, please."

I seriously need a condom.

But she's kissing me, soft little kisses that are getting hotter and wetter and deeper, her pelvis grinding against mine while she makes those moans in the back of her throat.

This.

This is what's been missing from my life for the past eight years.

Waverly.

Publicly a superstar, but privately as big of a dork as I am, looking for something she's always known she couldn't have because she has so much else, how could she trust *this* too?

I wrap my arms around her, tangling one hand in her crazy messy bedhead, and shift us to our sides.

Must. Grab. A. Condom.

Must. Keep. Kissing. Her.

Must—

"Oh my god, get your hands off my niece!"

Waverly shrieks.

I shriek.

She lunges for the sheet while I'm trying to duck—it's instinct after one too many close calls in my early career that I don't like to think about or talk about—and my forehead cracks against her elbow.

"My eyes," Zinnia shrieks. "Oh my god, Waverly, *what are you thinking?"*

"Out!" Waverly snaps. "Get *out!*"

"You heard her!" Zinnia hollers.

"I was talking to *you*," Waverly yells back.

Me?

I've slid off the other side of the bed and am trying to decide if I'm gonna look like a unicorn when I hit the red carpet with Waverly tonight.

Also, my eyes might be slightly crossed with pain.

And if this had happened on the road, I would *definitely* be on deck with the team doc.

Something bats at my dick, and I realize the cat's in here.

And he thinks my anatomy is a toy.

I cup myself with one hand.

He hisses.

Waverly and Zinnia are still shrieking at each other.

And one thing becomes blindingly clear.

If I have any chance at all of convincing Waverly that I'm worth it, it's time to call in reinforcements.

27

Waverly

I HAVE NEVER, *ever* been in such a foul mood before.

Ever.

And now I'm having to fake smiles as Aunt Zinnia and I walk the red carpet at the world premiere of *When Violets Bloom*, a beautiful coming-of-age story that I was thrilled to be asked to write three original songs for, and in which Geofferson unfortunately has a small role.

"You're carrying yourself entirely too stiffly," Aunt Zinnia murmurs through a fake smile of her own.

"I'm not talking to you," I murmur back while I wave to Avery Hart across the way.

"The press will smell the blood."

I ignore her and pose for the cameras.

Cooper's supposed to be next to me, but instead, he's sitting at my house with an ice pack to his forehead while I hope my cat doesn't try to dig into his pants.

Hashtag is very fond of dangly toys.

If he figures out where Cooper's hiding his now that the cat knows that Cooper *has* dangly toys, the rest of this weekend will only get worse.

"Waverly, where's your new boyfriend?" someone calls.

"She doesn't have a boyfriend," Aunt Zinnia replies before I can open my mouth.

"I am so furious with you," I manage to say out of the corner of my widely smiling mouth, sincerely hoping corner-talking will prevent the press from reading my lips.

"This is best and you know it."

Swear to god, if she's having Cooper evicted from my house while I'm here, I will go on strike.

"Stay. Out. Of. My. Love. Life."

"Waverly. Even if the man was serious about you, neither of you have time for each other."

"I've waited eight years. What's another eight until he retires? And it's not like I'm ever having children. *Ever*. It was bad enough growing up as Evelyn Sweet's daughter. Do you have any idea what it would be like for my kids to be *Waverly Sweet's* daughter?"

"Now you're being ridiculous."

We make it inside the theater, and I drop the smile as soon as there's no press watching me.

"Where are you going?" Aunt Zinnia asks me.

"To get a drink."

Kiva cuts her off when she tries to follow me, and since clearly, I'm safe from the danger that is Cooper Rock here, Aunt Zinnia lets me go without fuss.

Or maybe she knows I am absolutely in throw-down mode and I *will* make a scene, regardless of what anyone says about me later.

We've had our ups and downs. She's done countless amazing things for me.

But I'm still furious enough that the chocolate martini I order at the premiere's bar is probably a terrible idea.

Alcohol and my stomach don't go well together.

And *I don't care*.

Which is why I slam the first one right there at the bar and ask for a second.

Kiva doesn't so much as twitch a single eyelash, but she does slip her arm into mine as I head into the theater lobby.

"She better be on the other end of the aisle," I tell Kiva.

"I don't think you have anything to worry about," she replies.

My stomach is angry, but I'm starting to feel more mellow already as I sip my second drink much slower and greet old friends and acquaintances. Avery Hart, the star of the movie and the woman recently covered in the tabloids for taking an entire two-week vacation in Fiji, stops me for cheek kisses.

"Oh my god, I would *die* to be you tonight," she breathes in my ear before the director whisks her away to say hi to Sunny Darling.

Sunny Darling, whose role in this film was playing Geofferson's character's mother.

"I want to talk to Sunny," I tell Kiva.

She and her husband, Judson Clarke, who are both Hollywood royalty, live next door to me. I don't see them or their daughter, Sarah, nearly enough. I miss them.

They were always kind when I was growing up, and now I'm not sure I've seen any of them in two years.

"Waverly?"

A dark-haired white woman a little shorter than me

approaches. She's in a pantsuit instead of a dress, and I gasp out a cry that has people turning heads our way.

"*Sarah!* I was literally just thinking about you."

"Oh my gosh, I didn't think you'd remember me." She laughs as I tackle her in a hug that's probably overkill. "Or know to call me Sarah."

I should *not* drink. "Of course I remember you. And Levi talks about you and Beck all the time. I got the name memo. You smell amazing. I'm sorry I missed your wedding reception. I was in Europe. How's Beck? How's *the baby*? Can I talk to your mom or is she like, completely booked all night? Should I have my people call her people to see when we'll both be home for tea or something?"

Sarah rolls her brown eyes. "Mom's probably completely booked. C'mon. I think you're sitting near us. Have you ever met Beck? I feel like you should've, but I also know you're both crazy busy."

"I don't think I have. But I *feel* like I know him." I follow her deeper into the lobby, where half of Hollywood seems to be milling around.

I spot Sarah's husband, Beck, who made a name for himself modeling underwear after his Bro Code boy band days with the Wilson brothers and Cash Rivers, but seeing him in person for the first time isn't what has me blinking.

Is that *Cooper* next to him?

Both men are tall, with dark hair and bright smiles, and clearly interrupting each other while telling stories and cracking up.

Cooper is wearing a *Baby Ash suit*.

"I cannot even tell you how badly the two of them make my stomach hurt from laughing too much whenever we're out in Shipwreck and they get together," Sarah says. "Do *not* ask about the dead sheep. *Ever*. And say no if they ask if you want to hear about it. At least, that's my advice if you never want to know what it feels like to laugh until you puke."

"Am I that drunk?" I whisper.

She laughs. "You are not. I assure you, you heard all of that correctly."

"I assure you, I'm reasonably certain I'm drunk and having a very weird conversation in my head with you right now."

"Sarah," Beck calls, waving at us. "Cooper's a *unicorn*!"

"Oh my god," I whisper.

Sarah grabs me by the hand and pulls me through a curious crowd. Kiva's right behind us, but she falls into the background.

"Show her," Beck orders Cooper, who turns sideways, displaying the slight bump on his forehead courtesy of my elbow.

He slides one of those grin-winks at me, and *oh my god*, I have to hug him and kiss him and wrap myself around him *right now*.

I can only get in the hug. "You're here."

"I know people who know people who know the people who run the back door." He squeezes me tight. "And I heard this would make less of a scene."

"I'm so glad you're here." I peck his cheek, then rub the lipstick off, almost spilling my martini on his suit in the process. "And you wore Baby Ash!"

"Goes well with the unicorn horn."

"He got the bump chasing a runaway goat down Rodeo Drive this afternoon," Beck says to Sarah.

I choke on the martini that I'm not even drinking at the moment.

"Cooper has lots of practice chasing goats," replies a dark-haired man who's definitely not Hollywood but bears a striking resemblance to Cooper.

"Only because I love my big brother and hate to see him hurting when his pet goat disappears." Cooper shifts us so he has an arm around me, but I'm not hanging on him anymore. "Grady, you know Sarah and Beck, but have you met Waverly?"

The other man gives me a full-dimpled, blue-green-eyed grin. "Not formally. And definitely not anytime we've been in the same room together."

"*Stop*," a brunette woman hisses at him. She extends a hand. "Hi. I'm Annika. I'm Cooper's sister-in-law, which means we mostly like each other, but sometimes merely tolerate each other and can really hand over the dirt if either of us gets pissed over something the other does. And I've known him since before he was in high school, so I have *way* more dirt stored up than he thinks I do."

"Undoubtedly true," Cooper says without an ounce of shame.

I lean into him, absorbing the fact that he's here and I don't have to do this alone tonight.

He squeezes my hip.

"Grady, sweetie, you have spit-up on your backside," an older woman whispers as she pushes through the crowd to us.

"That's life, Mrs. Rock," Beck says.

Mrs. Rock? Cooper's *mother* is here too? And—oh my god.

Is that his father behind her?

I gape up at Cooper.

His ears go pink at the edges, which I swear is one of my favorite things about him. I apparently have a lot of favorite things related to Cooper.

"Sorry for the ambush," he says. "They're on Team Wooperly, I promise."

I start to laugh as another dark-haired woman pushes between us. "Hi. I'm Tillie Jean, and I'd like to *assure* you that I have *zero* interest in *ever* again having Cooper pretend to kiss me in public, even if it would give me great joy to picture Max finally retiring from baseball and tormenting the hell out of him if he ever *does* try it again."

Max Cole gives me the *what's up* chin lift behind her.

"Exactly how did you do this?" I whisper to him after stuttering out a *nice to meet you* to his sister.

"Cooper Rock magic."

Grady grabs Tillie Jean by the back of her dress, which is a drop-dead gorgeous shimmery green sheath, and tugs her back. "Breathing room, TJ."

"Hands off," Max growls at him.

"Waverly, you look lovely." Cooper's mom gives me a quick hug around my drink. "I'm Libby, and I know even more dirt on this one than Annika does, though I don't have her military training. She might have more recent dirt."

"It's nice to meet you," I stammer to her as well.

She smiles, and it's pure *kindness*. "I'm so thrilled to meet you too. Sunny played us a tease of your new song—the second one that the rest of the world hasn't been teased with for weeks—for the movie tonight, and we can't wait to hear the whole thing."

It's like she knows exactly what to say.

I'm friends with Hollywood people outside of knowing you, and I'm not going to get weird if you're seriously dating my son since this isn't my first brush with famous people. I understand that you're normal under that designer gown and jewels.

I wonder if my mom would've had that same note of pride

in her voice if she'd been here to watch a movie with my original songs in it too.

My eyes get hot and my throat tightens. I look at Sarah. "Where are the babies?"

"Home with my dad." Her eyes sparkle, and it's hard to miss the way Beck goes completely mute with total adoration anytime he looks at her.

God. I hear he barely travels at all anymore and is basically home with her all of the time, and he still looks at her like she holds the key to his happiness, and he's utterly smitten.

I glance at Annika too, who's being beamed at by Grady, and I have to take a large swallow of martini before I can ask my next question. "Both of them? You both have babies, right?"

Annika nods. "He knows he's only needed until one of the new dads here get separation anxiety."

"So probably another thirty minutes," Sarah says. "If Annika and I both last that long too. And she's breast-feeding, so she might have other issues."

They both laugh.

Then sigh.

Then laugh again.

It makes me miss Aspen.

"I hear Cooper's modeling your new wedgie-proof underwear," I say to Beck.

He blinks once, clearly confused, then grins broadly like he has no idea why I'd say that, but it sounds fun, and he's game. "It's not ready yet. We still have a lot of wedgie testing to do."

"A lot," Tillie Jean agrees. "I'm on the wedgie-puller team. Part-time. All volunteer. It's a lot more unpleasant than people think, considering Cooper's diet, and how close I have to be to his—*mmph!*"

"Thanks," Cooper says to Max, who's holding a hand over Tillie Jean's mouth.

Max gives him a full-on *I'm not doing this for you* look. "Beck, you know Dax Gallagher?"

I start to open my mouth—Dax and I collaborated on the final song I did for the movie tonight—but Cooper squeezes my hip again while Beck nods. "Oh, yeah," he says. "We go deep sea fishing every other year or so."

"Tillie Jean wants to ask him to be the grand marshal for next year's Pirate Festival Parade."

"*Dude.* He'd freaking flip. I mean, as much as he ever flips over anything that's not Willow. C'mon. Let's go talk to him."

"Seriously?" Tillie Jean squeaks. "We can just go do that?"

Beck looks offended. "TJ, have I *ever* let you down?"

"There was that one time you voted for Annika's sister's banana pudding in the bake-off…"

"Because hers was better," Annika murmurs with a smile.

Sarah steps between them and turns Tillie Jean to follow Beck. "Go on. Talk to Dax. It's your only chance. Ever. Go now, or forever be disappointed."

Our group shrinks.

Cooper tightens his grip around me and presses a kiss to my overdone hair like it's no big deal that he's claiming me in a room full of my peers and a select number of the press.

Like this is where I belong. Like I'm home.

This is what I want *all the time*. "You have no idea how much better my night is for you being here," I whisper to Cooper.

"I'm glad you don't mind claiming a unicorn in a baby dragon suit."

Is this love?

Or is this infatuation?

Whatever it is, I'm leaning all the way into it tonight.

"Do you like banana pudding, Waverly?" Mrs. Rock asks me.

"I don't know that I've ever had it."

Annika gasps.

Grady gasps.

Mr. Rock gasps.

"Nice knowing you," Cooper jokes. "I thought we had a chance there, but now my whole family's horrified. Did you know that ten out of ten of my ex-girlfriends have left me for my sister's banana pudding? Pretty much means—"

"The next time you're in Shipwreck, we are treating you *right*," Mrs. Rock interrupts. "And don't listen to him. None of his girlfriends ever left him for banana pudding. Mostly, they left him because he wasn't ready to be the man he's grown into today."

"Libby. Gross," Annika says.

Sarah cracks up.

Cooper does too.

"Ah, Waverly, you showed up," a cringe-inducing voice says behind me. "I'm honestly surprised."

Cooper's grip tightens on mine. Seven people around us pause and watch. I spot Aunt Zinnia noticing and making a beeline for us.

And I sigh.

For the first time in forever, I really don't care that Geofferson is here. I don't care that he wants to make a scene.

He can't hurt me.

Not if I don't let him.

And the rest of these people, all turning to stare?

Who are *they*?

Why do I let *them* hurt me?

So I turn, not at all certain what I'm about to say, but knowing that I *don't care* what anyone thinks of me being here with Cooper, of me seeing Geofferson, or *anything*, because these people around me?

They care in the *good* way.

But I've only half-turned when I feel something snap under my heel, and then I'm lurching on my broken shoe, and then—

And then I'm being swept off my feet by two strong arms draped in fabric covered in little baby dragons before I fall.

I squeak and wrap my arms tight around Cooper's neck, his earthy, warm, pine-and-butterscotch scent grounding me even as I realize I've spilled my drink all down his back.

"You okay?" he murmurs.

"My heel broke."

"Not your foot?"

I shake my head. "My foot's fine." And then I squeeze him tighter as that once-everything, now-annoying voice speaks again.

"Dramatics, Waverly?" Geofferson says.

I'm debating which version of *get the fuck away from me* I want to go with first when Cooper turns us to face my ex.

"Geofferson," he says brightly, like this is the best part of his day, "it's so nice the way you always make sure to say hi whenever we're together."

"What happened to your face?" Geofferson asks in that dry way that says he thinks he's being witty.

"Little Slugger got me in the forehead at a charity thing. What happened to *your* face?"

Max audibly chokes behind us. Geofferson's fiancée gives Cooper a second look. I stifle a surprised whimper and bury my face in Cooper's neck.

And Sunny Darling, Sarah's mom, easily the biggest

star here tonight, slides between us all. "Geofferson, if you require attention from the woman you cheated on in order to make a name for yourself in this industry, then perhaps this industry isn't for you. Run along. Go on. Shoo."

And then a commanding voice behind us starts in. "Put my niece—"

"Oh my goodness, are *you* Zinnia?" Libby Rock interrupts. "It is great to meet the woman who helped raise Waverly. What an amazing person you've given the world. You must be incredibly proud of the strong, independent, intelligent woman she's become. It's so hard to let go, but when you know they're very capable of taking care of themselves, that helps, doesn't it?"

Cooper's shoulders relax while Aunt Zinnia stutters.

Stutters.

"What is happening right now?" I whisper while Cooper subtly shifts and sneaks me away from the group making the scene.

"First meeting of the Team Wooperly Support Group. Awesome, isn't it?"

"You…you set this up?"

"I made a couple phone calls to get my family here. I did not sabotage your shoe—though I'm pretty grateful it means I get to carry you around like this—and I didn't even realize who all would be here, but I know good things happen when good people are around."

"Can you sneak us out whatever door you snuck in through?"

"Can and will, and I'll even do you one better. Sunny says no one notices if you sneak out once the movie starts, so we'll head on into the theater, and after we hear your first two songs, we have a date for fried chicken next door to your place."

I lift my head and stare at him.

He's not wearing a cocky grin. Not telling me we *have* to do anything. He's watching me, waiting, like he needs to hear what *I* want, regardless of what he's set up, and then we'll do it.

I could tell him I want him to take me out for ice cream.

I could tell him I want to go to the beach.

I could probably tell him I want to go to the moon, and he'd do everything in his power to make it happen.

"Thank you for being you," I whisper.

And there's the smile.

My favorite smile.

"Fried chicken?" he asks as he carries me into the theater.

I kiss his cheek. "It's a date."

28

Cooper

I'M STARING at the illuminated LA skyline from Sarah's parents' pool deck next door to Waverly's house when Grady drops into the seat next to me and offers me a light beer. "I can't decide if you're in over your head, or if you actually live a life that's much bigger than I thought."

The ladies are inside changing out of their fancy clothes. We snuck out of the premiere one by one after Waverly's first song played. There's fried chicken on the way, along with banana pudding ingredients.

"Yes," I say to the skyline.

There's a soft *coo* noise, and I glance closer at my big brother.

He's cradling Miles, who's barely a month old. I set the beer aside and make the *hand him over* gesture.

"I'm not letting you hold my kid."

"You think I'm gonna drop him?"

"No. But it's my turn."

"You *live* with him."

"And I like it that way. He didn't like the airplane and needs daddy snuggles."

"He needs to learn his Uncle Cooper is hella dependable when his dad's being a butt."

Grady growls.

"Fine," I say. "I'll go hold Beck's baby. She's cuter anyway."

"Sunny has her."

"*Fuck.*"

"Watch your mouth around my kid."

"People who cuss are smarter. You could be giving him a head start, but instead, it's *no, don't do this, don't do that.*"

Grady doesn't answer.

Not right away.

And when he does, he says the worst thing possible.

"You know you could fit in her world if you wanted to."

"Fit just fine, thanks." I don't fit.

I don't belong at movie premieres. I can fake it, but I don't fit. Not really. Not when the best thing to happen at her movie premiere was her heel breaking off.

Tomorrow, I'll be on the sidelines at her concert, completely helpless when it comes to whatever she might need in the middle of the show.

Helpless to be the one at her side if she's hurt or sick, because she's *bigger*.

Helpless to be the one putting her ex in his place for fear that anything I said would reflect poorly on Waverly—and yeah, I cringed *hard* to myself when I realized I'd pulled a total grade school move. What to say and what not to say when I'm out in public on a date with one of the world's top ten most famous stars is not a cheat sheet I've been given yet.

And it's not only that she has this big life.

It's that this big life *suits* her.

Watching her sign autographs for those kids at the baseball diamond yesterday was the exact same as watching her interact with my adopted Little Sluggers back in Copper Valley. She looks at you, and you're the center of the universe.

She makes people feel important. She makes them feel valued and loved.

And it's not just in person.

It's in her music.

The world's a mess. It *needs* art like Waverly's.

She has a mission, and it's bigger than me, it's bigger than baseball, and it's bigger than even she is.

Grady sighs and offers me the baby.

I take him, remembering all over again how tiny and fragile he is and how I need to treat him like the most priceless baseball in the universe.

Babies are awesome. Love holding this little guy.

But it's not enough to pull me out of my *I don't belong here* funk.

"Whoa, dudes, heavy atmosphere," Beck says.

Max grunts. Ava, Beck's baby, gurgles in Max's arms as he takes the seat on my other side.

"You grew up normal," Grady says to Beck.

"As normal as someone as fabulous as me can," he says.

Ava starts crying.

So does Miles.

"Quit pinching my kid," Grady says to me.

"I'm not. Beck's horrifying him."

"I could try singing," Beck offers.

"I could try punching you in the face," Max mutters.

Ava stops crying and coos at him, and after a minute of me

patting Miles on the little tushy and bouncing in my seat, he calms down too.

"As I was saying," Grady whispers in the darkness. "Ryder, you grew up *not in Hollywood*, even if you've always had a Cooper-sized ego."

"I was joking about being fabulous," Beck whispers back. "I was just *pretending* I was Cooper. Weird experience. I don't think I want to do it again. But you do you, Coop. Seems to be working for you."

There's another growl in the darkness.

"Ah, shit. Okay. It *was* working for you." Beck's still whispering. "I've gotten really good at interpreting Judson, and he says if you hurt Waverly, he'll kill you."

There's a grunt of agreement from much nearer behind me.

"Can you save murdering him until *after* the Fireballs win the World Series?" Max asks. "We kinda need the asshole."

Beck gasps. "*Dude.*"

"Jesus. Way to curse it," Grady says. "Now you'll never win."

Judson chuckles.

Guy's scary.

"Dad. Knock it off." Sarah steps out of the house to join us on the deck too. "The entire world saw you kissing Mom's pet pig on *Good Morning America* this morning. No one's buying the idea that you're scarier than the six bodyguards hanging out in the foyer."

"I was totally buying it," Beck says.

"We're already married. You can quit sucking up to him anytime."

"But then he might not buy me ice cream the next time he takes me to the park. Oh! Is that the fried chicken? Is food here?"

A soft light clicks on, illuminating all of us.

My mom, my sister, Sunny Darling, Annika, and Waverly all gape at us.

And I'm pretty sure it's not because Judson's crouched like a tiger about six inches away from my pool chair with a pet pig crouched next to him.

Not entirely, anyway.

"Why are men with babies so hot?" Tillie Jean whispers.

"TJ, I've told you, I'm not interested in brother-sister stuff," I say. "Sorry, Waverly. I told you she was weird."

I think I'm safe.

I'm holding a baby.

Max is holding a baby.

He's not gonna slug me.

TJ won't slug me.

Grady won't even slug me on TJ's behalf.

But Miles—

Oh. My. God.

My sweet little nephew, who weighs like maybe twelve pounds, goes full and total exorcist with whatever it is Annika fed him a little bit ago. He opens his mouth, flops his head to look straight at me, and then his mouth morphs into a firehose of you don't want to know. It's on my chin. Down my neck. Sliding under my shirt.

And I can only sit there gaping at him.

While it just. Keeps. Coming.

Annika cracks up. So does my mom.

And Judson.

Grady's laughing so hard he's hyperventilating. I haven't heard him hyena-laugh like that since high school.

"Aw, man, Sarah, that takes me back," Beck says from the doorway into the house. He takes a massive bite off a fried chicken breast and keeps talking. "Remember that time I handed you a baby right as she had that massive—"

A noise coming from Miles's mid-section cuts him off, and a moment later, what was formerly only coming out of Miles's mouth is now also leaking out of somewhere decidedly south of there.

Grady falls off his chair.

Sarah squeaks. "Oh, god, Cooper, I have *been there*. Do you need—"

I rise, carrying the soiled demon child with me. "I—"

Miles makes another noise, twists in my arms, lets out a noise from his diaper region, and then there's more carnage coming out of his pants.

Annika's trying to muffle her laughter, but she, too, sounds like a hyena.

Tillie Jean's crying through her hysterical laughter.

So's my mom.

Sunny Darling.

Judson Clarke has broken character and is also laughing until he has to wipe his eyes.

And Waverly—my beautiful pop princess who deserves way more than even a guy as successful as I am can give her— flashes me a smile that tells me this is my moment to shine.

This is my moment to prove that I, Cooper Rock, the man who went and got her security team when *she* was sick, can handle what the human body sometimes dishes out.

29

Waverly

HE'S LEAVING.

I need to leave too—I'm due in Toronto for another video shoot and then it's on to Boston and New York for back-to-back shows this weekend.

But all I want is for Cooper to get on my plane with me, for us to fly to Shipwreck and then ignore all of our commitments until we're either hungry or interested in seeing other people again, and when we see those other people, I want them to be Sarah and Beck, and Grady and Annika, and Libby and Clay—yes, Cooper's dad's name is actually *Clay Rock*—and Pop and Nana and Tillie Jean and Max.

"What about that first week in August?" Cooper asks me. "We have a three-game series in Seattle and you'll be in Vancouver."

"Music festival. Non-stop press when I'm not doing meet-and-greets or performing. What about your series in

Minnesota here? I have a drop-in at a fair in Wisconsin, but I could move it earlier in the day so I can spend the night in Minneapolis."

"Could probably work. Oh, hey, you have four days off right before Labor Day. What's that?"

I sigh.

And then I sigh harder.

Cooper's brows lift.

We're hanging out in my bed, unfortunately fully-clothed since Kiva and Scott One will be shoving us into my car for a ride to the airport sometime in the next thirty seconds, and *I don't want to go.*

Is this what it's like to have never rebelled against anything in your life and get all the way to your late twenties before letting loose all of the temper tantrums you've held inside for years, or do I need to get a grip?

November isn't *that* far away.

Sob.

"It's the annual Waverly Sweet Empire Retreat." I drag the words out like I'm saying *I'll be walking on hot coals and sleeping on a bed of high-heeled shoes*, which isn't fair at all to my employees. I love them, and I love doing the retreat every year.

I'll be excited about this tomorrow. I will.

I'm just *tired*.

And sad that Cooper has to leave.

He raises his hand.

I sigh once more, because clearly I haven't been melodramatic enough. Hashtag agrees. He lets out a long sigh from his perch in the window, and then follows it with a mournful yowl.

"Yes, I'm the boss," I say without calling on Cooper to let him ask his question. "Yes, I can cancel. Yes, I can skip. But this is literally the only time all year that I take the time to say thank you and sponsor a break for all of the people who work so hard, and—"

And it's hard to keep talking when he's kissing me this thoroughly.

I loop my arm around his neck.

He pulls me tighter against him.

One of us deepens the kiss.

Maybe both of us. We seem to share a wavelength when it comes to being physical and intimate.

"Time to go," Kiva announces from my doorway.

I groan.

It's Cooper's turn to sigh.

Hashtag rolls his eyes and flips over to lick his butt.

Cooper drops his forehead to mine. "It's sexy how you look out for everyone around you, but don't do it to the detriment of your own health. Bet they'd love a long weekend pass to an all-inclusive with their families as much."

"Accurate," Kiva says. "Now move."

My stomach grumbles in a way it hasn't since right before I went on stage Friday night.

Yesterday, I blew off everything and stayed home in bed with Cooper, and it was *glorious*.

Also, it wasn't totally in bed.

We also spent time in my pool. And in my sauna. And in my movie theater. And in my shower.

I definitely liked the shower the best.

And we spent time reading each other Fiery fanfic, and watching *Who's Your Family?*, and talking about our families, and telling stories about growing up and being on the road, and having *fun*.

"Your cat isn't ready," Kiva says.

Hashtag lifts his face from his butt and gives her a death glare.

"I've got him." Cooper drops one more kiss on my forehead, then scoots off the bed. Since he played superhero cleaning up the baby Thursday night, he's also played superhero with charming my cat.

Hashtag flops onto his back and shows Cooper his belly.

"Who's a good kitty? Who's such a good kitty who can't wait to go get on an airplane with his mommy?"

Cooper Rock makes me want things.

He makes me want *home*. He makes me want *family*.

He makes me want a life.

And he makes me want *him*.

He flashes a grin at me as Hashtag plays the role of a limp rag in his arms. "See? All it took was catnip, kitty treats, a new cat bed, a new cat tree, a fishing pole toy, sixty-three varieties of play mice, and some fresh salmon—but only the salmon from that one market, not the other salmon—and he's the happiest cat on the planet."

"I honestly can't believe I'm going to miss him, but I think I am," Kiva mutters.

Don't ask me how many times I've randomly burst out laughing this weekend.

I couldn't even begin to count.

But it's one more reason that I almost make Cooper late for his flight when we pull up to the airport.

"Why am I not giving you a ride in my plane?" I ask before I let him out of the car.

"Because you're flying to Seattle and I'm flying to Florida." He leans over and kisses my jaw under my ear. "I'll call you."

"*Video* call," I remind him.

"Can't wait."

"Hornball."

"Okay, kettle."

I laugh, but not for long. Not when he lingers with his mouth near my jaw and inhales deeply, like he's memorizing the scent of me.

"I have to go." *God*, the utter despair in his voice.

I feel it too.

Once we go our separate ways, will it ever feel the same as it has this weekend?

Is this the end of the magic?

I grip his hair one more time and kiss him hard. "Go kick some baseball ass."

"As if I'd do anything less."

He grins at me one more time like it doesn't hurt for him to pull away and climb out of the door that Kiva opens for him.

Cameras flash.

"Cooper! Cooper, over here! Did you move in with Waverly? Are you leaving baseball? Are you getting traded to LA? Is that Waverly in the car? Waverly! Waverly, here!"

Kiva slams the door, and Scott One pulls away from the curb, leaving Cooper and Kiva behind with the sharks.

"But—" I say.

He meets my eyes briefly in the rearview mirror, and I sigh and fall back in my seat.

This is how it goes.

Kiva will get Cooper through the paparazzi and security, then she'll meet us at the private hangar where my pilot is waiting with my jet, and all will be normal.

But does *Cooper* know that?

Will Cooper be okay?

He's a grown-up. He's strong. He deals with the media all the time.

But not like this.

And as I'm staring at the crowd in the rear window, for once, I want to wade in.

I want to be there to make sure he's okay and not overwhelmed and that they're not messing with his head before he has to get back on his game for the second half of the season.

"He'll be fine," Scott One says.

"But—"

"If he's not…"

Then he's not cut out to be in your life.

So those are my options.

Make above-average-but-not-A-List guys deal with insane press coverage, or break up with them.

Or walk away from all of the mess, a voice whispers.

My stomach rolls over.

Hashtag yowls in his carrier.

And I remind myself that I have to breathe.

Cooper will be okay. Kiva's with him, and he'll probably call in another fifteen minutes and be like, *Wow, I knew I smelled good, but I had no idea I smelled THAT good*, and we'll laugh, and he'll get on a plane, and I'll get on another plane, and maybe we'll see each other again sometime in August.

Hashtag yowls again.

I unzip his carrier enough to slip my hand inside and rub his furry head. "Same, buddy. I don't understand exactly what you said, but *same*."

30

From the text messages of Team Wooperly

COOPER: I swear on my favorite baseball glove, it was a one-time only thing like five years ago, and I didn't know she was a paparazzo when we hooked up, and I didn't know she'd publish that, and I still don't understand how they made YOU look bad and ME look like a saint, and I'm seriously pissed on your behalf, and I promise, IT WAS YEARS AGO.

Cooper: Right. You're on stage right now and you won't get this for a few hours. Hiramys, I sincerely hope you're on phone duty tonight. Ignore everything else I'm about to text so that you can have plausible deniability.

Cooper: Pop, my grandpa, has gone full pirate. He's PISSED. And he's old. And sometimes he forgets to wear pants, but we're pretty sure he doesn't like pants, so he goes without but tells us he forgets when really... Okay. Not the point.

Cooper: Starting over. Pop's been standing on the crow's

nest above Grady's bakery, using a bullhorn every day to tell everyone to sign the petition Nana's been overseeing to have all tabloids banned from Shipwreck. He might've made the news in Copper Valley yesterday. And then some of the national news networks might have picked it up.

Cooper: So, basically, I'm sorry about Pop and the OTHER coverage in the tabloids too. But none of what he's saying is wrong.

Cooper: Also, for the record, when that fucker standing on second insulted my nail polish and you all in one breath tonight, I wasn't smiling because I was amused. I was smiling because I was picturing myself smacking the shit out of the ball the next time I was up to bat and hitting it so hard and fast that it knocked him on his ass.

Cooper: *gif of the fucker landing on his ass after trying to catch Cooper's line drive in the game earlier tonight*

Cooper: This gif is me reminding you that you can manifest any fucking thing you want to manifest. Except, apparently, removing that godawful story about me and that paparazzo that's circulating faster than my line drive.

Cooper: I am really sorry about that.

Cooper: And I'm more sorry that they keep publishing shit that makes you look like you're the bad guy here. You're not the bad guy. YOU ARE NOT THE BAD GUY.

Waverly: Wow. A girl goes to put on a show and comes back to a novel. Are you okay?

Cooper: Am I okay? AM I OKAY? No, I'm not fucking okay, because I don't know if you're okay.

Waverly: *selfie of herself in a bubble bath, sans makeup, but with a cat sitting at the side of the tub*

Waverly: Have you slept with any other women since we hung out at your house in Shipwreck?

Cooper: Jesus. No. I don't even SEE other women anymore. It's like there are baseball players, there are dudes in other parts of my life, and then there are these genderless other people who are sometimes nice and sometimes ask me questions and we hang out if we were already friends or if we're related, but they're just like, globs of human beings who hold no interest for my libido.

Waverly: And have you told anyone any massive major secrets about me that will show up on the gossip pages soon?

Cooper: *jaw dropped emoji* You even have to ask?

Waverly: I think you needed me to ask so that you could remind yourself that you're not the bad guy here, and I know it.

Cooper: ... So... You're okay?

Waverly: This is just one more day in my life.

Cooper: BUT THIS IS NOT OKAY. This shouldn't be your normal. For the record, when I go talk to Mackenzie, it's because she says she knows people who can curse people, and I am getting the paparazzi fucking CURSED.

Waverly: Are YOU okay? This feels like more than you've ever had to deal with before on a publicity front. Even bigger than the airport last week.

Cooper: Totally get where you're coming from with keeping a stock of antacids on hand. Jesus. How do you live like this?

Waverly: Practice. And faith that the good I'm doing in the world outweighs the bad that comes with the job. Where are you? We could video chat...

Cooper: *selfie of himself on an airplane with a bunch of sleeping teammates around him*

Waverly: You look tired.

Cooper: I miss you. Kinda wish I'd punched that asshole so that I would've gotten suspended and had a few days off to come see you.

Waverly: No, you don't. You handled it exactly the way you should've, and that was even better than stupid caveman antics. Thank you for wearing my nail polish, by the way. That was really sweet.

Cooper: All Diego's idea. He's pissed that they're so relentless they even attacked the color of your new nail polish, he almost couldn't smile for an entire minute before he declared the whole team was painting our nails for good luck tonight. Management's putting him front and center for all of the media calls this week so he can be the one ranting about societal norms and assholes. Also, they've informed me I can't even record my usual advice bits for the kids until I get my emotions under control. Apparently telling kids to kick reporters in the knees if they say bad things about pop stars isn't Fireballs-sanctioned advice.

Waverly: Deep breaths. This will pass. It always does.

Cooper: Sorry I'm being an ass all over again. I just—FUCK. I feel so helpless right now.

Waverly: Sometimes the right thing is ignoring what's wrong. Take joy in knowing that Diego will get a chance to shine here. It's good experience for him. Especially since a cutie-patootie like him will most definitely be getting a few phone numbers from people in my world.

Cooper: He's a really good dude. I should warn him against anyone who tries to tell him he's not good enough. And I swear, that wasn't shade. I know everyone in your circles wants what they see as best for you.

Waverly: I should write a song about him.

Cooper: *side eye emoji* Do I need to worry about something?

Waverly: Only that I stealth-ordered myself a new water-proof vibrator and I'm trying it out in the tub tonight by myself.

Cooper: *sweating emoji* I take it all back. You're evil incarnate. You know I'm on a damn airplane with my entire team right now? That selfie? REAL TIME.

Waverly: The Cooper Rock I've heard about from his sister wouldn't be embarrassed by a natural physical reaction to the idea of his girlfriend naked and pleasuring herself.

Cooper: I'm not embarrassed. I'm frustrated as hell. Popping a boner? It happens to all of us. Rubbing one out on the team plane? Crossing a line. Crossing. A. Line.

Waverly: I'd say this is why I have a private tour bus and my own plane, but you know a little too much about where my interests haven't been for the past year.

Cooper: Until now?

Waverly: Very much until now. *winking emoji*

Cooper: *dead emoji*

Waverly: When do you land?

Cooper: Three hours.

Waverly: *selfie, pouting, surrounded by bubbles*

Cooper: Be honest. Is this revenge for the tabloids today?

Waverly: Nope. I'm just lonely and there haven't been any new Love on Fire episodes and yesterday's Who's Your Family? was super depressing and probably how my story would end if I ever met my sperm donor, and I'm thinking about you and really wishing that when I had my palm read at my label's anniversary party last year, that I would've listened when she told me I'd be happy if I gave it all up and went to live on a mountain.

Cooper: Seriously?

Waverly: She also said I'd one day have a dog named Fluffy, my mother was secretly a reincarnated toad, and that if I sent her four bitcoin, she'd show me where the government hides the aliens, so I assumed she wasn't reliable all around.

Cooper: Did you send the bitcoin?

Waverly: Yes, and I ended up with a treasure map that led me to the bulk nut section at the Whole Foods in Beverly Hills.

Cooper: *nut emoji* Sounds like a real treasure.

Waverly: I'm lying. Of course I didn't pay. I never do anything fun or impulsive like that. I'm boring.

Cooper: You're texting me photos of yourself in a bathtub, talking about giving yourself orgasms with sex toys, giving me the boner of all boners on this never-ending flight, and calling yourself boring? I'd say you're pretty much queening it right now.

Waverly: I don't feel like a queen.

Cooper: And I once again feel like an ass because I should be making you feel like a queen instead of bringing more trouble to your doorstep.

Waverly: If it wasn't you, it would be someone else, and that someone would be far less entertaining and likeable.

Cooper: Is that code for "you're worth it, you sexy beast", or is that code for "I guess I'll take what I have since you're easy right now"?

Waverly: I'm thinking about you and touching my clit right now.

Cooper: *panting emoji* I'm trying very hard—hard, heh— to remember I'm supposed to observe that you didn't answer my question and not get distracted by the images in my head right now.

Waverly: I have a house in Montana that came with a heart-shaped tub big enough for two. I'm imagining you in it with me right now. With candles all around the tub. And your tattoos all wet and glistening. And you kissing me while you're stroking my clit.

Cooper: Fuck. Fuck fuck fuck.

Waverly: You'd be doing magical things to my breasts too. Like that thing you did to my nipples last weekend? I get so horny every time I think about that.

Cooper: How are you typing right now and not drowning while fingering yourself?

Waverly: Dictation.

Cooper: Oh god oh god oh god, now I hear you saying that to yourself in that amazing voice of yours while you're all wet and I AM NOT OKAY, but I sincerely hope you are feeling fabulous.

Cooper: Jesus. I suck at dirty talk. WHY DO I SUCK AT DIRTY TALK?

Cooper: I hope silence means you're ignoring me and giving yourself the orgasm to end all orgasms.

Cooper: And I wish I was there with you.

Cooper: You're fucking amazing, you know that? I don't know another single person in the world who could tackle everything you take on every single day and still be standing at the end of it. It's probably not sexy or a turn-on for me to say that when I hope you really are coming right now, but I wanted you to know. You're a fucking rock star. And I don't mean literally. Clearly, you are, literally. I mean that if you weren't the famous amazing pop goddess that you are, you'd still be doing something else to make the world a brighter place no matter the obstacles anyone threw in your way, and that's fucking amazing. You're fucking amazing. I can't stop saying it, because it's true, and I hope you know it.

Cooper: Okay, can you at least send me proof of life? I need to know you didn't drown.

Waverly: *selfie of herself still in the bathtub, the bubbles messy and all up in her hair, cheeks flushed, eyes dark, and a soft smile on her lips*

Waverly: You give good text. And I think I'm going to sleep better tonight than I have any night since we both left LA.

Cooper: You're so fucking gorgeous.

Waverly: Thank you for believing in me.

Cooper: Jesus. Who wouldn't believe in you?

Waverly: *heart-eye emoji* I'm climbing into bed now. Safe travels. I'll ping you tomorrow. *blowing kiss emoji*

Cooper: Sweet dreams. *blowing kiss emoji* *heart emoji*

31

Cooper

HOLY BALLS, this is a rush.

I'm out with the whole team at a local video arcade-slash-karaoke bar after we clinched our division with tonight's win, guaranteeing us a spot in the play-offs.

Step one to the World Series is complete.

So we're singing and drinking and throwing down at the Skee-Ball lanes and darts and any video game we can find. No spouses. No partners. Just us guys, celebrating one step while still being exceedingly aware that we are not there yet.

We still have work to do.

"Coop! Coop, check it out!" Diego bustles to my side, all grins, and shoves a video in my face showing him and Max karaoke-ing together to one of Waverly's early hits. "He likes me."

I pause in schooling Frankie in Skee-Ball to fist-bump Diego. "You won him over, D. Told you it'd happen."

"Phone away, rookie." Robinson loops around and gets Diego in a headlock. "No cheating."

"I turned off cellular data!" Diego's still grinning as he fights the headlock.

I love that kid.

Waverly's right.

He needs a song written about him.

Jesus.

I miss her.

"Nuh-uh, Romeo," Francisco says. "Quit making moon-eyes. You can see your girlfriend after we go all the way."

"Who's moon-eyeing?" I grin a grin I don't feel at all. "And who's winking at the ladies across the bar? Yeah, I saw you too. C'mon. You're up."

Luca and Brooks race through behind us.

"You lost!" Luca yells. "Hand it over!"

"Never!" Brooks yells back, clutching the meatball porn hat.

Darren's crowing over something Emilio's saying, both of them at the bar having drinks. Max is back on the karaoke stage.

Dude has a voice.

If being the mayor's husband doesn't work out for him once Tillie Jean's running Shipwreck after Max retires, he could go on tour as one of Waverly's backup singers.

Francisco gives me a light punch in the arm. "*Dude.* Cooper. You hit two home runs and saved Baby Ash from Spike and totally made that one kid's day when you signed his shirt. *Quit mooning.*"

I haven't seen my girlfriend in two months is not the right answer here.

Nor is *I'm fucking tired of phone sex and I don't know if that'll get me through the play-offs and I'm starting to get afraid she's tired of it too and she doesn't want to be with me anymore because I'm a high-maintenance asshole who keeps making the news for old shit that makes her look bad.*

"Sorry, Frankie. Past my bedtime."

It's the lamest excuse in the history of lame and also in the history of excuses.

He slings an arm around me. "Aww, you miss your boo. Dude, if I was dating someone who made me smile like she makes you smile, I'd miss her too."

Fuck.

Now I'm getting choked up.

"Elliott! Greene! D! The Coop-meister needs you!"

Every single last one of my teammates across the entire sports bar drops what they're doing to head our way *immediately*.

So do four women.

Nope.

Nuh-uh.

"Do *not* let the women near me," I beg Francisco.

The words haven't even left my mouth before Diego and Max tag-team to intercept the small group.

Luca appears at my side, grabs me in the same headlock Robby was holding Diego in two minutes ago, and ruffles my hair. "C'mon, slugger. We're getting drinks with you surrounded by all of us in the corner booth so you don't make the news again tonight."

We spend another three hours hanging out, and yeah, it's fun.

It's what I need. It's what the team needs. And I love this part of my life.

Mackenzie told me once that the Fireballs were what made

her feel normal after growing up getting picked on for being raised by two drag queens. That even—or maybe especially—in our losing years, we were the other family, the other connection, she needed, and I know she's not alone.

Baseball's in my blood, and the thing is, *it matters*.

I love playing a game that makes a difference in people's lives. I love giving them hope. I love helping them believe.

I love working with kids who want to feel that. I love working with the Lady Fireballs and the Fireballs Foundation to do for Copper Valley what my family's always done for Shipwreck.

No one else could've done what I have for the Fireballs, and that's not ego. That's *action*. And I'm not done with the Fireballs. Not even close.

But I love Waverly too, and I don't know how we can be together when one of the things I love most about her—her mission, her belief, what drives her—is the same thing that drives me, and also the same thing that keeps us physically apart nearly every damn day.

We're both *make a difference in the world* people.

The team finally breaks and all of us head home around two in the morning when the bar closes. We have a game today, yeah, but there's no pressure to win right now, and celebrating a milestone like making it into the play-offs is important.

Also?

I'm banking on management letting me out of a few games and practices to go see my girlfriend before the play-offs start.

Which is the first thing I intend to tell her as soon as she picks up the phone.

But when I dial her number the minute I'm in the back of

Max's big-ass SUV—he's a voluntary designated driver and is dropping a bunch of us off—it goes straight to voicemail.

Duh.

She's in New York.

And she's probably sleeping. Same time there as it is here.

But as my phone comes fully back online, it's not the three voicemails in my inbox that catch my eye.

Nope.

It's the alert on my security system at my house here in Copper Valley.

Someone in a big hoodie and baggy pants, carrying a giant duffel bag, let themselves in thirty minutes ago.

I shoot a look at Max.

He's driving through the dark, nearly-empty streets of downtown Copper Valley like there's nothing going on at all.

Like Tillie Jean isn't plotting something *huge* now that we're in this window where she can fuck with my game with no repercussions.

And they still owe me for the glitter bomb.

I debate telling him I need to pee and asking him if he can drop me off at my place first, decide he'd drop me off last just for shits and giggles, and instead poke Emilio next to me. "Is Marisol gonna kill you for being out late?" I whisper.

Loudly.

Max's eye twitches as he shoots a look at the backseat.

And it works.

I get dropped off first.

But I don't head into the house the normal way.

Oh, hells, no.

Not when Tillie Jean's here causing trouble.

I'm going in the back.

And I'm gonna show her who's the prank boss.

32

Waverly

COOPER'S COUCH in his house in Copper Valley is every bit as comfortable as I'd expect it to be.

While I haven't been here before, I know it's definitely his house. The code got me in the door. His kitchen is stocked with Fireballs paraphernalia. He's sent me selfies from this living room.

Bonus, it smells like him.

Extra bonus, it's the one place I've actually been able to doze in the past forty-eight hours.

Pretty impressive, considering I ditched my entire security team eight hours ago and feel like my entire world is upside down.

They lied to me.

They all lied to me.

You're not eating right, you're not sleeping enough, and frankly, as much as I want to believe Cooper Rock can be a one-woman guy, you're miserable. Yes, I've been expressing my concerns to Zinnia. Yes, I suspected she was behind a few of the media reports about him. But no, I had no idea she was fucking around in his endorsement deals.

I shake my head to get Kiva's voice out of it, and instead hear her asking if this place is actually safe enough for me.

It's Cooper's house. It has to be.

While I don't know if there are alarms on the windows, the blinds are all closed and nobody saw me come in. I *feel* safe here.

Hashtag is sprawled across me purring loudly, and he'll make a complete and total ruckus if anyone comes in the house.

"Thank you for being a cat," I whisper to him.

He lifts his head, purrs in my face, licks a paw, and then puts his head back on my chest.

I check my watch.

Two-thirty in the morning.

My security team will realize I'm missing soon, and I'm well aware they'll track my phone and find me here, but what I don't know is *where the hell is Cooper?*

Is it normal for him to be out this late after a game?

It's definitely not normal for him to have not texted or called me back.

And—*fuck.*

Seriously?

I have no cell signal.

Why do I have no cell signal?

I—*dammit.*

My phone is still on airplane mode.

I toggle the switch to turn it back on, and that's when I hear it.

There's someone in the house.

Hashtag's ears go flat. He lifts his head, then lumbers to his feet, still on top of me.

I cradle him while I sit up. "Cooper?" I whisper.

There's no answer.

No noise either.

Hashtag growls.

The hairs on the back of my neck stand up.

And that's all the warning I get before a gigantic, massive *thing* appears that has to duck and twist to get through the eight-foot doorway from the kitchen area into the living room.

I scream and reach blindly for anything I can find.

Hashtag yowls, hisses, puffs up his fur so he's three times his normal size, and darts for the stairs.

The *thing* freezes in the doorway, like it's stuck, then shoves all the way through.

I have no idea what I'm throwing, but it's hard and heavy and I fling it at the *thing*.

My heart is racing. My mouth is dry. My lungs are too small and my legs are frozen and I can't get off this couch and I'm trapped in a blanket that was complete comfort three seconds ago and now is going to be the reason I die.

I scream and throw something else.

Maybe my phone.

I don't know.

"Waverly?"

"Get out before I kill you!" I yell.

"Fuck! Waverly! It's me!"

I fling something else at the *thing*, beaning it in the head before the voice registers.

"Cooper?"

The thing twists and bounces back against the wall, making

326

a picture frame fall. "I thought you were Tillie Jean!" Cooper yelps.

"What are you doing?" I shriek back.

"Pranking my sister!"

"*I am not your sister!*"

"I know! But I didn't know! Jesus! Fuck! How do I get out of this thing?"

I'm crying.

I am full-on, pop diva sobbing.

The *thing* hits a light switch, and— "*Oh my god!*" I gasp.

"Why—how—hold on, I'm getting out of this thing. The zipper's stuck."

He's dressed up like Ash, the baby dragon mascot, except...*bigger*. And where the Ash I'm used to has adorable little dragon horn bumps and cute little ears and a diaper, this Ash has two pigtails and baseball pants and sneakers.

And tomorrow, or maybe the next day, or sometime in a few months, I might think she's cute.

Right now?

Right now, that costume is between me and a Cooper hug, and I hate it.

"Why do you even have that?" I gasp as I try to stop myself from sobbing. My heart is still on overdrive and my arms are shaking.

"So management can't age her up yet."

Only Cooper.

And the crazy part is, *this is why I like him so much.*

He doesn't let conventions and rules and *you don't do that* stop him from what's important to him.

So am I not important?

"Hey, hey, it's okay. I'm gonna get out of this thing and

Jesus, I'm so glad to see you. I missed you. Are you really here or am I hallucinating?"

"You signed on for the Ritz-Carlton endorsement deal," I sob.

"What? Yeah. My agent said—"

"Aunt Zinnia picked you—*hic!*—so that I'd get mad and think—*hic!*—you're using me."

Dammit. Hiccups do *not* make this better.

And suddenly I have a 9-foot teenage dragon girl kneeling in front of me. "I'll quit. I'll walk away. I won't do it. I—*fuck.* Can I be a high-maintenance asshole and ask you to unzip me?"

"You're not—*hic!*—high maintenance."

"I can't even hug you right now because I was trying to prank my sister."

I don't know how I make my fingers work to get the costume's zipper unstuck, but I do. And the minute Cooper's half-free of the damn thing, he's tackling me in the warmest, tightest, safest hug.

And it makes me cry harder.

"I'm texting my agent the minute I let you go to tell him I won't do it," he murmurs into my hair. "*God*, I missed you. I can't believe you're here. You smell amazing. It's okay. It's okay. I've got you."

"I have to fire my aunt."

"Aw, Waverly."

"She's getting worse. And worse. And the past—*hic!*—few weeks—and I thought it was all in my head—and then—*hic!*—she keeps putting things on my schedule and—*hic!*—Kiva says —Kiva says she made them say—*hic!*—made them say my —*hic!*—nail polish—*hic!*—was ugly."

He's stroking my hair and peppering my head with kisses

and letting me sob all over his shoulder and tightening his arms around me with every word I utter, and *this is what I want.*

God, I missed him.

I missed his touch. I missed his strength. I missed his hugs and the way he smells like a warm mountain pine tree and the way he doesn't hold anything back. I miss his kisses. I miss making love to him, and I miss just *being* with him.

"What can I do?" he asks. "What else can I do?"

"Take me away," I whisper. "Just take me away."

His grip tightens even harder, and I know what it means.

I can't, Waverly.

You can't either, Waverly.

But what if we could?

What if we could?

He shifts, slipping one arm under my knees and the other around my back, and then he's lifting me and carrying me to the stairs. The costume is crumpled on the floor. All of the lights are still on. I have no idea where Hashtag is.

But everything's okay.

I'm safe.

Even though neither of us has said the words, I know I'm loved.

And tomorrow, I'm fixing what's broken in my life.

No matter how hard it is.

33

Cooper

My life has finally caught up with me.

"Three reasons I shouldn't kill you right now." Levi Wilson drops into the seat Waverly has just vacated inside Crusty Nut, my dad's restaurant in Shipwreck, and glares at me. "Go."

"I love her."

The glare coming from one of my oldest famous buddies goes darker than a cloudy moonless midnight. "Do not make me murder you. I have *way* bigger things to live for, but I swear—"

I shoot a look at the bathroom, where Giselle, Levi's lead protection agent, is standing and waiting for Waverly to come back out, then lean across the table and say the one thing that I can't say to anyone else. "What the *fuck* is in this for me if I don't?"

Levi makes a *go on* gesture.

So I do. "She's gone more than you used to be. I'm never

home. I'm bored on the road. Pranks aren't fun when all I want is to be with her. I spent six hours hanging with the team after we clinched the fucking *division* last night and couldn't stop counting the minutes until I could be done and call her. Food tastes like shit when we're apart. *Torres* zinged me in the locker room with the easiest crack about pirates I've ever had aimed at me. Management's pissed at the optics of me taking two days off right after we secured a spot in the play-offs to *go play with my girlfriend*, and I'd play like shit if I hadn't, and *I hate playing like shit.*"

"So you say you love her because you don't want to play like shit."

I glare right back at him. "I had to call in a favor from you to get security on her and I feel like an inept asshole for not being able to take care of her myself, and I feel like the four other favors I'm calling in so I can call off the favor I called in from you won't be enough either. So yeah. Go on. Murder me, but before you do, promise me you'll take care of Waverly when I'm gone."

He leans back and rubs his chin, still glaring at me. "I'm really fucking pissed that I believe you."

"We've been tabloid official for two months. Where the fuck have you been?"

"I thought Tripp was going along with shit her team was making up to piss me off, and there's this code," he mutters. "You don't ask your friends if it's fake. They'll tell you if they want you to know."

I barely stop myself from slugging him. *"You fucking knew they did that?"*

Giselle looks at the bathroom door, takes two steps toward me, then stops when Levi jerks his head back toward the women's bathroom door.

Swear to fuck, Dad's place is getting an upgrade this winter. No more of this one-seater, locked bathroom shit. When Waverly's in Shipwreck, she's using any bathroom she wants with a guard standing in the same room but not in the actual stall.

"Everyone knew Zinnia did that," Levi tells me. "Maybe not to the extent she's apparently pushed it, but sometimes, you have to take advantage of the press the same way they take advantage of our privacy."

I scrub a hand over my face. "Jesus."

"So what's the end game here?" he asks. "How are you even seeing each other?"

And isn't that the question? "Season's over in another seven weeks or so."

He stares at me without blinking.

Doesn't have to say what he's thinking next.

And what happens when you leave for spring training in February?

We go all the way, the team gets about three months off.

And if we *don't* go all the way—

Jesus.

My nuts just shriveled and every part of me answered that for me. *If you don't go all the way, you keep playing baseball until you do.*

No pausing.

No hesitation.

And the play-offs?

We're in them, but *nothing* is guaranteed. This is when shit gets real. When three of us having alternate off-nights can sink us in the first round of the play-offs, before we even get close to the World Series.

And if we still go all the way?

I'm not done. *I'm not done.* I can *feel* it, and the one thing I've never questioned in my career is how I feel.

So my three months with Waverly will pass in the blink of an eye, and then we're right back where we started with her on the road, me on the road, and maybe our schedules will cross once or twice a month until we get a couple months together all over again at the end of the season.

We can't keep doing this.

We can't.

One of us has to give something up, and that someone's gonna have to be me.

"I'm gonna deal with that when I have to deal with it," I tell him.

The bathroom door opens. Waverly steps out in short jean shorts, a Shipwreck shirt she stole out of my closet in Copper Valley this morning, no make-up, and a ponytail, and my heart rolls over and asks her to rub its belly.

She's goddamn gorgeous.

And it's not her curves, not her makeup, not her exercise or skincare routine.

It's this inner glow that says *I believe in the good in the world, and I want to be the good in the world.*

"Fuck," Levi mutters again.

"You like hamburgers?" Dad asks Waverly as she passes the bar, Giselle right behind her. "Fried chicken? Meatloaf? Cooper might not offer you more than French fries, but it's only because he took a ball to the head last night."

Her eyebrows shoot up as she looks at me.

I shake my head.

"Well, he's *acting* like he took a ball to the head last night," Dad amends. "All loopy and big-eyed and swoony. It's like he has a concussion."

"Did your father just tell her you're crazy about her?" Levi asks quietly while Waverly smiles and charms him even more while she asks him for whatever his favorite menu item is.

"Are you bad with subtlety, or is he?" I reply. "Because that was really not-subtle subtle."

Levi flips me off.

Waverly slides into my lap since Levi's sitting in her seat. "Hey, you," she says to him. "I thought you were busy all day."

He murders me with his eyeballs. "Something came up."

"Don't be a dick," she says. "Did I come after you when you were dating Violet Quinn and I warned you that if you were using my friend as a publicity stunt, I'd hunt you down and cut off your balls? No, I did not. *Back. Off.*"

I squeeze her leg. "I didn't know you were friends with Violet Quinn."

"Girls gotta stick together, especially when one of us is having a hard time."

"How's Aspen?" Levi asks.

She grins at him. "Aww, look at you changing the subject. She's good. You looking for someone to boost your visibility with another collaboration? I heard a few sample tracks for the next album she wants to cut, and if you want to stay relevant…"

"Trash-talker. You okay?"

Waverly sighs. "Today."

"Let me know if you need anything."

And that's supposed to be me too.

But I can't help with this one.

I can do a lot.

But not enough.

Not when I'm due on the ballfield eight or nine months a year.

"Here." I hand her a cookie off the tray we brought over from Grady's bakery. "Cookies help."

"Can you not sit on his lap?" Levi says.

"You're in my seat," she replies around a mouthful of chocolate chip cookie.

He points to the other two chairs at our four-top table.

She shrugs. "You're in *my* seat. And also, Cooper tells me siblings annoy each other, and you're the closest I have, and I also don't like the look you're giving to the guy who scared the shit out of me in a mascot costume last night, so…"

Levi glares at me. *"You have the fucking secret missing mascot costume?"*

I gape at Waverly. *"Did you just sell me out?"*

She laughs so hard she almost chokes, and Levi, Giselle, Dad, and I all trip over ourselves to find her something to drink.

"What are you doing?" My mom hollers from the kitchen. She hustles in looking horrified. "What are you doing to Waverly? This is her day off. *Quit tormenting her.* You poor thing. Here. Cooper said you love green tea."

Waverly stops coughing long enough to smile at my mom, who's shoving a to-go mug from The Muted Parrot, Mom's coffee shop, at her. "I do. Thank you, Libby."

Mom fusses.

Dad fusses.

I fuss.

Giselle hovers and Levi watches us all, until he shoves to his feet, shaking his head.

"Whatever it is, don't do it," Waverly says.

I want to punch him for having a silent language with my

girlfriend that I can't have because we're never in the same fucking place at the same fucking time.

He shakes his head again. "I'm leaving. Promised Ingrid I'd get Hudson from aftercare. You're in good hands here. You need anything else, call me."

"Levi?" Waverly prompts.

My friend looks at me.

And I suddenly get it too.

He never thought he'd see the day Cooper Rock would fall. Definitely not fall this hard. And never, *ever* for a woman so high above him in the stratosphere that it's a small miracle she's sitting here, with me, in my dad's small-town restaurant, fitting in as naturally as if she were born here.

"Don't make that face at my son," Mom tells Levi. "We have *always* believed in him, and we don't tolerate anyone who doesn't. Even the fancy-pants big-shots like you."

"Just gonna take a minute, Mrs. Rock." He smiles at her.

Waverly drops her head against mine. "Your parents are adorable," she whispers.

"Wanna borrow them? Anytime. Say the word."

"Can I borrow you for a while first?"

"Absolutely."

She smiles and kisses my cheek, and yeah.

I'm so fucking deep in the hole that is love that I don't know if I'll ever get out.

And I don't care.

34

From the text messages of Team Wooperly

WAVERLY: I'm back in LA, safe and sound. Amazing game tonight. I can't believe there's only two weeks left in the regular season. I told Hiramys to rearrange my schedule so I can make at least one of your playoff games, but things will be TIGHT. *frowny face emoji*

Cooper: It feels like you've been gone for seventeen years.

Waverly: I sent Tripp and Lila a massive thank-you basket for them letting me have you for two days more than I should've kept you away from baseball.

Cooper: Did you send yourself a massive thank-you basket for taking a little time off?

Waverly: No.

Cooper: Good thing I did then. Better news? There's more where that came from. Anytime you're missing Shipwreck, text me. Or Grady or Annika. Or my parents. Probably not Tillie Jean. She's still super pissed that she didn't get to participate in stealing that mascot costume. I'm pretty sure I need to go into hiding after the season's over. Usually, I take her pranks like I deserve them, because I do, but I have this awful feeling she's upped her game and I'm a dead man.

Waverly: *selfie of herself with her jaw dropped in front of the largest box known to man, stuffed full of goodies from Shipwreck*

Cooper: Dammit. I told Grady the BIG box. He must've kept the pirate ship for Miles. Not that I can blame him. Kid's cute.

Waverly: Oh my god, you are utterly ridiculous, and I could not love this more. I thought I had everything money could buy. I was wrong. I was so wrong.

Cooper: Most of what's packed in there is love.

Waverly: Stop. I swore I was done crying until I've finished my badass boss list, and you are not helping.

Cooper: You tackling that today?

Waverly: *GIF of Ares Berger sighing*

Cooper: Not to be that guy, but I noticed your stomach didn't bother you at all once we were settled in Shipwreck...

Waverly: *gif of someone shaking out the Tums*

Cooper: *gif of himself wearing a Fireballs cape*

Waverly: My last four shows of this tour are in the next four weeks, and then I have a week of press stuff to tease my next album, and then you'll be king of the baseball world a week or so after that, so I'm going to do what I have to do. But not yet.

Cooper: I hate this.

Waverly: She's the only family I have. It's complicated. And I don't want to end up getting so upset that I cancel my shows. It's not my fans' fault that I haven't done what I should've done years ago. Another few weeks won't hurt.

Cooper: You okay with Kiva and the Scotts?

Waverly: They're on notice. Scott Two cried. I didn't expect that. But we cleared the air and they know who the boss is. They said Hiramys has been so busy worrying about me that she was totally in the dark. So good news is, Hiramys is still amazing. Bad news is, there might be a lot of turnover in Waverly Sweet, Inc., this winter.

Cooper: Tell me what I can do to help.

Waverly: Make me laugh. Distract me when I complain. Spend your off-season with me.

Cooper: In case I wasn't clear – I'll be there the minute I'm free. And if I haven't told you, the play-offs are where things get weird. Upsets happen. Miracles happen. I might be seeing you sooner than I thought, which I have very, very conflicted feelings about. And I shouldn't tell you that, but I want to be honest.

Waverly: *laughing emoji* *crying emoji* Oh, god, if you go all the way – you'll have parades and other appearances, won't you? Have you ever done the late-night circuit? YOU WILL BE ON ALL THE SHOWS.

Cooper: Eh. If they want me, they can wait for when I feel like showing up.

Waverly: COOPER. Completely serious here. Do you know what that could do for post-career opportunities?

Cooper: Yeah, it'd turn me into Roy Kent.

Waverly: Roy Kent?

Cooper: Oh Em GEE! Gasp! No! WAVERLY. Tell me you've seen Ted Lasso. TELL ME YOU'VE SEEN TED LASSO.

Waverly: Yeah, but... Roy is like, Mr. Grouchy. You wouldn't know grouchy if it donned a pirate hat and a baby dragon mascot costume and pantsed you at second base.

Cooper: I just mean I don't see my future involving TV, so why would I spend my nights anywhere but with you?

Waverly: DAMMIT again. I'm walking away from my

phone because every time you say sweet things, it makes me tear up. I miss you. I miss you a lot.

Cooper: By December, you'll be completely tired of me. I'm best in small doses. Ask my teammates. They have to live with me for like nine months of the year.

Waverly: I have this text message from Diego who says the locker room wasn't the same without you, but that he's glad I got to have you for a few days. And then he sent me other videos of the whole team saying nice things about you, and none of them appeared to be under duress, so…

Cooper: All CGI.

Waverly: You are such a goof.

Cooper: *gif of himself having a twerk-off with an umpire after getting called out at first base*

Waverly: Hiramys just got here. She has outfits for me to approve and a schedule to discuss, and then I need to get to bed. Sleep well. Xoxo

Cooper: *heart emoji* You sleep better.

35

Waverly

ONE MORE WEEK. *One more week. One more week.*

My stomach is cramping constantly and I haven't eaten anything but crackers in three days. My head hurts if I think about anything too hard. And after a completely tumultuous play-off season, Cooper's first World Series game is tonight.

But all I can think is *one more week.*

Tops.

"You're releasing your tenth studio album in twelve years soon," Calista Finley says from her pink velvet seat across from me on the set of her daytime talk show in Burbank. She's a tall Black lady who started as a comic about the same time that I got my break in music, and as much as I adore her, I don't want to be here right now. "How does it feel to be on top of the world?"

"I think I could ask you the same, Ms. Seventh Emmy in a row, *plus* your third Critics Choice Award. High five, rock star." I smile at her and lean in for that high five while the audience goes crazy.

She slaps my hand but waves her other like I'm embarrassing her.

I probably am.

But come on. *Seven Emmys*? In a row? And so many more accolades under her belt than I could even begin to name?

She *is* a rock star.

"That was months ago," she says.

"And it's still amazing." I look at the audience expectantly. "Isn't it?"

They burst into wild applause again, and I give them my pop star smile.

It's the one I don't feel, but that I have to fake for *one more week* because this is only the first of seventy million appearances I have to promote my new album, and if I have a nervous breakdown on set because it's one more week until I see my boyfriend again, and one more week until I demote Aunt Zinnia to just being my aunt, then maybe I don't have what it takes to be in this business.

"Stop changing the subject." Calista gives me the friendly evil eye. It's like she's trying to be mad but she's incapable of it.

"How's your puppy?" I ask her. "Is she potty trained yet?"

"You are *still* changing the subject."

"Let's be real here. Betty Bite is *way* more interesting than me. Cuter too. I could *not* pull off bangs the way she does."

A picture of Calista's puppy flashes on the screen. Betty Bite's a young mutt with fluffy brown and black fur, and I want to squeeze her every time I see her picture.

"Oh, she's gotten so big," I squeal while a wave of *aaawws* and cheers sweep through the live studio audience again.

Thank you, Hiramys, for giving me ten thousand talking points today that are *not* my career or the tabloid coverage wondering how long I'll keep Cooper around once I don't have the excuse of our schedules to keep us apart.

I've spent a grand total of fewer than two weeks total with him in person since we ran into each other again in March, but we've texted and called each other so much that I feel like he's both been by my side this entire time, and also like he's been living on the moon.

Calista laughs. "That's Betty Bite. She's big and trouble. She's the best. But don't leave your…unmentionables…where she can get them. Or your vintage record collection. But if you have a weird gift from that relative that no one talks about that you need to dispose of in an innocent way, Betty Bite has your back."

"Is Betty Bite what really happened to that full-size Beck Ryder pillow that Levi Wilson got for Christmas?"

She makes a terrible poker face. "I have no idea what you're talking about. I would never have loaned my dog to a pop star so that he could innocently dispose of a terrible gift from an underwear model."

The audience laughs.

"Speaking of Levi, I hear he has opinions on you having a boyfriend for the first time since your big break-up," she says.

The audience goes apeshit crazypants like all of these teenage girls love Cooper as much as they love me.

And honestly, who wouldn't?

He recorded a podcast with Brené Brown that aired last week, and if I wasn't head over heels for him before hearing him talk with her about how important failure is to success, I would've been now.

Also?

Yes, that was totally me arranging it. No regrets.

Cooper might be a goofball, but he's also grounded. He prioritizes what matters, and he understands *why* it matters, and he recognizes that when people are given the freedom to be who they are and thrive without having to make excuses or justify their choices, *that* is when magic happens.

But we have an agreement, and I'm sticking to it as much as he did on the podcast.

We're not discussing our relationship in public.

But that doesn't mean I can't joke about it.

"I mean, Levi's a man?" I shrug. "He has a lot of opinions on things that are out of his control."

"Oooh, snap with the comeback about men!" Calista cackles. "So there's trouble in paradise for you and Levi Wilson?"

"Oh, no. Not at all. We adore each other." I launch into a story about how Levi's girlfriend's kids' pet squirrel almost got itself a starring role in our collaboration video, which I have full permission to share from my dear friend who called me last week and told me he never would've picked Cooper if I'd asked him if he had any friends I could date, but that I couldn't find a better guy who'd be a more committed partner if I contracted the most brilliant geneticists in the world and asked them to create him in a petri dish.

And then he'd added *not that you need my permission. But you have my and Ingrid's support on whatever you need.*

My nerves are fading as I get more comfortable in the chair, so when Calista asks if I'm up for taking questions from the audience, it's an easy yes.

It's always an easy yes, even if I'm still feeling the nerves.

"Hi, Waverly," the first audience member says as she approaches the microphone in the aisle. She's probably nine, maybe ten, with white skin, freckles, braces, and a quivering voice. "I'm—wow, I love you so much."

I smile at her. "Aww, you are too sweet. What's your name?"

Her chin wobbles. "Yolanda," she whispers.

"Hi, Yolanda. I love your glasses. Those are super cute."

She touches her glasses and beams. "I love you," she says again. Her mom nudges her, and she takes a huge breath that the mic picks up, and I want to hug her and promise her I'm a normal girl too.

"How do you sing for three hours straight without having to pee?" she asks.

"*Yolanda,*" her mom whispers while the rest of the audience laughs.

"Oh my gosh, that is the *best* question," I say. I drop my voice. "Wanna know a secret?"

Yolanda nods while her mother mouths *Oh my God, I'm sorry.*

"I am the world's fastest pee-er." I screw up my face and look at Calista. "Is that a word? Pee-er?"

"It is now," Calista replies. "How fast can you pee?"

"So I have, like, about forty-five seconds for costume changes between sets, and I have this signal for my team if I need to use the bathroom, so they know to follow me straight to the toilet if I need a break between sets, right?" I look back at Yolanda. "I have to change costumes so fast that I have people helping me pull off one outfit and put the other on and I have to pee in front of them."

She wrinkles her nose in horror.

The audience laughs uncomfortably.

But you know what?

No one's laughing at Yolanda.

"We only recommend that when you're over eighteen and give consent for people to watch you and help you change clothes," Calista says.

"Oh, for sure," I agree. "There are only about six people in my life that I'd trust to help me with costume changes."

"My cousins helped me pee when I got married," Calista says. "Do you know how hard it is to pee in a wedding dress?"

"I do, actually."

"Back up, back up." She smiles at Yolanda. "Hold two seconds, sweetie, because we need to find out when Waverly *got married*."

"Oh, no, I didn't get married. It's for my next video. And I am probably in a ton of trouble for saying that."

"Psh. You're the boss."

"Good point. We shot that video in this plane that makes it feel like you're in space. I had to take three practice flights on it first so we'd be sure I wouldn't throw up, and *then* I had to pee mid-flight, when we were shooting, while I was in the dress, and do you know how small airplane bathrooms are?"

"Was it one of those dresses with the massive skirts?"

"I had like six crinolines on underneath this thing. I barely fit in the airplane bathroom by myself, and my aunt's there yelling *don't let the hem touch the floor*, and my publicist was on her first flight, so she'd actually puked already, but she was guarding the door because we couldn't close it and there were cameras everywhere, and video of me stuffed into an airplane bathroom, peeing in a wedding dress is the *last* thing anyone wants to see."

I make a face.

The audience laughs. I realize *that* will be the clip about me all over the internet in approximately six hours, and you know what?

Fuck it.

Yolanda's beaming at me like I'm her hero.

Totally worth it.

"Okay, now that we've grossed everyone out talking about bodily fluids, next question." Calista turns to a brown-skinned teenager wearing a T-shirt from my last tour who's standing in the next aisle. "What's your name, sweetie?"

"Hi, I'm Hayami," she replies.

"Hi, Hayami." I smile at her too. "Oh my gosh, is that glitter on your boots? Those are amazing. Where's my stylist? Is she backstage? We need these boots in our lives."

"For real?" Hayami asks. "My cousin says glitter boots are over."

"Glitter boots will never be over as long as I have breath in my body. We're gonna be eighty-year-old ladies rocking the glitter boots together. Own what you love."

Her smile lights up the whole studio. "I have a question."

"Go right ahead."

"Do you really have a boyfriend?"

There's a titter from the younger members of the audience and a chuckle from their mothers.

"I do, but I don't like to talk about him, because some things should stay private."

"I think you should date that guy from the superhero movie."

"Aww, I'm sure he'll be flattered."

"He is *really* cute," Hayami says.

I know exactly who she's talking about, and she's right. He's very cute.

He also knows it.

"Cute doesn't always make the best boyfriend." Calista points to the audience, sweeping her finger and her gaze around like she's making eye contact with half the teenage girls in here today. "Demand what you're worth from your partners. Don't settle for what looks good. Go with what makes you *feel* good, inside and out."

"Are you an inspirational speaker when you're not being funny?" I ask her.

"The truth is in the comedy, and sometimes, that's the only way people will hear it." She points to the last aisle in the audience. "And now—oh. Well, look at this. We don't see this very often when you're visiting, do we?"

The next audience member with a question is a white man who looks about fifty. He has salt-and-pepper hair, a husky build, and he's wearing a button-down white shirt over jeans.

Don't be creepy. Don't be creepy. Don't be creepy.

I shouldn't judge.

I shouldn't.

But after this many years in the business, I get a vibe, and I am getting a vibe.

"What's your name, sir?" Calista asks.

He clears his throat awkwardly in the microphone, winces, does it again, and then blurts, "Norm."

"Hi, Norm." I smile, but I'm still silently begging him to not be creepy. My stomach rumbles, and I catch sight of Kiva hovering off-stage, like she knows it.

"You a big Waverly Sweet fan?" Calista asks.

"I—" He pauses, his eyes go shiny, and then he smiles.

Déjà vu washes over me and my gut tightens.

Have I met this guy before?

"I—can I sing for you?" he asks me.

If a teenage girl asked me that, it's a no-brainer. It's a *yes*, and I'm going to tell her she's amazing no matter what.

When a middle-aged dude asks?

"You sing?" Calista asks him.

His cheeks are going ruddy. He meets my gaze, and that déjà vu hits again. Why do his eyes look familiar? "Yeah," he says. "I—I sing a little. I—"

He stops stuttering, and suddenly launches into the chorus of "You Gotta Believe," one of my early hits that I wrote when I was struggling hardcore with the press covering every last embarrassing thing I'd ever done, when record sales weren't as strong as my label wanted, and when I felt like all of my dreams were out of reach.

It was my reminder to myself that I could get through the tough times to make my dreams come true, and it took on a life of its own when it released.

Chills are rushing all over my skin as Norm sings it.

The entire studio has gone silent, save for his baritone voice, right on pitch, his rhythm perfect.

Did I say chills?

What do you call it when your chills get goosebumps?

Who *is* this guy? Why do I feel like I know him? And why do I want to go throw up?

He stumbled over the last line in the chorus, glancing around at the gape-mouthed audience of mostly moms and young girls around him, and abruptly stops. "I—sorry. And thank you. I just wanted—"

"Oh, wow, that was *amazing*." I beam at him and clap. That's what you do, even when every system inside your body is squirming and roiling and yelling *something is wrong*.

The audience erupts in cheers too, and I shoot a glance off-camera, to where Kiva is standing ready.

We've been on shakier ground the past few weeks, but I know she sees that I'm nervous. Hiramys pops up behind her too, clearly ready to leap into action if need be.

Aunt Zinnia's hovering beyond them, her face pale.

I hope the audience can't tell how creeped out I am, especially since I can't even define why I'm creeped out.

"Norm, what was *that*?" Calista says as the audience's cheers die down. "And how have you been hiding from the music industry for all these years? Someone get Simon Cowell on the phone. *Well done*, sir. Well done."

He blushes so deep that it goes all the way down his neck, and he looks at me again. "I—thank you. For letting me sing. I've wanted to sing to you ever since—well, ever since I found out I'm your father."

Yep.

Full alarm bells.

Kiva rushes the stage. Calista's security people quietly move to the top of the stairs leading down this man's aisle.

He shoots a look around. "I'm sperm donor number one-four-six-seven-three from the *Next Gen* facility in San Francisco," he blurts, talking faster and faster like he knows he's about to be thrown out. "I registered with *MatchDNA*, and they sent me a new match with your name last week, and I—look." He points to his face. "We have the same eyes. And—"

"And we'll be cutting this part before it airs," Calista says quietly as the show's security team surrounds him and removes his access to the mic.

"I don't want anything, Waverly," he yells. "I don't want anything. I just wanted to say I'm proud of you and making that donation is the best thing I've ever done with my life."

I touch my face.

Then my throat, because it's the closest thing to my voice.

Then my stomach, which is in absolute panic *what the fuck just happened* mode.

And I look at Calista.

You okay? she mouths.

I open my mouth to answer her—*no, I've never done a DNA test*—but I suddenly can't.

Because my stomach is doing what it does best.

And there is no way I'm going to reach a bathroom in time.

I rise, ready to bolt, and I make eye contact with Aunt Zinnia.

She knew.

She knew.

Oh my god.

I try to stumble off stage before retching, and I don't make it.

Stupid stupid stupid stomach.

"You knew," I gasp at her as the crowd makes horrified noises behind me and more production staff and security rushes around us. *"When? How? What the ever-loving FUCK, Aunt Zinnia?"*

Oh god. Oh god oh god oh god. My stomach isn't done.

And it's not the only thing upset.

"I just wanted to protect you," she stammers. "I can't protect you if I don't know."

I clutch my midsection. "You're fired."

"Waverly—"

The nausea is winning. The nausea is winning, and this life is completely and totally losing.

I want to be alone.

I want to be safe.

I want a hug.

I want *Cooper*.

And instead, I have people I don't know finding out that other people know where I came from, and me puking all over will be front-page news in three seconds, and I can't have Cooper, because he's getting ready for the game of his life.

"Waverly—"

"When?" I demand. "How? Is this real?"

"You asked me to."

"*When?*"

"After your laser eye surgery," she whispers.

"Oh my *god*, Zinnia," Hiramys gasps as she shoves a bucket at me. "*She was high as a kite.*"

"Waverly—" Aunt Zinnia starts, all of the placating, *you know I know what's best for you* baloney hovering in her voice, and I can't do it anymore.

"*No.*" Oh, god, here it comes again. I try to dart around her, clutching the bucket, which isn't enough. I know the bathroom is close. But *where is it*? "No. You are *fired*. And I—"

I'm alone.

That's what I am. I have people who want to be my family. I have people who are paid to protect me. I have people I want to be with.

But I'm all alone.

36

Cooper

HOLY. Fucking. Shit.

This is it.

This is the game.

The Fireballs are playing in the World Series. We start tonight.

"We're *here*," I whisper to Diego and Max as we stand at the railing of our home dugout at Duggan Field. The stands have been draped with official banners and flags wherever they can find room to drape banners and flags.

Max claps D on the shoulder. "You have no idea how lucky you are to be doing this in your very first year in the show."

"I know, Happy Max," Diego replies reverently. "I know."

I snap a picture of the empty field and text it to Waverly.

We did it.

She knows we did it. She knows we're here. We've been talking every day, multiple times a day, usually for about four minutes at a time as one of us is rushing from one commitment to another.

She has back-to-back tapings to start the hype for her next album somewhere in LA all day today and probably won't see this for a few hours.

I text the photo to my family group text next.

My mom replies with a crying emoji.

Everyone does. Mom, Dad, Grady, Annika, Annika pretending to be Miles, Pop, Nana, Tillie Jean.

Even Max, who's standing right next to me.

"Whoa," Francisco says behind me. "This is like, *ours*. It's our home field."

"We're doing this," Brooks says behind him.

"We are so fucking doing this," Emilio agrees.

Four games.

We have to win four of the next seven games, and when —*when* we do—we'll do what no one ever thought possible.

We'll do what *I* never thought possible.

I mean, I thought it was possible.

But I'd started to doubt I'd see it in my career. I'd started to wonder if the Fireballs were truly cursed and if I'd wasted the best years of my baseball career reaching for something that no one else around me believed in.

I'd started to wonder if I *didn't* have what it took to make it happen all on my own. If I wasn't enough. If even my over-whelming belief in what was possible wasn't big enough to overcome the obstacles.

But then I heard Tripp wanted to buy the team, and yeah, you're damn right I made sure I spent as much time as I could telling him what I thought the team needed.

And then our former owner died, completely unexpectedly, and he left the team to a woman none of us had ever heard of.

A woman who came in like a bulldozer, scaring the shit out of us with all of the changes she implemented on day one and kept making on days two, three, four, etc. What was hope at new management turned into temporary fear that she'd make it worse.

As if things could get worse.

But Tripp believed too, and he got himself a role as the team's new president.

It was the only way the commissioner would agree to not move us to Vegas, and even then, we only had last year to prove we had what it took to stay in the league as the Fireballs.

And it turns out, Lila's a lot like me. She's never met a challenge she couldn't take on.

With style.

And so the two of them found a way to work together to rebuild the coaching staff, invested in players, launched what everyone thought was an insane mascot contest that would ruin everything and instead brought fans back in droves, even fell in love and got married, and now here we are.

Despite superstitions. Injuries. Illnesses. The teammates we lost to trades, the family members with health scares, our own egos getting in our own ways.

Arguments with coaches.

Slumps.

Fans who couldn't even talk to us becoming part of the Fireballs family, like Mackenzie.

Players who didn't want to be here last year, like Brooks, who'd sacrificed his own personal life for the sake of his own home team that traded him to the worst team in baseball. Luca, who's more or less the most-traded guy in baseball and just wants a home team and still doesn't trust that he gets to stay.

Darren, who's been with the team so long that he has that same fear that we'll wake up and find out this is all a dream.

We've all had our ups and downs, our doubts, our hopes, our worries on and off the field.

But *we're here*.

Game fucking One of the World fucking Series.

From worst of the worst to best of the best in two seasons.

Doing the absolute impossible and bringing a city back to baseball in the process.

I swipe my eyes.

God, I wish Waverly were here.

Third game. Third game of the series, she can make it.

Until then, I'm playing like she's here, and I'm calling her the minute every game is done.

Not for phone sex.

But because I want to hear her voice.

And for as much as I want this series to be over so I can be with her, I'm also taking in every single damn minute.

This is a once-in-a-lifetime event.

Thrice, my subconscious whispers. *We're doing this every year until your contract is up.*

The way I get on board with that makes me feel like my heart is splitting in two.

Will Waverly wait that long for me?

"Surreal, isn't it?" Tripp says.

We all turn and find him sitting about ten rows behind the dugout. Didn't see him when we came out.

His two kids from his first marriage are with him, both still young—James is in first grade this year, and Emma's two years behind him—but they're both clearly taking in the moment too as they realize their daddy's getting choked up.

"We're gonna make you proud, Mr. Tripp," Diego says reverently.

Levi's older brother shakes his head. "Already did, Diego. You already did."

Sobbing breaks out in another part of the bleachers, and we all collectively turn to see Mackenzie Montana Elliott sitting by herself, hugging a Baby Ash plushie while the tears fall.

"You did it," she says. Maybe to us. Maybe to Baby Ash.

"Not yet, baby," Brooks replies thickly. "Give us four games. What are you doing hiding up there? Get down here. We need our lucky charm."

Santiago, our head coach and team manager, strides out of the tunnel to the locker room. "You boys take it all in yet?" he asks.

"Getting there," Max says.

"Good. Time to suit up for practice. Just another game. And we're gonna crush it."

Just another game.

This is not *just another game.*

This is the first of the series of my life.

We win, our lives are changed forever.

We've done the impossible. We'll be legends. The Fireballs will never go back. Copper Valley will never go back. And that next mountain Waverly was talking about?

I can see it.

It's bigger. It's better. It's deeper in the community. It's opportunities for the whole fucking *world* that never would've existed without a team that proved how much failing was necessary to redefine winning.

It's getting World Series trophies as a coach. It's developing young players into superstars. It's making the Fireballs Foundation bigger and stronger. It's taking the benefits to Shipwreck.

And it's all being on the go.

Fuck. *Fuck fuck fuck.*

We lose, and management starts talking about what went wrong. What we should do better next year. How much harder we have to work next year, as if we won't work our asses off no matter what. Who should be traded and whose contracts shouldn't be renewed.

These guys?

They really are one of my families, and the off-season fucking *sucks* when trades happen.

I want to trust that they'll all be here when we show up for spring training. That they'll be the guys eating Grady's donuts on the one day that he sends us banana pudding donuts down in Florida for luck. That they'll all be there to do the annual de-cursing ritual that doesn't really happen because if you talk about it, you curse the de-cursing.

"We aren't cursed," I say as I stare out at the baseball diamond.

My teammates look at me.

"We're fucking *awesome*. Let's go kick some practice ass and have a goddamn good time playing some ball."

Whoops and cheers go up around me.

Next thing I know, we're rushing the locker room.

This is gonna be the game of our lives.

And what good is the game of our lives if we don't enjoy the hell out of it?

Morning warm-ups are perfect. We all bitch a little—it's tradition—we laugh a lot, we get stretched out and ready for our turns in the batting cages. And about four hours before the game, I cruise into the locker room, ready to switch into my interview jersey because I'm up with the social media team to talk about what it means to me to be here and hopefully not get too choked up on camera, when Diego makes eye contact with me.

He's not smiling.

He's *horrified*.

Every drop of blood in my veins turns to ice, and then I'm in motion.

I can solve this.

I can talk him down, and he's gonna have the series of his fucking young life.

"D-man. Talk to me. You okay?"

"Coop." He shoves his phone at me. "I wasn't supposed to look. *I wasn't supposed to look.*"

I shouldn't look either, but I can't help myself.

Waverly Sweet, Princess of Puke, the headline reads.

"Jesus motherfucking *assholes*," I growl.

And I skim.

And it gets worse.

It gets much, much worse.

It gets worse enough that I shove Diego's phone back at him and lunge for my own.

When Waverly doesn't pick up, I call Levi. "Where is she?"

"Fucking hell, you weren't supposed to see that," he groans. "Tripp's gonna kill me."

"Where. The fuck. Is. She?"

"I don't know."

Los Angeles.

She's somewhere in LA, and if she's not in LA, she's closer to California than she is to Virginia.

Fuck.

"She fired Zinnia the minute she walked off the set, texted

me to make sure you didn't know a thing, which is the only reason I know something happened, and she's not answering and I can't get anyone to tell me where she went after that, but *I will*," Levi says. "Cooper. We've got her. I'll find her. Play the game. It's the World Series. This is your dream. We've got her. It's okay. We've got her."

Right.

World Series.

Play the game.

Play the—

"What the *fuck* is wrong with you?" I snarl. "Would you say that if some weird-ass dude showed up claiming to be Ingrid's dad and then the tabloids covered her getting sicker than sick all over herself on a talk show set while people broadcast it live all over the internet? *Jesus.* Fuck. *Fuck the game.* Where the fuck is she?"

Luca stares at me from the other side of the locker room.

Darren slowly sits down on the bench two lockers down.

Max tries to look in on us, but Brooks is blocking him, frozen in the doorway.

"It's the World Series, Coop," Robinson breathes. I don't even know where he came from.

"I love her and she's hurting and I can't fix it. *I can't fucking fix it.*"

My eyes are wet.

My hands are shaking.

Whatever Levi's saying on the other end of the phone doesn't register, because it's not *this is where you can find her.*

I can't sit, but I can't stand.

I need to *move.*

"We got you, Coop," Brooks says. "Let me make a phone call."

"If it was Henri, I'd move heaven and earth," Luca says. "World Series be fucking damned."

"If it was Henri, we'd all move heaven and earth," Francisco says.

"If it was *any* of our family, we'd move heaven and earth," Darren says. "That's why we're Fireballs. Because we're family."

"I love her," I whisper again.

"Then you know what you have to do." Robinson hands me a towel. "We got your back. You go do what you have to do."

The World fucking Series.

Everything I've ever wanted my entire life.

And I know if I walk out that door, I might never come back.

But if I don't walk out that door—

I don't finish the thought.

I can't.

Because I've finally found that one thing that will always —*always*—be more important than baseball.

37

Waverly

MY FAVORITE THING about my mom's house is that it has the very best security system known to man.

Aunt Zinnia is completely and totally locked out now that I've changed the gate code to Cooper's parents' anniversary date. She won't guess that one.

My security team is banished to the exterior perimeter too.

Before I kicked Hiramys out, after I told her what I need her and the rest of my team to do, I made her block the internet from my phone completely, lest I'm tempted to look at all the tabloid reports, and I made her take my computer and tablet as well.

I could check the baseball game, but I'm so mad for so many reasons, not the least of which is mad at myself for not blowing off my schedule today to be there for Cooper, and then being mad at Cooper for doing the impossible and leading his team to the World Series.

I'm so damn happy for him and nervous for him, and I'm so damn angry that I can't get to him in time.

I had too much to do after that disastrous interview.

I would've called him to tell him that I'm packing right now, that I'm on my way and I've finally just *snapped*, but I don't want him to hear the panic in my voice.

I don't want him to know this is the scariest thing I've ever done.

I don't want to mess with his dreams when he's on the cusp of the one thing everyone but him thought was impossible only two years ago.

What if he feels it while he's playing and I'm watching and then I mess with his game?

What if he doesn't feel it and I start to fear we have no future because the man I'm supposed to be with would be able to psychically feel it when I need to be with him this badly?

What if losing my mom at a young age and then being raised by my aunt and put on a path to succeed succeed *succeed* means that I'm physically, mentally, and emotionally incapable of loving another person and putting them first, and I need to let him go instead?

I need a partner who can be here.

He does too.

He *deserves* someone who can be there for him.

This is the biggest night of his life, and I'm not there for him.

It shouldn't have taken *today* for me to realize how much I need to be there for him, and that there *is* a way for this to work out for us.

A way that doesn't involve only seeing each other for twelve hours overnight this month and three days next month and god only knows how little time the month after that.

And a way that still involves both of us doing what we were put on this earth to do. With just a few tweaks that I sincerely hope he'll understand and agree with.

If he doesn't—

Well, if he doesn't, I'll somehow pick myself up and go on, but I won't change a damn bit of the tasks I assigned to everyone who works for Waverly Sweet, Inc.

My mom's voice surrounds me as I head to the closet to gather everything I need for Hashtag too. I've had her album on repeat since I kicked everyone out, and for the first time since I left the studio earlier today, something really hits me.

I have a father.

No—I have a man who donated sperm once, and I happen to be a byproduct of his deposit.

And he knows that because Aunt Zinnia snuck a DNA sample from me when I was drugged up after getting my vision corrected and sent it to a DNA matching service so that she could investigate who might one day come after me if they ever thought we looked similar, and instead, a data breach at the matching service means that the entire world probably knows more about everyone I'm related to by blood now than I do.

"Why?" I whisper to my mom's voice. "Why does everything have to feel so *hard*?"

The song answers me, exactly like I need it to.

NOTHING *worth it is ever easy*
Everything hard is always worth it

MY BREATH CATCHES in my throat again.

I wish she was here.

I wish she could've met Cooper. I wish she could've seen what Aunt Zinnia was doing, and I wish she would've told me there's an expiration date on family as career managers in this business.

I wish we could've gone on tour together.

I wish I'd listened to her songs more instead of letting the lyrics slowly fade into the background as words I'd hum along with instead of *hearing*.

She told me everything I needed to know in her last album, and it wasn't until *today* that I truly listened.

Maybe I'm being a romantic fool. Maybe I'm reading things that aren't there.

But my mom's last album tells the story of a woman who wanted love, never took a chance on it, and wouldn't get another opportunity.

It's the story of a woman who hopes her friends and family live every minute to the fullest.

My life has been busy, and my life has been successful, and parts of my life have been rewarding and fulfilling, but my life is not full. I don't live it to make me happy, and until I add myself into this equation, I will never *be* the kind of happy that every human being deserves to be.

And that ends today.

I swipe away my tears, tell the fear to shut the fuck up, and drop my bag onto my bed next to my cat. "You ready, Hashtag?"

He's high on catnip. I tossed him an entire bundle the minute we were alone in the house, since he was obviously upset at how much of an emotional and physical tornado I turned into, and now he's clearly having an out-of-body experience. His eyes are glazed over, tongue lolling out, as he lies on his back and bats lazily at imaginary pixies.

"I love you, you goofball," I whisper to him.

He yowls a slow, soft, lazy, *it's like I'm making this noise because some force in the universe is making me and I can't find the energy to fight what the universe wants me to do* noise.

And I smile.

Just a few hours ago, I had a complete both-ends stomach revolt and total career meltdown on stage after a stranger announced to the world that he was my sperm donor.

I have zero doubt that's all anyone's talking about right now, and when my team gets done with their tasks, the gossips and the tabloids will have even more tea.

They won't stop talking about me for weeks.

And for the first time in my life, I'm aware that the outside world is fully focused on me having what they'll call a psychotic episode or a mental snap, some of them reporting it with glee, and *I don't care.*

Not only do I not care, I'm *smiling.*

What can they *actually* do to hurt me?

In all the years of the ugly reporting, I've never once had a young fan ask me if I really secretly have a sex room in my pool house. They never ask me if I stabbed Geofferson's mother with a chopstick at dinner or if we broke up because I didn't like the way he manscaped.

They don't give two fucks about what the tabloids say about me.

They want me to hold their hands and look them in the eye and tell them that they're good people worthy of love and that they can make their life into anything they want it to be, and that I believe in them.

And *that* is what matters.

Not what strangers on the internet think about me, or the people who take delight in thinking that I must be an awful person if I'm a woman with a successful public career.

So let them say what they'll say.

I'm over it.

I'm over living my life for what other people say about me, and I'm ready to live my life for what will bring *me* joy.

And what brings me joy isn't what I expected or even *wanted* right now.

That doesn't mean I'm not going for it.

I sling Hashtag's bag over my shoulder and pick him up, cradling him like a baby while he sings a song to whatever imaginary cat angels are circling his head.

"You are such a beautiful, hilarious, perfect kitty," I croon to him.

He sings back to me.

We're descending the curved staircase when I hear it.

Banging.

Someone's banging on my door front.

How?

There are walls and security and more security and— "*Oh my god.*"

Either Cooper has an identical twin, or he's banging on my door.

I never open my door when someone randomly knocks on it, but then, no one ever randomly knocks on it. Security is always pre-screening, and the one time someone climbed a fence undetected and got halfway to the front door, they were tackled and hauled away and I didn't find out about it until three days later, because I was on tour and Aunt Zinnia hid it from me.

But *Cooper is at my door*.

I toss Hashtag up onto my shoulder, dash across the wide foyer and fling it open. "What—"I don't get to finish my sentence because he's wrapping me in those solid arms and lifting me off the floor and burying his face in my neck, all while not disturbing my very high cat.

"Are you okay?" he gasps. "I got here as soon as I could. *God*, it feels so good to hold you. Are you okay? What can I do? What do you need? I'm here. I'm here, and I swear to fuck, I am *never* leaving again."

"Cooper—*what?*"

"The sharks, Waverly. The sharks came for you and I'm here to punch them in the face and shove them back in the water where they belong. *Are you okay?*"

"*Why aren't you playing baseball?*"

"*Who the fuck cares about baseball when the woman I love is hurting?*"

My breath catches hard in my throat and my eyes go hot.

He tightens his grip. "That's not how I meant to—"

"You love me."

"I love you so much it hurts. I love you so much I can't stand the way we've been apart. I love you so much, I'll spend the rest of my life carrying your bags and your cat everywhere you go so that I can be next to you, wherever you go, no matter what time it is or how far away it is from home. *You* are home. You're my home. I walked away from you once. I won't do it again. I love you. I love you above all else, and I always will."

Hashtag, who's still hanging out on my shoulder like a baby, sings a drunken yowl.

"And I love your cat too," Cooper adds. "Are you okay? I haven't shut up. I need to shut up. What do you need? What can I do?"

"I'm perfect," I whisper.

"Are you sure?"

"Aside from the part where you're supposed to be playing baseball *right now*. I should've canceled everything this week. I *did* cancel everything else this week. How did you get here? Never mind. My team's getting my plane ready. We can be in the air in thirty minutes."

"I'm not fucking leaving you."

"I'm coming with you. All week. I'm all yours. I love you, and I am *all yours*." I shift and press my lips to his, Hashtag yowls out a protest and leaps off me, and then Cooper's kissing me back, a rough rumble coming from the back of his throat that feels like relief and adoration and *everything*, all in that one perfect sound.

And everything inside me settles into sheer peace.

At least, for all of half a second before my hormones take over.

I don't know if I'm devouring him or if he's devouring me, but we're all over each other. I'm wrapped around him as he kneads my ass and carries me back upstairs to my bedroom. I pull his jersey over his head while he tackles the buttons on my loose blouse. I barely get his pants unbuttoned before he's tugging my leggings down.

And then we're rolling over my bed, kissing and hugging and laughing, both of us lunging for condoms, and I will never, *ever* get over the feel of him sliding inside of me, driving deeper, driving me wild, until I'm coming so hard I can't see straight and nothing matters but the feel of the two of us together, as if we're all that there is in the world.

He's everything in my world.

And he's *here*.

And he's solid and dependable and coming inside me with

a groan, squeezing me so tight I shouldn't be able to breathe, but he's my oxygen. He's my purpose. He's everything I want and even more than everything I need, and *we will make this work.*

He's still holding me, both of us on our sides, while I explore his back with my fingers and breathe in the scent of him, long after we've both quit panting.

"I canceled my next three years," I whisper as the sun sets and shadows fall across my bedroom.

He goes still. "No, Waverly, I'm done. I'm telling Tripp and Lila—"

"That you're finishing out your contract with the Fireballs while I take some *much* overdue time off to figure out what parts of my business I need to keep for *me*, and what parts I need to let go of because they don't make me happy, and while I just *breathe*. I can't *business* my way into happiness. That comes from *here*." I press a kiss to his chest.

And once again, Cooper proves that he is the best hugger on the planet. "We can talk this out and make sure—"

"Cooper, your *life's dream* is to take the Fireballs all the way to winning the World Series. You need to go back. I'm going with you. And *next week*, we can talk about next year. And next week, you can lose this argument with me all over again."

He chuckles into my neck, but it's not all laughter.

There's some sniffling too. "I love you."

"I love you."

Hashtag hops onto the bed and yowls that he loves us, and also air, and also occasionally falling in the swimming pool, which he doesn't really, but he's still high.

"Oh! He's right," I say to Cooper. "We should watch the game."

He winces.

I point at him. "That? That right there? Yes. You're going back, and you're finishing this series."

He snags my finger and presses a kiss to the tip as he stares straight into my eyes. "I love you more than baseball."

"I know," I whisper. "And I love you more than music."

"You might get tired of me. I'm a lot."

"Cooper Rock. *I* am a lot. We're a lot *together*. And we're going to change the world."

"We are, aren't we?"

Gah, that dimpled grin. I grab him by the face and kiss them both. "I love you."

"Even when I'm too much?"

"You are *never* too much."

"Ask you a question?"

"Always."

"You gonna be okay with Zinnia?"

I sigh as I lean into him and let him wrap me tight again. "Remember you told me how you met your family all over again as adult people instead of authority figures?"

"Mm-hmm."

"I think I need to do that with Aunt Zinnia. Eventually. When I'm not so hurt and angry."

"Do you *want* to?"

"Do *you* want me to?"

He strokes my back and presses a kiss into my hair. "People are complicated. She's your aunt. She raised you. She's fucked up here and there. She hurt you. She probably regrets it. That's how relationships go. Hell, Waverly, I'm gonna hurt you sometimes too, and when I do, I'm gonna make it right."

"I know you will. And I will too."

"What I want is for you to be happy, however you find that

happiness. If you set your ground rules and get to know her and like her and want her in your life, I trust your judgement. Same goes if you set your ground rules and get to know her and find out you don't like her and don't want her in your life. Or if it lands somewhere in between. Whatever you want. However long it takes you to figure it out."

I breathe a slow sigh of relief. He's right. I don't have to rush solving my relationship with Aunt Zinnia, and it makes me feel better knowing the only pressure he'll put on me is the question of what *I* want, not what everyone else wants for me.

That's a new kind of support for me.

I like it. "You're very wise."

"Nah, I'm just really good at knowing people are complicated."

I smile against his side, tracing the dates tattooed across his ribs.

His first day in the Majors, and the day the Fireballs clinched their first division championship.

Championship.

Championship. "Cooper. The game."

I fumble for the remote I keep in my nightstand, hit three buttons, and everything shifts into motion to open the cabinet hiding my television.

I don't have to change the channel.

It was already set from when I watched the Fireballs win their league championship last week to advance to the finals.

But unlike last week, I've missed the game.

"My heart just stopped," Cooper whispers as my gaze flies to the screen, where Diego Estevez isn't smiling as he's being interviewed.

There's no score listed.

What's the damn score?

"You're so serious," the reporter says to Diego.

"Doing this for Coop is serious business," Diego replies. "He's the whole reason we're here."

"You wish he'd been here tonight?"

"We all do."

Cooper doesn't say a word.

"You certainly showed him how much you care," the reporter says.

Luca Rossi walks past behind them, and we distantly hear his voice. "We love you, Coop!"

"Seventeen to one is a blow-out score for a World Series game. You think you're gonna tell Cooper to stay away so you can wrap this up in another three games, or would you rather he come back? Any superstitions there?" the reporter asks.

Cooper and I both let out simultaneous breaths.

"*Fuuuuck.*"

Nope.

No idea if that was me or him.

If he's feeling half of what I'm feeling in this moment—*should he or shouldn't he go back? Will they really do better without him?*—then it's probably both of us harmonizing.

Darren Greene shoves into the camera view. "What kind of idiot question is that? We can win with Cooper. We can win for Cooper. We can win without Cooper. We're the damn *Fireballs*. And I hope he gets his *bleep* back here before the next game, but every last guy on this team and fan in these stands knows he'd be here unless whatever kept him away was major, and every last one of us has his back. Ask Diego about starting us off with his homer and do your damn job."

"Fuck, I love that guy," Cooper whispers.

"Is he gonna get fined for that?"

"Probably."

"Can I pay it for him?"

Cooper snorts with laughter. "I'm gonna sit in a corner and watch you offer to do that for him, and then I'm gonna enjoy the hell out of the show. I honestly don't know which of you will win that argument."

We both lean back against my pillows and watch the rest of the post-game coverage.

Three games to go.

The Fireballs still have to win three more games to win the whole series.

"You're going to do it," I whisper to him.

He presses a kiss to my hair. "We're going to do it."

"No matter how many times I need to have sex with you to make sure you're on top of your game."

He snort-laughs, and then I'm beneath him once again, laughing while he kisses me until I'm not laughing anymore.

But I'm still happy.

So very, very happy.

38

Cooper

Ask me the last time a baseball game gave me butterflies.

No, wait, don't.

Might jinx it.

Heh. Kidding.

I'm Cooper Fucking Rock. I play for the Fireballs.

And we're in the top of the ninth in the seventh game of the World Series, all tied up at three games apiece in the series, leading by a single run with two outs to go, back at Duggan Field with my family in the stands.

All of my family.

Waverly.

My parents and siblings and in-laws and aunts and uncles and cousins and grandparents.

My Mountain Lions Little Sluggers team, who still finished worst in their summer league, but won two games this year, which is two more than last year.

The baristas from my favorite coffee shop in town.

Beck and Levi and their families.

All of them.

Cash Rivers too.

Even Davis Remington, the elusive, camera-avoiding fifth former member of Bro Code.

Pretty sure I even saw Zinnia when the camera panned over to the owner's suite, where Waverly's tucked away with her security team and Aspen, who insisted on being here to support her friend while Waverly's supporting me.

Taking the business part out of their relationship was a good move. Or should be, long-term. Waverly and Zinnia have been discussing boundaries, and I have high hopes for their future.

Also a good move?

Me getting my head back in this game as Trevor Stafford, our relief pitcher who was called up after spending most of the year in rehab in the Minors, finishes warming up.

There's a man on first, one out, and we're leading two to one.

If we can hang on to this lead, we'll have done it.

We'll be the champions.

Trevor rubs the ball in his hand and turns to look around at all of us. "Ready?" he asks me.

I nod and punch my fist into my glove, squatting into position. "You got this, Trev."

Brooks gives a *bring it* from third. Frankie bounces twice on the balls of his feet at shortstop, then squats too. Emilio, Luca, and Darren are in the outfield. Robby's guarding the runner at first.

Diego squats behind the plate while the entire rest of the

team, coaching staff, pitching staff, *everyone*, hangs out at the dugout rail.

The first pitch is a ball.

Second's a strike.

My balls are sweating.

I can feel everyone else's balls sweating.

Two more outs. Two more outs. Two more outs.

One more ball.

One more strike.

One more ball.

Fuck.

No, concentrate, Rock.

Concentrate.

We're fucking doing this. And then we're doing it again next year.

Trevor puts his foot on the rubber on the pitching mound, shakes his head twice at Diego's suggested pitch, then nods.

He tucks the ball into his glove, lifts his leg, pulls back his pitching arm, and lets it fly.

A split second later, there's a *crack*. A blur of a ball streaking between me and Brooks.

I don't think, I just move. I miss this, we're tied, because I miss this, and it's going in the corner in the outfield, and that runner on first will make it all the way home.

Don't miss don't miss don't miss dive dive dive dive —

I dive.

It's far.

It's so far. I don't know if I can—

And then it's there.

The ball is *in my glove*.

It's an out.

It's an out.

"Coop!" Robby yelps before my body hits the ground.

I land. Roll.

I come up and fire the ball to him at first a split second before the runner dives back for the bag.

Everything hangs in slow motion while I look at the first base umpire.

I *feel* everyone around me holding their breath.

Dude curls his hand into a fist, and I barely hear the word leave his mouth. "*Out!*"

He's out.

Double. Fucking. Play.

Game.

Over.

Game over.

We won.

We won.

The Copper Valley Fireballs, loserest of the losers, have won the World Series.

We did it.

We did it.

I'm still on one knee.

Robby's bouncing with joy. Darren hollers in the outfield. Frankie and Brooks and Diego rush the mound, everyone throwing gloves and whooping and celebrating.

And I bend over and I kiss the grass.

This grass.

This grass.

This is the grass I watched as a kid. The grass I've sweated on, bled on, cried on.

It's been here as long as I have.

And then the grass is gone because I'm being pulled to my feet by my teammates.

Not the mound.

Jesus.

They were rushing *me*.

As if it didn't take every last one of us on this team to get here.

And *here* is gonna take some time to process.

"We did it!"

"*Champions!*"

"Fireballs! Fireballs! Fireballs!"

Holy fuck.

We did it.

I join in the whooping and screaming and hugging, sparing a look up at the owners' suite, which has cleared out.

What feels like seconds later, all of our families stream onto the field too. Management. Coaches. Parents and siblings and nieces and nephews and aunts and uncles and grandparents and friends.

I grab Mackenzie when Brooks has let her go. "You did it, Mac!"

"I can't stop crying!"

"Don't talk to me about crying," Tanesha sobs.

I hug her too.

Then Henri. Marisol. Tillie Jean.

"I'm so proud of you, you big pain in the ass," she says through tears.

Max growls and steals her back.

He gets the win for tonight.

My mom's suddenly there, hugging me tight, and not for the first time, my throat goes tight.

"Thanks for believing in me," I choke out.

"You're a winner to me no matter how many trophies you do or don't have."

"Where's Waverly?"

"Hiding in the dugout."

Thought so.

I make my way through the massive crowd of the entire Fireballs organization, family, and friends—getting stopped every single step of the way.

Tripp Wilson hugs me.

Lila hugs me.

Levi Wilson hugs me. "Why the fuck isn't anyone making a fuss over *you* stealing the spotlight out here?" I grunt to him.

"People are asses. Need Giselle to get you through?"

"I'm Cooper Fucking Rock. World Series champion, thank you very much. I can do anything."

Except get to my girlfriend quickly.

But when I finally sneak down the stairs of the dugout and find her hovering beyond the door to the locker room, it's all completely and totally worth it.

"Oh my god, I thought you hurt yourself." She flings herself into my arms, peppering my face with kisses. "Hey, are you okay? For real? Do I need to kiss any booboos?"

And that's when I break.

There, in the arms of the woman I love, all of the emotions I can't hold back any longer break free. "I love you," I gasp into her neck.

She squeezes me so hard that the rest of the world ceases to exist. "*This* is what *you* were always meant to do too, you know." Her voice is thick, her hands threading through my hair, her lips still on my cheeks. I have no idea where my hat went, and I don't care. "I am so proud of you. I love you and I'm thrilled for you and I'm so proud of you."

"This all feels too good to be real. You. The team. Winning. You. You. You."

She laughs. "So what do you see on top of your mountain, Mr. Rock?"

"The whole world. The *entire* world. Right here. With you."

"That's what's on top of my mountain too."

Someone calls my name. We have things to do. Trophies. Interviews. Celebrating with the team before I go home and celebrate all over again with Waverly, then head out to Shipwreck to celebrate with my whole town tomorrow.

But for one more minute, I kiss the woman who means more to me than all of it combined.

"Thank you for coming to see me," she whispers when I finally pull back, that sense of duty—and excitement—pulling me back to where I only temporarily need to be.

"Thank you for waiting for me," I whisper back.

I don't know if we're talking about tonight, or if we're talking about her concert this past spring, or every minute of the eight years that we were apart, but I do know one thing.

For her, for this moment, for *us*, I'd do it all over again in a heartbeat.

EPILOGUE

Aka, the rest of the story of what really happened in the final epilogue of The Grumpy Player Next Door

Cooper Rock, aka a man on the way to the top of his mountain. No, really. He's driving up his mountain.

"THERE ARE seventy million things I love about Thorny Rock Mountain, starting with, it's where I came from," I tell Waverly as I steer my truck around a corner on the mountain that I still don't own all of since Beck Ryder is stubborn.

But. I have most of it, and now, I also have the woman of my dreams beside me, a World Series trophy nestled in between the groceries we grabbed before we left Copper Valley this morning to head to Shipwreck for Thanksgiving, plus a cat in his carrier, and there's so much happiness in my heart that I can barely contain myself.

"You came from the mountain?" she teases.

"Yep. I was birthed by this very mountain, and I gave it no

labor pains, and we high-fived each other the minute I came out, and we've gotten along great ever since."

She cracks up.

"Don't tell my mother I'm making shit up, okay?" I say. "Not that she'd be surprised. I tell her something like this every Mother's Day to watch her laugh at me."

"Oh my god, I love you," Waverly says. "Promise me you'll stay this goofy forever."

"I promise."

Much as I love the city, home is where my heart is, and I'm almost home.

Also, home feels way, *way* homier when Waverly's with me.

We pass the first house I bought once I decided I wanted to own the whole pile of dirt that birthed me. This one's a normal-size two-bedroom log cabin that families from the city come out and rent on weekends.

"High five, Bear Cottage," I call to it.

"You named your rental properties?" Waverly asks.

"Hell, yeah. Rents better when it has a name. Plus, who wouldn't want to stay in Bear Cottage?"

She squeezes my hand. "What if I want to stay in it?"

"You'll have to have your people check out when it's not booked. It's very popular. As you'd expect of a place called Bear Cottage."

Her smile lights the entire freaking morning.

"High five, Cedar Chalet," I call to my next rental property down the way.

"Did you buy out locals when you bought your mountain?" Waverly asks.

I shake my head. "Nope. They were mostly weekend getaways. All those people in the city have no idea what they were doing giving up their weekend properties to me."

"I heard Grady and Tillie Jean saying that you owning a whole mountain is bad for your ego."

"Waverly, be real. There are very, very few things in life that can ding my ego."

She laughs through the last two switchbacks, and there's one more driveway.

"High five, Beck Ryder's house," I call to one of the few properties I don't own.

"High five, Cooper, you magnificent beast," I reply to myself in my best Beck Ryder impersonation.

Waverly laughs so hard she snorts coffee out her nose.

Good timing, because I'm slowing down to turn into my driveway, except my driveway isn't there, and now I'm slamming on the brakes, angled hard in the middle of the road, staring at my mailbox.

Waverly coughs. "Cooper?"

"Hold on a second," I murmur. "You okay?"

"Gonna live."

She'd better. It's more or less the first time I've been allowed to drive her anywhere myself. And yeah, Kiva and the Scotts are in an SUV right behind us, but we're *alone*.

In a car.

With me driving.

Except I can't find my driveway.

"Is there a reason we're stopped?" Waverly asks.

"This is…my house."

She looks at me.

Then at the mailbox, which is definitely there.

Then back at me.

"My driveway is supposed to be here," I say.

Shit.

Am I losing my mind?

Where my driveway belongs, there's no driveway. It's undergrowth and a giant pine tree and fallen leaves and—

"Oh, *fuck.*"

"Cooper?" Waverly says again while Kiva climbs out of the car behind us.

I start to laugh. Stop myself.

Shoot a chagrined look at Waverly. "So, ah. About how you hate pranks…"

Her brows go up.

"Are you, ah, gonna be okay with…me getting pranked?"

Also, *how the fuck did she pull this off?*

I look up the road.

Then down the road.

This is definitely where my driveway belongs.

I am *not* confused.

That's my mailbox.

She didn't just move my mailbox, did she?

Oh, and make no mistake.

She is not Waverly.

She is Tillie Jean.

Waverly looks at me again, then at the mailbox, and I see the moment the light dawns. "Did someone remove your driveway and replant it with nature?"

"Looks like."

"Oh my god."

"I can disappear. I can make both of us disappear. I mean, I love my family. They're the best. They really are. But we can recreate Shipwreck and family somewhere else. I know a bunch of retired baseball players who'd love it. We can survive this if you don't want to get caught in the crosshairs of a prank war between me and my sister. Or if you want me to give up pranks, I can do that. I would. For real. I will submit to only being pranked without doing prank-backs for the rest of my life. For you. But *only* for you."

"She replaced your driveway with nature," Waverly repeats in awe.

I scratch the back of my neck. "We kinda have this thing in the off-season…"

Her eyes light up with utter joy and more than a little mischief. "What are you going to do to get her back?"

I blink. "Seriously?"

"She replaced your driveway with nature."

We stare at each other a beat, and then we both crack up.

That's a good one.

That's a *seriously* good one.

"You hate pranks," I remind her.

"But this is *not* just a prank. This…this calls for creativity and Cooper Rock Awesomeness."

I chuckle.

And then I cackle.

Waverly doesn't suddenly change her mind, which means mine's made up.

Tillie Jean should know by now that you don't awaken the beast in November.

Not if you don't want to spend the rest of your life looking like a toddler who had an accident in a glitter factory.

I whip out my phone and send a quick text. "I've got an idea or two for some epic revenge," I tell Waverly.

"Can you make sure the revenge that comes back doesn't involve anyone jumping out of dark enclosed spaces and scaring the actual shit out of me?"

"Ground rules will be re-laid just for you. Also, in case a

prank ever goes too far, the safe word is *dad's balls are saggy today*. Sorry. Awkward. But it works for all of us."

God, she has the best laugh.

And she's still cracking up as she swings the truck door open.

"Where are you going?"

"C'mon, Mr. Thorny Rock Mountain. I need to write a song, and then I need to kiss you until I can't breathe, and before we can do that, looks like we have some hiking to do."

I catch her hand, pull it to my lips, and kiss her knuckles. "I love your sense of adventure."

"And I love your sense of *life*. I want to absorb it and learn to live it too, so when you need me to remind you, I'm there." She leans back into the truck, across the console, and kisses me. "Last one up the hill has to make dinner naked."

"We're having Thanksgiving dinner down in Shipwreck."

"Then it's gonna be really awkward for you, isn't it?"

This woman.

A few weeks of sleep, shutting out the news, and lots of television, sex, and laughter have made her so happy that I'm not sure I can keep up.

She's the woman of my dreams, and I intend to do everything in my power to keep living this dream with her.

BONUS EPILOGUE

Waverly

IT'S BEEN months since the last time my stomach was this upset, and I've forgotten how to deal with it.

"We don't have to go," Cooper says. It's early April in San Diego and we're in the back of my SUV. He's on a family pass from the Fireballs after the most amazingly fun spring training before the regular season starts in a couple days. We're sitting at the edge of a park where there's a picnic going on that I both desperately want to attend and also desperately want to avoid.

"Seconded," Aspen says from the third row of seats behind me.

While Cooper and Kiva will be getting out to go with me if I decide to take all the steps necessary to get to the picnic pavilion, Aspen's gotten too famous and will be staying here with Scott Two.

"I want to go," I say. "I just need a minute."

Cooper squeezes my hand. Aspen squeezes my shoulder.

Kiva and Scott Two wait patiently, offering no judgment or advice.

"Okay, I need five minutes," I say.

All thirty-two of your known half-siblings are having a picnic and you're invited is a lot more appealing in theory than it is when I'm sitting here looking at actual people who share my DNA.

Cooper shifts to stretch an arm behind me. "Take your time."

Who I am is obviously much more than just my DNA, but I'm also incredibly *curious*. How many of them can sing? Do any of them also have serious nervous stomach issues? Is loving cats genetic, or do my half-siblings have all manners of pets?

Would any of them treat me like a normal human and welcome me into their lives as a friend?

I don't *need* them to be my friends.

But I'm curious. And after being warmly welcomed into Cooper's large family, I want to know if I can be a friend to someone else like me who wants to learn where they came from too. And where better to start than with people that I share actual genetic material with?

I blow out a slow breath. "Okay. I'm getting out."

Cooper waits.

Kiva waits.

I don't reach for the door.

"No one has phones or cameras." Kiva points to the security checkpoint where Hiramys is charming everyone into turning in their electronics. My genetic half-siblings are aware there's a possibility I'll show up. I've seen the posts in the family channel on the MatchDNA site, and I'm taking comfort in how many of them are excited to meet each other, with relatively few mentions of me specifically compared to mentions of the rest of them.

Aunt Zinnia registered me under one of the fake names that I use when I check into hotels. Unfortunately, though, she used her own real credentials to pay, with her Waverly Sweet, Inc. credit card, and that's where things got messy with the data leak.

Clearly, Aunt Zinnia wasn't young enough to be the daughter in question for my sperm donor.

I could call him Norm.

I could.

But I'm not there yet.

He's also not invited today. As my half-sister Laurel put it, he's not our dad. He didn't raise us, and he crossed a line.

We all get to choose what we want to know, and he took that choice from you, she messaged me privately. *He won't be there.*

I blow out another breath, and this time, I slip on my sunglasses and reach for the door.

Cooper follows me out of the car with his normal ease and grace, like he's not sweating this at all, and his calm confidence settles my stomach. I'm sure he can feel my uneasiness. He picks up on the subtlest changes in my mood, sometimes before I even realize I'm feeling it.

"You think I can have a tumble-off with anyone in there?" he says as we head toward Hiramys's checkpoint. Yes, we're following the rules like everyone else, going through the one entrance to the roped-off pavilion, but we both left our phones in the car already.

"Cooper..."

He squeezes my hand and flashes me a grin. "What? I won't *start* it. But I'm happy to make a scene if it takes any pressure off of you."

"I know."

We take our nametags from Hiramys, who squeezes me in a quick hug. "They're all very nice, sweetie," she whispers. "You're gonna be fine."

I inhale deeply, and then we push past the entrance and into the picnic, where probably seventy-five people are already milling about. Many of my half-siblings have spouses and kids, and family was invited, probably so none of us felt totally alone or weird.

"Waverly?" a woman with dark hair and brown eyes and light brown skin says. "Hi. I'm Laurel. We had a small private conversation—"

"About shrimp," I finish with a smile, because we talked about that too.

"Yes." Her shoulders relax, and she smiles back at me, and it's spooky to realize we have the same smile. But also good.

I have connections here.

"No shrimp here," she tells me. "At least seven of us get sick every time we eat it, even though we didn't when we were younger. Let me know if you have any questions about anything else on the menu. And I wanted to introduce you to Jean. Her mom passed away when she was young too. I thought you two might have a lot in common. More in common, I mean."

We slowly make our way through the picnic area, meeting my half-siblings and their families and finding out that a bunch of us hate pickles—who knew?—and that over half of us always sneeze four times anytime we sneeze once.

Nobody crosses lines or presses boundaries or makes me feel uncomfortable when they ask what I'm working on in my time off. I'm not asked for my autograph or pictures. When people congratulate Cooper on the World Series, he takes it in stride.

This *is* our life.

But here, I get to just *be*.

Not quite as easily as I get to just *be* with Cooper's family, but there's no pressure to have to perform, and nothing feels weird.

Until about thirty seconds after I give him the *I've had enough and am ready to go home and decompress* signal.

We're making our way to the exit when one of my younger half-siblings whispers Cooper's name. I don't remember meeting her, but her nametag says she's Maple. She's slightly taller than I am, with dirty blond hair that's cropped short, pale white skin, and wide green eyes. She's wearing a plaid flannel shirt open over a plain white crop top, cargo pants, and army boots, and I have this instant sense that she and Aspen would be besties, and not just because they both share names with tree species.

Provided Maple's not someone who doesn't understand boundaries.

Not gonna lie.

The way she whispered Cooper's name was kinda creepy.

He and I both stop and glance at her.

Her gaze darts between us.

"Mac," he says quietly to me out of the corner of his mouth as we both turn to face Maple, and after the number of stories he's told me the past few months, I understand exactly what he's saying.

Maple reminds him of Mackenzie back in the days when Mac couldn't talk to him.

I squeeze his hand. *Go on. Make her comfortable. We have a minute.*

And here it comes.

That dazzling Cooper Rock smile, dialed down to human levels that won't intimidate. "Hey. Maple, right? Nice to meet you. You grow up around here, or are you one of the siblings from somewhere else?"

"I have to tell you something," she blurts. Her voice is smoky, and I wonder if she can carry a tune.

"I'm all ears," Cooper says.

She darts a look around and steps closer to us. I feel Kiva coming up behind us, clearly getting the *something's off* vibes too.

Cooper's relaxed posture doesn't change.

And Maple stares at his feet while her words come out in a rush. "You made me famous."

Cooper blinks.

I blink.

Kiva stops beside me, and she doesn't blink. Pretty sure she's sighing internally.

"How's that?" Cooper asks.

Maple reaches behind her, under her flannel, and then everything gets a little blurry.

Kiva doesn't really fuck around when someone's reaching behind their back.

"*Gack!*" Maple squeaks from the ground beneath my security agent, where she's been pinned so effectively, so quickly, that it's a wonder she can still make noise.

Cooper shoves me behind him and starts backing me toward Hiramys, who's still manning the only entrance to the picnic area.

My half-siblings and their families all gasp and turn to stare at us.

"Why do you have a phone?" Kiva barks.

"To sh-show C-Cooper the s-story," Maple pants.

"What story?"

"*L-love on F-fire!*"

Cooper stops.

I stop.

Hiramys whips her head around.

"Kiva, let her go," I say quietly as I peek out from behind Cooper.

"I didn't take pictures," Maple says. "*God*, you're cranky. I get it. Look, *I get it*. But I just wanted to show him."

"Show me what?" Cooper asks.

"How it ends."

I gasp.

"How *what* ends?" Kiva growls.

"Kiva, *let her go*," I repeat.

"Wow, she's hot," my half-brother Harold mutters.

I might not claim him.

Maple shoots a look at Cooper, then at me. Her face is red and splotchy like she's embarrassed.

Possibly mortified.

"You wrote *Love on Fire*," Cooper says reverently.

Kiva backs off, and Maple pulls her legs under herself and stares at the ground. "Yeah," she mutters. "And you made it famous."

"Dude. Maple. That story is *awesome*. You made it famous yourself."

She lifts a squint at him. "Did you just call me *dude*?"

"It's a Cooperism when he's temporarily speechless," I interject. "Highly complimentary."

"You wrote *Love on Fire*," he repeats.

Kiva heaves a heavy sigh.

I stifle a smile.

I know that tone.

So does she.

"You're a Fireballs fan," he says to her.

"I mean, duh. Who isn't in this country?"

"She is *not* like Mackenzie," I whisper to him.

But his mind is racing. I can *feel* it. "Can you write other mascot fanfic? Like, give poor Meaty a happy ending? I didn't mean that the way it sounded. Can you give him a love interest? My buddy Zeus tried that once, and it was ugly. Meaty needs a better story. You write it, I'll share it. I still have nightmares about the story Zeus tried to write."

"Is he serious?" Maple asks me.

"Wait, wait, is *she* serious?" one of my other half-siblings or one of their family members asks. "Maple. Are you for real? Not having the end of that story is *killing* me."

"It's not done yet," she mutters. "I don't know which ending to use, okay?"

"*The happy one,*" someone else shrieks. "Use the happy one!"

"They're all happy!" Maple shrieks back. "I just want Cooper to tell me which one *he* wants me to use because he's *Cooper Fucking Rock* and this is like the best-worst day of my life, *okay*?"

"I did not have this on the Waverly Sweet Weird Family Reunion Bingo Card," Hiramys whispers to me.

"Have you not known Cooper long enough?" I whisper back.

"Right. I forget he's more famous than you in some circles."

"Holy shit. I can't believe I'm finally meeting the brain behind *Love on Fire*," he says reverently. "Waverly. Go get your phone. I need a picture."

"Aspen's gonna die if you don't introduce her too," I murmur to him.

"Shit. Right. Maple, sorry to do this to you when you have no idea what it means, but you're coming with us. You're officially a member of the Rock family now. And we need new family photos. Over there. With other people. Kiva, apologize. Waverly, remind me to text Henri. All of the rest of you, nice to meet you. Hope to see you again. I gotta go call my mom. Best day ever." He glances at me, and that spark of mischief dancing in his face makes it impossible to hold back a laugh.

Every day is Cooper's *best day ever*.

And really?

I can't argue with him about today.

I love *Love on Fire*. Meeting the author and finding out we share DNA?

Totally the best day ever.

Until tomorrow, when Cooper and I are headed back to Copper Valley for baseball season to start.

And then it'll be another string of best days ever with the man I love.

PIPPA GRANT BOOK LIST

The Girl Band Series
Mister McHottie
Stud in the Stacks
Rockaway Bride
The Hero and the Hacktivist

The Thrusters Hockey Series
The Pilot and the Puck-Up
Royally Pucked
Beauty and the Beefcake
Charming as Puck
I Pucking Love You

The Bro Code Series
Flirting with the Frenemy
America's Geekheart
Liar, Liar, Hearts on Fire
The Hot Mess and the Heartthrob

Copper Valley Fireballs Series
Jock Blocked
Real Fake Love
The Grumpy Player Next Door
Irresistible Trouble

Standalones
The Last Eligible Billionaire (An Amazon #1 Bestseller)
Master Baker *(Bro Code Spin-Off)*
Hot Heir *(Royally Pucked Spin-Off)*
Exes and Ho Ho Hos

The Tickled Pink Series
The One Who Loves You
Rich In Your Love

The Bluewater Billionaires Series
The Price of Scandal by Lucy Score
The Mogul and the Muscle by Claire Kingsley
Wild Open Hearts by Kathryn Nolan
Crazy for Loving You by Pippa Grant

Co-Written with Lili Valente
Hosed
Hammered
Hitched
Humbugged

Pippa Grant writing as Jamie Farrell:

The Misfit Brides Series

Blissed

Matched

Smittened

Sugared

Merried

Spiced

Unhitched

The Officers' Ex-Wives Club Series

Her Rebel Heart

Southern Fried Blues

ABOUT THE AUTHOR

Pippa Grant is a USA Today and #1 Amazon Bestselling author who writes romantic comedies that will make tears run down your leg. When she's not reading, writing or sleeping, she's being crowned employee of the month as a stay-at-home mom and housewife trying to prepare her adorable demon spawn to be productive members of society, all the while fantasizing about long walks on the beach with hot chocolate chip cookies.

For more information, visit Pippa's website:
www.pippagrant.com